Dicky, Richard, and I

A Story of Madness in the Making

Robert Banfelder

BB
~
Broadwater Books
Riverhead, New York

Broadwater Books
141 Riverside Drive
Riverhead, New York 11901
E-mail: broadwaterbooksinfo@gmail.com

www.robertbanfelder.com

ISBN: 978-0-9915912-1-3

Printed in the United States of America
10 9 8 7 6 5 4 3 2 1

For my loving partner Donna and my son Jason

PRAISE FOR THE NOVELS
OF ROBERT BANFELDER

The Good Samaritans

"One of the powerful aspects of this book are the wonderfully short chapters. I found myself saying for two days and one night, 'Oh, just one more chapter.' And one more, and one more. Banfelder expertly weaves the subplots together at the end, and delivers a thrilling denouement. This book is one of the best crime thrillers I have read in a long while." ~ Russell F. Moran, author *The Gray Ship*

The Author

"*The Author* is filled with twists and unexpected turns that will keep readers on the edge of their seat until past where you think this one will end. But wait, this is just the beginning. Outstanding! Unspeakable crimes, a thrilling chase and a mesmerizing tangled plot. What more could you ask for? Banfelder has written another winner!" ~ Mark Reid, editor, NewBookReviews

"Robert Banfelder does a masterful job of providing the reader with every detail regarding the unorthodox murders committed by the sinister Colomba. An excellent read." ~ JMHunter, NJ

"Banfelder's descriptions are detailed, the novel well plotted, and his imagination without bounds." ~ Donna L. Gestri, author, *Sweet Figs, Bitter Greens*

"Horror fans that enjoy Stephen King, and suspense fans that enjoy Scott Turow will find a lot to savor in this rabid chiller. Five stars for me." ~ Eva Ercolani, NY

"You will think twice before shutting off the lights at night. Banfelder is unrelenting in his ability to move you along, and into his pages. You are running fast, and just when you think it might be safe, Banfelder hits you with another curve. Not to be missed. The story is action-packed, the characters are driven, and the ferocity of the story will stay with you long after it ends." ~ Patti Ann Bengen, author, *New Beginnings*

The Teacher

"As a forensic psychologist specializing in psychopathy, I have been researching authors who write fiction in the field of forensic psychology. I am impressed with Banfelder's well-researched, credible, and unique plots regarding the criminal mind. *The Teacher* was an easy, enjoyable read. The author painted an excellent picture of a psychopath through Clarence Emery. I noticed quite a few subtleties such as his inability to be nervous, always in control, and establishing relationships only for secondary gain. Bravo! It is always nice to see the field advanced." ~ Dr. Jason D. Dunham, Licensed Psychologist, Fellowship Trained in Forensic Psychology

"At once, and throughout the book, you get more than a glimpse into the mind of the serial killer. Banfelder captures your attention and never lets go. I hated for the book to end." ~ Betty Fitch., N.C

"The big questions for Justin Barnes, covert operative for Suffolk County Homicide in *The Teacher*, are how does Emery manage to elude the police, and is the killer working alone? Another haunting question is can Justin stop him? This story will bring you to your knees." ~ Patti Ann Bengen, author, *Sex*

"If you like psychological thrillers or loved *Silence of the Lambs*, then *The Teacher* will prove to be a story that keeps you interested and reading until the very end. You will find yourself wanting to be a character in the book to actually help with the capturing and doing away with Clarence. Banfelder does an excellent job of keeping the reader on the edge." *Armchair Interviews*

Knots : A Justin Barnes Thriller

"As usual, Robert Banfelder has captured the true essence and criminal profile of the serial killer. This book is very fast-paced and difficult to put down. As a professional in the field of forensic anthropology and cultural anthropology, I can see the amount of research time that goes into all of his novels. His writing style makes reading all of his novels a great adventure. He is a master of his craft! I recommend his books without reservation." ~ Linda Chase, Forensic Anthropologist

"An excellent thriller. Mr. Banfelder is quite a master of the suspense." ~ C. Betancourt, NY

"I love the Justin Barnes character; hes the rebel we'd all like to be, and I found myself cheering him on and rooting for him to succeed. Robert Banfelder's details and descriptions are wonderful and make the scenes come alive for the reader." ~ Candy, NY

"A true thriller written by a master of the genre." ~ Russell F. Moran, author, *Justice in America, How It Works, How It Fails*

Trace Evidence

"Lots of twists and unexpected turns. A great read and I love the ending!!" ~ Candy, NY

"Be prepared. The ending brilliantly takes yet another unexpected turn involving the least likely of suspects." ~ B. Fitch, NC

"Almost to the last page, you will question the choices made in the name of justice. A terrific read." ~ Donna L. Gestri, author, *Time Takes No Time*

"Robert Banfelder captures the essence of the serial killer. I could not put down this book." ~ Linda L. Chase, Forensic Anthropologist

Books by Robert Banfelder

Fiction

The Richard Geist Trilogy

Dicky, Richard, and I

The Signing

The Triumvirate

The Justin Barnes Four-Book Series

The Author

The Teacher

Knots

The Good Samaritans

Trace Evidence

Battered

Nonfiction

The Fishing Smart <u>Anywhere</u> Handbook for Salt Water & Fresh Water

The North American Small & Big Game Hunting Smart Handbook:
Bonus Feature: Hunting Africa's & Australia's Most Dangerous Game

Acknowledgments

My thanks to Christoper Paparo (www.fishguyphotos.com), friend, fellow angler, outdoors writer and photographer for his graphics expertise.

For allowing me to live my dream, my deepest gratitude goes to my soulmate, Donna Derasmo, and my son, Jason.

Author's Note

Dicky, Richard, and I is the revised and expanded version of *No Stranger Than I*, published in 1991 by Hudson View Press. This new novel paves the way for the upcoming titles *The Signing* and *The Triumvirate* as part of the Robert Redler trilogy.

Robert Banfelder

Table of Contents

Prologue

North Shore State Hospital for the Criminally Insane
Havenwood, Long Island, New York
1969

The eighteen-year-old boy lay semiconscious, badly beaten and bleeding, strapped to a hospital bed. A river of red spilled freely from his mouth as four male attendants entered the room. Coal-black faces contrasted sharply against bloodied white sheets and walls as the patient's sea-green eyes danced insanely in his head. Suddenly, the duty nurse burst into the room and over to the patient's bed.

"My God! He's bitten off his tongue," Nurse Crayford exclaimed, exploring the rictus wide.

Richard Geist shook his head of clay-red curls, baying, gurgling, and choking on his blood as the nurse pushed his face back down and to the side.

"Get these restraints off fast before he drowns in his own blood," the head nurse ordered, struggling to hold the young man still, reaching across the patient's plaster cast. But no one moved an inch. Black faces stared back at her defiantly, resolute and unanimous in their intent. "Oh, no. We're not murderers," she stated firmly. "I'll not burn in hell for this. Now, we'll move him into Emergency, and I mean now," she added flatly, challenging each and every glare.

Finally, one of the orderlies stepped forward. Then another, reluctantly. A third flatly refused, storming out of the room angrily. A fourth remained standing in the corner, quite distraught.

"Now!" she repeated.

The orderly, shaking his head firmly from side to side as if against better judgment, approached the edge of the bed cautiously, staring down at the grotesque figure that appeared to be leering up at him in hideous triumph. Carefully, the man removed one of the restraints when suddenly Richard screamed and smashed his cast into the black face with a force that sent the orderly back into the corner from where he came. Bottles of IV toppled then crashed against the floor as the patient tore the plastic tubing from the stand, single-handedly coiling and stretching the lengths of transparent line around the nurse's neck, trying to rope her in, trying to enunciate but a single word. But she would not hear of it and broke away. So he plunged a finger into his bloody bottle of a mouth before withdrawing it, managing to scrawl a cryptic word upon the shadowy wall—before they were upon him.

The following week came patient Geist's handwritten letter of request to North Shore State's director.

North Shore State Hospital
Psychiatric Unit
Room 743
Oct. 7, 1969

Dr. Thomas Kirby
Director, North Shore State Hospital
Havenwood, N.Y. 11768

Dear Dr. Kirby:

The hospital administration has confined me to this institution, insisting that I am not, in so many words, of sound mind. It would, I am sure, prove fruitless for me to give an accurate account of all events from start to finish so that I might set the record straight.

As I am labeled 'multiple,' not unlike an array of Campbell's soup cans wrapped in red and white—Chicken Noodle, Cream of Celery, or Consommé—so, too, am I distinct. Not being able to see that we are all in the same soup is certainly madness in itself.

They tried to kill me, but as you can see, I am still here. By the end of this tale, I ask only that you look deep into my soul, and ask, "What power or providence sustains thee?" If the answer conjures up pure evil, then, perhaps, you will want to kill me, too! But as I set forth a moment ago, they tried.

Hereupon, I humbly petition North Shore State

Hospital for its consent to proceed with this document in order that certain dark truths be established concerning the matter of Dicky, Richard, and Victoria Geist vs. the State of New York and its enemies within. I request one (1) typewriter; one (1) unabridged dictionary; one (1) package legal size pads (8½ x 14); ballpoint pens, pencils, and soft eraser.

Respectfully submitted,
Patient 2751

The psychiatrist set aside the letter for a second time that morning, staring at the middle-aged nurse sitting across the desk from him. "And why is this so important, Nurse Crayford?"

"Catharsis, perhaps. The patient wishing to write his story is probably his own best medicine."

"Is it now?"

"I used qualifiers, Doctor."

Doctor Kirby smiled. "Yes, so you did."

"Also, I feel it might tell us things about him that they didn't have time to learn at the King Foundation. Dr. Bianco said that Richard only recently merged another personality."

"Yes, his mother. I know all about that. I spoke with the new director at length. Very strange case, indeed."

"Doctor, Richard's story may hold the key to what we're looking for," she stated matter-of-factly. "It may shed some light on his other personalities. Besides, writing is the only way he can communicate now."

"No argument there. By the way. What was the word he finger-painted for us on the wall?"

"Lark."

"Lark?"

"Yes. It's the name of the detective who was on the case."

"I see. What do you suppose it all means?"

The nurse shrugged her shoulders. "Why don't we let him write his story?"

The psychiatrist hesitated a moment before leaning back

uneasily in his chair. "Just so long as you keep a close eye on him," he cautioned. "And take care of that eye," he added, gesturing toward the bruise above her brow.

"Aye, aye, Doctor." She smiled wearily, stood up and headed for the door.

"Oh, just one more thing."

The nurse paused. "Yes?"

"Please. No more Shakespeares. We've already got several on the second floor."

Nurse Crayford nodded with a smile. "Good day, Doctor. 'Parting is such sweet sorrow.'"

"'That I shall say good day till it be morrow,'" the psychiatrist spirited back playfully.

Book I

Emerger

Chapter 1

PLAYTIME PAST

The story necessarily begins in the late spring of 1956, for little Dicky was but five and could not go back in time as yet. Nevertheless, the quiet little town of Lake Hiawatha, New Jersey would once again swell with families escaping the exhaustive heat of summer from the cities. Most of the sheets of plywood that boarded up many a bungalow had been taken down around Memorial Day, and the musty smell of those cold, wet seasons, better left forgotten, would linger at the edges of yards for weeks thereafter.

The older children would be the first to fill the empty lots and fields with bats and balls and baseball gloves, the boys' crumpled shirts and folded jackets serving as makeshift bases. The overflow of younger children would soon be taking to the streets, chalk lines marking many a tarmacadam diamond. Boys were the participants. Girls were the spectators. Those who didn't play ball or watch the games simply rode their bicycles around all day. Of course, there was the lake itself, but it was five miles away (which might as well have been a million) and cost money to get in to swim. Besides, it was baseball that was foremost on everyone's mind.

And there was little Dicky, a year-round resident, excitedly anticipating the arrival of city children within a week or two. He waited patiently for Mother to serve him breakfast before asking her permission to get in an hour of early batting practice with the twins who lived several blocks away. It was a Saturday, and his only hope to escape the drudgery of household chores and studies. The only other neighbors were the old couple, the Millers, who lived across the street.

"Mother, may I go out after breakfast and play ball with Jimmy and Brian for a little while?" Dicky asked, sitting at the tiny kitchen table.

"No! Now, you know that's too far away for a little boy to wander. We've been through all this before. Besides, I want you concentrating on your words and phrases," his pretty mother answered in a crisp voice, handing him a glass of milk and a bowl of cereal. "And I want to see penmanship not chicken scratch. Learn to shape your a's and o's properly instead of running around with your playmates. Chasing after a silly ball is a complete waste of time. Playtime's over. Learn to read and write well, and you'll make something of yourself. Maybe you'll even write a book one day. I want you way ahead of everyone. Is that clear?"

"Yes, Mother," he answered up unhappily, spooning out a heap of sugar from a ceramic bowl sitting on a corner of the table.

"Reading, writing and arithmetic. Work out problems in your head. Add up license plate numbers as the cars go by. Those are the games I want you to play. I want you to read everything that you can get your hands on. Read. Read. Read. Go on, now. Otherwise, I'll find some work around here for you to do. There are mirrored tables in the parlor that need dusting."

Suddenly, the sugar bowl went sailing off the table, smashing to pieces across the checkered tile floor. Dicky stared down at the mess,

"Jesus Christ, Dicky! Can't you even sit at a table without making a commotion? You know your father's sleeping. If I'm not listening to his goddamn bellyaching about working nights and weekends, then I'm cleaning up his crap. Now, you're giving me more crap to clean. Well, you're going to clean up after yourself this time. Clumsy little bastard," she muttered.

"That wasn't me, Mother."

"What?"

"I didn't knock the sugar bowl off the table, Mother. Honest."

"Oh, I suppose it was that imaginary friend of yours. I hear the whispering in your room at night. Dr. King tells me it's quite normal. Well, I'm telling you to your face that there is nothing normal about it. If you wish to whisper, do it down a well—directly to the devil—till you sound the depths of hell," she rattled off in sing-song fashion. "You had better stop this kind of behavior immediately. Do you understand?"

"I understand, Mother."

"I mean it, Dicky. If you had woken your father, there would be hell to pay. He only has another week or so before he's switched to days. Now, I want you to promise me that I won't witness this kind of behavior again. The lying. The clumsiness. The whispering and all. None of it! No more whispering into your pillow, hours into the night. Or that infernal rocking back and forth. Or I might have to smother that little demon deep inside of you while you're fast asleep. A little pillow talk you might say. YES!"

Dicky nodded his head anxiously.

"Good. Now let that be the end of it. We don't need a psychiatrist around here. Just a good talk now and then. You're five years old, Dicky; it's time that you grew up. Now let's get the dustpan and broom out of the front hall closet. Later on, you'll come outside and take another picture of me if you want some air."

Dicky went down the hallway, peering up at the framed photographs plastered across the parlor wall. "You're very pretty, Mother."

"Why, thank you, dear. That's such a sweet thing to say." She smiled, opening the closet door and handing over the items before marching him abruptly back into the kitchen. "After you clean up here, you can mop the floor with a mixture of ammonia and water. Mother will show you how."

Chapter 2

THE WEED GARDEN

Scores of black and white as well as colored photographs of Mother filled the parlor walls within the modest two-bedroom ranch. Many of the pictures were shot out of doors and were taken over a period of time by any number of men friends whom Mother called admirers. Posing in the yard in tights and high-heeled shoes, she caused quite a stir throughout the neighborhood, especially during summer months when Father's shift was switched to days.

Women gossiped, and the men drove themselves crazy, driving back and forth in front of the house till Dicky knew those license plates backwards and forwards, inside and out. One man actually passed by the house seven times on foot, pretending to be going here and there or doing this and that, watching Mother's every move out of the corner of his eye.

One of her admirers was a thin man who would always trail behind her for the day, camera in hand, trying to keep her still. CLICK. Kicking off her heels, she'd laugh and run playfully across the weedy lawn, showing off with somersaults and splits. She, pausing now and then to freeze the action. He, swearing to capture *all* her acrobatic feats. CLICK. CLICK. Cartwheels and graceful leaps. CLICK. CLICK. Backbends and kicks that seemed to touch the sky and defy the heat of day. Suddenly she'd disappear into the house with her camera-carrying admirer close behind.

She, off with her tights and stepping into stockings made to snare. He, focusing in on all her wonders, wondering if he'd dare. Mother would turn to admire herself in the back hall mirror, bending forward from the waist, touching her toes at the very floor, stretching her arms and wiggling her fingers toward the ceiling, finally standing still. She'd stand there stately and proud. Pretty as her pictures, with long, lustrous hair and large, expressive dark eyes. "Dicky, be a darling and go outside now and play for a while," she'd say softly. "Hear?" Click went the sound of the lock behind him as he exited through the cluttered porch to the front stoop.

Dicky threw his ball high into the air, wondering if it would ever,

ever come down again.

If you watched closely, you could actually see each and every picture in the parlor come alive—vibrant and dimensional—collectively covering the giant green-leafed wallpaper pattern peeling at the corners of the room. Each photograph seemed to camouflage the very leaves themselves. Those suffocating leaves, with their choking vines climbing and twisting behind each and every frame like restless serpents hiding in the grass. Yes. Mother did her acrobatics in a giant weed garden.

There was one picture that hung by itself in the far corner of the room; it was a picture of little Dicky, all alone, wearing a cowboy outfit. He is four—four years after they pulled him from her like a weed. He is pointing a pair of six-guns, staring wide-eyed, focusing in on all the pictures along the other wall. Dicky knows that she sees him because she is smiling in his direction, her back arched, her head touching the ground, though her smile appears as a frown, you see, for her head is really upside down. He wants to run to her; however, he is bound within the very frame.

Mother kept lots of photos in albums and boxes, too. Her favorites were those of the gazebo she used to play in as a child. It wasn't really a photo, though. No. It was a negative. Mother and Dicky were standing together on a blanket of light. She was holding him by the hand like a little doll, their heads ridiculously inclined heavenward. Eyes closed. Laughing silently like performing minstrels with painted faces. Aunt Helen had taken the picture the day she came to meet Mother and Dicky near Yankee Stadium. He was so happy. It was to be his very first ball game, but Aunt Helen had lost the tickets, or so she said. Instead, they'd all be going off to the zoo. Dicky didn't dare say anything, for he knew better. Besides, by five he had learned to deal with disappointment. He seemed positively paralyzed by the sounds reverberating from the stadium as a woman's voice sang the National Anthem, her words echoing behind the music spewing forth from speakers crackling high above them in the street. Dicky listened carefully to the sounds—just standing there and shivering as if frozen.

A group of little boys around Dicky's age, dressed in Yankee baseball uniforms, hurried toward the entrance with a pair of grownups at their heels. The children carried bats and balls and gloves and wore their brimmed caps backwards. One of the boys kept swinging his baseball bat back and forth while the child's mother screamed down at the little Yankee fan in her Spanish tongue. Dicky clicked his own tongue, trying to imitate the foreign words.

Close to the ballpark still stands the courthouse on 161st Street. Dicky marveled at the columns that support the architrave, so Aunt Helen took another picture. Of course, you can't see the inscription, but Dicky can set forth the words for you:

THE ADMINISTRATION OF JUSTICE PRESENTS THE NOBLEST FIELD FOR THE EXERCISE OF HUMAN CAPACITY -IT FORMS THE LIGAMENT THAT BINDS SOCIETY TOGETHER-UPON IT BROAD FOUNDATION IS ERECTED THE EDIFICE OF PUBLIC LIBERTY

It was Dicky's first time on a train, and he grinned broadly, amusing people as he swung around and around the white enameled pole, loudly chanting verses from silly school songs as the rail cars lumbered noisily aboveground on the way to the Bronx Zoo.

The only animals that really fascinated Dicky were the zebras. He watched their dizzying stripes move back and forth between the bars like prisoners in uniform. He begged Aunt Helen to take a picture, but she told him flatly that there was only black and white film in the camera. Both she and Mother thought that to be the funniest thing in the whole wide world, bending forward with sidesplitting, idiotic glee.

"Now why in God's name would you want a picture of a bunch of horses in pajamas?" Aunt Helen had asked, laughing insanely. "Come, I know something he'll go crazy over," she said, passing the camera to Mother, half dragging little Dicky by the hand. Dicky's mind reeled violently.

The two of them sent Dicky into a dusty outdoor cage, all by himself. Suddenly, an attendant lifted him under the arms then lowered his little body upon a loathsome, mottled shell, holding him from falling off the infernal creature as it crept along on scaly limbs. Just beyond the bars, Mother and Aunt Helen stood there laughing insanely as Dicky sat crying, riding out his rage, in doubt as to which side of the cage he was to regard the beasts. So afraid. Dicky was so afraid.

But Mummy kept right on snapping pictures just the same.

CLICK-CLICK. "Smile, Dicky darling." CLICK. "Oh, come on now and smile for Mummy."

Oh, how Dicky wanted to smash that repulsive reptilian shell. How he wished he'd had the boy's baseball bat. He would have smashed its ancient shell quicker than the Spanish woman could have ever clicked her foreign tongue. But he somehow managed to remove himself from that tortoise through the power of his mind. Somehow, he could stand back from it all . . . as though the horror were happening to someone else. It was the way he learned to deal with fear.

Early that afternoon, Aunt Helen and Mother found a restaurant-bar somewhere in the neighborhood. Dicky stood momentarily mesmerized, staring up at the giant meats on the steam table in the front window when he was jolted back by a group of men just leaving, positively reeking from the smell of booze and beer. Mother and Aunt Helen pulled him inside by his little hands. There he saw other men behind a counter, sharpening knives, carving and slicing meats, making awesome sandwiches. Another group of men with stoic faces formed a line and filed past, sliding trays along a brass railing. They carried tools and wire cable strapped to thick leather belts slung low around their hips. Western Electric, he shivered, triggering a brilliant fireworks display that flashed across his brain: bursting, splintering, fragmenting, falling through endless space before finally melding into tiny beads of frustration that he simply could not comprehend as yet.

On the other side of the narrow sawdust path, others in plaid shorts and soiled trousers sat facing the wall on wooden stools: smoking, drinking, laughing, exchanging glances and comments over their shoulders as Mother and Aunt Helen bustled by with little Dicky sandwiched between them as the only two women in the entire place made their way to one of the tables in back.

During the course of the afternoon, they both had lots to drink. Mother kept peering over her glass of scotch at one of the men seated across the room. The man kept looking at her. Smiling. Mother smiled, too, hiking up her skirt and suggesting things that made Aunt Helen very angry.

"Not in front of the child, for God's sake," Aunt Helen pleaded angrily.

Mummy practically somersaulted out of her seat, and yanked

little Dicky by the hand, half dragging him through the gray, palling, smoke-filled scene and out into the light, pulling him toward the subway station.

"YOU'RE A WHORE," Aunt Helen shouted, stumbling down the street behind them. "DICKY'S ILLEGITIMATE—YOUR FATHER'S A CUCKOLD, DICKY. CUCKOLD-CUCKOLD," she crowed, waving her arms excitedly like a great bird. Aunt Helen turned and walked away.

By the time they descended the staircase, throngs of people in bright clothing were everywhere. Laughing and shouting. It was like a carnival. Children were jumping around excitedly, holding on to half-eaten hot dogs and pretzels, blowing into the tops of empty Coke bottles while making sounds like a choo-choo train, tossing and catching Cracker Jacks in their mouths, waving red, white, and blue pennants and flags, yanking steadily on the strings of their helium-filled balloons. The Yankees had won the pennant!

Dicky felt something then that he had never felt again. He didn't know what it was, except that it made goose bumps all over his flesh. It was the first and only time he felt alive. He felt American. At five he was alive and American. And then at six—pick-up sticks.

Chapter 3

SCRUPLES

The following year a family was having a house built in back of Dicky's. Not just another summer bungalow, but a year-round residence. Dicky was so excited because he thought he'd finally have a friend close by. The new neighbors had settled into their home before it was actually finished off on the inside, let alone furnished, for they had no other place to stay, or so said the older boy whom Dicky put in the hospital the very first week the trio arrived, recalling how the fat boy had tried to do dirty things to Dicky's little thing as the two of them sat quietly atop a new foundation going up on an adjacent building lot.

Dicky went off the wall altogether, returning a moment later with a standard one-by-two in both hands, delivering home the power and promise of a Louisville Slugger. He knocked the obese lad clean off his perch, opening up the back of the boy's head like a shattered sugar bowl.

A home run, indeed! For the boy went running all the way home, screaming bloody murder and crying for his mother. And a thick, yellowish-brown fluid oozed just beneath his nape like maple syrup, although everyone else insisted it was red and bled profusely.

When Mother, along with the police and the boy's parents, had asked Dicky for his side of the story, he simply told the truth. But the fat boy's father insisted that Dicky was lying, maintaining that his son was a good boy who sang in the choir every Sunday back home. He demanded a full apology and suggested that Dicky should follow his son's example. So Dicky said that he was sorry for the batting practice and promised to be good, singing the National Anthem in a crackling voice for everyone.

That's when Mother packed their bags again and took little Dicky all the way out to Long Island to visit her old friend, Doctor King, leaving Father behind to stew for the summer and to see to the fat boy's doctor bills.

Humpty Dumpty sat a wall,

Humpty Dumpty had a great fall,
And a lousy summer convalescing.

Dr. King's house. That king-size house. Quiet as a mouse. Mother and Dr. King had gone upstairs while Dicky waited in one of the quiet and cooler of the air-conditioned rooms below. He became intrigued with an apothecary scale. On the table, beside the balance, was a little book. *Weights and Measures*. Dr. King and Mother were up there quite a long time, but Dicky waited patiently in the study as he was told.

When the two of them finally came down the winding staircase, Dicky asked Dr. King if he had any scruples. They both looked quite upset at the remark. Mother tripped and lost her balance, but Dr. King caught her by the arm, holding her steady as she adjusted the strap on her shoe. And then he laughed, explaining, "He means weights for the scale; they're called scruples." Mother laughed, too . . . although she really wasn't sure.

Suddenly, an old, thin black woman appeared in the doorway and handed Dicky a small box filled with golden graduated weights with which to play. Then, just as suddenly, Dr. King and Mother disappeared from the room again, leaving Dicky all alone with the strange woman. Kneeling before a low oak table, as if in prayer, Dicky weighed things very carefully, not saying a single solitary word.

Across the table sat a golden mortar and pestle surrounded by three golden frogs. Or were they brass toads? At the center stood a statue of a young man holding a winged staff with two serpents entwined around each other. Around and around.

"That's Hermes," the woman said smiling, introducing herself as Dr. King's housekeeper. "Messenger of the Greek gods and conductor of souls. That there staff he's aholdin' is a symbol of the medical profession. A caduceus. Ya hang 'round ol' Sarah, she gonna give ya a real education. Of course I ain't got none of them fancy degrees like Dr. King. But I tell ya one thing," she said, pointing to the other objects throughout the room. "A lot of this here culture done rub off on me. Yes, siree. And why not? I's been a rubbin', a-brushin' and' a-cleanin' everythin' in sight for years. Ah, hee, hee, hee," she declared and laughed enthusiastically.

Dicky looked up at the taut black face, peering into the woman's dark, mysterious eyes. Eyes set deeply in their sockets. Eyes that held a keen intelligence.

"Of course I ain't gonna push nothin' on ya," the housekeeper assured the boy, sitting herself down beside him. "Now take Hermes, here. Yeah. Ol' Sarah take 'im in a minute," she affirmed, narrowing her eyes and becoming very serious. "Hermes," she said softly, pointing to the statue, "was the conductor of souls to Hades. That be the world of the dead," the woman whispered eerily, "separated from the land of the livin' by five rivers; the rivers Hateful, Forgetfulness, Woeful, Fiery, an' the Wailin'," she added, tracing five fingers along a coal-black hand as though they were, indeed, the very rivers themselves. "Ya see," she continued, her eyes burning deeply into his, "the newly arrived dead was ferried 'cross the river Hateful, to be buried by a greedy old man who gots paid with a coin left in their mouths, 'long with honey cakes to keep them quiet. And anyone who tried to enter or leave Hades was challenged by the fearless dog, Cerberus: a three-headed hound that guarded its gates." The woman bobbed her head affirmatively before continuing.

"Then all the dead drank from the river of Forgetfulness, and the judges of Hades gave each soul its proper place. The good and heroic was rewarded in the Elysian Fields. Them's at the edge of the world. But the wicked gots sent to the lowest regions," she declared solemnly. "You see that there black and white bird behind ya?"

Dicky swung around, acknowledging with some degree of caution written across his face.

"That there's an ibis. Ain't no ordinary bird. No siree, bobtail. He be the embodiment of the Egyptian god, Thoth. A moon-god. He credited with the invention of writin', geometry, and astronomy. Darn tootin'. And when those archeologist folks finds them Egyptian tombs, where the mummies is kept, they finds them birds in there with 'em. Of course ya know what a mummy is, don't ya?"

Dicky nodded.

Sarah smiled. "Well now, them mummies is all wrapped up like that 'cause one day their soul gonna come back to their body. Ya see, them Egyptian people, they believes in life after death. And Sarah gonna tell ya a little secret. Everybody wanna believes that. I mean deep down inside oneself. That be the hope of all mankind. Yes, siree. And I'll tell ya another thing. From what ol' Sarah can see, them

17

Egyptian people spent so much time preparin' for death, why I don't see where they found the time for livin'," she swore and laughed heartily.

"Sarah!" Dr. King called, his tone ringing a note of concern.

Sarah immediately picked herself up, standing on thin bowed legs before hurrying out of the room. There was a lot of commotion. Dr. King ran up and down between the floors past potted green plants that hung in front of large windows along the staircase like giant apothecary scales. Dicky remained kneeling beside the oak table, playing with the graduated weights, balancing the scales precisely. Glancing up toward the great bay window, he saw a pair of seagulls soaring in the distance before turning his attention back to the scene coming from the living room. From the study, Dicky studied the three of them intently.

"Ya sure you's all right, ma'am?" Sarah asked, helping her houseguest over to the couch.

"I'm fine, really. Thank you, Sarah." Mother forced a smile. "I—ouch—twisted my ankle coming down the staircase before. I'm afraid it's somewhat swollen now. I'm sorry to be such a nuisance."

"Nuisance, nonsense. Now, you jus' lies back here an' takes it easy. Dr. King gonna fix ya up good as new."

"I always had weak ankles ever since I can remember," Mother fibbed. "Oh, but I used to love to ice skate, though; only I'd have so much trouble walking on them," she prattled, lying down on the couch.

"Yea, I know jus' how ya feel. Ol' Sarah feels like she been walkin' on ice skates all her born days." Sarah smiled broadly, displaying perfect white teeth.

"Oh, I bet both of you girls cut quite a figure," Dr. King declared and winked, stepping into the room and unwinding a wide roll of bandage from a box.

Dicky watched curiously from the study as Dr. King sat at one end of the couch, winding the bandage around Mother's swollen ankle. Around and around. Why, he could have wrapped her like a mummy right then and there, Dicky grinned.

"Now, we'll just put these on like so." The good doctor smiled, fastening the end of the bandage with little metal clips.

"Thank you, Doctor." Mother smiled amorously. "It's nice to know you can handle anything from head to toe. And you have such a lovely bedside manner, too," she cooed, blowing him a gentle kiss.

Dr. King grinned boyishly. "You do like Sarah said now and rest awhile. Let's put this pillow underneath your foot. There you go. How's that?"

"Just fine," she said, reaching for his hand.

"Well, if yous two excuse me, ol' Sarah gonna whip up a little somethin' to eat. Ya like curry, ma'am?"

"Please call me Vicki, Sarah. And yes, I love curry."

"Well, that's good, 'cause Sarah gonna surprise ya with a special chicken curry dish. Yes, siree." Sarah disappeared from the room.

"Oh, this is so silly. I just can't lie around here like this," Mother protested, starting to get up. "Let me at least help Sarah with a salad or something."

"I heard that," Sarah said, appearing again with her hands placed firmly upon her hips. "Now, ain't no room but for one woman in Sarah's kitchen. Ya bes' set her straight on that point from the start," Sarah insisted, grinning up at Dr. King.

"Ah, I forgot to warn you," Dr. King declared, gently reclining his houseguest upon the couch. "The kitchen is Sarah's territory. Otherwise, it becomes a battleground," he cautioned with a smile.

"Sarah?"

"Yes, ma'am—I mean Miss Vicki."

"Is Dicky behaving himself in there?"

"Oh, he's jus' fine. A fine young gentleman. Yes, siree. Now don't you fret none 'bout him, hear? Me and him's gettin' 'long real fine. He gonna like it here jus' fine."

"It's just that I worry about him. He's been too quiet lately."

"Too quiet?" Sarah frowned. "Count yo' blessins, child. I raised two Indians. O' course, their father came from India. A real tiger, too. Till one day I cook 'im up a steak, and he wanna know what he's eatin'. He done pass out cold when I tell 'im it was from a cow. Ah, hee, hee, hee. He never did like Louisiana much anyhow. I used to call 'im My Great White Hope, seein' as where we met and how he was always wearin' them white robes. Why, he prayed more than any man I ever knowed. Didn't do him much good, though. Died in a car accident 'long with our two boys. Long time ago."

"Oh, I'm so sorry, Sarah," Mother said sincerely.

"Count yo' blessins, child," Sarah repeated softly, leaving the two of them alone.

"They met in Africa as she was traveling around the Cape of Good Hope," Dr. King explained. "Very tragic story. Makes you stop and think."

"Yes," Mother said with a distant stare that meant she was a million miles away. "David."

"Yes?"

"I have something to ask you."

Dr. King smiled. "Well, ask away."

"Promise me you won't get upset."

"Now, how could anyone get upset with someone as beautiful as you?"

"David, can we go up to the gazebo this evening?"

"Victoria!"

"Just for a little while," she pleaded. "Please?"

"I really don't think it's a good idea. Especially with that ankle. Besides, everything is covered up."

"Pretty please?" She smiled brightly.

Dr. King said nothing for a moment, about to be taken in completely by her charm. "No doll?"

"No doll," she promised. "I'm over that now. That's all in the past. I have Dicky now. He's my baby doll," she assured him, gently clasping his hands between her own. "I'm strong now, David. You're the one who gave me strength."

"All right," he said. "Just for a little while. Agreed?"

"Agreed."

That was a long, long time ago. Dicky had spent that summer in a kingdom by the sea, but things grew quite confusing there. Especially during one hot summer's night. The sky was filled with stars. The moon all round and white. He had grown quite restless and couldn't fall asleep, listening to the pounding of waves that seemed to draw him to the distant shore.

Dicky dressed quickly then quietly scurried out the back, panting as he raced across the grounds toward a familiar structure looming against the sky. A gazebo, similar to the one in a family album, lured him like bait. Only the structure seemed much larger and sat high upon a knoll. Otherwise, it was very much like the one that Mother used to play in as a child.

Dicky made his way stealthily up the stairs and along the circular deck. Around and around he crawled till he was almost dizzy. Swept away in an unexplainable delirium, he crept over to one of the openings and pressed his little face against a narrow floor-to-ceiling screen, arms outstretched to either side, appearing like some sort of giant insect with its wings spread wide across the breadth of the frame.

On the far wall, he saw a painting of a woman in a chair with her legs up in the air, wrapped around the body of her beau like those serpents snaked around the staff in Dr. King's study. Suddenly, the painting seemed to come alive, as though the woman was performing acrobatic feats . . . shedding her silky garment to the floor . . . gliding up and down . . . twisting and turning . . . slithering along the other body rhythmically.

Dicky closed his eyes tightly. His mind became a reeling merry-go-round of madness; his gut turned into a bubbling pit of molten glass. The puzzle of the picture was incomplete. Those missing years before the tender age of five, forgotten. Erased from memory. Three-four, "Shut the door!" One-two, "Buckle your shoe."

> All the King's horse,
> And all the King's men,
> Couldn't put your Dicky
> Back together again.

Chapter 4

PRAYERS UNANSWERED

When Mother and Dicky finally returned home from that "kingdom in heaven," as she put it, Father was quite upset with them for having spent practically the entire summer there at the King Foundation. But Mother said that she was through being kept under lock and key, claiming that Father had imprisoned her in a concentration camp through their years of so-called marriage. She even denounced Satan with such ferocity that she became the more diabolic, railing against the infernal forces for not delivering her Nazi-Hitler husband to the very gates of hell. As a last resort, she appealed to a high authority.

Kneeling in the parlor before one of the mirrored tables, eyes closed, hands locked together in prayer, Mother raised her arms toward the heavens. "Oh God, how I beg You to take that Nazi-Hitler from me," she pleaded. "He used me to do his goddamn cooking and cleaning—never gave me a vacation—made me wait for him for seven years before he married me. Now I come home to find the son of a bitch on early retirement. Now I have him on my hands both day and night. And I'll still have to do everything around here myself. Oh why, oh why did I ever marry an old man, anyway? He never wanted any children—had a kid by his first wife—never told me he was married during those seven years—never told me the truth about anything. That good for nothing Nazi-Hitler!" Mother brought her clasped hands down hard upon the reflective surface, smashing the mirrored table again and again. "TAKE THAT NAZI-HITLER NOW! STRIKE THAT NAZI DOWN!" she screamed, the blood dripping from her elbows onto the colorless threadbare rug. "I don't need that Nazi anymore. I have my admirers. Scores of them."

Unmoved by her petition and form of supplication, Father just stood there silently, staring down at the splinters of glass, finally realizing that a part of his life had shattered before his very eyes.

From that day forth, Father retired altogether, spending his days and nights in semi-seclusion, dwelling in the dark and gloomy world Mother would prepare for him. Shades and curtains were drawn throughout the room like a parlor for the dead. That decrepit father figure who was more than twice her age was aging rapidly. He'd rest day after day in his green vinyl recliner, sitting or reclining quietly in yellow crotch-stained long johns, regardless of whether it was January or July. Occasionally, he'd lift himself up with great difficulty, journeying from parlor to porch, nibbling and dropping pieces of smelly Limburger cheese along the way, moving like an oversized, crippled rat.

The enclosed and cluttered porch, which Mother commonly called his junk room, was the boundary of Father's domain, housing the skeletal frames of television and radio sets. Dead, dusty tubes lay strewn across the workbench. A large and tattered Ohm's law chart, its corners curled with age, hung from a pale, beige, once white, musty wall. In the corner of the room on a chipped yellow-enameled cabinet sat an oscilloscope. Volumes of faded book bindings and old copies of electronic magazines filled the badly warped, wooden shelving above the work area. Stacked below the shelving were hundreds of radio and television tubes stored away in faded red, white and blue RCA boxes, like little colored coffins.

Father grew sickly and quite depressed. One day Dicky told him certain secrets as the ancient figure stood silent before his workbench, listening carefully while examining a smoky-gray tube from years gone by, scrutinizing the fine filament wires that ran the length of the glass, squinting feebly at its broken tungsten thread. Perhaps he sensed that everything in that antiquated room was dead . . . everything . . . except for the potential energy entombed within those sealed glass tubes that lay tucked away in those little red, white and blue RCA boxes.

As time went on, Father spent more and more hours out of each day gazing about his dense metallic graveyard. He appeared quite weak on the afternoon that Dicky turned him toward the filmy window in the door, leaving him to wonder if the world at large still held a sentiment or two, or if his fate was somehow sealed within the very space he occupied, void of any matter anymore.

It wasn't long before Father turned incontinent. Disgusted, Mother finally moved him to the porch. Vinyl chair and all.

Chapter 5

HAPPY BIRTHDAY, MOTHER DEAR

Another spring and the end of April's rainy season brought Mother into bloom. Tearing about the house insanely she went, yanking and suddenly releasing window shades wound tight as they flapped around violently in the air. Around and around. And then again, around the room she'd come, carelessly tying back the curtains to the wall as Dicky's eyes grew accustomed to the light.

A warm afternoon in early May brought Mother's accountant friend around to help celebrate her thirtieth birthday, showering her with expensive gifts. Horatio Gladstone was a rather large man with a huge heart, and something of an armchair philosopher, not to mention a Sunday sailor of sorts. He even brought a present for Dicky. A good-sized sailing ship. Horatio sat sprawled out in the sunny parlor, shades rolled tight across the opened window tops like furled sails, white curtains reefed to either side. The man's massive frame filled the new leather chair while Father sat sequestered in the cluttered porch, sickly and silent.

"You see, my boy," Horatio began, "we limit our horizon by adopting and advocating one particular doctrine. You must learn to borrow from all doctrine, rejecting what does not fit the situation today. You must learn to formulate your own ideas. But you mustn't make rules for others. Moses sat on that goddamn mountain and gave us ten 'shall nots!' Between his audaciousness and the cold, it's no wonder his hair turned white," he roared.

Hot air blew over Dicky's head, but he sat listening patiently to the pitch, sitting on his hands upon the couch, swaying to and fro. Seasick, you might say.

"You must learn to fill your life with *you*, you see."

"Me?" Dicky asked, seated beside his sailing ship, its keel set deep between two big blue bolsters, the boat rocking unevenly as though trapped within giant waves, sending Dicky and his imaginary crew to one side and then the other.

"Yes, you, son."

"Sit still," Mother ordered, passing among the many opened

presents that lay scattered along the floor like sunken treasure.

"Close your eyes a moment. Go ahead," Horatio insisted.

Dicky pulled his hot little hands from underneath his sweaty legs and covered his eyes.

"Good. Now stand back from yourself. Go on. Concentrate. You can be anything or anyone you want to be. All right, now tell me what you see."

Dicky's head was swimming. He sat rigid. His eyes closed tightly. He had played this game before.

"Well, my boy?" Horatio coaxed. "Doctor? Lawyer? Indian Chief?"

"The butcher, the baker, the candlestick maker," Dicky recited and shivered, peeking between his fingers.

"WHATEVER!" Horatio exclaimed, laughing heartily, his huge barrel of a stomach rising and falling in wave-like fashion.

"Sir, do you believe in God?" Dicky asked, going back to toying with his ship.

"God?!" Horatio exclaimed incredulously. "God is either dead or in shock or never was but should have been. I believe in life, my boy. Life! Not man's folly. We believe what we believe because of ideas. That is all. You see, ideas thrill and chill and kill. Ideas melt and seduce. Ideas are like the rudder of a vessel, forever changing the course of our lives. A man is not the product of his environment, but of environ ideas. Ideas are the substance of life. There are neither good nor bad spirits hovering over us. Only ideas of the mind which subject our bodies to the soul of that phenomena. Ideas, my boy. Ideas live on until they are modified by the influence of other ideas."

Dicky sat across from the monumental figure. Listening carefully, now. Getting the drift of the harangue.

"Through the natural order of things prevailing, we complete a cycle as do the seasons," Horatio continued. "Every phase of our life is charted at varying points like stars plotted throughout the heavens. Some of us believe we can control our destiny by holding to a true course, keeping things on an even keel. Unfortunately, most of us are but poor navigators, gazing up at the stars while sailing whimsically through life. Note that I didn't say *breezing* through it," he bellowed, expelling a watery sheet of wind and spray into a meaty, cull-like claw, the other hand suddenly disappearing inside his blazer, withdrawing a handkerchief as though signaling in semaphore. "Ideas govern the course, my boy. Ideas! And the only thing that can diminish the power of our own ideas is the influence of another. Now, you remember that, captain.

"You see," Horatio went on forever, breathing rather heavily, "there are as many concepts of God and religion as there are varieties of frozen foods. Money is the god of our society, and poverty is judgment day. Oh, we claim to be one nation under God. Yet we strive to be so individualistic, segregating ourselves into different sects of religion, organizations, and philosophical orders, enhancing our cultures or establishing our very own personal code or creed. And there we stand. Not as brothers, but as intrepid warriors ready to tear at each other's throats with our iconoclastic swords. You see, my boy," Horatio expounded, leaning forward in his seat, "the only power man truly possesses is the power within the idea. And it is man's *idea* that created God, in order to create the idea that God created man, in order to explain the order of the unexplainable. What a job the gods must have! Thank God there are so many of them," he roared, reaching for his drink.

Mother came back into the parlor carrying a pot of tea and a plate of little pastries. "Dicky, be a darling and take these boxes and wrappings out to the porch for your mother, but be sure to save the ribbons and bows. Oh, and don't forget to give your father his medicine."

"Please excuse me for a moment, Mr. Gladstone," Dicky said politely, gathering up all the boxes and wrappings his little arms could carry, ribbons sinking to the floor.

"—Uhm! What's this Mr. Gladstone nonsense?" Horatio declared, calling after him. "Hell, my boy. Why you and I go back before you were even born," he stated enigmatically. "When you were but a mere twinkle in your father's eye. Isn't that right, Victoria?"

"How about a sweet, Horace?" Mother smiled uneasily, serving him one of the tiny treats.

Chuckling, he answered haughtily, "And why not—you look positively delicious."

Dicky disappeared into the porch.

"Ah, he's turned into a fine young man," Horatio said with a sigh, leveling his fork against the thin layers of crust and cream.

"Horace—"

"How old is that little bugger, now?"

"He was seven in February."

"Seven years old. I can't imagine where the years have gone, Victoria. Can you, my sweet?"

"Horace, listen to me. I don't want you saying things like that in front of him," she insisted. "Do you hear me?" Dicky could hear his mother from the next room. "He remembers and repeats everything. He's not stupid."

"Why, I should say not. What, with your looks and my brains—"

"I mean it, Horace. And I wish you'd kindly refrain from those sermons of yours. I have enough things to worry about without you filling his head with such notions."

"You're right. You're right. He's got plenty of time to explore and expand that wonderful mind of his. Come on now. It's your birthday. Let me see a great big birthday smile. There, that's better."

Dicky came back into the room for the rest of the boxes and bows, then back out to the porch he disappeared, carefully separating pretty ribbons from the trash. He stayed there in that dusty room for quite some time, just staring down at the ashen figure in the chair before finally returning to the parlor.

"Well, that takes care of all the garbage," Dicky announced most pleasantly. "Oh, by the way. Daddy's dead in there. Happy birthday, Mother dear."

The weather had turned unusually cold, and a storm was brewing on the day they buried Father, which became the excuse for a very private ceremony. As the hour grew dark, a dead silence prevailed. Suddenly, animated, hoary boughs boldly blew against the blackness, their fingered branches pointing toward a neighboring slab of stone that deflected the steady, pounding downpour. Mother moved nearer Father's grave while Dicky's brave little eyes focused on the anonymous shadowy forms standing to either side. Four shivering figures silently lowered the coffin with canvas straps into the frothy earth.

Dicky ceased listening to the insignificant words of the minister, mesmerized by the meticulous descent of the coffin into its obscurity. Dicky sensed the awful strangeness of the moment. No memories. No sad feelings. None whatsoever. A strong and steady wind swept across the small graveyard, and lightning abruptly lit the heavens. That very picture, framed against the sky, engraved itself in Dicky's mind forever as time stopped. A word: frozen silently upon the lips of the minister. Pairs of cold eyes: peering into a sparkling grave. The silent widow: smiling fixedly into the eternal abyss. The casket: resting peacefully at the bottom of a hellish hole.

Chapter 6

THE HOME

It was strange how Horatio Gladstone suddenly disappeared from the scene (Mother said it was his health) and how Dr. King kept weaving in and out of the picture over the next few years, in and out of the family albums as well. There he was, appearing again and again. Birthdays. Holidays. Valentine's Day. Any occasion at all. Especially right after Father was killed. Of course, the family doctor had explained that Father had suffered from involutional melancholia before it finally took its toll; that he was exceedingly depressed, entering into early senility. All that doctor talk. Only, Dicky never told anyone that it was sugar shock that actually killed Father. You see, Dicky told Daddy how sweet Mummy had become. He told him that she had another Sugar Daddy; he had told him many secrets there in the porch. You should have seen his reaction. Understandably, he slipped away, farther and farther, until the darkness finally swallowed him up altogether. Dicky had given him his medicine, all right.

Mother enjoyed her new-found freedom, but she was receiving quite a bit of pressure from Dr. King, who wanted something of a more permanent relationship. She wouldn't hear of it though. After a period of time, Dr. King stopped coming around so often. Oddly enough, that's when Mother became more violent than Dicky could ever remember. Consequently, Dicky suffered at her hand practically on a daily basis; at times, with both her lovely, perfumed hands wrapped resolvedly around his little neck, fingers interlaced, thumbs pressed determinedly into his tiny throat till he thought his soul would soar away forever. Screams of mercy were silenced mercilessly over the slightest infraction. So Dicky learned to keep his distance. To keep everything bottled up inside.

Whenever Mother wanted to be alone at night to entertain a gentleman caller with the assurance of a good degree of privacy, she would send little Dicky outside to his jungle hammock hung between two giant elm trees alongside the house. And without a single complaint, he would snuggle down deep inside his mummy-shaped sleeping bag in coldest winter, listening to frozen rain pelting the sewn-in single sheet of plastic that formed the roof with wooden spreader sticks or sheltered the gossamer walls of mosquito netting when draped like a cozy, temporary coffin. And in the early morning, before the first sound of any life, he'd unzip the cold rows of metal teeth that cocooned him, contorting his frigid body from the bag, crawling about his shaky shelter for a peek at the world below. He'd watch his frozen breath spew forth, then most magically disappear, thinking how wonderful it would be if he could make the gloomy world around him vanish just as easily.

On summer nights, when warm and gentle breezes tarried through the transparent olive drab netting, voices carried with it. Voices and other familiar sounds of pleasure emanated from the opened jalousie windows of Mother's room. And Dicky would lie awake, quietly mimicking those sounds for his own amusement, rocking himself to sleep by poking and pushing at the ground with one of the spreader ticks. Back and forth.

One night, as Dicky lay fast asleep, Mother and her new beau approached his hammock in a drunken stupor. Dicky's reverie became a reeling nightmare as his world went topsy-turvy, the two of them turning his hammock around and around like a winding sheet, twisting it tighter and tighter until the lengths of line creaked madly before suddenly unwinding and rapidly propelling him in the other direction. Faster and faster. Dicky rose in a whirling frenzy to pairs of hands that spun him around and, at the same time, supported his little body save he come falling through the flimsy screen. He heard their laughter mounting as he unleashed sheer madness, tearing insanely at the wall within and landing precariously upon his feet. Dicky reeled to the right then stumbled backward as though he were the one intoxicated. Mother and her beau roared until they grew short of breath while Dicky fought to regain his equilibrium, faltering about the piece of property with pieces of tattered netting clutched tenaciously in his tiny hands.

Finally, Dicky was told to go inside the house and directly into bed. It was really quite a night. The Millers from across the street had called the police, but Mother's beau had driven off shortly before they arrived. So everything was dark and quiet. That is, until the police were gone. Then Mother started up again, dragging Dicky from between the sheets, screaming and punching him wildly for having created such a terrible scene and ruining his jungle hammock. She ushered him into the parlor and made him stand in the corner, instructing him that he had better not move a muscle till morning.

Late that morning, swollen and sore, Dicky still stood in the corner of the room, facing the giant green-leafed walls, pleading with Mother that he'd be as good as gold, begging her to let him sit a spell. But there was only silence. So he closed his eyes tightly and set his mind a million miles away, peering into a world of galaxies before finally realizing that there was no relief in sight. His mind was losing concentration by the minute, and his skinny legs felt as though they were about to fold. He had no place to go, yet he knew he had to run away forever.

He ran out of the house and across the yard as Mother ran to the phone to call the police. Within minutes, two patrol cars came to a screeching halt several blocks away. Dicky fled as fast as his little feet would carry him. Over a fence and between many a neighborhood home he flew, the police in full pursuit. He cut across Farmer Ferguson's property, plowing through gardens and gates, tearing insanely across lawns beneath lines of laundry and up another block to where a patrol car thwarted his escape. One of the police officers threw Dicky into the car and drove him home to Mother.

Mother was standing on the front stoop crying as they pulled up. "Take him away. Take him away," she pleaded over and over again, showing them her self-inflicted wounds, her badly bitten hand, and the scratches on her face. "You have no idea what I've been through," she cried and carried on, telling them a pack of vicious lies. "You don't know how I had to run down to that school of his and fight for him. You don't know what a summer I've had to endure. You don't know what a time I've had since the day that Nazi father of his dropped dead. Not that I would want him back for a minute, mind you. Take him away, I say. Take him the hell away from here forever."

Dicky sat shivering in the corner of a room at police headquarters, giving his tender age of ten while trying to explain what a jungle it really was back there. Half listening, the desk sergeant made arrangements with a parental home in another county. The sergeant hung up the phone, explaining directions to the two patrolmen who had taken Dicky into custody.

The officers took Dicky outside and put him into the backseat of the same patrol car. One of the patrolmen climbed in beside him and put a pair of shiny handcuffs on Dicky's skinny little wrists, clicking the stainless steel cuffs closed until the metal pinched his skin. The officer settled back in his wrinkly uniform for the long drive ahead of them.

It was dark when they arrived at the parental home, but Dicky could discern the structure set in heavy Gothic stone. Gloomy and grotesque. The police officers led him inside the building and down the end of a long corridor before removing the handcuffs. The vestibule reeked of disinfectant. A huge bald-headed man, garbed in a dull-gray uniform, stood at the top of the stairs, his thick arms folded across a massive chest. He shouted down at Dicky, ordering him up the steps. The voice echoed off the dreary walls, ringing violently in Dicky's ears as he moved toward the staircase. But one of the policemen grabbed hold of his arm while the other officer recorded information in an open log book that rested on a stand. Its pedestal rocked unevenly. Dicky could sense the giant's impatience. The policeman finally dropped the pen between the pages of the book before leading the lad up the flight of stairs. Dicky didn't dare take his eyes off the awesome form. He could still hear the ringing in his ears and taste the pervasive odor in the air. He stood there awfully scared. Suddenly, the policemen were gone. The giant ordered him to strip down and get into the showers, but Dicky insisted on a bath.

"I'm a bad boy, so I must sit in my own filth," Dicky said, shivering violently. "Mummy beats me, so I must be bad." He ripped off his clothes, showing his bruised and battered body. "Last night she beat me for at least a quarter of an hour. I must be terribly bad. But I'm not mad. Though if I'd had a hammer, I'd have bashed her brains in."

Outraged, the giant turned on a row of steaming showers then threw Dicky under the scalding water; the child's screams carried insanely throughout the building.

In the morning, Dicky found himself standing on a long line along with many other boys waiting for a second seating. Breakfast. If you could call it that. He found the trays and utensils greasy. The food revolting. The milk chalky. The bread stale. Afterward, he was given a physical examination then assigned to an outside work detail: policing the area along with another older boy. The boy walked over to him.

"Hey, Red. That you they brought in last night?"

Dicky looked up. His back and legs still burned from the scalding shower. "I'm not sure," he answered.

"You know, you woke up the whole place with your goddamn screaming," the boy complained, stooping over and picking up several cigarette butts. "Give you a piece of advice," he said, depositing the butts into the coffee can, concealing the larger ones in the elastic of his sock. "If you're smart, you'll keep your troubles to yourself. Otherwise you'll find yourself being transferred to Menlo Park, West of the lower bay," he advised. "They've got a nuthouse over there. Home away from home. Ya dig? The shrinks down there will wire your skull and shoot the juice. Mess with your head till you're nuttier than a fruitcake."

Dicky stared off into the distance.

"What's your name, carrot-top?" the boy demanded.

"I'm not sure."

"What?"

"I just can't be sure of anything anymore," Dicky told him. "Mother beat me. I showed the police my bruises, but they said I fell when I tried to run away. I showed the giant, too. I told the nurse this morning that the giant scalded me under the hot showers, but she said that I didn't know how to adjust the water. Then she took my blood," he added, rolling up his sleeve and pointing to the single needle mark along a bluish vein.

The boy looked queerly down at Dicky. "Hey, get to work. One of the screws is coming, screwball."

Within the next few days, Dicky was sent down to Dr. Roche's office. Dr. Roche was a clinical psychologist assigned to the parental home. Dicky was directed to a small desk where he was told to have a seat. He informed the doctor that there was nothing wrong with him. Dr. Roche smiled complacently, assuring him that everyone who comes to the home undergoes a series of tests, and that it doesn't mean there has to be something wrong. They had a quiet little chat about this and that. Then Dr. Roche handed Dicky a question and answer sheet and asked that he circle the letter which best answered each question. Dicky studied the questions carefully.

1. If you had an evening to yourself, would you

a) go to a movie
b) go to the opera
c) stay home and read a book

Dicky circled the letter c, crossing out the first three words. After he completed both sides of the sheet, Dr. Roche escorted him to a table filled with many blocks of different sizes and shapes. Before the psychologist could explain what he wanted, Dicky had inserted each block into its corresponding slot with remarkable speed and dexterity.

Dr. Roche stared down at the table in fascination. "Well, it's obvious you've had some experience with this sort of thing before," he declared.

"Yes, sir. Can I get a drink of water?" Dicky asked.

"That's, 'May I,'" Dr. Roche corrected.

Dicky removed one of the blocks from the table, placing it squarely upon his shoulder. "Choose one, Doctor: a) Chip off the old block. b) He's got a chip on his shoulder. c) Knock this chip off my shoulder, and I'll knock your block off." Dicky stood there grinning.

"Please put the block down, son. I'm not about to play," the psychologist stated apprehensively.

Dicky set the block down then went to get a drink of water from the fountain just outside the door. When he returned, Dr. Roche sat Dicky at a desk, handing him a booklet and a blank sheet of paper.

"Each section of this booklet deals with an area of mathematics," Dr. Roche explained. "Certain sections are more difficult than others, but I'd like for you to try and answer each problem. However, if you get stuck, don't waste time. Just go on to the next. I gave you a scratch sheet to work out your answers. Please do *not* write in the booklet. If you need more paper, I'll gladly give it to you. When you finish a section, you may go on to the next section. Now open your booklet to the first page; you'll find an answer sheet inside. If you have to erase on the answer sheet, do it thoroughly, then fill in your next choice darkly. I'm sure you've taken tests like this in school."

"Yes, sir."

"Good. Now please read the example at the top of the page."

Dicky read the example.

"Are there any questions before you begin?"

"How long am I going to be here, Doctor?"

"You mean here at the home?"

Dicky nodded.

"That depends on how well you cooperate," he said matter-of-factly, handing Dicky a pencil. "You may begin whenever you're ready."

Dr. Roche sat down at his own desk, and Dicky began the test. Fifteen minutes had passed when Dicky put down the pencil and closed the booklet.

Dr. Roche looked up. "I said you may continue whenever you've finished a section."

"I finished all the sections."

Dr. Roche looked bewildered. "You finished *all* the sections?"

"Yes, sir."

"There must be some mistake. There are over a hundred problems."

"One hundred nineteen, sir. And there are no mistakes."

Dr. Roche stood and walked over to Dicky's desk. He thumbed through the booklet then picked up the scratch paper, turning it over. "But your scratch sheet is blank, young man. Where did you work out the problems?"

"In my head, sir."

Dr. Roche looked at Dicky rather dubiously before walking over to a file cabinet and removing an answer key from the drawer, returning and laying the manila card over Dicky's answers. He stared down in amazement. "This is extraordinary!" he exclaimed. "I've never seen anything like this."

"Numbers are an extraordinary language," Dicky explained. "I have an attraction for the order of things. Mathematics is simply order in its purest form. Mother had a nice form before she had me."

"Yes, well, can we get on with it please?" the psychologist suggested, somewhat overwhelmed. He placed a stack of inkblot cards in front of Dicky. Dr. Roche turned one card over at a time, asking Dicky what each form seemed to suggest.

For Dicky, they triggered an unpleasant or violent reaction, but he responded carefully and deliberately, depicting objects of beauty and serenity. Flowers. Trees. Birds. Yes, seabirds . . . soaring, sailing, swooping down in profuse strains of premeditated art.

A final test, similar to the other, called for the subject to select an item from a choice of three, circling the one which best represented the image depicted above the examples given. The abstraction seemed to suggest a missile projection, with blotches boldly outlined adjacent to its base.

> a) rocket
> b) phallus
> c) laboratory flask

Dicky added the letter d), than wrote: "giant rhubarb in the garden." Across the face of each page he scribbled, "none of the above," handing back the booklet with unerring calm.

The psychologist's face turned red with anger. He studied Dicky for a moment before speaking. "You know, I think it's safe to say that you are deliberately trying to be difficult."

Dicky smiled and nodded his head in agreement. "*May* I go now, Doctor?"

Dicky did not see Dr. Roche's face again, which made no nevermind to the little prisoner of the State, although he figured the psychologist held the key to just how long he'd be confined. Oddly enough, the only face he anxiously awaited after waking each morning was the angry giant's puss. For whenever the colossal form saw Dicky filing past, along with all the other boys en route to breakfast, the man would express the look of sheer astonishment, as if to say, *Why, you're still here!* And each morning, Dicky would look for that look of amazement on the giant's face as confirmation that he, Dicky Geist, had not been shipped off to Menlo Park in the middle of the night to have wires attached to his head.

After a month, Mother and Dr. King brought Dicky home to Lake Hiawatha, but only after they made him promise that he'd be especially good. Of course, he said he would.

Chapter 7

PASTIMES

By the age of thirteen, Dicky had developed a passion for literature, devouring everything from Homer to Hemingway, escaping into worlds far beyond his own. On Saturday and Sunday mornings, Dicky would read the Bible in bed. For afternoon amusement, he'd work on complicated crossword puzzles in his head. During the week, he'd run the mile into town to the local library, check out three books, then off to school he'd go. In school, he'd read voraciously during homeroom, lunch hour, or any chance he had. To say he didn't learn from his teachers would be inane; to say he outshined them was understood without a doubt. His math teacher would try to trick him in front of the other students, but Dicky would work out complicated problems in his head that left his instructor frustrated and in the dark. When it came to literature, his English teachers tried to have him see things *their* way, but Dicky came up with his own interpretations that were nailed down with such support that they usually couldn't help but hem and haw. The question of whether or not Hamlet was insane was Dicky's favorite theme. The lesson Dicky learned from all his teachers was the fine line between envy and jealousy.

In addition to the classics, he also enjoyed reading and collecting comic books. Hundreds filled his closet or were found just beneath his bed until the day Mother burned them along with the leaves in the backyard. Piles of leaves and stacks of comics went up in smoke as Dicky returned home from playing ball one afternoon.

"Time to put childish things aside," Mother insisted, smiling like a pretty daytime witch, standing beside the burning wire basket with her bamboo rake. "I have to go into town for a little while to do some grocery shopping, so I want you to dust the mirrored tables while I'm gone. I spent a good part of the morning cleaning up your room, and I want you to keep it that way."

Dicky ran inside the house and to his room for fear that Mother had discovered certain materials hidden beneath the strip of linoleum in his closet: booklets and pamphlets collected over the years. But everything was there. All the secret materials sent away with coupons cut from the back of comics, paid for with money Dicky had pilfered over a period of time from Mother's pocketbook when she was fast asleep.

On the day the very first envelope had arrived, addressed to Dicky Geist, he had simply satisfied Mother's curiosity by explaining that the package contained nothing more than advertisements for various Christmas card promotions as well as membership invitations to secret clubs, which was certainly true in part, for the advertisers were always trying to sell you something. What he didn't tell her about were the materials concerning magic. Illusion. Pure and simple.

Starting out with coins and cards, lengths of clothesline and Mother's scarfs, Dicky would practice secretly in his room, well into the wee hours of morning, sometimes wrestling with a trick for days or weeks on end, becoming quite proficient as time went on.

In the schoolyard, you'd think that he'd be quite popular among his classmates. Actually, it didn't turn out that way at all. Oh, he'd show them tricks, all right: illusions employing sleight of hand. And the tricks worked like a charm, drawing them to him in droves. The only problem was that the children insisted on *knowing* how the magic was performed, which Dicky flatly refused to reveal. Needless to say, their frustrations mounted by the minute, till finally one girl from the upper grades stepped forward and threatened to blacken both his eyes if he did not divulge the *magic*. That's when Dicky pulled out packaged coils of clothesline from a plastic pouch, warning the girl that she was a direct descendant of Medusa and that her hair was actually crawling with squirming, slithery snakes—a nest of vipers about to burrow deep within her ears and out the very eye sockets of her skull.

The girl giggled as did the other children, yet stood absorbed in the mystique of the moment. "And why would they do that, dickhead?" she questioned patently.

"Why? So as to pass their deadly venom off as crocodile tears," the young illusionist cast in *sotto voce*, misdirecting her attention to the sudden lifting and shifting of a Slinky before the girl's face and curly head of hair, the toy's helical spring of concentric rings rising and falling and actually seeming to snake freely through her curls along with coils of cotton clothesline before she ran screaming hysterically across the playground in absolute terror. Not so much from fear of myth as from the mixture of ammonia and water that had burned her angry eyes as Dicky had gently squeezed the saturated coils high above them.

And when the booklets on ventriloquism arrived the following year, he studied diligently during every spare moment he could find, practicing his substitute sounds, working quietly in front of the mirrored tables in the parlor by day (when Mother wasn't around), or speaking very softly into his pillow for fear he'd alert a soul.

After a while, he knew that he had learned his lessons well. Like the time Clarabell the clown appeared on *The Howdy Doody Show* as a rather questionable form of entertainment for children, squeezing high-pitched obscenities from his horn as Mother came into the room, disbelieving her ears and threatening to write NBC and the producers, immediately killing the picture and permitting Dicky to go outside to play for half an hour.

Then there was the stupid talk show that Mother had made him sit and watch with her practically every Saturday afternoon. He would sit quietly by in the parlor, confined to a narrow wood-framed chair off to the side of the TV. Across the room, Mother would be nestled comfortably on the couch.

As the show began one afternoon, a pretty assistant appeared with a caged bird that she placed upon a table in the far corner of the stage before bringing on a special guest. No sooner than the man sat down, after having been formally introduced by the host, did the bird start chirping away and talking excitedly.

"Hello. I talk. Can you fly?" the winged creature went on incessantly, interrupting the guest speaker and mimicking the host, upstaging both personalities and becoming the center of attention although distanced from the screen. A second camera zoomed in for a close-up, and Dicky observed the creature's dilating black pupil as the bird cocked its brilliant head quizzically to one side. Listening for all its worth before parroting the words and phrases of both host and guest, mimicking the laughter of its audience.

Finally, the bird was introduced as Chewy, a three-year-old, green-feathered, yellow naped Amazon, with the expected longevity of sixty some odd years.

"Hello. I talk. Can you fly?" it repeated, preening beneath its wing.

    Dicky laughed aloud, for he absolutely loved that bird. But Mother, somewhat bored by its antics, suddenly got up and changed the channel. Then another. Yet, there on every station came the voice of Dicky's feathered friend, Chewy, laughing away insanely or engaged in repartee.

> Channel 5: "How're you?" came a voice that carried over the air waves above the call of Jungle Jim's.
> Channel 7: "Hi. I'm your feathered friend," it screeched.
> Channel 9: "Come fly with me," it sang along with Frank Sinatra.

> Mother could not believe her ears.

> Channel 11: "We're birds of a feather."
> Channel 13: "Gonna fly this coop forever."
> Channel 2: "Ah, hee, hee hee," it chortled madly, coming in loud and clear, imitating Sarah, Doctor King's housekeeper.
> Channel 4: "Hello. I talk. Can you fly?"

    And once again around the dial it flew till Mother thought the bird would drive her bats. In frustration, she switched off the set and sent Dicky outside to play.

    The day after the TV repairman came and reluctantly adjusted the antenna on the roof, explaining that there was nothing wrong with the set, Dicky started making the sound of a single drop of water in the kitchen sink about every sixty seconds or so. Even the plumber thought her something of a lunatic after having changed the washers in the faucet at least half a dozen times that month.

    It wasn't long before Dicky tried his hand at hypnotism. Nothing quite captured his attention as those pamphlets he received regarding hypnosis. How nicely things were coming together for him as he studied before the mirrored tables in the parlor. He had no one to practice with, so he practiced on himself whenever he knew he was alone, first dusting one way with his magic rag, and then the other, poring over the information, practicing for hours at a time over a period of months, improvising as he went along, until he had finally mastered the technique.

Those had been rather trying years; the years he lost himself in time. Dicky couldn't be too careful, for his secret pastimes seemed to be melding themselves into a single, solitary force—seemed to be taking little Dicky over.

It was on a cool and quiet afternoon as Dicky was kneeling over one of the mirrored tales in the parlor when he heard Mother returning from grocery shopping. He was busy dusting up a storm with his magic rag, wiping his reflection in wide clockwise circles while staring down at his image intently. He heard her coming into the house by the side door, so he quickly ran the rag in the other direction, listening to the sounds emanating from the kitchen as Mother unpacked and put away the groceries: the sound of cabinets opening and closing, the sound of the refrigerator and freezer doors, the sound of running water in the sink. Dicky whispered furtively, fixing his eyes sharply upon the image in the glass:

"From where do you come when I summon you forth?
Are your words that which I actually hear?
Where do you go when I wipe you away?
To where does your voice disappear?"

"Through time," came the enigmatic reply across the room from Dicky. "Through time," were the words that ushered in ever so faintly, rustling the curtains, brushing back and forth against the sash and sill while seeming to mingle there for a moment. "Through time," came the whisper again and was gone.

"Yes. Through time," Dicky said ever so faintly through motionless lips, gazing into the mirrored table.

"We're not heating the outside," Mother said, coming into the room and winding the jalousie window tightly. "I wonder if this will grow at all," she mumbled to herself, setting down a tumbler of water upon the narrow sill. The top of the glass contained a partially submerged oval object, held in place by toothpicks resting on the rim. "Did you finish dusting the other tables like I asked?"

Dicky focused on the convoluted pit, noting the submerged portion magnified by the water. "Not yet, Mother. But I will."

"Well, see to it that you do. I don't want to see a single speck of dust. Hear?"

Dicky lowered his eyes to the mirrored table; its border faceted with squares shattered his reflection, multiplying his image to form a series of distorted vignettes. "Yes, Mother."

Mother took an appreciative glance at her avocado seed before leaving the room. Dicky went over to the window, gazing at the object in fascination, observing the tiny crooked white root emerging from its world. He was deep in thought when suddenly there came a loud crash that shattered the window beside him and sent the tumbler flying across the room. Dicky neither flinched nor moved an inch. A baseball had struck the far wall with a thud, and Mother's avocado pit rolled across the floor.

Mother came running in from the kitchen, screaming hysterically at Dicky as she dashed over to pick up the pit and ball. "Those are your goddamn friends and their lousy baseball," she swore.

Dicky swallowed hard, insisting he hadn't a single solitary friend in all the world.

"Well, you could have if you weren't so goddamn strange," she hollered. "Whispering into your pillow when you think there's no one else around."

"I don't whisper, Mother."

"I see," she said, stooping over and carefully picking up the larger pieces of glass. "Then I'm just imagining things. Yes? I know you do things with your voice. I hear you in the yard."

"I don't know what kind of things you're talking about, Mother."

"You know exactly what I'm talking about. I know, for instance, that you can imitate Fat Billy's voice. When his mother was calling him in for dinner the other evening, you answered her in his voice. And don't deny it! I heard you distinctly. Billy was coming up the block, and before he cut across our yard, you answered her in his voice. I heard that profanity. I heard what you said. I also heard him screaming bloody murder when his father got ahold of him. And I watched you grinning from ear to ear. You want to stand there and tell me that isn't so?"

"That wasn't me, Mother."

"Oh, so now we're back to that again. I'm afraid I'm going to have to call Dr. King. I think this business has gone far enough," she said, walking away angrily. "Thirteen years old, and you still behave like a child!" she exclaimed, storming out of the room.

"Thirteen years old," Dicky thought aloud. "But where did all the years go?" he asked of no one in the room, trying desperately to recollect. He knew there were important missing pieces of a puzzle that simply came or went with the voices, and he was determined to put together the picture of the past. So many missing pieces he thought, staring down at the shards of glass.

Chapter 8

THE TIME CLOCK

Having skipped two grades, Dicky was only sixteen when he graduated high school. Smart as they come. But he couldn't hold a steady job in town. As an oddball, he could find only odd jobs to do around the neighborhood, such as mowing lawns a mile a minute like a lunatic in summer; violently shaking little trees in autumn so as to rake in a little cash; shoveling walks in winter; and a little landscaping in the spring. There was some talk of college, but Dicky really wasn't interested.

By seventeen, he had suffered severely. Sitting down in the parlor, he went through the family albums, trying desperately to sort out the past. There was Father, *reposing* in his green vinyl chair on Mother's thirtieth birthday, or so she had told a friend. An aged brown and white portrait of Dicky's maternal grandparents, posing stone-faced with their daughters, filled a single page. A candid picture of little Dicky dressed up like a devil for Halloween stood out from the others. Pictures of many men filled subsequent pages. There was picture after picture of Mother posing in sexy bikinis, standing by a tranquil bay alongside Dr. King. Pose after glamorous pose. There were other pictures, too. Not the kind you would find in any family album, to be sure, but rather images fixed somewhere in the back of Dicky's mind, tucked away in time; images too painful to reveal as yet.

Dicky had experienced years of abuse since the day his so-called Father died, all because Mother wanted to play house. Yet she didn't want the responsibility of having to raise a child alone. The neighborhood men wanted to play house, too. Only they knew when playtime was over.

Through those difficult years, Mother had ambivalent feelings about rejecting Dr. King's persistent invitations to spend the summers together at his Long Island estate. But she was stubborn, which was something Dicky couldn't understand at first. As he grew older, he began to understand her single fear. It was for fear that the good doctor would have a taming effect on her, and it was the very wildness within her soul that would not submit to any sort of compromise. Not yet, anyway.

Mother would phone Dr. King only when she needed a favor or his soothing advice concerning Dicky, who was getting out of hand. She'd keep in touch, yet she'd keep him at a comfortable distance until it was she who decided otherwise. Always on her terms. Always by her rules. And when the local traffic became too congested for her to handle, when her men friends started to drive her crazy, smothering her, suffocating her, she'd suddenly pull her disappearing act, directing Dicky to the door or phone.

"No, Mother's not home now," he'd lie. "She went to Florida to visit her sick sister and won't be back for several weeks," she'd have him swear. "No, I'm fine. The neighbors are looking in on me," he'd assure the caller.

And if her men friends were persistent, if they kept phoning or coming around, she'd simply reach for the bottle of Scotch or more prescription to calm her shattered nerves. Actually, it was Dicky's prescription, so she'd take a double dose. When the pills ran out, she'd call Dr. King, who'd call the pharmacist in Lake Hiawatha. Then she'd walk down into town with an empty prescription bottle and a roll of film in one hand and little Dicky in the other, flirting outrageously with the druggist behind the counter, fast developing another relationship.

Only on a rare occasion could Dr. King convince Mother to at least have dinner together. He'd drive all the way in from Long Island, and they'd have a quiet little chat. Somehow she had managed to keep the patient doctor on a string for all those years, and for very selfish reasons to be sure. Dicky grew to understand those reasons perfectly, reasons that had to do with a new and full-blown fear. It happened shortly before Mother's fortieth birthday. The year of fear for a woman as vain as she. Oh, she was still as attractive as any model who graced the fashion covers, as shapely as the pictures in the family albums taken when Dicky was but wee. And nearing forty, not a blemish on her pretty face or a wrinkle anyplace. Flawless. Regardless, age had become her enemy.

Actually, Mother grew even more attractive and, like a honey pot, drew more and more of those mindless drones to her side. But just before her fortieth birthday, something had happened. Her alacrity toward those local yokels suddenly diminished to nothing more than mild indifference. For the time clock in Mother's head had told her that it was time to get serious. Time to secure a nest egg for her future. She was now ready to be tamed.

Of course, there was another factor, too. Mother was finding it more and more difficult to control Dicky, especially with his being around the house most every day. She needed help, so she phoned Dr. King who was delighted to have them spend the summer at his estate. Dicky was reluctant to go at first, but he thought it might be interesting to see what kind of web she'd weave.

Dr. King sent his chauffeured limousine around that June.

Chapter 9

CABBAGES

No sooner than the limousine came barreling through the gate and up the drive to Dr. King's estate, did Sarah come stomping out of the house, quarreling with Max the chauffeur as the middle-aged light-skinned black man stepped from the car, coming around to open the door for Mother and Dicky. Sarah followed, hands placed firmly on her hips. Dr. King's housekeeper had aged considerably over the years since Dicky had last seen her.

"Why, I wouldn't go from here to the corner with that ol' fool," Sarah declared, walking up to the limo on old bowed legs. "You see the way he drives, Miss Vicki. Like a crazy man," she insisted, as though she were continuing a conversation with someone who had just returned from market instead of a ten-year hiatus. "He wouldn't drive that way if Dr. King be in the car. Or would you, fool?" she demanded, glaring up at Max with indignation. "If I was you, Miss Vicki, why I'd —" Sarah's sharp tongue suddenly stopped in mid-sentence as if someone had lifted a needle off a recording record before switching to a slower rpm. Her words mystically transformed themselves into music, for there were notes where a moment ago was noise. Sarah was practically singing, "Oh, good Lord, will ya look at you, Miss Vicki. Why, you's prettier than a picture postcard. Like ya haven't even aged a day," she crooned, giving Mother a warm and welcome embrace.

Mother smiled, basking in the compliment for all its worth. "How have you been, Sarah?"

"Pretty good fo' a leathery ol' lizard." Sarah turned her head.

A tall young man with a healthy head of clay-red curls stepped from the limousine. Towering over everyone; six-foot even. Sarah just stood there, shaking her head in disbelief before throwing her arms around him, squeezing him with all her might, tears streaming down her coal-black face. The young man stooped over to embrace her and felt the wetness on his cheeks. Warm, wet tears.

"You's all grow'd up. I knew a little fellow called Dicky, but I see Richard now." She pulled him even closer. "Still, I know that Dicky's hiding away somewhere in there," she whispered queerly, patting him gently on the back.

Richard was standing there with Sarah, cheek to cheek, smiling past her, enjoying the sound of his name and the way she said it. Strange was the only word for the sudden friendship which magically manifested itself and secured a silent yet sacred bond between them. He stared uneasily at the brick facade with iron bars which stood looming in the distance: The King Foundation.

"Well now, let ol' Sarah have a good look at ya here," she said, smiling brightly, wiping away the tears on the back of her sleeve. "Dang if ya didn't grows up to be the spittin' image of Hermes. You remember how ol' Sarah feels 'bout him, now don't ya?" she swore and winked.

Dr. King, coolly clad in cotton and wearing a warm and winning smile, came forward. Congenially. The personification of gentility and hospitality. The perfect picture of a host. Tall, trim, and well-tanned, he gracefully took Mother's hand and kissed her gently upon the cheek. Then he took and shook Richard's hand most masculinely. Sarah invited everyone inside to freshen up, for lunch was about to be served on the patio. Both she and Max took the bags from the trunk, still arguing with one another as they disappeared inside the house together.

It was a beautiful summer's day. Sarah served drinks from a silver oval tray bordered and ornamented in filigree. Sparkling drinks in crystal goblets glistened. Sarah disappeared, returning a moment later with a large silver platter filled with rings of kielbasa, salads, and homemade breads.

"Oh, Sarah, you shouldn't have gone to all this trouble," Mother declared.

Sarah smiled then left again, returning with yet another dish. "Now jus' you feast yo' eyes on these, Miss Vicki. Ol' Sarah made one of yo' favorites as I recall." Sarah held the colorful stuffed cabbage entrée before Mother, each plump green leaf stuffed beyond capacity with meat, rice, onions and raisins, held together with toothpicks. A dozen servings sitting in a dish of rich red gravy.

"*Gołąbki!*" Mother cried in Polish. "They look absolutely delicious. Oh, Sarah. David. Thank you. Thank you both so very much."

Sarah smiled broadly, and Dr. King went inside to turn on some music. "Polka time everyone," he announced. And the music blared in duple meter. Suddenly, Max jumped up and grabbed Sarah around the waist with one hand, pulling up his baggy pants with the other.

"Let go o' me you ol' fool," Sarah insisted with annoyance, pushing Max away. "Man ain't got no shame, flirtin' with an ol' lady. Ol' fool."

"Ain't no fool like an old fool," Max declared.

And everyone danced and ate and drank and laughed at Max who was laughing and dancing merrily by himself across the patio. Richard looked around amusedly, thinking how *polished* everything seemed. Then Mother told stories about when she was a young girl and how her mama and five sisters would all sit around the kitchen table waiting for their papa to come home from the tailor shop each night. And how everyone was forbidden to speak anything but Polish in the house.

"Oh, and the fights it used to cause," Mother went on. "Papa would throw out every gentleman caller who wasn't Polish, or who was, but couldn't speak the language fluently. Mama would always prepare golumbki for him on special occasions. God, how we loved golumbki! And all of Papa's girls would stand in line to wait on him hand and foot. Oh, he was such a fine tailor. He even made most of Dicky's clothes for school, and he taught all of his girls to sew. All I ever wanted was my own sewing room," she sighed.

> Tailor-mades and
> Tailor maids
> All in a row.

Later that afternoon, Sarah served tea along with her special dessert that Richard simply devoured. Honey cakes. Mother made Sarah promise to write down her recipe for stuffed cabbage. Sarah smiled broadly, informing everyone how many thousands of years old cabbage is, and how it had been seen floating down the Nile by explorers.

"That be the longest river in the world, Richard," Sarah said. "It flows from a lake named same as yo' mother's. Lake Victoria. Flows all the way to the Mediterranean Sea. Yes, siree. Lake Victoria be the second largest freshwater body in the world. Sarah been all through Africa. Been all 'round her, too. Darn tootin'." Sarah made a great sweeping motion with her arm. "From the Gulf of Guinea off the Ivory Coast, on up and through the Mozambique Channel. Finally, 'round the Cape. Yes, siree. The Cape of Good Hope. Ah, hee, hee, hee. That's where Sarah met her 'Great White Hope.' More tea, Miss Vicki?"

The military was Richard's means of escape from all that madness and hullabaloo. Besides, he really wasn't doing anything with his life since the day he graduated high school. Mother was against the whole idea at first, but Dr. King convinced her that it might be for the best.

"But why the Marines?" she protested, for it was the height of the war in Vietnam. "He could be killed! He should be thinking about college, not playing soldier."

"Maybe they'll make a man out of him," Dr. King suggested. "Richard has a lot of growing up to do."

By the end of summer, everything had been arranged. Max drove Mother home to Lake Hiawatha for a spell, first dropping off Richard in Manhattan to be sworn in. Sworn in as Private Richard Geist, he was.

Chapter 10

COMMITTED TO AN IDEA

The sun was already scorching the station platform as Private Richard Geist stepped off the train in Yemesee, South Carolina, along with many other young men who had enlisted in the United States Marine Corps. The new recruits were swiftly rounded up by a barking bulldog-face marine sergeant, distinguished from the lower form of animal in three respects: a) sergeant stripes; b) the fact that the figure paced back and forth on two legs instead of four; c) the man's ability to coordinate thumb and forefinger; thus, enabling him to remove an offensive piece of lint from his utility trousers. Yes, trousers.

"Thumbs along the seams of your trousers when standing at the position of attention," the sergeant barked, trotting up and down the ranks as though examining livestock. "Bunch of cock-sucking, long-haired, fairy fucking freaks is what they sent us this time out," he growled. "You! You think that's funny, lady? You think you're here on holiday, you sorry sack of shit?" he hollered into the face of a heavyset recruit wearing baggy pants. "You got a pussy or a pecker beneath that petticoat, fairy face? You better answer up immediately because I'm in serious doubt."

"Pecker, sir."

"This is the United States Marine Corps, not a goddamn breeding ground for freaks and faggots; not a fat farm for sorry-ass fucking fruits. Do you know what a faggot is, lard-ass?"

"Yes, sir," the heavyset youth replied.

"Of course you do," the sergeant snapped, ordering the rest of the recruits to line up in single file, *asshole to bellybutton*, sending *lard-ass* to the rear, double-timing his charge of *sorry shits* to the mess hall, instructing everyone that they had but five minutes in which to *trough down chow* and fall back into formation; those last on line had less than three. Everyone ate while standing, wolfing down their food without bothering to chew. "One minute to go, girls. You're gonna be running all afternoon, so you don't wanna barf up on the lady next to you. Now do you?"

"No, sir," several voices mumbled.

"Bunch of goddamn cunts and cattle. I can't hear you, assholes."

"No, Sir!" everyone shouted in unison.

"Let's go, shitbirds. Outside. I said move it, lard-ass!" the sergeant hollered, branding the heavyset recruit in the rear end with the shiny tip of a combat boot. "Today, maggots."

Moments later, everyone was herded like cattle onto to a poorly ventilated bus and shipped off toward the Recruit Receiving Depot on Parris Island.

"You keep those goddamn windows closed," the voice commanded.

Several of the recruits mumbled things beneath their breath. Others forced a smile while whispering among themselves. Richard said nothing, enjoying the ride, covering the span of years it had taken him to reach this point in time. He stared at the bridge and body of water they were steadily approaching.

When the bus finally stopped and its doors flew open, two angry men in campaign covers (hats like those the Mounties wear) and khaki uniforms quickly boarded and ordered everyone off. "Get those sorry-ass hides of yours into high gear," one of them shouted, pushing and prodding the entire pack forward with short wooden clubs, stampeding the disoriented lot out onto the tarmacadam.

"Faster, you fuckin' red-haired flag of shit," another swore, driving the butt end of his club into Richard's rear. "Fall in, faggot. I mean, now! You filthy turd."

Richard giggled, certain that the men were anally fixated, fascinated with the way the sergeant ran his f's together.

"Oh, I have a surprise for you, asshole," the sergeant swore.

The new recruits stood sweaty, rigid and wide-eyed, corralled by several other stone-face marines standing tall in spit-shined boots and shoes. The two men in khaki uniforms and campaign covers walked around the new recruits threateningly, smacking their clubs into the palms of meaty paws.

An older marine, bearing the stripes of years of service, stepped forward in green utility trousers and bloused boots. Like an awning, he lowered the front of his olive drab campaign hat onto a pair of bushy brows. A stolid, shadowy countenance contrasted sharply with a sardonic grin. "You find this amusing, boy?" the chevroned sergeant snapped at Richard.

Private Geist stood firmly planted, squinting at the taunting fleshy lips and angry mouth. "Me?"

"Yes, you, shit-for-brains! You find this amusing?" he repeated, raising Richard's chin several inches with the think end of a wooden club.

"Fascinating," Richard responded.

"Fascinating?" the sergeant grimaced, his jaw tightening with disapproval. "First and last word I better hear outta that smart mouth of yours is, Sir. You got that, scum?"

"Sir, yes, sir."

"I can't hear you, boy."

"Sir, yes, sir!"

"I still can't hear you, maggot."

"SIR, YES, SIR!"

"I wanna know why a shitbird like you joined the Marines."

Richard considered the question carefully.

"You deaf, boy?"

"I want to be a professional, Sir."

"Boy, I just got finished telling you that the first and last words outta that sewer trap of yours is, SIR! When you talk to me, you better be standing at the position of attention. You keep those eyeballs glued straight ahead—feet at a forty-five degree angle." He slammed the toe of a highly-polished boot between Richard's shoes. "Get those thumbs along the seams of your trousers. Stomach in. Chest out. You want to be a professional? A professional what?"

"Sir, I want to be a professional killer, SIR!"

The sergeant's face lit with genuine fascination. He stared at Richard intently.

"You a Yankee, boy?"

"SIR, YES, SIR!"

"What's your name, scum?"

"SIR, PRIVATE GEIST, SIR."

"Private Geist. You are on my shitlist, shitbird."

"SIR, YES, SIR!"

All three men were standing in front of Richard when lard-ass suddenly swatted something on his neck. Two of the three figures were immediately at the fat lad's throat, spinning the recruit around to face the ranks, sandwiching the boy between them while barking away insanely like a pair of rabid dogs, funneling their fury down each ear as fright took hold and shook those flaccid cheeks.

"What's your name, asshole?" an angry sergeant shouted.

"Sir, Private Swanson, Sir."

"Sand fleas are sacred to this island, Swan-shit," a second sergeant volunteered.

"And you just killed one, scum," a third exploded in Swanson's face.

"Sand fleas are essential to your training here," the first assailed.

"They teach you respect."

"They teach you discipline."

"They're God's little creatures."

"Do you believe in God?"

"Sir, yes, sir."

"Then you have no respect."

"God would have your ass for this."

"That is if we weren't here to claim it first."

"God is a second-rate citizen around here, maggot."

"We are your salvation."

"Do you understand?"

"Sir, yes, sir."

"God doesn't frequent foxholes."

"Or assholes."

"Or any place that's dark."

"You swat that sand flea on patrol, or in a hole, or up a fucking tree, and you're dead, dead, dead!"

"And your men are dead with you."

"Charlie and his slanted gook-eyed gang are going to be pickin' at your goddamn bones, boy."

"Are we getting through to you?"

"Sir, yes, sir."

"Well, let's see about that."

"Do you put your trust in God, or men like us who will teach you how to save your ass one day?"

"Men like you—Sir, men like you, Sir!"

"Then you're an atheist bastard."

"Sir, yes, sir."

"Well, let's hear it, by God. Loud and clear."

"Sir, I am an atheist bastard, Sir."

"I think he's got it."

"I think so, too," another barked, turning to face the group. "And if I ever see any one of you lay a hand on another sand flea, or scratch your balls, or move a goddamn muscle when you're supposed to be standing at the position of attention, I swear I'll rip your fucking head off your shoulders and shit in your neck. Do I make myself understood?"

"SIR, YES, SIR!" everyone answered up loud and clear.

"Get back into formation, scumbag."

"Sir, yes, sir," the recruit responded sharply, fighting back the flood of tears dammed up at the very corners of his eyes.

The marine in green came forward, and the other two in khaki stepped aside. "All right, all of you listen up and listen up good," the mean green marine commanded. "We are your D.I.'s. Drill Instructors. I am your senior instructor. My name is Gunnery Sergeant Walker. To my right is Staff Sergeant Pierce. To my left is Acting Sergeant Mascal. It's our job to transform the lot of you mangy creatures into something resembling marines. From here on in, you will think marine. You will act marine. And maybe in time, you will become marines. We have thirteen weeks to accomplish this. Thirteen weeks of pure hell. Some of you won't make it. Some of you will be sent back after weeks or months of training only to start all over again. But all of you will do things you never thought possible. Some of you will wish you were dead. Others of you will think you are. And if anyone gets any ideas about leaving here, may God have mercy on your soul."

Clothing issue and haircuts down to the scalp were next on the agenda. Private Geist reflected on how he and all the others seemed so completely strange. Powerless. An army of little Samsons about to be programmed before their hair grew back again. He thought about how well those military minds played their games: humiliate, intimidate, and provoke. HIP was their acronym and their way. Breaking you down before rebuilding. Molding and reshaping personalities were, indeed, the order of the day.

During indoctrination, presented in an auditorium that first week, Private Geist half listened to some lieutenant's lecture concerning the Marine Corps as a military unit and a branch of the

U.S. Armed Forces. Richard's attention wandered from the lieutenant's chart on stage to a large emblem hanging on a wall: a colorful plaque of an eagle, globe, and anchor—symbolizing the presence of marines in the air, on land, and sea.

". . . and so, men," the lieutenant continued, walking back and forth across the stage, punctuating his sentences with a wooden pointer, poking at the chart, "it's important for you to understand that the United States Marine Corps is a division of the Department of the Navy, generally employed in amphibious landing operations under the authority of the Secretary of the Navy. You men are paid by the Navy. You are, in essence, a police force for the Navy. In wartime, you are essentially a group of paid professional killers. And we are, indeed, at war, I need not remind you."

Richard imagined himself running through a field with an enemy's head impaled like a cabbage on the end of a bayonet.

"And men," the officer bellowed, snapping open a silver lighter in a single motion, pausing to light a cigarette, "we are the finest fighting organization of the face of the globe. We're in there first, so we've got to be the finest.

"Now, there's just one more thing I want you to bear in mind before you leave this room; and that is, there is no such thing as *can't*. You can do any task you put your mind to. Always remember that. That's all, men. Good luck."

"COMPANY—TTEN—HUT!" commanded a voice from the rear of the auditorium as the officer crossed the stage. "DISMISSED."

Richard remained standing in the front row while scores of young recruits started filing out the back of the building in an orderly fashion.

A young corporal, who had been standing patiently by, came bounding up the steps toward the officer. "Excuse me, Lieutenant," he said, saluting sharply. "There's a Captain Mathews on the phone who's insisting on immediate delivery of those condiments he requisitioned last month, sir."

"That goddamn idiot," the lieutenant roared angrily. "He knows I *can't* do that. I already told him so. Tell him to call Captain Burrows over at the commissary."

"I did, sir. But Captain Burrows *can't* help him either."

"Well if he *can't* help him, how the hell am I supposed to?

Where the hell am I going to drum up cardamom and cumin seeds around here anyway?"

"I *can't* help you there, sir."

Richard couldn't help but smirk at the lieutenant and his lackey on the stage, especially after listening to that laughable lesson then having the officer negate his own decree. Horatio Gladstone was right. You had to inject your own ideas into doctrine.

But much to Richard's dismay, his ideas were not permitted. He was not allowed to think for himself. He soon learned that his thinking was done for him. Disenchanted, Private Geist was constantly being singled out for special duty assignments, which made him responsible for being the finest. He soon grew to despise being the finest, being responsible and being first. Inevitably, he came to despise his three drill instructors who volunteered his services for the worst of all possible work details. Latrine machine; and Richard was all the moving parts: scrubbing and mopping and polishing everything from floor to ceiling. They had him working long into the night when everyone else was fast asleep. There came a point when he imagined himself running through a field with all three cabbage heads impaled on the end of his bayonet.

But Richard soon learned how to get the help he needed with those assignments, either by belching or simulating the sounds of breaking wind loud and clear whenever lard-ass happened past one of the instructors. Like the time the famished recruit stood on the chow line in front of Richard, disgusting sounds emanating from the fat boy's gut, or so it seemed. Or in the middle of P.T. when the exasperated lad completed a set of sit-ups, flatulating quite loudly. But the final straw was during a grenade exercise when lard-ass evidently and dramatically exploded his asshole before the entire platoon. Doing it was one thing. Denying it was quite another. But blaming it on Private Geist, or any recruit for that matter, was tantamount to treason, and the instructors threw a fit, sending lard-ass to sickbay, rationing his chow, making life as miserable as they could for the innocent slob.

Lard-ass swore to Richard that he'd get even.

On the parade ground, Richard and lard-ass were constantly under Sergeant Pierce's scrutiny.

"One — three — three-by-yo-left. Left-right-left. To the rear — — March. Double to the rear — March. Close it up. Close it up.

Three-by-yo-left. Left shoulder — Arms."
                snap snap snap snap
"Right shoulder — Arms."
                snap snap snap snap
"Le-ft — le-ft — three-by-yo-left. Column right — March."
But Richard had piped a "column left" into the fat boy's ear, sending the reckless recruit crashing headlong into the sergeant's side.

"— — —Pla-toon — Halt. Right — Face. Order — Arms."
                snap snap snap snap
"At ease. Get up here, Swan-shit."
"Yes, sir."
"What?!"
"Sir, yes, sir."
"I can't hear ya, boy."
"SIR, YES, SIR!"
"Do ya know what a fuckin' column right is?"
"SIR, YES, SIR!"
"So why did ya start flankin' to the left, maggot?"
"Sir, I thought—"
"Ya don't get paid to think, Private!" Sergeant Pierce shouted in Swanson's face. "You get paid to listen up and follow orders. Whattaya gawkin' at, boy? You get those eyeballs straight ahead. You are at the position of attention. If I see ya movin' those eyes around again, I'll knock them outta your head like marbles. You understand me, boy?"
"SIR, YES, SIR!"
"This is close-order drill, not a fuckin' hometown parade. Twice around the parade ground, scumbag. DOUBLE TIME — HUT."
Private Swanson rifled through the ribbons of heat rising off the macadam, glaring angrily at the hot noonday sun that soaked his trousers and shirt, sweat pouring profusely down his rubbery-flaccid face.
"Now the rest of you listen up," the sergeant shouted. "Some of you may think it's hot out here. Well, let me tell you somethin'. In another hour, it's gonna seem like a fuckin' inferno. And if we don't get it right, we'll be out here till after the sun goes down. That'll give you time to cool your heels. Platoon — tten-hut. Right shoulder —

Arms."

snap snap snap snap

"Left — Face. Forward — March. One — three — three-by-yo-left. Left-right-left. To the right flank — March."

Late that evening, Private Swanson was the recipient of a blanket party. Soap bar-filled socks toned his fleshy body brightly. As the weeks wore on, lard-ass Swanson had drawn the wrath of the gods upon him, steadily weakening under the drill instructors' steady dose of discipline. He was about to crack.

Richard, on the other hand, was pretty much left alone. He showed a remarkable talent for handling himself in tight situations, especially during hand-to-hand combat, taking on two or three combatants at a time, batting their heads and bodies to hell and back with a pugil stick: a padded weapon that simulated the butt end of a rifle at one end, the blade of a fixed bayonet at the other. And he fought them all, refusing to wear the protective headgear during practice, insisting that its confinement would drive him mad. This, his instructors had to see for themselves, ordering the recruit to wear it on the day they invited the top gunnery instructor on the island for the challenge, figuring that Private Geist would lose control; lose the competitive edge. But they were wrong.

Private Geist did, indeed, go mad. But it was a madness that he was in touch with from the start. The only control he lost was in not knowing when to stop. The top gun never knew what hit him, although Richard hit him twenty-seven times. Finally, they had to pull Richard off the badly battered form, for the recruit was desperately trying to tear the padding from the stick in order to finish his opponent off for good. His instructors said he was a natural. Richard also qualified expert with the M-16 rifle and the .45 caliber pistol.

After graduating Parris Island as an infantryman, Richard was off to Camp Lejune, North Carolina for combat training. He really seemed squared away. But when the war games commenced, Richard was reported missing from his squad. No one knew a thing. Therefore, he had been considered captured. Defeated from the very start by the *enemy* team. Actually, he had buried himself earlier within a shallow, swampy grave, five hundred yards to the north, covered over with a sheet of corrugated cardboard caked with muddy earth. Patiently, he awaited the seasoned rival team, carefully listening for their sound. As he knew they would, they came and probed the area. Apparently satisfied, the fire-team lined itself somewhere along a berm lying adjacent to the soupy land. From either direction, the *enemy* would surely take its toll. But Richard had other plans, for he was about to emerge victorious.

A quiet kind of madness began to unearth itself from within a gloomy corner of the marsh. Sliding out from under what seemed a den of vipers snaked along his limbs, Richard slowly emerged with slime-soaked strips of burlap across his forehead, face and hands, inching his way out of the swamp and toward a waist-high wall. He slithered on his back beneath barbed wire obstacles, his cherished weapon cradled lovingly in his arms.

As Richard reached the peak, he quickly established his field of fire behind enemy lines, mercilessly cutting down the unsuspecting column of ambushers who freaked then dropped their silly heads in sheer disgrace.

"Dead! Dead! Dead! Dead! Dead!" sounded one of the alert yet otherwise startled field observers, pointing a very disappointed finger at each and every sorry soul.

Richard was congratulated for his unique display of camouflage, grotesquely featured from head to toe in slimy moss and burlap. Standing posed for pictures beside his cruddy piece of cardboard, he was commended for making the most of available cover.

"Out-fucking-standing, Private," was the praise a lieutenant colonel paid, for Private Geist was meritoriously promoted to Private First Class.

The following day, Richard received a telegram from home:

WESTERN UNION

DARLING DICKY,

TRIED TO CALL YOU THIS MORNING. MR. GLADSTONE PASSED AWAY LATE LAST NIGHT FROM A HEART ATTACK. I FEEL YOU SHOULD MAKE EVERY EFFORT TO COME HOME FOR THE FUNERAL. MR. GLADSTONE WAS VERY GOOD TO YOU OVER THE YEARS. MORE THAN YOU'LL EVER KNOW. PLEASE HURRY HOME AND HELP YOUR POOR MOTHER. FUNERAL IS TOMORROW MORNING. CALL ME AS

SOON AS YOU GET THIS TELEGRAM.

LOVE,
MOTHER

Richard stood in the renovated office before his commanding officer, desperately explaining why he believed Horatio Gladstone to be his real father.

The officer looked up impatiently, his face fixed firmly in an unyielding disposition. He pushed the telegram back across his desk toward Richard. "Look, I'm sorry Private Geist. While I can appreciate your situation, I'm afraid I'm going to have to deny your request for an emergency leave. This Mr. Goodstone—"

"Gladstone, sir."

"This Mr. Gladstone isn't even related. He was your mother's friend. You have to understand that even in situations where, say a close uncle dies . . . ."

Richard stopped listening, glaring angrily at the large plaque of an American bald eagle hanging on the wall behind the officer's desk, its enormous wings spread wide. He tried holding back the tears, biting his bottom lip, closing his eyes, connecting pieces of the past and present.

> *Hell, my boy. Why you and I go back before you were ever born. Isn't that right Victoria?/Horace, I don't want you saying things like that in front of him . . . He's not stupid./Why, I should say not. What, with your looks and my brains—/That Nazi never wanted any children./YOU'RE A WHORE. DICKY'S ILLEGITIMATE . . . CUCKOLD-CUCKOLD/He was very good to you over the years. More than you'll ever know . . . more than you'll ever know . . . more than . . . .*

"HE'S MY FATHER!" Richard shouted uncontrollably, the tears falling freely down his face.

"Listen, Private," the officer snapped. "You're supposed to be a marine. And you're on your way to becoming a damn good one. I'm not here to wipe your nose for you. Would you behave this way if your father were here now? Act like a man, son. If your mother got herself knocked up by some Goodfellow, it was still . . .” Richard stared in disbelief at the officer. “. . . who raised you and put food on the table and a roof over your head. Do you understand what I’m saying, Private?”

Richard glanced furiously around the room. Near the desk, a large unassembled plaque of the Americas lay beside a metal anchor, along with lengths of chain.

“Are you listening to me, Private? I’m talking to you. What do you think you’re doing? Get the hell away from there,” the officer ordered, pushing back his chair, the veins bulging in his neck like wild vines. “Put that down you goddamn son of a—”

Suddenly, an angry beat of feathers seemed to emanate from the eagle perched above, and the high and mighty military man raised his brow in awe. In that instant, the force from the heavy chain sent the officer sprawling spread-eagle against the wall beneath the great bird.

CUCKOLD-CUCKOLD!

The next blow ripped the soft flesh from the corner of the captain’s mouth. Several teeth shot across the room and hit the wall like bullets. Blood spilled freely to the floor. Bleeding profusely, the officer slowly dragged himself into a corner before he collapsed. Richard folded the chain in two then brought it down hard upon the helpless form. Smashing him over and over again.

Suddenly, the room fell still. Richard could hear footsteps coming down the hall. He quickly knelt beside the body, coiling the thick length of chain around the captain’s neck, tightening and twisting the silver links of steel, strangling the man, suffocating him, silencing even the slightest chance of breath to bear as two orderlies burst into the room, pulling Richard off the badly battered form.

“YOU MOTHERFUCKERS,” Richard screamed. “I WANT TO GO HOME TO SEE MY DEAD FATHER. I’M ONLY A LITTLE BASTARD,” he cried.

One of the men threw Richard face down on the floor, pinning his arms behind his back, handcuffing him as the others hurried over to assist the officer.

“Jesus Christ,” a corporal cried. The officer gasped for air. “Get a medic—fast! He can't breathe!" the enlisted man shouted, applying mouth-to-mouth resuscitation.

Everything happened so fast. From just outside the window, Richard could hear the sound of drummers and buglers marching by as he was severely clobbered with nightsticks and fists. He offered no resistance, but shivered to beat the band. Still handcuffed, they dragged Richard off toward another building, throwing him into a dark and dismal cage. He was in a terrible rage, recalling the very first time that little Dicky was beaten until he learned to stop shivering from the cold. He wasn't very old. Yes! Things were coming back to him now. Richard lay shivering but silent on the cold steel floor of his cage, confined to a nightmare of early childhood when Mother had beaten little Dicky senselessly in the snow.

Private Geist awoke from what he had hoped was another nightmare. But he was all bloodied, battered, and bruised. He was in severe pain and had no idea of how long he had been confined. That morning, two marine guards came for him, roughly escorting the senseless soul out of the building and into the blinding light. They marched him across the compound to an infirmary where he was cleaned up and carefully examined before being taken back and thrown into that solitary cell.

Several days later, Richard was driven by jeep to a building some distance away. He was led down along a corridor and ushered into an anteroom. One of the guards knocked officiously before ordering the prisoner through the set of double doors, marching the prisoner across the large office, ordering that he stand at the position of attention before sounding off loud and clear as instructed.

"Sir, Prisoner Geist reporting as ordered, Sir." Richard stood handcuffed before a figure seated at the desk. Two flags hung from tall staffs, framing the window behind the officer.

The man spoke without raising his eyes from the folder in front of him. "Assaulting your commanding officer!"

"Sir, I—"

"Shut up!" the officer snapped, looking up from his report, his eyes glued to Richard's. "We have very serious charges against you, Private Geist." Sharp creases scored the officer's shirt, dividing the breast pockets evenly. A tropical tie held back an angry knot in the man's throat, bowing the neckwear forward. A golden clip of polished brass held the tie in place at the center of the shirt. Razor sharp creases ran each length of sleeve. Gold leaves adorned the collar. The major stared back down at the report. "Just where the hell do you come off, Private? Assaulting your commanding officer. Calling your commanding officer a 'motherfucker.'"

"Sir, I—"

"Maybe they've got motherfuckers where you hail from. But not down here, by God!"

Richard tried to explain that such an endearing term showed great Christian love, and that it would be rather unchristian-like to pass judgment for one's vernacular, especially for such a righteous man as he. But the major's eyes lit with murder as he had Richard expelled from his office before the officer did something he might later have regretted.

Private Geist sat in the brig for over a week before he was brought before a naval psychiatrist. After listening to Richard bitterly complain about the myth of southern hospitality, the doctor put his notes aside.

"Listen, Richard. May I call you Richard?"

Richard smirked.

"Richard, I'd like to ask you a direct question." The prisoner did not respond at first. "I'd like for you to try and tell me why you joined the Marine Corps."

"What do you mean?"

"Why the Marines? Why not the Navy? The Army?"

Richard shifted in his chair uncomfortably.

"Maybe you were trying to prove something to someone."

"I don't understand what you mean by 'prove something to someone.' To who? Or is it whom?" Richard giggled.

"That's what I'm asking you."

Richard looked around uneasily. "What are you getting at?"

"At what's troubling you."

"And what do *you* think is troubling me?"

The psychiatrist observed Richard carefully. "You seem to be harboring a great deal of hostility."

"My commanding officer refused to let me go home to see my real father for the very last time," Richard said defensively.

"I don't think it's your commanding officer who's upsetting you,

Richard."

Richard thought for a moment. "Look, Doc. I joined the Marine Corps to travel, but find it rather difficult trying to defend my condition of sanity for not having taken Greyhound. May I go now?"

During a Special Court-Martial, Richard received an Undesirable Discharge and was sentenced to ninety days in the brig. Early each morning, he worked an eight-hour laundry shift. In the afternoon, he volunteered his services and was assigned to a pressing detail where he learned how to operate everything from old-fashioned ironing equipment to the more modern types of pressing machines. There, from a window overlooking a courtyard, he had the opportunity to observe a reconnaissance unit training every weekday afternoon. Precision killing machines. Executing each and every movement with deadly flair. Richard watched intently, never missing a single show.

"Off again, I see," said the turnkey.

"A way of letting off some steam," he told the guard who insisted on knowing why Richard always volunteered.

After evening chow and showers, Richard was returned to his cell. A dreary little space with a canvas cot. And when most everyone was fast asleep, he'd practice every single exercise he'd seen demonstrated earlier in the courtyard, feverishly absorbed in the perfection of his art. One-arm then two-arm pushups upon his fingertips till the sweat poured off his back. Karate punches and kicks. Foot sweeps and flips. He'd practice, not in a fury, but with deliberate, controlled sequences, four to five hours into the night, every night, until he knew he was proficient. The emergence of a maggot into a deadly fly. An aerial acrobat. Flying soundlessly from wall to wall of his claustrophobic cell. Horse stances. Roundhouses. Ceiling-high kicks and whirls. Till the metamorphosis was complete. In the mornings, the guards would always wonder why he smelled so bad.

Richard also found the time to do some thinking. He thought about the irony of his short-lived rank of PFC. Private Geist was becoming very private, indeed. He had made no friends among the other inmates. Most of them had the good sense to stay away. Somehow they knew to fear him.

However, there was one new prisoner who came looking for trouble for no apparent reason. It happened one afternoon while Richard was busy pressing sets of utility trousers. The heavyset youth came at him fast with a flashing blade from behind, but Richard had turned and saw lard-ass out of the corner of his eye, and in that instant, flattened him; that is to say, he flipped him horizontally onto the scorched pad of the pressing table, then brought the hot steel plate down hard upon the fat and wrinkled body. Stepping onto the pedal near the floor, Richard sent up a shot of scorching steam that seemed like a thousand vipers hissing as the smell of burning flesh and the sound of torturous screams filled the room completely. Only then did Richard tear the figure off the table, and with a smashing blow, managed to send the blubbery bastard headlong into an ancient iron mangle.

Later, when asked by the psychiatrist if he knew what he had done to the two hundred ten-pound prisoner, Richard calmly stated that he had *mangled* him, reducing lard-ass to a level of humiliation only he would understand.

The psychiatrist told Richard that he had probably forfeited time off for good behavior normally accorded a three-month sentence, and that he should have thought twice about his actions, having burned and scarred the young man severely. Richard explained to the psychiatrist that very little thought goes into reflex conditioning. And although Private Swanson's weapon was blunt, a butter knife as it was learned after the fact, it was hardly the point. For he would rather lose some time than lose his life, now that it had a purpose, now that he had so many things to do, now that the Marine Corps had served its purpose perfectly.

Of course, the psychiatrist thought he'd have a field day. But Richard ended the conversation abruptly by declaring that he was *private* Geist, civilian, or soon to be, anyways.

Chapter 11

DISCHARGED

Richard had spent his eighteenth birthday behind bars, having received neither cake nor card; nor did he really care. He was released in the middle of February, incidentally, without having served additional time for his questionable behavior concerning Private Swanson. Apparently, his action had been viewed as self-defense. What Richard did lose, however, was the benefit of Father Morley's prayers, for the young chaplain had been unsuccessful in trying to persuade Richard to attend mass. 'Morley sorely needed souls to save' was the homily preached on Sunday mornings by several prisoners whose only salvation was a break from an otherwise dull routine.

The morning was cold and windy, and Richard overheard one of the guards saying that it was snowing up north. No one spoke to him directly as they led him toward the main gate. He had been up half the night thinking. He thought about Horatio Gladstone, wondering what it was like to be dead, lying forever still in some box beneath the frozen earth for all eternity. He wondered if there really was a soul, and if it actually left your body when you died. He thought about heaven and hell, certain that he was experiencing the latter right here on earth. He didn't need a priest to tell him what no mortal man truly knew for sure.

A black limousine was waiting just beyond the gate. For a moment, Richard thought it was a hearse. Max stepped out without a word, opening a rear door, and Richard slid into the backseat beside Mother.

"You lost weight, dear," she said, kissing him quickly on the cheek. "And you look so tired. I think what you need is a nice long rest."

Dr. King extended his hand, but Richard just sat there passively before he spoke, asking Mother if he could visit Horatio Gladstone's grave as soon as they got home. Dr. King lit a cigar and told him that they had a long drive ahead of them and wouldn't be arriving until late that evening. Richard asked the doctor why they hadn't flown, why they had to drive all that distance, which didn't make any sense whatsoever. He asked why they had even bothered to come at all.

Dr. King informed Richard, almost apologetically, that he had a fear of flying and had to drive everywhere he went. He also told Richard that they came because they cared.

Richard looked around uneasily, then closed his eyes . . . dozing off every now and then.

Early that afternoon, when the four of them had stopped for fuel, food, and bathroom facilities, Richard asked Mother if perhaps they could visit Horatio Gladstone's grave the following day. But Dr. King interrupted, saying that it wasn't a good idea just yet. Richard was about to say something, too. But something told him to keep a civil tongue.

It was a long, tiresome drive for everyone. Dr. King relieved Max at the wheel for a while. Late that evening, Richard saw signs for New York. Max was back in the driver's seat heading east, away from New Jersey, barreling along at seventy miles per hour through a light but steady snow.

"Where the hell are we going?" Richard insisted, sitting up straight.

"We're just going to Dr. King's for a while, dear," Mother answered. "Now just relax."

Richard could sense that something was brewing, but he was too numb to start an argument. If he didn't like what was going on, he'd simply leave after a good night's rest. He wasn't anyone's prisoner any longer. He wasn't under lock and key. He saw a sign for Long Island then settled back in his seat.

Shortly before they were to arrive, Dr. King reached back for the car phone and put through a call. Moments later, the limousine bounded through a pair of open iron gates. Seagulls stormed the snowy sky, and hardy ivy snaked along a cold stone wall. Max drove past Dr. King's estate, toward the tall buildings in the distance. Impersonal brick facades with iron bars loomed against the sky. Richard gazed at the stars, wondering what was up.

"It'll just be for a while," Mother said uneasily. "Just until you're well enough to come home. You have your own private room. I'll see you as often as I can," she promised. "All right, dear?"

Richard stared at this mother incredulously. "You're crazy if you think that I'm going to be put away in there. I served my time. Wanting to go home to visit my dead father was my only crime."

"I'm afraid that you haven't much of a choice, Richard," Dr. King interjected.

"What Dr. King means, darling, is that he went out on a limb for you. You don't know the trouble you caused everyone. They were going to sentence you to several years for what you did to that officer. Only David stuck his neck out for you."

"They were going to throw the book at you, Richard," Doctor David King rejoined.

"But David made some kind of deal with them where you would only have to serve three months, along with the understanding that we'd take care of you until you're—feeling better. It took a lot of convincing, dear. People didn't want to go along."

"But David, here, broke out his checkbook, I suppose."

"That's not fair, Dicky. Now, you apologize to Dr. King this instant. Do you hear?"

"No, let him have his say. Then I'll explain to him how the real world works if he really wants to know."

"What the hell does a little problem in North Carolina have to do with New York? I paid my dues. I have my walking papers, as they say. Now, let me the hell out of here. I'm walking. I don't have to listen to all this crap. I'm not going to be put away in there. I have my rights."

"And I have my reputation, son. I gave some people in Washington my word. I didn't write any checks. No one in my realm is on the take as you may think. It's a world of favors, Richard. Some people in Washington owed me favors; through them, I made some contacts. Only now, I'm in their debt. That's how my world works. That's how I built this place."

"Do me a favor, Doctor," Richard said.

"Name it."

"Save the sermon."

"I'm telling you, Richard. You haven't got a choice. You have to go along. I'm going to help you—if you let me."

"And what if I say no? What if I flatly refuse?"

Dr. King smiled, sending down his window while lighting up another one of his cigars. "Max, here, will help you with your things."

Max brought the car to a sudden stop in front of A Building, turning around with a wide grin. A grin that told of a hidden kind of madness. A grin that Richard understood only too well. Two burly men in white coats waited near the entrance.

"I see," Richard said, grinning back knowingly. "Sir, Private Patient Prisoner Geist reporting as ordered, Sir!" he snapped as Max discharged his passengers along a white wet walkway leading to a distant door.

Book II

Adult

Chapter 12

PATIENTS AND PATIENCE

Spring arrived, and the last of the snow had finally disappeared. Crocuses were starting to perform their magic beneath budding limbs that patiently awaited the early morning sun. Patients were encouraged to spend part of their time outdoors; however, Richard kept to himself and his room. It was a very private room, not unlike his military cell in size. Actually, a bit larger, with a sink and toilet sectioned off behind a small partition toward the back. Along a length of wall sat a metal bed in lieu of a canvas cot. Directly across from the bed stood a blonde-colored wooden chifforobe. Propped along its top sat half a dozen handsome hand carved frames of different shapes and sizes. Black and white photographs of Mother performing her acrobatic feats filled five of the hardwood frames; the sixth frame bordered little Dicky brandishing a pair of six-shooters. The photographs, taken from several family albums, had been Richard's only request. The frames were given to him by Mr. Wyszynski, one of the patients on the ward who claimed he didn't need or want them anymore.

Richard was resistant to treatment of any kind, but Dr. King was patient, keeping a watchful eye. So, too, did Richard, who stood framed behind the barred window situated on the top floor of A Building. Early each morning he could be seen gazing down and around the seventeen-acre parcel, its maze of magnificent hedgerow bordering perennial gardens which were about to explode in Technicolor. He'd study Carl Gustafson, observing the caretaker's handiwork gradually unearth itself from rows of sleepy, wintry beds.

In the afternoon, after the grounds had dried up nicely, Richard would watch groups of young school children playing baseball and other sports in a nearby park. On weekends, an energetic priest usually came by to help organize teams and coach the happy boys. But it wasn't until an unusually warm morning toward the end of March that Richard finally emerged from the building. He walked up to the iron fence, watching a group of youngsters playing fly-ups in the park across the boulevard, vehicular traffic moving busily back and forth.

From out of nowhere, a gang of teenagers appeared on the scene and started lobbing small stones at the children, taunting them and disrupting their play. Richard hollered for the teenagers to stop, so they turned on him instead. From over passing vehicles, they threw stones in his direction. But he did not flinch or move an inch, not even when one of the stones struck the iron railing directly in front of him, its pitch ringing insanely in his ears. He stood firmly planted, staring, listening intently to a series of pinging sounds resounding in his head until the group was distracted by two young women strolling past them. The teenagers cursed Richard insanely before heading along the busy boulevard. The teenagers quickly followed behind the pair of switching skirts, shouting and whistling their approval.

Suddenly, a powder blue mini-van, flowered with bright colored petals and the word LOVE crudely arched above a garish rainbow, bucked and jolted out of the park and across the boulevard amid the sound of blaring horns and screeching brakes. The passenger of the van was playing *Strawberry Fields* on an invisible harmonica buried somewhere within a blond beard. The man's filthy feet hung out the window; tattered, bleached-out bell-bottom trousers ballooned in a gentle breeze as he played on forever, oblivious of his girlfriend who was freaking out at the wheel. Apparently, she was trying to gain control of the vehicle, grinding gears and pumping pedals before man, machine and music came to an abrupt halt, her full bare breasts bounding freely into view. The boyfriend laughed and fought and fondled her, when suddenly their door flew open and the young woman fell naked onto the pavement, screaming hysterically in the midst of traffic above the cacophonous blend of curses and catcalls coming from other motorists.

A moment later, the man pulled in his feet, slid over, and started up the engine as the buxom woman clambered toward the vehicle, managing to reach the running board a split second before the van veered sharply to the right of an oncoming car. Richard watched the woman holding on for her life, her heart-shaped buttocks bouncing bountifully up and down as the reckless driver weaved in and out of traffic along the busy boulevard. A young couple in a passing car extended their fingers to form a V, shouting 'flower power,' while other motorists gave the hippies but a single sign. Finally, the blue van, filled with its insanity, faded in the distance, but the Beatles' number played on in Richard's mind.

Richard turned around and saw the Foundation's caretaker ascending the basement stairs between the buildings, the man's powerful arms wrapped around a large, rusty trash barrel heaped with garbage.

Carl Gustafson was a strapping Swede who sported a magnificent pepper-and-salt handlebar mustache, along with a bountiful head of snow-white hair. He had spent nearly a quarter of a century at the King Foundation. From early spring to late fall, Carl tended to the gardens and the grounds as well as the connecting property of Dr. King's estate. When he wasn't busy gardening or emptying cans of garbage, he'd be in his basement room with his face buried in a book, or in the patients' library, pestering Mr. Schimmel about ordering certain newspapers, periodicals, and such. Books and beauty were Carl's first love, but the caretaker staunchly maintained that before there could ever be any real beauty in the world, people first had to learn to rid themselves of their garbage.

Carl set the barrel down, wiping off the front of his rust-streaked T-shirt. The caretaker looked over at a group of men heading toward a clearing. Men in dark suits and construction helmets were busy everywhere. A surveyor in a bright shirt and khaki pants was leaning forward, peering through an instrument, signaling to his partner in the distance.

"You see them over there?" Carl addressed Richard. "Contractors and engineers looking to put up more buildings by the end of the summer, I suppose. Now that's what I call insanity. I could create another Eden here. Say, have you ever been to the Kingdom of Sweden? That's its official name. I was once its King, you know. What a paradise. Not like this country. People don't seem to realize that it's the GODDAMN SHANTY IRISH THAT RUINED THIS COUNTRY," he hollered through cupped hands, loud enough for Mrs. O'Brian to hear him from her nearby window in adjacent B Building. Several of the men in the group looked around uneasily. "Everyone is so busy keeping an eye on the niggers, they can't see that it's those GODDAMN SHANTY IRISH. Can't seem to see the forest through all that goddamn greenery. Of course, the niggers are bad enough, not to mention the spics. '*MIRA! MIRA!*' Look at their goddamn cars!" he exclaimed, pointing to two dilapidated Chevrolets parked along the service road just outside the gate. "Believe me. They need Christ on their dashboard, if only to guide them through Monday morning traffic, for heaven's sake."

Richard didn't say a word. He stood and watched a middle-aged woman dragging a large bag of garbage beside her, winding a steady course between a hedgerow and a tulip path, heading toward Dr. King's estate. He glared at the king-sized house in the distance.

"Ever wonder why the Irish don't particularly care to drive?" Carl ranted. "Because they're either in civil service or public transportation. And why not? Either way it's a free ride! They're the ones you always see parading through the subway gates without having to pay the fare, waving their passes in the air. I tried that once when the city raised its fare, pushing through and protesting with all the spics, niggers, and guineas. All of a sudden, this mick cop grabs hold of my arm. So I dropped my pants in protest, waving you know what at the people on the IRT. All the minorities made it through, but this red-faced rookie latches onto me, insisting that I'm off my trolley. *Ja.* But the guineas are the worst. No one moves faster than a guinea in distress. You should have seen them during World War I. Neither the Germans nor the Austrians could get any information from them because most of them didn't know anything; and the few who did, couldn't possible say a word; not with their fingers laced on top of their heads they couldn't.

"Anyhow, this one fat guinea kept screaming 'A-FA-NAB-BA-LA,' chipping tartar from his teeth with his thumbnail at one of the German soldiers before the Kraut finally put a bullet in his gut. Poor bastard moaned for a priest for thirty minutes before he died. Goddamn dumb guinea bastards. Most of them wind up in sanitation anyhow. Did you ever watch those scavengers collect the garbage? They actually take half of it home with them, running to the driver with a find.

"There's only one person dumber than a guinea, and that's a Polack. Do you know why they don't have coffee breaks in Poland?" he queried. "Because it takes too long to retrain the help," Carl carried on, his bright blue eyes dancing wildly in his head. "You should have seen Wyszynski's face when I told him that one. Stupid Polack.

"You know, we even had a crazy Chinaman here once. Little almond-eyed creature with tiny feet. Went around collecting

76

everyone's laundry with a big smile, and our socks came back with heavy starch. So administration assigned him to the kitchen. Now, who's crazier? Them or us?" he insisted. "Showed the cooks here how to make chicken egg drop soup. Only thing he knew how to make. 'Rittle bit of this and a rittle bit of that,' he'd say with a big wide grin. Oh, Schimmel was in his glory, all right. Sure, the goddamn Jews love their cooking. And why not? They own all the Chink restaurants, for Christ's sake. By the way," he asked haughtily, "what nationality are you? No, don't tell me. Let me guess." Richard walked away. "American Indian," Carl called out. "You know how I can tell? BECAUSE YOU'VE GOT A FEATHER UP YOUR ASS."

It seemed that no one really knew very much about Carl, except for his nemesis, Mrs. O'Brian, who lived in B Building. The old woman claimed she knew more about the caretaker than anyone, including his doctors. Richard learned that she had been a music and history teacher for over twenty years, committed to the King Foundation for blowing up the principal's office of her school one rainy night, insisting that she was finally in harmony with the world. Whenever anyone spoke to her in an authoritative tone, she would hum very loudly, drumstick-like fingers planted firmly in each ear.

According to Mrs. O'Brian, Carl Gustafson had been born in a small village in the northeast corner of Sweden, near the Finnish border. As a young man, he had worked in the great forests before migrating southward, seeking education and employment at a college just outside Copenhagen. It was there that he met Sonjia, a young and beautiful language student with whom he had fallen madly in love, proposing to her in more than a half a dozen languages. They were married in short order and lived together for over a year before her mysterious disappearance. Mrs. O'Brian would say no more.

Apparently, the old woman had been Carl's confidante; that is, up until the time he learned that she had gossiped to the others about his personal life, and especially about his estranged wife. He felt a strong sense of betrayal and threatened to boot her butt from 'here to Blarney Castle.' So out of anger, the old woman started rumors about a medley of young men who would drop in on Carl during all hours of the night.

Like that very evening while Mrs. O'Brian had been resting quietly in her room when suddenly she heard a loud commotion coming from the passageway between the buildings. She also heard what she believed to be the clashing of cymbals and the roll of distant drums. When she went to her window to investigate, she saw the caretaker conducting himself rather peculiarly, waving his arms excitedly as two Spanish youths scaled the basement stairs in a frenzy. She watched them as they fled past Mr. Schimmel, who stood near the top of the stairs trembling in his shoes. A moment later, she witnessed a tall black man encircling his arm "affectionately," was the word she used, around Carl. Then the two men disappeared through the entrance off the passageway leading to the caretaker's quarters in the basement.

Late the next morning, Mr. Schimmel came briskly along the garden path on his way to open up the library. He paused for a moment to consult his worthless, handless pocket watch that he always carried with him, deciding he had time enough to relate the evening's incident (as he perceived it) to Mrs. O'Brian as well as all the other women seated along the benches:

"I vas coming home from verk yesterday evening," Schimmel declared in a thick Yiddish accent, tucking the timeless piece securely in his vest-pocket, toying anxiously with the pewter fob, "vhen I saw this hippie, hoodlum gang vaiting for me in the alleyvay," he stated assuredly. "They tried to assault me. Maybe tventy of them," he declared. "But vhen they saw I vas not afraid of them, and ready to stand my ground, they turned and ran avay." The frail man proudly puffed out his chest and strutted past the women like a resplendent peacock, as feigned enthusiasm carried through the group. "I vas not a coward!" he cried, scurrying off in the direction of the library.

Everyone knew that Mr. Schimmel was afraid of his own shadow. Quite literally, in fact. "There were times that he would actually cower and quake whenever he saw it," Mrs. O'Brian had told Richard. "But there were also times when he would scream out in a rather frightful rage, stamping his very own shadow mercilessly until the attendants came to carry him away." The old woman went on to explain that he had gotten better over the years. "But I liked him a whole lot more when he first came here years ago and tried to run away from himself. I'd see him making tracks around four in the afternoon, so I'd holler down from my window, telling him that the very devil was at his heels. God, could he run in those days. As the years went by, he started chasing himself all around the Foundation, grabbing at the ground and zigzagging across the gardens till Carl Gustafson finally set him straight. Of course, the silly doctors saw Schimmel's antics as a step in the right direction. So, Schimmel had this plan to catch his own shadow." Mrs. O'Brian paused to giggle. "Well, one day the idiot climbed up onto a picnic table as the afternoon sun had cast the little man's shadow clear across the lawn, you see. Suddenly, he lunged off the table as far forward as he could, and broke his leg. Almost had himself, too, by God," she swore with great laughter. "The doctors insisted that he was making progress by leaps and bounds. Now, on a good day, he chases Carl Gustafson around the grounds instead."

Suddenly, the old woman's tone changed. Her face grew stern as she gave her interpretation of the incident concerning Carl Gustafson's behavior the other evening, supporting her conviction that the caretaker was a raving homosexual.

Although Mrs. O'Brian undoubtedly heard the commotion, the old woman could not possibly have known what the argument was about, for she certainly was not in proximity of the recreation room where the argument erupted, nor were her ears as keen as they had once been years ago. Furthermore, she did not understand Spanish which dominated a good part of the altercation.

Richard, who was fast becoming a recorder of such scenes and sounds, had been busy reading in the basement lounge on the evening that the loud disturbance began. There had been the blaring of Latin music coming from the recreation room down the hall, followed by a shouting match rising steadily above the strident sound, when suddenly a needle raked across his nerves and the music stopped. Clearly, he could hear Carl Gustafson hollering back and forth in both Spanish and English while Spanish voices hollered back.

Richard had gotten up and went quietly over to the door. Peering down the hallway, he witnessed Carl march two boys out of the recreation room, flatly informing them that the room was closed for the evening, and that they had no business being in there at that late hour playing spic music. He gave the youths a brief lecture on Strauss then waltzed the pair along the corridor, explaining that tomorrow was another day. One of the boys shouted something in Spanish, the other spit at the Swede, calling Carl's mother a whore. Carl went positively crazy, chasing the pair around the hallway, carrying on insanely all the while.

"Come on back here you rum swizzlin', noon snoozin', night prowlin' spics," Carl had ranted. '*Si, Señor—Por favor. You don't say nothin' 'bout mi madre.* Hear?' he mocked and sneered in an exaggerated tone. 'She bring me 'cross the border so I may find op·por·tun·ity. How you say, 'Stick 'em up!'? Up both your asses when I get my hands on you," he swore with the unmistakable look of murder in his eyes.

The two boys ran for their lives. One of them flashed a middle finger high above his head without the satisfaction of looking back for fear he'd lose a step as he fled past Richard standing in the doorway of the lounge.

"Up your sisters' kazoos, Raul!" Carl shouted. "You just wait till Sunday's visit when I see those two God-fearing, cross-bearing, olive-skinned, black-haired beauties. Identical twins? Until they open up their mouths. '*Mira, mira, aquí. Madre. Padre. Maria*, she's engaged! *Comprometido*. Oh, Maria. I make for you *una mantilla*. We have a fiesta. *Maravilloso. Estupendo.* That makes four christenings—two communions—and an engagement party this month alone! Oh, Maria. My twin sister. Oh! *Dios mio!* I'll be an aunt before I'm eleven! Oh, Maria. Oh, *Madre!* Oh, *Padre!* Oh, Cisco! Oh, Poncho!'"Carl ridiculed, practically out of breath, intermingling flawless Spanish and English on the run, coming around the hallway for a second time before chasing the two out into the alley.

Richard had quickly followed to a point just inside the doorway where he saw Carl seize a lid from one of the garbage cans that lined the alley wall and angrily hurl the giant discus through the air, set on destruction rather than distance as the pair fled up the stairs between the buildings past Mr. Schimmel who stood there shaking in his shoes. The cover crashed against the stairs in front of the frightened librarian. Clanging and banging and rolling back down. Around and around. Until it finally settled upon the ground.

"Fifty *pesos* for your asses, hombres!" Carl hollered.

It was at that point that Paul Johnson, a young, virile black attendant, intervened, escorting Carl back to his room while trying to reason with him calmly. Mrs. O'Brian stared down from her window and drew the conclusion that the argument had been over money, thereby reinforcing her belief that Carl Gustafson was engaged in deviant relationships with young men. Then, through innuendo, she continued planting seeds of suspicion, affirming that, "those Swedes certainly do like their smorgasbord," especially when she saw Carl paying close attention to other women.

With few exceptions, everyone seemed to get along reasonably well with one another. Of course, everyone had their prejudices, but they somehow learned to couch their biases and other behaviors in less dramatic terms. And so, for the most part, a harmonious coexistence prevailed throughout the active patient population. Active because Dr. King simply did not believe in pushing piles of pills and other forms of medication down patients' throats. So not everyone walked around the institution in a stupor like one might imagine. Consequently, many of Dr. King's patients could hold a pretty intelligent conversation now and then. And it didn't take Richard long to discover that the King Foundation held several remarkable patients. Patients who would serve his needs quite nicely. All he'd need was patience.

The greatest hurdle among the patient population was in trying to comprehend one another's ethnic background. Even men like Mr. Schimmel and his Polish comrade, Mr. Wyszynski (both of whom had suffered and survived Nazi concentration camps), often found difficulty understanding one another's behavior. For example, Mr. Schimmel, for the life of him, couldn't fathom why it had taken Mr. Wyszynski seven days to have his first wife buried six feet in the ground or why he had partied for a week thereafter. And Mr. Wyszynski simply could not comprehend Mr. Schimmel sitting shivah in a lugubrious state for seven days over the recent death of his older brother, who, as Schimmel himself proclaimed, had given him nothing but aggravation during the last years of his life. What astounded the Polish refugee even more was the fact that Schimmel's family had the body cremated! Actually had the body cremated. A body that in life had also suffered and survived the holocaust. It went beyond his comprehension that a family would carry out such a deed. And family was everything to Wyszynski; that is, until the day he lost that very faith.

Mr. Schimmel had sat shivah for seven days and would have sat for seven years had it been tradition, aside from the fact that he worshipped his departed brother dearly. Though at times you'd never know it from some of the remarks he made in anger. Mr. Schimmel mourned, and Mr. Wyszynski had partied, yet no two men could have suffered or grieved for their respective losses, nor shared a greater hatred in their hearts toward those responsible (or resembling those responsible) for the mass extermination of their people, howsoever long ago. For in their minds and hearts, they despised Carl Gustafson. Mr. Schimmel detested the caretaker's Germanic features. That commanding presence. The snow-white hair that had once been blond and slick as corn silk. Those piercing blue eyes and florescent smile. Mr. Wyszynski loathed Gustafson's arrogance, his assured manner, and those despicable, caustic ethnic comments. Carl was prejudice personified.

Although Richard got out more often with the warmer weather, he remained quite reticent, so Dr. King decided to hold off on any sort of formal therapy for the moment. Mother tried to alert Dr. King to the fact that whenever Richard went into an uncommunicative, introspective state, it generally signaled the 'calm before the storm.' Nevertheless, the good doctor was quick to suggest that it would, at most, amount to nothing more than a 'tempest in a teapot.' He assured Mother that there was absolutely no cause for alarm—that it would simply take some time before Richard would come around, but come around, he would.

As the days passed, Richard spent more and more time exploring the Foundation, seemingly disinterested in the idle chatter all around him, yet always managing to collect a distinctive piece of information here and there, especially where it concerned Carl Gustafson.

Carl was busy cleaning up branches and other debris that winter had discarded when he saw Mr. Schimmel pacing anxiously back and forth before several women seated along a nearby bench.

"Ah, it is a fine day," the librarian declared, but with a degree of apprehension in his voice. "Vouldn't you agree?" he added, removing the worthless pocket watch from his paisley vest.

"Hey, Schimmel," Carl called out. "Are you going to open up early today or what?"

Mr. Schimmel ignored the caretaker, staring up at the clear blue sky in fascination, then down at his timeless piece. He raised the pocket watch as high as the pewter fob would allow, bending forward at the waist until the face of the watch was as close as possible to his own. Tilting his head to one side, he listened for all its worth.

"Time to repair that ticker, birdbrain." Carl taunted, screwing up his face and positioning his arms like the hands of a clock before turning his attention toward the black attendant coming out of the administration building. The caretaker watched with interest as the man read a folded newspaper in one hand, drinking a cup of coffee with the other while on the go.

"Hey, *schvartze*," Carl hollered over to the man. "That this morning's paper, Paul? You read about the old nigger woman they found lying in the laundry room of her apartment building? Found her stone dead on the concrete floor, facedown in a pool of Clorox. The super said that she looked white as a sheet when they discovered her. Guess they'll have to do her up in black face for the funeral," he funned.

The attendant simply ignored Carl and kept right on walking.

"Bye-bye." Carl waved.

"Real trash," Schimmel mumbled to himself, putting away his watch. "*Tobacco Road*. I'd vhip that Nazi in a minute if he vasn't so goddamned big," he added, waving his hand with disgust in Carl's direction.

Carl saw Schimmel's friend, Mr. Wyszynski, coming out of the infirmary. "Hey, Wyszynski. Do you know why there're only two pallbearers at a Polack's funeral? Because a garbage can only has two handles! Hey, here's one I made up myself. Do you know what a Polack's idea of higher education is? Answer: To elevate the building!" he said with a chuckle. "Do you know why they don't have coffee breaks in Poland? Because it takes too long to retrain the help. And I'm sure you can't tell me why they don't have pharmacists in Poland. They're still trying to figure out how to get the bottle into the typewriter. Hey, where are you going?" Carl called out as Wyszynski made an about-face and headed back inside the building. "I guess I made him sick again," the caretaker proclaimed with a certain satisfaction.

"That's the faggot," Mrs. O'Brian whispered cautiously to the other women as the caretaker passed by.

Carl walked over to another group of ladies perched along their bench like so many pesky pigeons in a park. "Good morning, my little chickadees," Carl greeted with a devilish grin, twisting and turning up the ends of his mustache like fine-spun filaments of thread being drawn from a spinning wheel.

"Good afternoon," corrected the middle-aged Italian woman, squinting up at the noonday sun.

Carl shaded his eyes with the back of his hand and looked up, too. "Why so it is, Mrs. Zammitti," he declared, exchanging dissembling smiles and nods of perfunctory courtesy. "So it is," he repeated, raising his arms together to twelve o'clock. "It was that shuffling Sambo with his morning paper and coffee that threw me off," he said, sauntering off toward the library.

"I wonder what homosexuals do with one another," one of the women questioned and giggled, smoothing out the fabric of her skirt.

"I wouldn't dare to imagine," another answered, biting her cuticles until they bled.

Yes, they all came with their customs and cultures. Their hopes and their despair. Their religious conceptions and notions of nationalism. And from that regard, they tried to understand each other's differences. From that preposterous position, they tried to incorporate their cultures and inculcate their teachings. No different than society at large, though at times certainly more intense, Richard reckoned.

Mrs. Ackerman, who lived on the top floor of B Building, couldn't understand why Mrs. Alvarez had worked for so many years as a secretary while her husband stayed home and looked after the children, or why the Spanish woman used to fry her pork chops in lard, grinding the spices with a wooden pestle. And Mrs. Ackerman certainly would not have understood or accepted the fact that Mr. Alvarez was having incestuous relations with his daughter. Mrs. Alvarez couldn't accept that either. Surely, Mr. Alvarez would not have understood about Mrs. Alvarez and her boss, although he had probably suspected. What the Jewish woman could never understand was why Mrs. Alvarez would say a prayer each day for her husband after having been separated for more than a decade, or why he still came by each week to visit, bringing her large bouquets of flowers. Mrs. Ackerman demanded to know why no one ever came by to pay *her* a visit or send *her* a lousy flower. She, an Orthodox woman of fifty some odd years. Fifty plus years of religious devotion.

While Richard was busy collecting and sorting all this data, Mrs. Ackerman asked one of the nurses if Richard could accompany her back to her room, if only for a minute. "It would be so much like a visit," Mrs. Ackerman pleaded.

Surprisingly, the nurse agreed, probably because Mrs. Ackerman was the only patient assigned to the ward while that wing was undergoing renovation. So the three stepped off the elevator on the eleventh floor, and Mrs. Ackerman proudly showed Richard her mezuzah, a tiny parchment rolled within a silver case, affixed to the door frame. She polished the object energetically with the sleeve of her robe as the nurse unlocked the door. Mrs. Ackerman asked the nurse if Richard could take a little peek inside her room. "If only for a teeny-weeny moment. Pretty please, with sugar on it," the woman begged excitedly.

"Only for a moment," the nurse instructed then went across the hall to the water fountain to get a drink.

Richard stood just inside the sparse but immaculate room while Mrs. Ackerman went on to explain why she alone stood closer to God, confident in the fact that it was she who occupied a space at the very top of B Building, whereas her good friend, Mrs. Alvarez, was confined to the second floor, thereby concluding that the Spanish woman was several levels beneath her in station as well. Mrs. Ackerman avowed that she alone would be the first to serve God. If only He would give her some sign. Some word. However, she warned of her increasing impatience and frustration. Suddenly agitated, Mrs. Ackerman grabbed the menorah off the bureau, frantically rubbing the candelabrum up and down the front of her ragged robe while insisting that she had kept herself pure too long, and in the process, failed to consummate her marriage to Alan, the man of her dreams, who eventually sought comfort and satisfaction in the arms of her very own sister.

"Visit's over, Mrs. Ackerman," the nurse announced, removing Richard from the room and locking the woman within.

The following week was warm and sunny. Carl stood busy in one of the many gardens, spreading handfuls of fertilizer from large bags that he had carted over in a wheelbarrow from a nearby shed, carrying on quietly to himself about the role of God in man's illustrious garden of the world. Warming up for his delivery. After a period of time, the caretaker dropped what he was doing and broke into a series of dramatic monologues. Mrs. Zammitti heard his ranting and pulled Mrs. Alvarez along for the entertainment.

"God was here!" Carl exclaimed. "Schimmel saw Him with his own eyes. Right out there," he declared and pointed, "hovering over the service road, the traffic backed up from here to kingdom come," he continued, setting the stage. "Schimmel went running over to Him like a crazy person, creating a terrible scene," Carl projected, acting out the role of both Schimmel and God, respectively.

Richard was quite impressed with the resounding quality of the caretaker's voice thundering down upon the patients who stood gazing up in awe as Carl unfolded the scenario—including stage directions. As a matter of fact, Richard deemed that Carl played the part of Mr. Schimmel to perfection: accent, demeanor, mannerisms and all.

> God: [calling down] LITTLE MAN.
> Schimmel: [looking up] Vhat is it?
> God: [looking down, and so forth] I AM GOD.
> Schimmel: *Vy iz mir*! Vhich von?
> God: THERE IS ONLY ONE GOD
> Schimmel: For us Jews, yes. But for the *goyim*, that's another kettle of fish, vhich, by the vay, we can eat seven days a veek if ve vant. So long as it's not crustaceous. You see, ve remembered after all these years. Besides, shrimp is up to seven dollars a pound, and lobster is criminal.
> God: I AM GOD ALMIGHTY.
> Schimmel: So how come You haven't got an accent? You have credentials? References? A high school diploma, maybe?
> God: YOU IMPUGN GOD'S WORD?
> Schimmel: Listen, don't get mad. You can't be too careful, you know.
> God: I AM BUT ONE GOD FOR ALL BUDDHISTS, CHRISTIANS, CONFUCIANS, HINDUS, JEWS, MUSLIMS, SHINTOS, TAOISTS AND

ZOROASTRIANS ALIKE!

Schimmel: Ah, that's nice. He said it alphabetically so as not to offend anyvon. Hey! Hey, God. Shaddai. Vhere do You think You're going? Ya give me a stiff neck and Ya leave? Listen, maybe ve could make a deal. I have a nice girl for You. You like *shicksahs*?

Carl walked over and put his arms around Mrs. Alvarez while Mrs. Zammitti giggled.

"Then what happened?" Mrs. Zammitti insisted, encouraging Carl to go on.

"Then? Then God suddenly reappeared over the park. Father O'Rourke was playing ball with all the boys, patting everyone good-naturedly on the ass when God suddenly called down to him." Carl stood on his tiptoes, cupping his hand over his mouth and calling down in a loud but benevolent tone.

God: OH, FATHER O'ROURRRRRKE.

Father O'Rourke [and all the children looking up]: Jesus Christ!

God [smiling down benevolently]: NO, ACTUALLY HE COULDN'T MAKE IT. WELL, THAT'S NOT ENTIRELY TRUE. YOU SEE, HE DIDN'T WANT TO COME. I'M SURE YOU CAN UNDERSTAND. THINGS BEING THE WAY THEY ARE AND EVERYTHING. GRAVEN IMAGES. ALL THE COVETING. THE KILLINGS. YOU KNOW HOW SONS ARE. DIDN'T WANT TO DISAPPOINT HIS FATHER. [moving down closer to Father O'Rourke and whispering] WELL, IF YOU REALLY WANT TO KNOW THE TRUTH, JUST BETWEEN US FATHERS, I THINK IT'S BECAUSE OF YOUR WATERS. YOU KNOW, WITH THE POLLUTION AND

ALL. HE WAS AFRAID THAT IF ANYONE ASKED HIM TO DO HIS WALKING ON WATER SCHTICK, EVERYONE WOULD BELIEVE HE WAS STANDING ON GUSTAFSON'S GARBAGE.

Father O'Rourke: Who are you, my son?

God: [raising his voice angrily] I'M NOT YOUR SON. I'M YOUR FATHER, YOU SCHMUCKY CELIBATE. YOU'RE NOT A REAL FATHER. [grabbing his crotch] ONE DAY YOU COULDN'T GET IT UP AND THOUGHT IT A PREREQUISITE TO THE PRIESTHOOD. ORIGIN OF *THE PETER PRINCIPLE*, BY GOD. DIVINE SACRIFICE!

Father O'Rourke: [horrified] Oh, my God!

God: NOW YOU'RE GETTING IT TOGETHER. A LITTLE FEAR, A LITTLE WORSHIP. SORRY TO TOUCH ON SUCH A SOFT SPOT, BUT YOU KNOW WHAT A JEALOUS GOD I AM. GOOD LORD, IT'S GETTING LATE. [looks around omnisciently] TELL THAT BLACK SON OF A BITCH STANDING OVER THERE [pointing] HE'D BETTER NOT THROW THAT BALL AT ME.

Boy: Howd's He know I's dinkin' dat, Father?

Father O'Rourke: [holding the boy's throwing arm]
God only knows, my son. God only knows.

Yes, a little fear, a little worship. How well Carl understood their differences. Führer of the Firmament, deploying those scattered souls, instilling forever the awesome powers of Providence, preying upon the basic fears of man: Nakedness. Impotence. Exposure. Castration. It all boiled down to vulnerability! Shame, shame. The dread of devils, demons, and death. But even more terrifying, the ever present uncertainties of life.

"*Ja*, the traps in life, my friends," Carl continued. "'Tis one of the reasons I don't play golf anymore." Carl grinned, driving an imaginary golf ball high into the air toward an attendant coming out of A Building. "FORE!" Carl hollered in the man's direction.

Marvin Gitlin ducked one way and then the other, raising his arms protectively, pretending that he was about to be struck, playing the patient's game. "Hi, Carl," Marvin waved good-naturedly.

"Off the fairway, you fucking faggot," Carl demanded, lining up another shot. A moment later, the caretaker was off across the green, heading toward the library.

Just around the corner of the building, Raul and his younger friend, Miguel, sat snoozing contentedly in the noonday sun. They sat with their backs flat against the brick foundation, soaking up its warmth, obscured behind several shiny garbage cans. Raul slept with his mouth wide open, snoring away loudly. Miguel slept peacefully at his side, absorbed in pleasantries that bore a certain satisfaction upon his gentle face.

Raul stirred lazily as Carl carefully untied one of the laces wrapped twice around the top of the boy's sneaker. Next, he undid the bow at Miguel's shoe, tying the two laces together securely. Stepping back quietly, Carl gingerly lifted off two lids from the cans in front of him. Holding the shiny shields firmly by their handles, he brought the set of aluminum covers crashing together within inches of the pair of sleepyheads.

"SIESTA'S OVER," Carl screamed at the top of his voice as the boys scrambled to their feet, wheeling in opposite directions before falling to the ground, fighting frantically with their footwear while Carl stood over them menacingly, delivering another thunderous clash that brought attendants and nurses hurrying toward the scene.

Chapter 13

THE LIBRARY

Unnoticed, Richard waited quietly in the stuffy vestibule of the library and watched as Carl took down the last of the books from the steel shelving. Books were everywhere, piled high along the floor and tables throughout the commodious room. Except for the reference section, filled to capacity and standing off in a corner by itself, every other stack stood bare. Bare and barren. A standing army of steel-gray skeletons picked clean. Perforated with perfectly round holes. Drilled decisively silly. Like an erector set. A dimensional metallic graveyard. Death with depth. Row after countless row. Down and across. Like a perverted kind of crossword puzzle.

Carl wiped the sweat from his brow, then finally went around the room and opened several of the windows for some ventilation before beginning the tedious task of separating the American authors from the prodigious piles, rearranging the books alphabetically, calling their names aloud.

Ade, Alcott, Alger, Austin —

Carl worked feverishly, placing one book beside the other along the top shelf, apparently hoping to finish up before Mr. Schimmel returned from the infirmary he'd visit routinely during lunch each day, for the librarian would invariably spend his lunch hour consoling his good friend, Mr. Wyszynski, who'd complain about any number of ailments to anyone who'd listen.

Richard stepped just inside the room, enjoying a refreshing cross breeze that tarried playfully through the opened windows and brushed his hair, putting a smile and a whisper lightly upon his lips. "Shh." Not a soul in the building except the two of them. He was very much amused.

Carl reached down for another batch of books, suddenly aware that Richard was standing there.

Charles Brockton Brown, William H.
Brown, Buck, Cooper, Crane,
Dickinson, Dreiser —

"Everyone needs to be classified," he declared. "A place for everyone, and everyone in their place. Everyone must know one's place."

Emerson, Faulkner, Fitzgerald, Hawthorne,
Hemingway, Hubbard, James, Kerouac,
Lardner, Lewis, London, Mailer, A. Miller,
H. Miller —

"We're in a class by ourselves," the caretaker stated sadly. "That's why you and I are here, I suppose. We're all in a class by ourselves. A collection of lost souls."

Melville, O'Hara, O'Neill, Poe,
Salinger, Steinbeck, Stowe, Thoreau,
Thurber, Twain, Villard, Wilder . . .
Tennessee Williams

Carl held back the works of Tennessee Williams, pausing to articulate the dramas and traumas of the playwright's past, filling in the space with volumes of black American authors and poets. Starting over alphabetically. Pigeonholing his prejudices. Keeping things black and white.

Baldwin, Cullen, Ellison, Gordone,
Hammon, Hansberry, Hughs, J.W. Johnson,
McKay —

"Everyone mus' remember from where he come," Carl drawled. "Then he know jus' who he be. Ol' Thomas Lanier Williams mus' remember dat he got roots. Ol' Tom mus' never forget he be a octoroon —dat's a fact—and mus' therefore stand among his native kind." Carl grinned satisfactorily, placing the works of the southern playwright before Richard Wright's *Native Son*.

Tennessee Williams, R. Wright, Yerby.

Carl went through the piles of books, searching for what he termed, "the contemporary crafty craftsmen of our time. My goyish taste," he bellowed.

Bellow, Malamud, Markfield, Roth.

"Ah, but what this place needs is a good shit-kicker on Jesse James and his gang. How the hell can you depict America without a biography on America's foremost American? Why, Jesse and his boys laid the very foundation upon which America was built. Of course the Irish had their counterpart." Carl grabbed an armful of books and paraded back and forth along the stacks, dancing a jig and singing verse from *Bold Brennan on the Moor* in a thick Irish brogue:

> "Tis of a fearless highwayman
> a story I'll tell,
> His name was Willie Brennan
> and in Ireland he did dwell.
> 'Twas on the Lim'rick mountains
> he commenced his wild career,
> Where many a wealthy gentleman
> before him shook with fear.
>
> Brennan on the moor,
> Brennan on the moor,
> Bold and yet undaunted
> stood young Brennan on the moor.

Beckett, Behan, Joyce, Moore —

> A brace of loaded pistols
> he carried night and day,
> He never robbed a poor man
> up on King's Highway.
> But what he'd taken from the rich

like Turpin and Black Bess,
He always did divide it
with the widow in distress.

Brennan on the moor,
Brennan on the moor,
Bold and yet undaunted
stood young Brennan on the moor."

O'Connor, Sheridan, Synge, Yeats.

Carl pranced around the room, selecting the English from the lot while muttering some gibberish about an infamous forest fag with a bow as though he were speaking with a mouthful of marbles.

Austen, Blake, Bacon, C. Bronte, E. Bronte, Byron, Carroll, Chaucer, Coleridge, Conrad, Darwin, Donne, Defoe, Dickens, Dryden, T.S. Eliot, Gissing, Hardy, Hobbes, Hume, Huxley —

Suddenly, Carl picked his nose, belched, scratched his crotch, then flatulated loudly. "Long Live the Queen!" he proclaimed. "Hail Robin And His Band of Merry Men."

Keats, Kipling, Lawrence, Locke, Marlow, Maugham, Meredith, Mill, Milton, Noyes, Orwell, Pope, Russell, Shakespeare, Shaw, Shelly, Spenser, Stevenson, Swift, Tennyson, Thackeray, Thomas, Wilde, Wordsworth.

Carl reached down for a tattered book near his feet. A book he had read many a time before. "Ah! Don Quixote," he cried. "Truly the last of our magnificent madmen. Committed to the glory of a dream. *Olé!*"

Cervantes

He worked methodically, filling in the shelves with an enthusiasm a rookie sorter of mail might display at a central post office. Richard realized that the caretaker was creating a linear map of sorts: the bough of Western Man.

"*Oui, oui!*" Carl exclaimed, toying pretentiously with his marvelous mustache while picking through the works of Camus and Sartre, reciting lofty treatises of existential thought before finally seeking solace in Voltaire's simple words of wisdom noted in the conclusion of *Candide*, elaborating on how the old man in the story finds contentment through the cultivation of his own garden, rather than pondering and trying to answer the unanswerable. "*Ja*, and that is what I must continue to do," the caretaker said, smiling quite satisfactorily. "I must simply cultivate my own garden."

> Balzac, Camus, Dumas, Dumas fils,
> Flaubert, Rimbaud, Rousseau, Sartre,
> Voltaire, Zola.

"Vhere are your papers?" Carl demanded with a perfect German accent, assuming the ostentatious bearing of a border guard.

> Engels, Grimm, Hess, Hitler, Jaspers,
> Kafka, Kant, Lessing, Mann, Marx,
> Nietzsche, Werfel, Zweig.

Carl sorted, selected, and swept his prejudicial map across the steel shelving—categorizing, classifying, and cataloging his predilections: Italy, Poland, Greece, Russia.

An overwhelming sense of nostalgia engulfed his being as he placed the last of the faded volumes along the shelving, carefully wiping the dusty spines on his pant leg: Finland, Sweden, Norway, Denmark, and Iceland.

Finally, he set the last book in place, stepping back from the monumental altar of ideas. "I wonder if people realize that Icelanders read more books than any other peoples in the world, or that the illiteracy rate in Sweden is nonexistent. *Ja*, that is a fact. Of course, our suicide rate is quite another matter," he sighed. "Fear is not knowing—or knowing too much, I fear."

Carl spoke of the days when he was a young man working in the great forests near the Finnish border, sitting around the campfire in the evenings, drinking Swedish beer along with all the other men, discussing women, logging, and politics.

"And as the night wore on," he reminisced, "and the flames fell low into the glow of white ash, we'd all tell stories, sing songs, and even recite poetry, usually about some girl, some quiet place, or just something that had touched our souls somewhere in time. Then, just for a moment, everyone would remain seated and silent, as if reflecting upon their very souls." Carl stood silent for a moment. "Suddenly, all would stand and raise their beer to cheer the very best and worst of prose or verse," he remarked, holding up an imaginary glass. "But most of all, I remember the silence. *Ja.* Sweet silence. She weighs heavy upon my heart," Carl said rather mysteriously, gazing around the room. "Where have all the poets gone?" he cried. "So little poetry left in the world today."

Suddenly, Mr. Schimmel entered the library, walking right past Richard, the look of bewilderment written across the librarian's face. "Vhat the hell is this?" the librarian demanded of Carl.

"Ah, Mr. Schimmel."

"Don't you 'Ah, Mr. Schimmel' me, you, you sauerkraut." Mr. Schimmel looked around the room in disbelief. "Vhat the hell did you do here?"

"Why, I put everyone in their proper place. Everyone must know one's place."

"GET OUT OF HERE!" Schimmel cried aghast.

"Oh, by the way." Carl grinned. "I'd like to talk to you about requisitioning some shit-kickers on how the West was won."

"You have no business being in here. Do you hear vhat I am saying? I am in charge here. You vill vait outside." Mr. Schimmel scrutinized the shelves in horror. "Spoiler! You mixed everything up! Everything is out of order."

"Poetry is the best words in their best order," Carl replied. "Where have all our poets gone?"

Mr. Schimmel turned to Carl angrily. "Do I meddle in your garden? Do I tell you how to grow flowers? VELL, DO I? You march in here like a Nazi stormtrooper. Like the Sturmabteilungen; the Brownshirts. This library is not open until I am standing in it. I am in charge here! Vhy should this day be different than any other?"

"*Ja*. Why indeed?" Carl agreed. "Perhaps for a thousand reasons or for no reason whatsoever. No matter. Listen." Carl recited.

"What matters is what is,
and not the reason why;
The question, not the answer,
the seeing, not the eye."

"I wrote that," Carl added proudly.

"May I come in now, Mr. Schimmel?" Richard asked politely, still standing near the threshold.

Mr. Schimmel turned and looked at Richard, then back to Carl. "You see the vay he vaits patiently and asks permission? A fine young man. A real gentleman. Come, Richard. Come in here and look at vhat this madman has done."

Carl brushed past the angry librarian, deftly removing the man's pocket watch from his vest, along with the pewter chain. Once outside, Carl filled his lungs with the fresh breath of spring, singing out gaily.

"One night he robbed a packman
his name was Pedlar Brown,
They traveled on together
till day began to dawn.
The pedlar seeing his money gone
likewise his *watch* and *chain*,
He at once encountered Brennan
and robbed them back again.

Brennan on the moor,
Brennan on the moor,
Bold and yet undaunted
stood young Brennan on the moor."

It was only then that the unsuspecting Mr. Schimmel happened to look down, suddenly noticing that his watch and chain were gone.

Carl kept looking back over his shoulder until he saw fury itself come storming out of the building. The caretaker laughed with delight, loping leisurely along the gardens, his long legs easily outpacing the little angry man.

It was a game that Carl enjoyed immensely, a game he never tired of. It was a routine the doctors, nurses, and attendants had retired from years ago, trying in vain to catch the harmless, elusive, singing Scandinavian. Besides, the watch always did turn up, although sometimes rather mysteriously, once reappearing in Mr. Schimmel's matzo ball soup.

Carl continued his singing on the run:

> "When Brennan saw the pedlar
> was as good a man as he,
> He took him on the highway
> his companion for to be.
> The pedlar threw away his pack
> without anymore delay,
> And proved a faithful comrade
> until his dying day.
>
> Brennan on the moor,
> Brennan on the moor,
> Bold and yet undaunted
> stood young Brennan on the moor."

Richard walked up to the card catalog, making a mental note of all the information he needed. A moment later, he headed toward the reference section, searching methodically for a half a dozen tomes. He carried the weighty matter over to a partitioned area located in the far corner of the room and settled down comfortably into a high-backed chair. He opened one of the books to the index, noting the items of interest. Completely absorbed, he propped his elbows onto the warm wooden surface, clamping his head between his palms, poring over the material bit by bit. Page by page. Committing it all to memory.

"Yes. In memory of Mother," Richard offered prematurely, raking his fingers satisfactorily through his clay-red curls.

Chapter 14

BLOWUP

It was a beautiful April morning, and the birds were chirping away excitedly as Mrs. Ackerman strolled quietly along the gardens, dragging a large plastic bundle filled with garbage. Althea Blythe, a young and very attractive black woman who lived on the third floor of B Building, observed the older woman closely. As closely as though she were judging an entry to some important contest. Suddenly, Mrs. Ackerman reached down and deposited something into the bag before continuing along with pompous bearing, primping the coil of hair at the back of her neck with one hand, trailing the bag of trash with the other. Althea followed at a reasonable distance.

Mrs. Ackerman always wore her hair up. Several of the women on her floor attested to the fact that she had long and lovely chestnut hair that reached the small of her back. The nurses had said that she could keep it long, just so long as she kept it clean. But Althea couldn't understand why Mrs. Ackerman went to such great lengths to conceal it in the first place, although Mr. Schimmel had tried to explain that it was a tradition steeped in the orthodox observance of turning pretty into plain except in private. Althea watched intently as one of the nurses went over to take the garbage away from Mrs. Ackerman, but the woman wouldn't give it up without an argument.

"That's my bag, bitch," Mrs. Ackerman insisted. "I spent the whole morning picking up after you little piggies."

"But the bag is full, dear. See?" the pretty nurse said pleasantly. "Come with me now," she coaxed, "and we'll find you a nice big empty bag inside. All right?" Nurse Marlow removed the bag from the patient's hand, setting the bundle down near the steps as she led the frustrated woman back inside.

Althea focused on the clear plastic bag that contained the morning's garbage, packed to the hilt with crumpled foil and saturated, greasy, green paper towels; gold and silver can tops, to which clung tiny pieces of meat and cigarette butts; broken egg shells, smooth and white as alabaster; potato and orange peelings; blood-stained meat packages laden with strips of marbled fat; and several large juice cans, one of which was filled with rendered grease and burnt matches. Althea looked up to see Carl Gustafson coming around the garden path from the direction of Dr. King's house, so she quickly grabbed the garbage then disappeared down the steps between the buildings.

Mrs. Ackerman was still arguing with the nurse just inside the doorway of B Building as Carl came by. But the caretaker was distracted by another commotion coming from the narrow passageway below. Setting down a small pail of fertilizer, Carl approached the steps cautiously, suspecting that the ruckus was caused by some stray animal rummaging through the garbage. For there were numerous reports about abandoned animals, especially dogs, roaming wild in packs along the nearby shores and highways around the institution. Many cats, dogs, raccoons and an occasional opossum had been killed along the busy boulevard just outside the gate, struck by speeding motorists as the animals tried to cross in heavy traffic. Carl heard the sound of whimpering and went down the stairs to investigate. There, he found Althea on her knees, sobbing and sifting carefully through scattered garbage on the concrete floor.

Richard had been watching the scene from a nearby bench when Mrs. O'Brian suddenly appeared before him, inviting herself to sit and chat a spell. Mrs. O'Brian related Althea's tale of woe, for she knew the story well.

"First you have to understand, Richard, that it had only been a year since Althea lost her natural mother in a tragic drowning accident, and under rather suspicious circumstances," the old woman began, knowing she had a captive audience of one. "Not to mention the fact that her well-to-do father had remarried quite suddenly," she continued, moving a little closer to Richard. "So Althea had tried to bury her grief by throwing herself headlong into her work, designing layouts and modeling clothes no less than fifteen to sixteen hours a day for a chic fashion magazine in Manhattan.

"It was there that she met Mark, one of the new photographers who saw the early warning signs of a nervous breakdown heading her way. He worked with Althea on assignments almost exclusively, capturing her frame of mind, showing her care and understanding, slowly pulling her back from the well-disguised depths of depression.

"And as the months passed by, Althea and Mark spent more and more time together, either at his place or the park, usually working on layouts or taking long walks on Sunday afternoons. One afternoon, Althea brought Mark home to meet her family. But she only did that once, for her father's reticence spoke louder and clearer than any words could offer," Mrs. O'Brian offered knowingly.

"Then on the anniversary of their courtship, Mark took Althea to an exclusive restaurant and presented her with a small silver film canister, like the ones he had taped to the strap of his camera. Althea unscrewed the cap, and out rolled a brilliant diamond ring into her palm of her hand!" Mrs. O'Brian exclaimed, sticking the palm of her own hand practically under Richard's nose. "Of course, Althea shed tears of happiness all through dinner. And although the ring was too big and had to be sized, Althea insisted on showing her parents and announcing their engagement.

"Well, before she went to bed that evening, she placed the ring back in the cotton-lined canister, which is a silly thing to do because the fibers get caught in the setting. Anyhow, Althea was so happy; that is, until she awoke late the next morning to discover the canister missing from the top of her bureau. Althea wept bitterly as her stepmother tried to explain exactly why Althea's father had thrown both the canister and ring in the garbage before he left for work that morning, having proclaimed that no daughter of his was ever going to marry white trash.

"Althea ran from the house hysterically, searching frantically through virtually empty cans of garbage. Up and down the street she went. She spent nearly a week at the city dump, tearing insanely through tons of trash. Shortly thereafter, a violent argument erupted between Althea's father and her fiancé. She never saw Mark again. Althea had sat in her room for over a year, but her family said that she would learn to adjust," Mrs. O'Brian explained, gesturing toward the steps.

Carl gently knelt beside Althea, showing the handsome woman that there was absolutely nothing in the garbage that would be of any interest to her, helping her to her feet and back up the stairs. Picking up his pail of fertilizer, he brought her over to the bench.

Althea removed a picture from the pocket of her pretty blouse and held it out for all to see. Mrs. Zammitti came over from B Building and stared down at the photograph: a black and white photograph of a sad young woman standing all alone in the middle of a meadow, gazing into space. Althea said she liked the picture because of the beautiful white dress the woman wore, explaining that it reminded her of the wedding gown she never got to wear. She said that her fiancé had enlarged the picture and that the blowup revealed the woman's hand placed gently on her stomach, suggesting that she may have been with child.

"Just like Althea had been before her father made her terminate the pregnancy," Mrs. O'Brian whispered.

But Carl told Althea that she was probably blowing things out of proportion, warning her about the illusions of life and art, along with the dangers of assuming the wrong interpretations, especially when tampering with distance and space. He tried to explain to her that an artist always runs the risk of reducing life to a series of dots and blurs.

"Like Mr. Wyszynski over there." Carl gestured toward the figure coming out of the infirmary. "You see, he suffers from the blurs. Oh, he has perfect vision, mind you. Like a hawk. Only his head is in the clouds. I SAID, HIS HEAD IS IN THE CLOUDS," Carl shouted in the man's direction.

Mr. Wyszynski stuffed his hands into the pockets of his robe and shuffled aimlessly across the grounds.

Carl shook his head in annoyance. "Depressing sort of chap. Doesn't hear too well either. Besides," he scowled, perusing the photograph, "the woman is holding her stomach—not because she is pregnant—but because she is looking for the itinerant guinea bastard who sold her the fucking frankfurter that made her sick to her stomach."

Mrs. Zammitti looked around nervously, poking at the picture and wanting to know if there were any mice in the meadow.

Althea asked Carl if he had anything nice to say about Italians, reminding him of the fact that they bestowed such wonderful gifts for all the world to see, gifts presented in the form of beautiful religious paintings and sculpture.

Mrs. Zammitti nodded affirmatively.

"And in return, we give them our garbage, daily," Carl argued. "So, by now, they should have quite a collection," he added with a certain satisfaction. "Besides, all their talent is over there. In Europe. Not here. What accomplishments have they bestowed upon us here? Tell me! No, I'll tell you," he insisted, reaching down for the pail of fertilizer near his feet, sprinkling a little pinch here and a little pinch there, listing a host of spicy ingredients and declaring Italian-Americans' sole achievement as the unprecedented combination pizza. "Seven strokes of genius and a hot oven is their only true contribution. Invented *here*. Try and get it over *there*," Carl affirmed, throwing an imaginary dough high into the air off floury-like fists while breaking into song. "When—the—moon hits a-you-eye—like a big pizza pie—that's a dago," Carl sang out gaily in rich baritone.

Mrs. O'Brian waved her hand excitedly as if begging to be called upon in class. "That's Amoré!" she exclaimed. "Music and lyrics by Harry Warren and Jack Brooks; from the film, *The Caddie*, recorded by Paramount—1953," she offered proudly. "But keep your ears open for Kander and Ebb," she added confidentially to Richard, inching herself a little closer to the quiet lad.

Carl told Mrs. Zammitti to tell Mrs. O'Brian to save her trivia for the isolation booth on the American game show, *The $64,000 Question*. And Mrs. O'Brian told Mrs. Zammitti to tell Carl that she, indeed, was already living in one, explaining to Richard that she and Carl hadn't spoken directly to one another in many years.

"Goddamn shanty Irish," Carl swore beneath his breath.

"And what do you say about us black folks behind our backs?" Althea criticized, putting away her photograph.

Carl, setting the stage, dramatically sprung behind Althea like a character actor out of a villainous scene, as though she were the damsel in distress and he the scoundrel. Conveying outrageously bawdy behavior, he darted his tongue suggestively, licked his lips lasciviously, and rolled his eyes desirously over her trim figure. Stooping slightly forward, his head alongside Althea's, he arched his bushy eyebrows haughtily while twisting up the villainous ends of his wildly wicked mustache. "Behind yo' back," Carl whispered with a drawl, "I says, looka dat fine ass on dat momma."

Althea cocked her pretty head to one side, her jaw set tight with disapproval. "You certainly delight in giving everyone the needle, don't you?"

"I'm afraid you fail to see that it's the guineas who are doing all the needling, sweet cheeks," Carl retorted, plunging an imaginary needle into Althea's arm. "It's their traffic you folks are tied up in. Guinea gangland traffic. Got it?" Carl winced, withdrawing the notional needle and pointing an accusing finger in Mrs. Zammitti's face.

"Oh, I got it all right," Althea said as Mrs. Zammitti backed away nervously, biting down upon the finger of a fisted hand.

"Bunch of junk collecting, drug pushing, racketeering, wop, dago, Sicilian-guinea gangland Cosa Nostra families; strictly speaking in generalities, of course," Carl ranted, following after the frightened woman. ". . . that are shoveling white shit down black throats, or coursing it through their swarthy veins. Well, there's no nativity scene on my front lawn, Mary! No one here can accuse Carl Gustafson of being a hypocrite. No bones buried beneath my gardens. And I can assure you that both the Swedish and Danish authorities dug everywhere," Carl assured everyone rather cryptically, walking off in a huff.

"White trash!" Althea snarled, causing Carl to stop midstride. She glared at him angrily.

"White trash?" Carl was taken aback. "White trash, you say? Now just a cotton pickin' minute here, my pugnacious pickaninny," he railed. "Why don't you jus' be gone with the wind and plant yo' Aunt Jemima ass down on some southern-white plantation where it belongs. Lots of trash for you to rummage through down there. I saw you pickin' through those sanitary napkins and tampons," he insisted, breaking out in angry dance around the bench, slapping his thighs rhythmically.

> "Gonna jump down, spin around
> Pick a bale of cotton.
> Gonna jump down, spin around
> Pick a bale of hay.
> Jump down, spin around
> Pick a bale of cotton.
> Gonna jump down, spin around
> Pick a bale of hay."

"Yea, and if you want to see the nigger in yourself, she insisted, "you need only examine your own negatives more carefully."

"BLACK TRASH," he screamed. "I can see the forest through the trees."

"I think you're projecting, honky," Althea shouted, hurrying back down the stairs before tearing insanely through another bag of garbage lined along the wall.

"Now, listen here, girl," Carl demanded, calling down to her. "Growing up back home you may have been privy to such importuning as, 'Black is beautiful,' and 'You *haves* an uptown address, my little pearl.' But you best get yourself straightened out, sister. And I don't mean by working that lye into your hair. I see those empty bottles of straightener in the trash. You can start right now by being your natural self. Hear? Get yourself back into pigtails or corn rows, sweet thing. Or else Mama Gustafson, here, gonna conk ya silly. Ya dig? You have no business acting or trying to marry white. You jus' find yo'self a nice cotton pickin', boot lickin', shoe shufflin', soul searchin', jazz jivin', juice shootin', coke snortin', ghetto gatherin' nigger, honey. One who'll escort you to your own kind of restaurant in your own part of town. One who *knows* how to order:

"'Hey sucker. Yea, I mean you, motherfucker. Ripple Collins here for momma, and an order of fried chicken, ham hocks, hominy grits, chitlins, collard greens, black-eyed peas, and the usual fo' dessert. What's you mean, melon only in season, man?'" Carl concluded, heading across the grounds with pail in hand, leaving Althea to her trash, knowing full well that Mrs. Ackerman would be by momentarily to clean up Althea's mess.

Mrs. O'Brian went on to explain that, like Mrs. Ackerman and Althea, Carl, too, once held a certain fascination for garbage. Mrs. Ackerman's obsession with it was founded in her firm belief that 'cleanliness was next to godliness.' Carl's attraction for garbage was simply that he liked to snoop. That is, until one day he discovered something that he hadn't quite bargained for. The old woman related that story, too. Practically sitting upon Richard's lap as she opened up her purse.

"Oh, it happened many years ago while Carl was attending classes and working as a custodian at the small college near Copenhagen, shortly after he had met and married Sonjia," she explained, painstakingly painting her fingernails a putrid shade of purple. "Carl would surreptitiously and systematically search through all the campus trash, discovering many secrets about students and faculty. He learned, for example, that around the end of every month, the chairman of the Foreign Language Department would pass by a certain trash receptacle located near the corner of the gymnasium, and there discard a large plain Manila envelope when he thought no one was looking. Concealed within the packet was a wide assortment of literature covering everything from Swedish films to Oriental ointments; offerings for monthly selections of books, magazines, erotic manuals, devices, and clothing of all sorts. Can you imagine?" she added coyly, brazenly stroking Richard's leg.

"Then on one particular occasion," she whispered, leaning over ever so close, "Carl discovered the pieces of a torrid love letter hidden among the literature in the chairman's monthly packet buried at the bottom of the heap. The handwriting looked familiar. So familiar, in fact, that Carl wept as he put the pieces together, for the letter had been written to the chairman of the Foreign Language Department and signed by his wife, Sonjia," Mrs. O'Brian said matter-of-factly, blowing upon the set of nails, holding them at arm's length for quick inspection. "How's that for art, handsome?" she asked and smiled mischievously, fishing for something more than just a compliment.

"Beautiful," Richard answered, taking her hand in his, lying to her eyes. "So how did Carl wind up here?" he asked, pumping her for further information.

Mrs. O'Brian giggled. "Well, it took a rotten marriage and two stinking wars, but he finally made it," she continued, explaining how Carl had immigrated to the United States after the First World War, managing to find some work as a janitor at a small apartment house in New York, while waiting to be naturalized. "Then when World War II broke out, he volunteered his services, winding up in German occupied Italy once again, fighting alongside British Eighth Army Allied forces under the command of General Montgomery.

"Only this time, he fought *against* 'those guinea bastards,' is the way he likes to put it." She went on and on, delving into the past delightedly, as though it were a house of history reopened only yesterday when she was as young and carefree as Carl. "Even though Italy surrendered and became a cobelligerent, declaring war on Germany some five weeks later, Carl insisted that the guineas were the real enemy, and even more of a threat than Hitler himself. After one of many battles fought at Anzio, Carl was left for dead, regaining consciousness several months later at a V.A. hospital in Maryland, of all places. Down there with all the other quacks. Get it?" She giggled gaily, poking Richard in the ribs. "Carl received treatment from several doctors for both mind and body. I don't think they did a very good job."

Richard forced a smile.

"Anyhow, shortly thereafter, Carl wound up here with two wicker suitcases in hand, handsome as can be," she swore. "Oh, and insisting all the while that he was General Montgomery, having been dispatched as head of the Twenty-first Army Group to commandeer 'this hotel,' demanding a private room away from all other guests, explaining that he was mentally fatigued and needed a nice long rest."

"That's what Mother said I needed," Richard offered in response and grinned.

The old woman nodded understandingly before continuing. "Then a year or so later, Dr. King appointed Carl his official caretaker, giving him added responsibilities as time went on. But as the years passed, Carl became more and more obsessed with the relationship between people and their garbage, revealing many personal details concerning all of us who live here, not to mention certain members of the staff. It got to be quite embarrassing. Especially for a young woman like myself as you might well imagine." Mrs. O'Brian smiled, absentmindedly running the second set of purply wet nails through her silver hair.

"That man, would, without warning or provocation, broadcast to anyone, the names and menstrual cycles of all of us young ladies here, nurses who were on the pill, as well as several doctors who used prophylactics by the dozen. I remember Carl handing a used condom to Mr. Schimmel on the very day they brought him here, instructing the new admission to pull it down over his head, insisting that the little man was the biggest prick he ever had the displeasure of meeting. But that was not until Mr. Schimmel cried and carried on, believing Carl to be the culprit who had kidnapped and murdered Lindbergh's baby, would you believe? However, I think Carl killed his wife, Sonjia," the old woman whispered, staring down in disbelief at the set of streaked nails. "I BELIEVE IT WITH ALL MY HEART," she blew up angrily, storming off the bench and marching briskly away.

"How do you think he killed her?" Richard called out.

"Find that out for yourself, and you've got the answer to the sixty-four thousand dollar question."

Chapter 15

ANALYSIS

It was the second week in April, and Dr. King had not gotten Richard to communicate, neither in group therapy nor in private. Patient Geist remained quite uncommunicative; that is, until *he* decided it was time to play the psychiatrist's game. So, opening up his mouth one morning while reclining on the couch in Dr. King's office, Richard started talking about when Dicky was first learning to read and write. Then, for no apparent reason, he closed his mouth in mid-sentence.

Dr. King sat behind his desk; he wore a stark-white lab coat that contrasted sharply with a healthy head of dark curly hair. He sat demurely, drumming a set of manicured fingernails upon the highly-polished mahogany surface.

Richard lay quietly on the dark leather couch, staring across the room at a group of framed photographs hung along the far wall. Black and white photos of outer space. He lay listening intently to the rather impatient cadence of finger tapping, his own fingers laced comfortably behind his head.

Dr. King took a moment during the interminable lull to light up one of his cigars before reaching for pen and pad. "I'm here to listen, Richard," the psychiatrist said evenly, puffing steadily on his cigar while jotting down a note or two.

"Then listen!" Richard said abruptly, absorbed with the scribbling of bits of information, aware of the pervasive odor in the air.

"Why don't you just start from the beginning?" Dr. King suggested, putting down the pen.

"The beginning?"

"Yes. You started telling me about when Dicky was first learning to read and write."

"Oh, I could tell you stories all right. I could tell you stories that would make your hair stand on end. I could tell you the ABCs of it. That's how she used to drill Dicky. 'A, you're Adorable. B, you're so beautiful. C, you're a Cutie full of Charms,'" he sang aloud. "She was an AWFULLY BITCHY CUNT, you see. Then she'd make little Dicky recite and write the alphabet. Backwards and forwards.

ZYXWVUTSRQPONMLKJIHGFEDCBA," Richard recited excitedly before calmly setting forth the letters alphabetically, singing out childishly to the tune of *Twinkle Twinkle Little Star*. "Over and over again. From big A to little z. Oh, she taught Dicky how to read and write all right. He wrote so nice. All over Mother's mirrored tables with her red lipstick. You should have seen her complexion. RED! Obscenities scribbled across her reflection. So angry was she. So many years ago." Richard recounted the years Dicky resided in that Hiawatha house, recalling the very first season they moved into the quiet, little town.

"It was spring, and there was no one else around, except for the Millers who lived across the street. That's because most of the houses were actually summer homes. We had corner property with lots of pine trees in the backyard. Hundreds of them," he exaggerated with childlike glee. "Dicky was only four," he said, holding up four fingers.

"When summer arrived, the neighborhood suddenly filled with children around Dicky's age, but Mummy would sit little Dicky in the backyard with his chalkboard and easel, working with him on his words and phrases. Oh, she was so proud, showing him off to all her new neighbors, explaining how she had taught darling Dicky to read and write from the age of three. Labels and signs. Signs and labels . . . most of them from soup cans. Chicken Noodle, Cream of Celery, and Consommé.

"Fall was just a cooler rendition of the summer season, whereby Dicky would sit outside with his little pocket dictionary, leafing through scores of vocabulary words. 'STOP!' Dicky had scribbled, deliberately raking his chalk across the slate and sending shivers up everyone's spine. Then Dicky wrote and rearranged the letters of the word. Backwards and forwards. Inside and out. STOP, POTS, SPOT, TOPS, POST, OPTS. 'My word! What a clever little bird,' they purred, moving cautiously across the lawn.

"Winter came early that year, and it was the first real snowstorm Dicky could remember. His whole wide world became a blanket of blinding light. He loved the crunching sound it made beneath his rubber boots. That is, until one night when he made the mistake of mentioning the smelly doody in his bed. That's when Mummy grabbed a box of soap flakes off the kitchen counter and dragged little Dicky outside the house, throwing him down half naked in the chest-high snow, cursing and beating him mercilessly, making him undress and wash his body, socks, and underpants thoroughly with handfuls of soapy, powdery snow. 'Mummy is going to teach you how to do a cold water wash,' she swore. Dicky stood there shivering insanely, trying to get his clothes and body clean. And when he finally did, Mummy refused to allow him back inside the house unless he stopped his infernal shaking. At first, he couldn't do it, but she said that he would remain out there until frozen stiff if necessary. I think that's when Dicky first learned how to send his mind a million miles away to balmy beaches that cooled the scorching sand between his toes. Finally, he stood still and silent, long enough to satisfy her rage.

"For the better part of winter, Mummy confined herself to the house, hibernating in dormant states of gloom until another spring arrived, when suddenly she became as vibrant as the viny, green-leafed pattern on the wall; that is, till the following fall when she tried to strangle little Dicky. Only he tucked his tiny little chin tight against his chest like this," Richard demonstrated, straining his voice and drawing himself up to the center of the psychiatrist's couch.

"It was around that time when Dicky started school. Mummy brought him in on the very first day and caused some sort of commotion with the kindergarten teacher. And all the children laughed at Mummy. So Dicky thought that if he lost himself among the group of laughing children, and laughed, too, no one would suspect he belonged to the woman who was making a spectacle of herself. But before he had a chance to hide amongst his classmates, the teacher singled him out, summoning him to the front of the room. Dicky didn't understand what was being said, but just before Mummy left, she blew him a kiss. He had to bite down hard upon his bottom lip, making it bleed, to stop the tears that appeared blood red as they fell upon his shoes.

"Near the end of the school year, the kindergarten teacher told Dicky that he was being promoted to the second grade the following term, that he would skip first grade because he had performed extremely well, and that everyone was very proud of him. Mummy was quite proud, too. First, she called the school to confirm Dicky's story. Secondly, she notified all the relatives, informing them of the news.

"Then came Christmas Eve, the one holiday that Dicky

remembered most of all. BRRRRR. Mummy turned cold as stone, arguing with Father over how to string the lights and where to hang the ornaments. Dicky shivered as he hung the silvery strands of ice. 'NO NOT LIKE THAT—LIKE THIS,' she shouted. 'Learn to do it nice.' Dicky tried, but Mummy looked dissatisfied. She left the room, returning a moment later with a kitchen cleaver in her hand. 'LET ME TEACH YOU HOW TO TRIM THE TREE,' she screamed, hacking off its branches with a spirit all her own, running throughout the house and ripping holly off the walls, cursing Dicky insanely till his little ears began to burn.

"Father grabbed hold of little Dicky's arm, leading him from the house, pulling him by the hand and across the street to the Millers. And through their picture window, everyone witnessed Mummy utterly destroy the contents of the living room. Hickory-dickory-dock. Down came the grandfather clock. CRASH! 'Oh, my dear—there goes the chandelier!' Mrs. Miller exclaimed. SMASH! Father tried to stop her from further destruction, for he ran back across the street screaming, 'PLEASE DON'T DO ANY MORE DAMAGE,' as a group of silent carolers passed by the house in shock. Then the Millers led little Dicky from the scene, hushing and comforting, and wishing him pleasant dreams. 'You're a fine young man,' Mrs. Miller said so softly, tucking him in gently upon their couch, drawing the drapes and switching off the light." Richard closed his eyes tightly and lay back upon the psychiatrist's couch, drawing his knees to his chin, curling himself into an inconsolable ball of grief.

"The following morning, Mummy phoned for her little man, and Father came and took him by the hand. 'Be careful what you say,' he pleaded. 'Your mother isn't feeling very well today.' Dicky saw their Christmas tree lying in the gutter with the trash. Decorticated. Like a dismembered green giant. Its spine and spindly branches were strewn along the curb, along with strands of silver ice and holly, hanging in the wind. Then Mummy opened up the side door off the kitchen. 'Come. See what Santa has brought you, dear,' she said with a grin, pointing to a box and a paper bag sitting on the kitchen table.

"Father helped unpack a phonograph from a plain brown cardboard carton. But Dicky wanted to know why the presents were not wrapped and if they could still have another Christmas tree. Father said that Santa had been very busy that year. And as for a Christmas tree, 'Why, we have a backyard full of them!' he declared, smiling and gesturing to the stately pines that filled the outer window frame high above the kitchen sink.

"After Father finished explaining to little Dicky how the turntable turned and how sound is recorded and reproduced, he removed a single record from the bag: *Rudolph the Red-Nosed Reindeer* and *Silent Night*. Mummy insisted on listening to the latter. Over and over again. Around and around it spun till Dicky turned nauseously dizzy. He asked Mummy if Santa hadn't left anything for her. Suddenly, he heard the sharp sound of a needle grate across his nerves. Without a start, Mummy ripped the cord from the outlet, picked up the phonograph then pushed it through the kitchen door window while Father stood in shock.

"Finally, Father led Dicky through the parlor and out to the porch, taking a dusty black box down from a shelf. 'This is a transformer, son. It transforms electric energy via electromagnetic induction. Someday I'll buy you a set of electric trains and show you what I mean.' You see, Mummy had her ABCs, and Father had his electronics.

Richard took a deep breath followed by a minute of silence. Dr. King remained silent, too, waiting patiently for Richard to continue.

"One day, Mummy turned quite mad and had to be taken away to a private hospital. But I'll bet you know all about that. You were probably one of the doctors who sent her there. So Dicky stayed with the Millers until Mummy was well enough to come home. Well! Mummy wasn't even home a day before she started in, dressing Dicky in garments Grandfather had made especially for him, tailored to a T: a short pleated jacket with matching knee-length pants; a frilled shirt with ruffled sleeves and collar made of lace, encircled with a large loose bow. Then she'd twirl and curl his clay-red locks before one of the mirrored tables in the room. 'There now, that's my baby doll,' Mummy said, beaming brightly. Little Dicky gazed down at the strange reflection in the glass, wondering if he even knew the little girl. And if Mummy wasn't looking, he'd wipe the mirrored surface with his sleeve, but the image simply would not disappear. Not at first. Of course, one had to know magic, but Dicky swore he'd never, ever tell a soul.

"Because Dicky skipped one grade, and then another, he was the youngest as well as the shortest child in the class. Even the girls would tease him about his size, making fun of his clothes, kicking his bony shins. Boys and girls together would torment him on the bus. Dicky would lie awake nights, terrified at the thought of going to school each morning. Then one day he turned positively mad. Digging through his chest of drawers, he found a plain flannel shirt and a pair of chino pants. Mummy didn't say a word, but he could read the disapproval on her face, both aware that a change had taken place.

"It was a rather cool morning. Dicky felt an air of confidence as he left for school that day. He held his head high, heading towards the bus stop. The children would no longer torment him the way they had before, he swore. But as he approached the corner, he could hear them whispering and snickering. He could feel the blood rush to his face. Dicky stood there alongside the road, prying loose a stone embedded in the earth with the side of his shoe."

Richard stood up on the psychiatrist's couch and dug his foot into its center, contorting his face and altering his tone. "'Where're your Sunday-go-to-meetin' clothes?' one of the boys sneered. 'Probably being taken in here and there,' a girl teased, pulling at Dicky's clothing. 'Is that a fact?' the boy persisted, towering over little Dicky, awaiting his answer. I guess Dicky kept him waiting too long, for the boy became very impatient and drove his fist furiously against Dicky's temple, knocking him to the ground. But Dicky pulled himself together, picking up the jagged stone and smashed it against the boy's skull, over and over again, until a series of wild explosions in his own head subsided, as though an evil force lurking within some corner of his skull was suddenly being released through some barbarous form of exorcism. Then Dicky dropped the stone and seized the bloody head of hair, smashing it hard against the smooth macadam, till only the whites of the boy's eyes were visible. Everyone stood as still as statues; no one moved a muscle or an inch. Dicky got up and wiped his bloody hands upon his chino pants, believing that he had actually killed the boy. Apparently, all the children did, too, for they suddenly started screaming bloody murder. Dicky ran into the woods to hide.

"He prayed that the law might be merciful, seeing as how he was the son of a mother with a diseased mind, praying they'd confine him to an institution in lieu of the electric chair. He couldn't bear the thought of that so-called father of his entering the death house, identifying himself as an electrical engineer and the father of the condemned, imagining the man asking the warden if it would be all right to explain to his son how death is actually caused by amperage— not voltage, while Mother stood in the background, screaming, 'DON'T LISTEN TO YOUR NAZI FATHER, DICKY. SPELL MISSISSIPPI FOR YOUR MOTHER.' Later that night, he learned that the boy was very much alive, but seriously hospitalized. For a while, Dicky really thought there was a God."

Dr. King puffed on his cigar while Richard watched the red glow brighten and fade, a gray pall unfurling a kind of genie, bowing and weaving its way through dust and light, curling and climbing, curving and carving through aery space, fuming and forming an eerie visage off the burning ash, the pervasive odor permeating the office curtains as well as Richard's clothes.

The psychiatrist set his cigar down in the ashtray just long enough to pass a hand along a closely shaven cheek. "Tell me, Richard, how did Dicky feel the day his father died?"

Richard considered the question carefully. "Feel? You want to know how Dicky felt the day his father died? Why don't you ask me how *I* felt?" Richard responded angrily. He waited for a reply, but there wasn't any. "No one would let me see him. You wouldn't even let me visit Father's grave."

"I'm not talking about Horatio Gladstone, Richard. I'm talking about your father, William Geist."

"No! You're talking about a father figure," Richard snapped. "My real father died of a heart attack while I was in the service of my country. He departed suddenly and left me all alone. But I've come to understand the world. I understand that it is held together with fascination. I'm not afraid anymore. I am my father's son, wherever he may be," he stated, getting up and walking over to the water cooler in the corner, dispensing a paper cup. He pushed the silver button and watched a single bubble rise from the mouth of the inverted bottle, bubbling its way through time, heading toward the surface before exploding into a chaotic galaxy of tiny, watery worlds.

"Why do you believe Horatio Gladstone is your real father, Richard?"

Richard looked up in silence, staring off into space. Other framed black and white photographs hung in the shadowy corners of the office. Meteors and comets. Craters, crescents, and moons. Stars. Suspended against the unearthly, shiny blackness of time. "Did you take these pictures, sir?" Richard asked cheerfully.

Dr. King studied Richard carefully, noting his evasiveness and sudden change of tone. "Yes. Do you like them?"

Richard nodded in fascination.

"Mr. Wyszynski made those frames in the workshop some years ago. I understand he gave some smaller ones to you for the pictures in your room. He was really quite a craftsman, you know. He even built that bookcase behind you. And those bookends over there on the shelf are hand carved."

Richard turned and stared at the pair of wooden masks that unquestionably captured the pain and torment tooled across each face, the mirrored look of madness imprisoned forever between the grains of polished oak.

"You know, you should have some sort of hobby, Richard. Something that would really interest you and give you a sense of satisfaction. Maybe one evening you'd like to help me take some photographs like these. We'll be putting a man on the moon next year. Isn't that a remarkable thing? What do you say? It would do you a world of good," he said with a smile. "We could even do some developing if you like. I use the gazebo on the knoll for a darkroom, and the deck around it serves as a sort of makeshift observatory where I have a telescope I made. As a matter of fact, tonight would be a perfect night to view the stars. Your mother's coming by to visit you this afternoon, and I'd really like to have the two of you as my guests for dinner this evening. Maybe you'd like to come by the house a little early. Think you might be interested?"

"Sir, yes, sir," Richard answered up with enthusiasm.

Dr. King beamed. "Then it's a date. I'll notify Dr. Bianco that you'll be coming by this afternoon. Sarah will be thrilled to see you. She asks about you every day. Well, it looks like we're out of time," he said, glancing at his watch.

"Time? What time is it? I have plenty of time, you see."

"It's just about lunchtime. And I do have other patients, Richard."

"Patients—patience," Richard said pleasantly.

****

Carl Gustafson had finished thatching a section of lawn and raking leaves that had collected along a tall hedgerow, leaving the pile for later. Next, he busied himself hoeing a patch of garden while Richard helped him pull some weeds.

"I see that you're left-handed," Richard noted. "I heard it said by older folks that years ago schoolteachers used to actually force students to write with their right hand."

"*Ja*, that is true," Carl confirmed, working the earth along the garden's edge. "I can tell you firsthand," he said. "If you attended school back in the old country and were left-handed, the teacher would tie that hand behind your back during penmanship. So just for spite, I wrote everything from right to left, making all my letters backwards. Just to let them know that I was DAMN MAD! Here, let me show you." Carl put down the hoe and took out a small piece of paper and the stub of a pencil from his shirt pocket, then scribbled something down. "That's mirror writing. See?

ᗡAM ИMAᗡ

"Damn near drove Mrs. Oglesby crazy. She actually graded my papers with a mirror," Carl reflected. "Well, I continued writing my letters backwards. So she left me back that year, insisting that I was backward. Of course, I had her again the following term. Only that year, I wrote from left to right and upside down. Like this:

DⱯWИ WⱯD

"You should have seen her reaction. Actually believed that there was something wrong with the mirror; that is, until she saw her ugly face," Carl roared, putting away the paper and pencil and picking up the tool.

Richard grinned. "Dicky did some mirror writing, too."

"*Ja*, they made us do everything with our right hand," Carl went on, ignoring Richard's comment. "But I can still throw a ball or swing a hammer with either," he offered reassuringly.

"I'm right-handed," Richard said. "Right is might."

"Right is merely relative," the caretaker continued, hoeing the garden vigorously. "Who's to say what's right? Were the wars right? Ah, why am I even asking you? You weren't even born then," he remarked, gazing off into the distance.

"Just a twinkle in my father's eye, I suppose."

"Did you know that I was once dead for an undetermined period of time?" Carl declared with vacant eyes. "*Ja*. Soldiers of indifference. Jumping around from body to body like grotesque toads. I was in a state of shock, the medics told me afterwards. Yet, I can still remember someone tearing insanely at my jacket and shirt, ripping the beaded chain from around my neck, shoving one of the metal dog tags between my upper and lower teeth, hammering a sweaty palm firmly against my lower jaw before ensuring it bloody closed with the toe of a combat boot. And long after the shelling was over, I, along with many other bloodied bodies, lay still and silent beneath the song and flutter of birds." Carl stared at Richard profoundly. "Yes. They found my body on a bloody beach. Gory as a ghoul. Me, among a multitude of mannequins. Marked for identification and glorification."

Carl unbuttoned his shirt and showed Richard the single silver tag hanging from a chain. "You see these grooves at each end? They put this part between your teeth—like so," he demonstrated. "Then whammo!" Richard could plainly see where the metal edges had cut deep into the caretaker's gums. "My medal of honor," Carl proclaimed proudly.

"When I first came here from the V.A. hospital, the doctors and nurses tried to take it away from me, but I told everyone present that it was my religious medal. See, it says Lutheran. Yet, they still persisted. 'GOD SHALL SMITE YOU ALL,' I screamed. Just then there was a loud clap of thunder. You should have seen Nurse Ryder's face, what with only two weeks on the job. Of course, I saw the flash of lightning seconds before any of them, as they were all so busy trying to take away my badge of courage. Then the skies opened up and in stormed Dr. King, angry as the Lord, informing them that I could keep my blessed tag. 'But what if he should swallow it or sharpen the edges and slit his wrists clear down to the bone?' Nurse Ryder cried with deep concern. Well, Dr. King assured her that I was positively crazy, but certainly not stupid," Carl affirmed. "And so, to alleviate her worries, he put Nurse Ryder in charge of me, assigning her full responsibility.

"The following day it was still raining, and most of us retired to the lounge. Nurse Ryder was passing through when she noticed someone lying on the couch, completely covered with a sheet. Ghostly. Not moving so much as a single muscle. When she pulled the sheet away, she uncovered yours truly, lying there with my tongue hanging out, naked as a jay bird, except for the chain and tag dangling from my big toe. Do you know she actually stood there for a full thirty seconds before she screamed bloody murder? Finally, she ran to get an aide. So I just grabbed my socks and slippers and trotted down the hall.

"*Ja*, it rained like cats and dogs that entire week, flooding everything in sight," Carl continued, breaking up clumps of grass and soil with the hoe. "We had a priest here then, by the name of Desmond, I believe. Grabbed Nurse Ryder's tits over there on high ground, insisting he was seeking two of every kind. So she swung her fists in a furious arc and blackened both his eyes." Carl laughed heartily. "Then there was that other guinea wacko who went running to her rescue. 'Nero the hero' we called him because he was always fiddling with her ass and alarming her about the terrible conflagration in his pants. Not exactly in those words of course, but his message rang clear as a bell. Nurse Ryder said that she thought she would go mad working here. That's when Dr. King took her off the ward and made her his secretary-receptionist.

Richard enjoyed the anecdotes, taking in every word like a sponge. Finally, he had to excuse himself in order to get ready for Mother's visit.

Later that afternoon, Sarah prepared tea for Mother and Dr. King, with Richard off about the house somewhere.

"I don't know," Sarah said, entering the study and setting the tea service upon the parquet table, shaking her head from side to side. "Don't make no sense to me a'tall, Miss Vicki. Sun shinin' out there jus' as bright as it can be, while you sittin' 'round in here drinkin' hot tea in a sixty-two degree air-conditioned room. Other folks be out there lyin' in the sun like lizards, tryin' to get all swarthy and beautiful like me. And you's no better either," Sarah added, scolding Dr. King. "Puttin' sugar in yo' tea to make it sweet, then squeezin' lemon in to make it sour. If that don't beat all. Course, I don't say nothin', him bein' a hotshot doctor and all. Everybody knows that sugar is a killer. But I jus' bite my tongue and looks the other way." Sarah frowned, walking from the room on old bowed legs and leaving the two of them to their afternoon tea.

Dr. King smiled warmly, sitting down on the couch beside Mother as she calmly sipped her tea. She looked especially beautiful that afternoon, sitting there quietly with long shapely legs crossed in ladylike fashion. Lustrous, lovely auburn hair rested softly on her slender shoulders. Brilliant and expressive doll-like eyes illuminated high-set cheekbones and a flawless complexion.

Mother leaned forward, setting her cup and saucer down upon the table in front of her, eyes shifting to the doorway as Richard passed by the room behind Sarah. "I just don't know what to do about him, David," Mother sighed with such concern. "He hardly said a word. And when he does, I don't know whether it's fact or fancy anymore. I didn't know whether or not to believe him when he said he was coming up here to the house for dinner. I just don't know with him anymore. I try and be a good mother. I honestly do. I try to talk to him. It's not easy though. He hardly said a sensible word during visitation. David, I just want you to know that I appreciate everything you're doing for him." She clasped her hands firmly on her lap. "I want you to know that I'm very grateful."

Dr. King smiled a handsome smile. "Victoria, I was going to tell you something after dinner as a surprise, but I'll share it with you now. When I spoke to Richard this morning, he seemed very interested in some recent photographs I hung up in the office. Planets and stars and such. I asked him if he'd like to help me take some pictures tonight, and maybe do a little developing. He lit up like a Christmas tree. It was the first time he's responded to anything like that since he's been here. Even Dr. Bianco was surprised when I told him. He's been trying to get him motivated for weeks now."

"That's odd because Richard didn't mention anything about it during my visit. Although he did mention something about space, being bounded or unbounded, or something like that. Crazy kind of talk."

"Well, that seemingly kind of crazy kind of talk may be a very healthy sign, Victoria. He was probably alluding to the expanding universe theory. He reads voraciously. The fact that he's starting to open up is certainly encouraging in itself, and perhaps the perfect opportunity for the two of us to work together on a project like father and son. But I'm going to need your help, too. I'd like you to be around here to help pave the way. I think that now would be a good time for you to start moving your things into the house like we discussed. It will give us both a chance to work closely with Richard. It will also give him the time he needs to adjust to things. I don't want to spring everything on him at once. I want Richard to see that we can all be a family together, and that we really care about him."

"Oh, David. I don't know. I thought we were going to wait until the end of summer."

"The end of summer is practically around the corner, Victoria. Another two weeks, and we're into May. In June the contractors are supposed to show, and it'll be another madhouse around here. That's if they even start as scheduled. Then I've got the Foundation's annual picnic celebration in July. Besides which, we still have a million and one plans to finalize before the wedding. It would make a lot more sense if you were here now," he reasoned persuasively.

"I still don't know, David. Do you really think it's a good idea? What I mean is, it may be too soon. It may have a bad effect on him."

"Let me be the judge of that. All right? Unless, of course, you impugn your doctor's judgment," he challenged playfully, taking both her hands in his.

"You know better than that," she deferred.

"Then it's settled. Doctor's orders," he teased. "Sarah can fix up one of the rooms for you downstairs; we'll have you settled here in no time."

Mother raised her hands in mock surrender. "Well, if you really think it's a good idea. I'm sure you know what you're doing, Doctor."

Dr. King beamed as brightly as the noonday sun. "As intelligent as she is beautiful," he professed, kissing her affectionately upon the cheek. "Oh, and I already took the liberty of telling Sarah to prepare the guest room, that you'll be staying here tonight. We'll all have a lovely dinner together. And afterward, Richard can help me set up the photographic equipment. It should be dark enough by then. How does that sound?"

"How does one say no to you?"

"One doesn't," he kidded.

"That's what I thought," Mother agreed and laughed excitedly. "Oh, David. I do love you so."

"Oh, and don't say anything to Richard about your moving in just yet. We'll find the right moment."

"You mean, *you'll* find the right moment," she said uneasily.

"Now, don't you worry your pretty little head. Everything is going to work out just fine," he assured her, kissing her tenderly upon the lips as Richard disappeared quickly down the hallway.

That evening, Sarah had prepared and served a beautiful standing rib roast for Dr. King and his two special guests. The three sat quietly by as Sarah paraded busily back and forth between kitchen and dining room, a room tastefully decorated with recessed lighting, expensive paintings and exotic plants, as well as comfortable seating for forty people islanded upon a Persian carpet; that is, if one had a mind to entertain en masse. Dr. King sat at the head of the table. Replete. Smiling. Mother sat immediately to his right. Sarah suddenly appeared back at the dining room table, serving up piping hot second helpings for everyone.

"Oh, my goodness! Sarah, what are you doing?" Mother exclaimed.

"For heaven sakes, Miss Vicki. You's skinnier than a broomstick. Now you got to put some meat on them pretty bones of yo's," she insisted, serving Mother another rib and a portion of fresh asparagus spears, spooning on a rich, white cream sauce.

"So help me, Sarah, I'm going to come apart at the seams," Mother swore.

"And what about you, young man? You don't like ol' Sarah's cookin' no more?" she scolded.

"I'm really not very hungry, Sarah," Richard said, staring down at this plate.

"Well now, if you want some of ol' Sarah's honey cakes for

dessert, which I knows you do, then you better eat somethin'. Hear? 'Cause you's even skinnier than yo' mother."

"Dessert?" Mother sighed. "Why, I can hardly breathe."

"Listen, why don't we all take a breather before we have our tea and cake," Dr. King suggested, coming to the rescue of his guests. "What do you say we go for a little walk?"

"Make that a long walk," Mother agreed, allowing herself another bite and a final sip of fine wine. "You stay here and finish your meal, Richard. You hardly touched a thing."

Sarah disappeared into the kitchen while Richard poked sullenly at his plate. He watched Mother and Dr. King strolling arm in arm along the path between a giant hedgerow and a garden of impatiens that went on forever, or so it seemed. The day was growing dim.

"You know, David. I think every little girl in the world should have a gazebo all their very own. Those were some of my fondest memories," she mused. "I used to pretend that Mama's gazebo was a great big doll house. I'd take my little doll out there with me, and we'd play house together all afternoon, sipping tea and talking about all sorts of wonderfully foolish things. Say, David! Do you think maybe we could have our tea and dessert at the gazebo?" she asked excitedly. "It's such a lovely evening for it."

"If you'd like," he said, with the slightest hesitation in his voice.

Mother beamed. "Oh, I'd like that very much, David. It's such a perfect place to be. I absolutely adore it."

"You know, we had a particularly interesting admittance here today."

Mother looked up curiously, for Dr. King rarely discussed any of his patients with her, excepting Richard, of course. "Oh?"

"Her name is Theresa Martinez."

"And why, might I ask, is this patient so particularly interesting?" she inquired teasingly. "Hum?"

"Well, for one thing, Theresa's only nine," he elaborated with a smile. "For another, she's brought along a companion with her."

"A companion?"

"Yes, her doll. And do you know what the peculiar thing is? The doll's name. Guess what her doll's name is?"

Mother looked up blankly.

"Her doll's name is Ruthie."

Mother stopped in her tracks. "Ruthie?"

"Yes, I thought it rather strange."

"Strange?"

"Well, wasn't that the name of your doll?"

"David, that's a very common name," she said defensively. "You know, like Barbie, Annie, Suzie. Why not Ruthie?"

"Yes, of course. It just struck me as odd. She also has a fascination for the gazebo. As soon as she saw it, she made a mad dash across the grounds, cradling her little doll."

"David, all little girls, and for that matter, big girls, too," she cooed, "would have a fascination for a gazebo as big and beautiful as yours." She held on to his arm as they continued walking.

"I suppose."

"You said she's only nine. I'm sure she doesn't have the same—problem I had."

"No, nothing like what you went through. She's certainly as overprotective of her doll as you were. But the situation isn't quite the same." His face took on a serious demeanor. "Theresa Martinez was raped," he stated gravely.

Mother flinched. "Raped?"

Dr. King nodded. "Only her mind won't accept that fact. For her, it was Ruthie who was raped, and so she must protect her vulnerable self by way of protecting her doll."

"Oh, David, I feel so sorry for the little dear."

"Tell me something."

"Tell you what, David?"

"About all those wonderfully foolish things you and Ruthie used to talk about."

"That's ancient history, darling. We've been all through that years ago. I told you everything."

"Tell me again."

"God, that was such a long time ago, David."

"Tell me anyhow," he pressed. "What would the two of you talk about?"

"Oh, you know. About everything, I guess. Mother and daughter things mostly. Love. Marriage. Children. Being a good mother. Things like that. You know something? That's the strange part."

"What is?"

"It was like I was always Ruthie's mother. I mean even after Dicky was born. I couldn't believe it when the nurse told me I had a baby boy. I always believed that I'd have a little girl and name her Ruthie. Mother had six girls, you know. No boys. Even my sisters had girls. Except for my older sister, Helen. She couldn't have any children at all. Am I babbling, David? I'm sorry. I bet this all sounds crazy to you."

"Sounds like a sorority, if you ask me," he kidded, holding her close as they continued along the garden path, narrowing nearer to the hedge.

"It's just that I felt so strange having a son."

"You know, you never really told me why you suddenly stopped seeing me. I wanted to bring it up a hundred times over the years, but I knew you didn't want to talk about it. After therapy, you just upped and disappeared. And I never saw you again until a few years after Richard was born. We shared very special moments, you and I. I guess Sally and the boy were very much alive in my mind. They still are, of course, but Sarah taught me how to let go. I don't know how she ever survived when she lost *her* family. She had absolutely no one, Victoria. She's been a real comfort to me. Like a big sister. Only now, we're all going to be one big happy family. When I think back over the years . . . God, you were so god-awful young when we first met. I think that's what held me back at first. I never meant to hurt you— "

"Darling, there's no need to— "

"Yes, there is," he insisted. "The first time that you returned with Richard, we spent the summer sailing and horseback riding at the ranch. Remember? I tried to keep you a secret from everyone. Including Sarah. That's why I didn't have you staying up here at the house. That's why I had you stay at the ranch. Can you understand?"

"Of course I can, David."

"And then I had to leave one evening on business for several days."

"Yes," she said uneasily.

"When I got back—well, when I got back, something had happened. I found you with that doll again. And Richard—how old was he then? Four? He was quite hysterical. You were very upset and wouldn't talk about it."

Mother paused and ran her hand along the side of a sculptured hedgerow. "Fourteen years ago, David. I guess at that point in my life everything seemed to upset me. My husband wanted no part of children. You know that. And if you must know the truth—I stopped seeing you—well, because Dicky—" Sensing something queer, Mother stopped and turned around abruptly. "Richard! Richard, is that you? What are you doing there?"

Richard stood just behind the darkened hedgerow that separated them. "I came along for the walk, Mother," he answered, peering through the lofty, budding wall.

"Well, you just turn right around and march straight back to the house this minute. Did you finish your meal like I asked you to?"

"I'm not hungry, Mother."

"You hardly touched anything on your plate. Sarah went to a great deal of trouble to make everyone a nice dinner. Now you go on back and finish your meal. Understand? I don't want—"

"Richard, would you do me a favor and tell Sarah that we'll all be having our tea and cake at the gazebo?" Dr. King interrupted, trying to prevent the argument from escalating. "Maybe you could give her a hand. Then later on us guys can set up the telescope and camera. How does that sound?" he asked, communicating through the hedge.

"Sounds like a fraternity if you ask me," Richard answered, grinning from ear to ear.

"No one is asking you for your snide remarks," Mother snapped. "Please do as I ask and go on back to the house. Now!"

"Mother."

"What is it?"

"I'm not a child anymore."

"Then stop behaving like one. Stop sneaking around like a thief in the dark."

Richard turned around and started back toward the house, disappearing along the hedgerow as dusk put day to rest.

"Don't you think you're being a little hard on him?" Dr. King admonished.

"Oh, David. I'm so sorry. I just don't like him sneaking up on us like that. You don't know, but he does that all the time. I've never had a moment of privacy with him skulking around. And those damn remarks of his. He was like that all through school. You of all people know the trouble I had with him. Always thought he was better than anyone else. Always ready with a smart answer."

"He's a smart boy, Victoria."

"Maybe too smart for his own good."

Dr. King took her into his arms. "God, you're shaking like a leaf, Victoria."

"It's nothing. He gave me quite a start is all. David?"

"Yes?"

"Let's forget about the past for the moment. Let's just think about our future together. I'll tell you everything in time. I promise. I had planned on telling you before the end of summer. But not like this. Not out here for little ears to hear. But in private. It's not that big a deal," she pouted with pretense. "Please trust me."

"I love you very much, Victoria," he whispered softly.

"And I love you," she declared, holding on to him tightly as they rounded the hedgerow and followed the open garden path leading toward the gazebo. Mother peered over David's shoulder to be sure they weren't being followed.

Moments later, Richard got up from beneath a pile of thatch and leaves, briskly brushing off his clothing. He headed back toward the house, sorting through the past, putting together the missing pieces of a sordid puzzle. One by one.

Back inside the house, Richard related Dr. King's instructions to Sarah as she continued clearing off the dining room table, with the exception of Richard's plate. Several minutes passed before Sarah returned. Smiling, she sat down next to Richard, adjusting her apron and slowly shaking her head from side to side. "Now, ain't but two ways that food gonna disappear from yo' plate, young man. And sittin' there gawkin' at it ain't one of them. So, we'll jus' put this rib back on the platter here like so, and nobody gonna be the wiser. If someone asks you if ya finished all yo' food, well you jus' smile and nod yo' head with satisfaction. And if anybody asks ol' Sarah, she don't see nothin' 'cept an empty plate. Because you see," she said with a wink, "one little white lie be better than a black one. Sure as shootin'," she swore and laughed. "Now, com'on in the kitchen and keep ol' Sarah company," she coaxed, carrying the platter back inside.

"Well now, let me see here," Sarah said, taking down sets of cups and saucers from a cabinet. "We all gonna have our tea and honey cakes up at the gazebo, you say. Then I bes' be fillin' up this here sugar bowl, else I be fetchin' back and forth all evenin'. Ya know how yo' mother takes her tea. I tries to tell her this afternoon that she's just as sweet as she can be. Ya wanna hand me that there plate behind ya, Richard?" He handed her the plate piled high with little cakes fresh from the oven. "See, ol' Sarah sweeten things up with a little bit of honey, raisins, and brown sugar," she explained, stirring the small saucepan over a low flame. "None of that there refined white sugar. No, siree. That be a real killer, ya know. Jus' like white flour. Devil's dust, my daddy use'ta say. He be the George Washington Carver of the North. A sharecropper. And distinguished in his field," she added wryly, pouring the syrupy contents over the plate of little cakes.

"Com'on over here and let 'ol Sarah tell ya a little story like she do when ya was jus' knee high to a grasshopper. Does you recall how ol' Sarah use'ta tell ya stories?"

Richard nodded, watching with interest as the old woman added the finishing touch, sprinkling honey cakes with crushed almonds.

"Well now, Sarah gonna give ya a little history lesson. One that a young and foxy lookin' Sarah taught in Africa. Sarah been all around Africa, you know. Up and down the Niger and the Nile; back and forth along the Congo. Each and every mile. Sarah be a missionary fo' a while," she said and smiled widely, wiping her hands on the corner of her apron. "Land sakes alive. Why I was jus' a pretty little thing. I loved the men, and the men loved me. How you think these ol' legs o' mine got so bowed?" she joked and laughed. "Wouldn't let any of them get away. Ah, hee, hee, hee. 'Sweet Sarah,' they use'ta say. Lordy be. Yes, siree. Foxxxy!"

Richard picked at the honey cakes, placing the bittersweet almond pieces upon the tip of his tongue while Sarah moved busily about the kitchen.

"You see, Sarah taught them natives back there that in the Western world, 'round the late eighteen hundreds, both peasants and poor city folk alike shared a common dark bread made from coarsely milled wheat flour, thought to be inferior on 'counta how it had all them there seed particles mixed up with it. Of course, the wealthy could well afford the very expensive white bead, reckoned to be all pure and everythin', after havin' been sifted again and again through bolts of fine cloth till most of the roughage be removed. Then, 'bout a score of years 'fore the turn of the century, man's technology done revolutionize the industry. Stone wheel gave way to steel, smashin' them seeds to smithereens and enablin' the millers to remove most of the fiber in order to produce low cost, high prestige, white flour. But Western man, he fail to realize that the fiber itself be fortified with God-given nutrients necessary to his diet; the pure irony of it bein' that the ultra-refined flour, thought to be so pure and wholesome, done barely kept alive the wheat flies that had for generations plagued the flour trade.

"Well, to make a long story short and sweet, 'bout the same time they removin' all that there good fiber, modern man's sugar consumption be on the rise, addin' a heap of ultra-refined flour and sugar products to a growin' list of fiber-deficiency diseases long as yo' arm, Richard. And in little less than a century, Western man done refine hisself into a state of pure, unadulterated hell," Sarah declared, her head held high with certain knowledge, her eyes wide awake with wisdom.

"Anyhow, Sarah taught that lesson to a group of native villagers in Uganda, explainin' how the African diet, thought to be inferior like the black bread of early Western man, was, in fact, superior and more wholesome than the white. But after Sarah finished doin' all that explainin', one of the 'White Fathers' saw the whole business as a subtle racial attack aimed at underminin' the very foundation of their work, accusin' Sarah of tryin' to segregate the factions of black and white in their converted Christian village. I's talkin' loaves of bread, and that ol' fool be accusin' Sarah of racial prejudice, by God! Well, yo' Sarah, here, saw red as she come racin' 'cross that compound like a Bantu warrior, threatenin' to serve God righteously by handin' over that Christian lunatic to the lions." Sarah laughed, her white smile brightening Richard's evening.

"Well now," she said, reaching into another cabinet for a set of serving trays, loading them up with cups and saucers, dishes, utensils and such. "I guess we bes' be headin' on up to the gazebo."

Richard carried the larger of the trays stacked with expensive bone china, following Sarah across the moon-blanched grounds. As they approached the gazebo, a cool breeze swept across the hillock, and he could taste the salty sea air tunneling into his nostrils as he took a hearty breath. He listened intently to the tumbling waves pounding the rocky shore below, funneling its tuneless chant up the towering cliffs, drawing him nearer the edge of the precipice. The sheer height of the cliff on which he stood offered its beholder a spectacular view of the magnificent watery world below. The panorama dizzied him, as though momentarily unleashing him from the very land itself.

"You comin', Richard? Or jus' rattlin' my nerves 'long with that tray of good china you's holdin'."

"Sorry, Sarah," he said, looking up to see Mother and Dr. King seated at a table on the deck beneath the stars. Mother stared down at Richard coldly.

"I don't know," Sarah said, climbing up the steps ahead of him. "Don't make no sense to me a'tall. Sun shinin' out there all afternoon while those two sittin' round inside jabberin' away. Moon come out and they's suddenly all starry eyed." Sarah laughed, setting down the tray and spreading a white linen cloth across the table. "Now you try and figure that one out while I go inside and put some water up for tea."

"Come sit, Richard," Dr. King insisted. "Put that tray down and have a seat."

Richard set the tray down carefully.

"Will you fix your hair, please?" Mother fussed, running her pocket brush through Richard's curls. "Stand still for heaven's sake!"

"You can all start on them honey cakes," Sarah called from inside. "Tea be jus' a few minutes."

"Come on, Sarah," Dr. King called. "A watched pot never boils."

"Unwatched pot liable to boil over this dang stove of yo's," she answered from behind the screen door. "I swear I hates these 'lectic stoves."

"Now you know darn well that's a very expensive range, Sarah."

"Oh, sure 'nough. It ranges somewhere between hot and fiery hell. Thing's got a mind of its own."

"Well, so do you, Sarah," Dr. King reminded with a grin. "Do you know that Sarah had me get rid of that stove the day she started here? Absolutely refused to cook on anything but gas. I had to go out and buy a new gas range for the house. So Max brought the electric one up here."

"How anybody can cook on these dang contraptions is beyond me," Sarah complained, attending to the tea.

"Oh, simmer down in there, Sarah," Dr. King quipped.

"Oh, hush up now and eat yo' honey cakes. You keep an eye on him, Miss Vicki, 'cause he sneaks one at a time when nobody's lookin'. Thinks no one's countin'."

"What I count is calories," Mother said through a girlish giggle.

"That's why I only take one at a time," Dr. King said sillily. "That way, I lose count. Besides, I'm not getting fat. Not yet, anyway," he added flatly, sucking in his gut.

"I'm going to get fat just looking at them luscious little cakes," Mother declared, helping set the table.

A few minutes later, steam whistled from the tea kettle, and Sarah reappeared with a pot of tea. "And what's the matter with you, young man?" Sarah chided. "You worryin' 'bout getting' fat, too, or jus' plain bein' polite?" she questioned, putting several honey cakes on Richard's plate before pouring tea for everyone. "Got me three bony maronies here, all worryin' 'bout getting' fat. If that don't take the cake," she punned. "Ol' Sarah past the age of worryin'. I learn a long time ago that worryin' jus' a short-cut to the grave. Life be filled with things a body ain't supposed to do. Always be somebody 'round to make a law against, build a fence around, or put a tax on somethin'," she declared. "Of course, ol' Sarah broke a few laws in her day. Tore down quite a few fences, too. Not exactly what you'd call a shinin' example, now would ya?" she said and laughed lightly. "And talk about taxes? Good Lord!" Sarah continued. "Why, Dr. King always complainin' 'bout taxes. See, what we need 'round here is another tea party like they had up in Boston, 1773."

"Well, as far as taxes go, and believe me they go sky-high around here," Dr. King assured everyone, "I'm afraid it's just something we all have to live with."

"Like death," Richard added calmly, watching Mother spooning heaps of sugar in her tea.

"The only difference is that we can recover from taxes," Dr. King replied.

"Could we please talk about something more pleasant?" Mother suggested, giving Richard another cold stare.

Dr. King went on endlessly about his plans for the Foundation. Richard listened to the waves crashing against the rocky shores below. He watched several sea gulls gliding high above, their wings spread wide while riding a crest of aery currents before suddenly vanishing from sight. He drew the salty sea breeze deep within his lungs once more, pondering the awesome forces that nature played upon the land. Finally, he took one of Sarah's honey cakes from his plate, savoring the bittersweet almond taste.

After everyone had finished with tea and dessert, Mother helped Sarah clear the table while Dr. King and Richard set up a telescope.

"Whew, it's getting' a might breezy out here," Sarah decided. "I left some honey cakes inside, 'long with the fixin's for more tea jus' in case you boys get hungry. Hear?"

"That'll be fine, Sarah." Dr. King acknowledged.

"We'll see you up at the house, David. You behave yourself, Richard," she said, taking the tray from Sarah as they both went down the stairs.

It was a perfectly clear night. Richard observed the stars strewn across the sky like brilliant treasure scattered throughout a steel-blue vault of time. A king's ransom, spent along an endless journey through space. Its riches extending far beyond the boundaries of imagination. "You know, it's fascinating."

What is?" Dr. King asked, removing a roll of film from a small silver canister, loading then mounting the camera onto the telescope.

"The universe. The way it's held together by fascination."

"Fascination?"

"Yes. Such harmony if you care to listen. Such form and structure if you dare to see."

"I'm afraid you lost me."

"I was lost and afraid, too," Richard stated matter-of-factly. "But I've come to understand the world. I've learned that even in the midst of chaos there is order. If you dare to look beyond."

"Look beyond what, exactly?" Dr. King asked, adjusting and focusing the instruments.

Richard gazed up at the sky. "Take the stars for instance. The galaxies outside our local group are receding at a velocity proportional to their distance from us. Systems of stars, moving at a fantastic rate of speed within an expanding universe, heading towards eternity, or eventual collapse."

Dr. King looked at the lad knowingly. "Yes, that's quite true, Richard. I was wondering if you knew about such matters because of certain comments you mentioned to your mother earlier today. Life is certainly filled with mystery. Is it not?"

"Death's an even greater mystery, which even kings have spent a lifetime trying to unravel."

Dr. King stared at Richard rather curiously.

"Yes, I had asked Mother about the universe during her visit. Whether or not it was bounded or extended infinitely. I asked her if she thought there was an end in sight."

"Those are certainly far reaching thoughts," Dr. King remarked. "But I'm afraid your mother is more down to earth," he said with smile, stepping aside for Richard to have a look.

Richard leaned forward, peering through the telescope at the luminous body in the night sky, observing its craters and seas of gray, absorbed in its powerful influence upon man's water-world below. Moonbeams enchantingly casted down their magic spell.

Dr. King pressed the cable release atop the camera when suddenly Richard stepped back into the shadows along the railing. zzzzzzzzzzzCLICK.

Richard shivered, tightly wrapping his arms about himself. "BRRRRR."

"Richard, are you all right?"

"I'm fine."

"You're shaking like a leaf."

"It'll be all right."

"It is getting a bit chilly out here. Why don't you go inside while I finish up the roll. Then we can develop and print some pictures if you like. You can help me by closing all the shutters. I'll be in, in just a few minutes. Okay?"

"Would you mind if I put a pot of water up for tea?" Richard asked, shivering uncontrollably.

"Are you sure you're all right? You look a little pale," he said, placing a hand on Richard's forehead.

"I'm fine. Really. A fine young man," he said then laughed.

"All right. I'll only be a few minutes."

Richard went inside the gazebo, scanning the entire space. Thermometer, trays, tong, timer and other equipment lay neatly arranged on a table behind him in a bath of light. An enlarger covered with clear plastic sat on a small cabinet against the wall. He fixed his eyes intently on the shadowy containers sitting on the shelves above the table, noting their labels carefully before going around the studio and drawing all the shutters tight.

Quickly, but quietly, Richard moved across the darkened room and over to the sink, sounding water in the kettle like a drumroll. Picking up a utensil off the counter, he flew back over to the shelf and took down one of the large containers, prying off its lid with the handle of the spoon. Stooping, he removed a silver object from the elastic at the top of his sock. Unscrewing its cap, he shoveled the mouth of the small container into the contents of the larger, filling the little silver film cylinder to capacity with tiny white toxic crystals then secured the cap and concealed the canister back within his sock. Richard pressed closed the lid of the large container and put it back atop the shelf. He crossed the room and replaced the utensil, shut the faucet then finally set the dripping kettle down upon the stove — sssssssssssssss was the sound of the sizzle.

zzzzzzzzzzzzzzzzzzzzzzzzzCLICK went the sound of the camera about a dozen times just outside the door.

Richard was standing by the glowing, crackling coil of heat when Dr. King pushed open the screen door and set the tripod and other equipment down in a shadowy corner.

"Well, I finished off the roll. By the way, you didn't happen to see a little silver film canister around here, did you?"

"How can I see anything? It's a darkroom," Richard answered, switching on the light, standing there nonchalantly, grinning from ear to ear.

Dr. King glanced around the room. "I guess the wind must have blown it off the railing while I was busy loading the camera. No matter. I just set them aside for Carl Gustafson; he uses them to separate and store his seeds along with other odds and ends."

"That's odd," Richard said, staring at the painting hung above the couch along the far wall.

"What is?"

"That painting over there, of a man and woman in a chair."

"Oh, *The Contortionists*," Dr. King explained with mild amusement, staring at the naked couple entwined around each other. "Max gave that to Sarah as a present many years ago, but she wouldn't have it in the house. Or Max either, for that matter. Especially after he told her that it reminded him of the two of them. Anyhow, it would up in here along with the stove. It's supposed to have been in his family for generations. Some goddess and slave, or so I'm told. They look more like a pair of serpents if you ask me. Terribly skinny. Don't you think?"

Richard looked suspiciously from Dr. King back to the painting, stepping forward for a closer examination of the naked woman and her half-clad, light-skinned lover. Suddenly, impressions of long ago flashed across his mind. Abstract, yet defined. Shades of light and dark contrasted sharply along the shapely form. Chiaroscuro. The painter had certainly caught the essence of their high-flown passion . . . surfacing a kind of madness within a perfect frame of mind. "I'M NOT AFRAID ANYMORE," Richard shouted. "Not afraid at all. No. I've come to understand the world. Not flat as a mat nor fixed in the center of the universe. No! Everything spinning and whirling around and around," he said shivering. "Like a merry-go-round. Up and down. Faster and faster. Lots of animals around. Like a zoo. No, near a farm! Moooo. Cows and horses. Nay. Yes! That's what horses say. Lots of horses. All corralled around her on the hay. Behind a great big barn. Yes. Things are coming back now. All around . . . ."

"Around who, Richard? Who are they?"

"Neigh," Richard whinnied flawlessly, "they really don't want to say."

"But you do, Richard. You want to say. They're all bottled up inside you, waiting to come out. Let's unleash them now," Dr. King cajoled.

"Faster and faster. Pumping her up and down. One at a time. Up and down as Dicky crawled along the ground with twin holsters strapped to either side." Richard got down on his hands and knees. "Dicky watched them as they formed a ring around her while she lay whinnying in the hay, drawing them all a little closer, staging them here and there when suddenly little Dicky drew his guns—CLICK— CLICK—CLICK—filling all of them full of lead as he fled back along the bridal path. Everyone trotting after him.

"'Hey! What's the kid doing here?' one reared. 'Get him the hell out of here fast,' another snorted through distended nostrils."

"Who are they, Richard? Who do you see?" Dr. King insisted.

"Seven stallions and a mare."

"One at a time, now. Who?"

"Whooo! Like an owl, one was wise. 'Whoa there, partner! Don't worry about your mommy, son. She's fine. Having a good time,' he panted. 'You'll understand better when you grow up. Probably even forget all about this in time. Pay it no mind. Just pretend it's all a bad dream. Hey, you know something. I have a little boy just like you. He's got another daddy now. Doesn't remember me at all. You'll forget everything in time,' he said with the smell of liquor on his breath. 'Come on now, partner. No need to cry. Giddy-up, here,' he ordered, lifting the cowpoke high into the air and upon his bare shoulders. And away he trotted, bouncing Dicky up and down like a bucking bronco. 'You ride me back to your bunk, and I'll have you fast asleep in no time . . . .'

"'Time? What time is it? WHERE'S MUMMY?' little Dicky had screamed till he was hoarse, screaming from inside *your* ranch house, Dr. King.

"Finally, Mummy came into the room and listened impatiently to his tale. 'Shh. Shh. There, it's all right now. You had a bad dream, darling. Mummy's right here,' she stated calmly with stable breath, rocking Dicky in her arms. 'You had a nightmare, dear. Go on back to sleep. Here's Mummy's doll to keep you company. You didn't see those things at all; and I don't want you telling anyone you did.' But Dicky tore all the clothing off the doll and showed her *exactly* what he saw."

Richard closed his eyes and sank slowly to the floor before Dr. King, rocking himself back and forth to the roll of boiling water on the stove. Some time passed before Richard opened his eyes and looked around the room. "What time is it?" he whispered.

"It's getting late, Richard," Dr. King replied coldly.

"Yes," Richard agreed, getting up quietly and walking over to remove the pot of tepid water from the stove. "Would you care to join me in a cup of tea? After all, this is a tea house. Is it not?"

Dr. King said nothing, putting away the rest of the photographic equipment and informing Richard that they were leaving. He closed and locked the door to the gazebo, walking back toward the house in silence with the boy. The psychiatrist wanted to rail out against his patient by calling him a liar to his face, telling him that he had sadistically fabricated that awful story about Mother, that something in the painting had triggered a sick sexual perversion which Richard had simply blown out of proportion for the sake of attention. Dr. King wanted to act impulsively. He wanted to put aside his training and forget about everything that he had learned in dealing with and treating the delusions of patients like Richard Geist. It took all the reserve the man had in order to keep from unleashing his own monumental rage.

Chapter 16

NESTING HABITS

May 1st showers drowned Carl's flowers, and the morning turned into a bloody mess. Heavy rain pelted a large picture window in the dining area. It came without warning and continued in a steady downpour, distorting Richard's view of the lush green landscape framed against a darkening slate-blue sky. Sheets of rain fell against the pane, and male patients moved steadily along the breakfast line. Mr. Wysznski stopped abruptly, raising a shiny tray before his face like a mirror, frantically rubbing his stubby gray growth of beard.

"Mr. Wysznski, please hold your tray properly and move along like everyone else," Nurse Harrigan said impatiently. "You're holding up the works."

Mr. Wysznski lowered his tray and shuffled forward, following the person in front of him. Several men in white aprons stood behind the serving counter, dishing out generous portions of biscuits and gravy along with an assortment of other breads, bacon, sausage, eggs, potatoes, pancakes and maple syrup. With one hand, Joseph Wysznski extended his tray like a discerning artist would hold a palette, a thumb and forefinger tenaciously holding and supporting the colorful array.

"Two hands, please, Mr. Wysznski," Nurse Harrigan said with a sigh.

When Mr. Wysznski reached the end of the steam table, he snatched the syrupy ladle from the server then mashed and mixed his fare within each section of the tray, quickly finger-painting a series of sweet impressions upon the countertop, capturing the mood and moment of the bleary scene presented just beyond the plate glass frame behind him.

Nurse Harrigan hurried over and pulled the tray from the patient's hand. "If you don't want to eat your breakfast, Mr. Wysznski, you can just sit down at a table by yourself," the head nurse insisted in her heavy Irish accent, leading him away by the arm.

Mr. Wysznski suddenly broke loose and fled down the aisle between a row of tables, smashing himself with considerable force against the far wall, falling immediately to the floor. Two attendants went running over to help the frightened figure, but he fought them furiously, kicking and clawing at the floor as though he were desperately trying to escape into some other world below. Finally, they managed to pull the terrified man to his feet.

"DONNIE!" he screamed, trembling at the flash of light and thunder resounding just outside the window as the nurse and attendants held him in a chair.

"It's all right, Mr. Wysznski. It's only a storm. No one is going to hurt you. It's okay. Everything is going to be all right," Nurse Harrigan promised, trying to hold the man's head back, encompassing his bloody nose with a handful of paper napkins.

But Mr. Wysznski crossed his legs and locked his chin against his bony chest, his arms outstretched like a Christ figure. He sat there trembling, listening intently to the pounding rain while the blood poured profusely down his face and robe.

Mr. Schimmel sat down with Richard at one of the nearby tables in the corner of the room and related Mr. Wysznski's sad story in detail:

"It vas many years ago on such a morning like this von as the heavy rains came and the thunder sounded," Mr. Schimmel began explaining in his thick Yiddish accent. "Wysznski vas home sculpting in his verkshop in the garage vhile babysitting his four-year-old grandson. A quiet suburban neighborhood home that he had built along a cul-de-sac. A home that his daughter, grandson Donnie, and son-in-law had shared. Suddenly, there vas the screeching of brakes just outside the home. Wysznski had looked up from his verk, staring apprehensively at the side door to the garage. It vas open, and Donnie vas gone. Wysznski dropped his tools and ran outside to see vhat had happened; vhat he saw vas his little grandchild sprawled against the curb. 'Dead!' several of the neighbors had announced moments later. Wysznski just stood there in horror, refusing to believe his eyes and ears before running back to the garage then inside the house, closing and locking the doors behind him vhile his neighbors vent screaming mad. Wysznski covered up his ears to shush avay the steady pounding on the doors and vindows . . . the bell-ringing at the front door . . . the nerve-shattering phone . . . the sound of screeching brakes and thunder resounding in his head; the pleading and insane shouting of his neighbors telling him that his grandson vas dead. Then those horrible faces pressed against the vindow panes, peering in on him like grotesque vater monsters. Lightening flashed across the sky, and thunder drowned out the sound of sirens screaming in the distance. He vas still standing there long after the neighbors had gone and his daughter had returned home from shopping, along vith the police." Mr. Schimmel pulled his chair closer to Richard's, stirring his coffee steadily while his eggs were getting cold.

"Actually, the boy lay in a coma at County General for a veek before he died. Wysznski hadn't slept, eaten or vashed for days on end, refusing to attend the funeral. He'd just sit quietly at home in his chair, staring out the vindow for veeks then months, jumping up periodically to check the doors, vindows and locks throughout the entire house vhenever he heard a car coming around the cul-de-sac.

"Von afternoon, his son-in-law returned home from the office to find all the doors and vindows nailed shut from the inside vith heavy planks of vood. It was then that Wysznski's daughter decided to have her father brought here to the King Foundation for psychiatric care.

"Vell, vithin a year, Dr. King had Wysznski verking vith his hands again, allowing him to use the verkshop vhenever he wanted, just so long as von of the shop attendants vould keep an eye on him. But gradually, he began to slip back into a state of depression, becoming totally disoriented, losing his vay along the corridors, unable to cross a room vithout bumping into things. It happened shortly after he learned that his daughter and son-in-law vere planning to sell the house and move to Australia. Dr. King tried to explain to Wysznski that the company vas transferring his son-in-law to Sydney, and that they vould be back within a year. But Wysznski vould shake his head emphatically.

"'No, don't you see?' he vould plead with Dr. King. 'They vant to be rid of me because I'm getting vell. They blame me,' he vould cry. 'They're running avay to the other side of the world. He's the von who put in for that transfer, you see. He's the von who's making her do all this. She swore to me on her mother's unmarked grave that she vould never, ever sell the house. I built that house vith my own two hands. She promised that she'd be there to take me back vhenever I got vell. Vell? I'm getting better every day. Isn't that right?' he vould say to Dr. King. 'I can just feel myself svelling up with sanity by the minute,' he'd veep, taking deep breaths and ballooning his bony cheeks until his face turned the color of borscht. Tears streaming down his skeletal face. Tventy pounds in von veek he lost, I svear to God.

"The sad part vas that vhat Wysznski had said vas true. He had been getting better. Vhat he said about his daughter and son-in-law vas also true. They vere indeed running avay! Dr. King tried desperately to discourage the couple from leaving the country at that particular time, explaining that their relocation to Australia vas, in the eyes of his patient, outright abandonment; especially at a time vhen Wysznski needed his family's love, support and forgiveness more than ever. But they vould not listen.

"So Dr. King reminded the voman of the fact that the only family she had vhen she came into this vorld, the same hour her mother departed it, vas her father: a man who, together with his second vife, had somehow managed to escape the 'production center' situated somevhere in the Silesia province of German occupied Poland; a man who, in hiding, had to half carry his pregnant vife through voods and fields by night, foraging for food by day; a man who, vith his own two hands, delivered his only child into a mad, mad vorld—with his own two hands, dug his beloved vife's grave, burying her on foreign soil on some forgotten hillside; a man who, consumed vith both grief and fear, found it necessary to scar his infant daughter's body before turning the child over to some farm family fifty kilometers from God knows vhere; a man who vent vandering aimlessly in near hysteria for days or veeks, or vas it months, who knows, vas captured and confined in a concentration camp shortly before the vor ended; a man who many years later found his daughter as vell as the courage and strength to bury the past and go on living through his only flesh and blood," Mr. Schimmel continued, pausing just long enough to consult his worthless watch, toying anxiously with its pewter fob.

"Vell, Dr. King told Wysznski's daughter and son-in-law that if they left for Australia, they'd be destroying all hope for a man whose only chance of a full recovery vas that he be granted forgiveness and understanding.

"Vell, a short time after Wysznski's daughter and son-in-law closed on the house and moved to Australia, Wysznski closed his mind, shutting out the vorld forever. If he spoke at all, it vas of prevor party days shared by his first vife and their intellectual friends who

140

tried to varn the world of a madman's rise to power. Or of his second vife and how her postvor verk had finally taken its toll before she died of tuberculosis in some godforsaken sanatorium in the mountains. He even bragged to me of how he had partied for an entire veek thereafter with friends and relatives, creating a hoopla at the funeral that vould put an Irish vake to shame, he claimed." Mr. Schimmel shook his head in sadness before taking a sip of coffee. "He tried to hide his pain and torment from me, his only friend. But I could see through all the bullshit! I could see the signs of sorrow and the scars across his heart as if they vas visible.

"Anyvays, Dr. King appealed to Wysznski's daughter in writing, reporting that her father's condition vas deteriorating rapidly, encouraging her to visit, or at least write more often. But eventually her correspondence amounted to nothing more than a birthday greeting or an occasional card around the holidays," Mr. Schimmel concluded, shaking his head in sheer disgust, biting into a toasted bagel and taking another sip of coffee.

Richard didn't feel like eating, so he politely excused himself from the table, preferring instead, to watch the bloody scene as the attendants and nurses finally led Mr. Wysznski away.

"Come along now, Mr. Wysznski," one of the men insisted, half carrying the trembling patient toward the gaping, moaning pair of elevator doors. "No one is going to hurt you."

Nurse Harrigan stepped inside and held the doors open before pushing a button, sending the car upward to the infirmary on the fourth floor as two attendants ushered the frightened figure within.

"NO!" Mr. Wysznski shouted upon ascent. "DOWN. PUSH DOWN. THEY'RE DOWN UNDER. THEY'RE ALL DOWN UNDER," he screamed. "DONNIE'S DOWN THERE WITH THEM, TOO."

Dr. Angelo T. Bianco entered A Building from the side entrance, dancing and dripping his way merrily across the lobby beneath a black umbrella. Muffled screams fell to the foyer as the cage of rage rose between the floors.

"There he goes; off to Greenland," the psychiatrist waved, referring to its geographic direction as well as the color of the rubber room they'd put Wysznski in until he'd calm down a bit.

The doctor strolled over to the reception desk, raking his fingers through his wavy black hair. He peered inquisitively over the shoulder of a man stooped over an electric IBM. A large open toolbox sat on the floor near his feet. "And who, might I ask, are you, sir?" the psychiatrist inquired suspiciously. "Careful how you answer, for it's sometimes rather difficult to tell the sane ones from the lot."

"Repairman," the man answered without looking up, tinkering inside the machine with a set of tiny shiny tools.

"Can you fix it?"

"I can repair anything," the man replied.

Doctor Bianco immediately stepped out of his shoes and, with a free hand, set the pair of soaking-wet loafers in the cover of the man's toolbox. "Full soles and half-inch rubber heels by three o'clock," he demanded. "And if you're really good, I've got a customer with a pocket watch who could use your services, too."

The man looked up and smiled.

Dr. Bianco turned to the pretty nurse, shaking his head with mild annoyance as she pecked away upon an outmoded manual typewriter. "Good heavens, Donna. Filling in as receptionist again, I see. How *do* you put up with these deplorable conditions around here?"

"Simply by resigning myself to the fact that everyone around here is crazy," Nurse Marlow replied with a winsome smile, trying to type upon a 3 x 5 index card with the index finger of each hand.

"Would you have dinner with me tonight?" the psychiatrist asked.

"Why, I'd have to be crazy. You know perfectly well that I'm a married woman."

"But I'm crazy about you," he insisted.

"Well, then why didn't you say so?"

"See you at eight."

"Just don't tell me later on that you're too tired."

"Are you insane?" he said with a wink and a nod.

"Oh, I almost forgot. Dr. King called earlier saying that Mrs. Geist would be coming by for Richard this afternoon," she related, handing over a phone message and gesturing toward the patient standing by the elevator. "She'll be escorting him to Dr. King's house for an early dinner."

"Again? He just had dinner there a couple of weeks ago," he said, glancing over at Richard.

142

"I certainly hope that the good doctor knows what he's doing," the nurse replied, erasing and retyping mistakes.

"No one in love ever knows what they're doing," Bianco declared, moving back across the lobby in a kind of dance fever, bobbing and weaving in soaking-wet stocking feet, setting down a series of steps that resembled the bossa nova one moment, a merengue the next. Across the green tiled floor he flew, twirling the umbrella around and around on his shoulder like a parasol, parading past a group of young nurses coming off their shift.

"Didn't anyone ever tell you, Doctor, that it's bad luck to carry an open umbrella indoors?" one of the nurses rebuked, shielding her pretty face.

"Sing-ing in the rain," Bianco sang out merrily, grabbing the nurse around the waist. "Just sing-ing in the rain. What a glo-ri-ous feel-ing, I'm hap-py again," he carried on, kicking up his heels as the set of groaning elevator doors opened and Nurse Harrigan stepped out, apparently in no mood for any kind of shenanigans.

"Listen, Gene Kelly," the head nurse snapped. "That bumbershoot of yours belongs over there in the umbrella stand by the front door," she stated firmly in her Irish brogue, failing to see any humor in the psychiatrist's behavior.

Dr. Bianco suddenly snapped his umbrella shut and gently bayoneted the buxom woman in her buttocks as she passed.

"Damn you!" Nurse Harrigan exclaimed, turning and throwing her weight around. "You put down that goddamn thing or so help me God—I'll teach you—stop it—a thing or two," she hollered, trying to wrestle the weapon away from the playful soul.

Dr. Bianco let the umbrella go and grabbed the woman from behind. "UP THE REPUBLIC!" he shouted, humping the head nurse madly against the wall while patients and personnel went about their business rather routinely.

"YOU LET GO OF ME! YOU SON OF A BITCH," she yelled. "What the devil do you think you're doing?"

"Close order drill," Bianco panted, nipping at the back of the woman's neck like a dog in heat.

"How do you spell hemorrhoid, Doctor?" Nurse Marlow called out from the front desk, banging the carriage in frustration across its track.

"HE—MO—double—R-H—O-I-D, spells *hem or rhoid*," Dr. Bianco sang out gaily to the tune of *Harrigan—That's Me*, gyrating against the head nurse's buttocks as she fought furiously to free herself.

"I'LL KILL YOU—WHEN I GET MY HANDS ON YOU," she screamed insanely.

"It won't fit," Nurse Marlow cried, ripping out the card.

"Try P-I-L-E-S," the psychiatrist sighed, feigning orgasm as the repairman doubled over the machine in fits of uncontrollable laughter. "And have that lunatic standing next to you committed just as soon as he's finished repairing my shoes."

Richard hung around the reception area for most of the morning, listening to the weather reports forecasting heavy rainfall over the next several days. Shortly before noon, an attendant came by to escort Richard back to his room in order to have him ready for his visit. As the elevator passed between the floors, one could still hear Mr. Wyszynski screaming and carrying on from his temporary cell situated at the opposite end of the building from Richard's room on the eleventh floor. Even at that distance, he could hear the man calling out for his grandson, Donnie. He could plainly hear the man pounding the padded walls and floor of his cell as though the man were confined but several feet away.

About an hour later, Mr. Wyszynski's screaming and pounding had abated; then finally, silence took its place. Richard stood in his room gazing at the photographs on the bureau: pictures of Mother as a young acrobat, gracefully performing somersaults and splits; a picture of Dicky as a small child wearing a cowboy hat, holsters slung low across his hips, western hardware held at arm's length in hot little hands.

CLICK.

A key turned in the lock, and the attendant pushed open the heavy metal door. "Let's go, Richard. Your mother is waiting for you downstairs," Marvin Gitlin said.

Richard turned away from the man.

"Com'on. You're going up to Dr. King's house for dinner."

"If you don't mind, I'd rather stay here in my room."

"Oh, I don't mind," the lanky man replied. "But I think Sarah might be a little disappointed if you didn't show. Not to mention your mother and Dr. King."

"We just had dinner there two weeks ago."

"I know, but today's supposed to be kind of special. Listen, I really can't say too much," he whispered, taking Richard into his confidence, "except that there's something in the air besides warm breezes, if you get my drift. Besides, Sarah made a goose with all the trimmings. Better than meatloaf, which is what you'd be having here."

Richard turned to the attendant. "Marvin, I'd like to ask you something."

"Shoot."

Richard drew two gun fingers from his hips.

Marvin smiled. "Hey, that's pretty quick there, partner."

Richard dropped his hands to his sides, stared at the attendant queerly. "Marvin. How long have you been with Dr. King?"

"You mean both here and at the ranch?"

"Yes. Tell me about the ranch."

"Dr. King's ranch house; just across the bay. Started there some twenty years ago, I reckon. The same year Dr. King lost his wife and child. Took him years to get over that."

"I'll bet."

"Yeah, that was a helluva time for him. Mrs. King died in childbirth. They tried to save the boy, only there were serious complications. Shortly after that, Max was released from the Foundation and became Dr. King's man servant."

"Max?"

"You know. The one who drove you up from the Carolinas after your discharge."

"Yes, I know Max. Are you saying that he was a patient here?"

"One of the craziest," Marvin assured him with a laugh, shaking a head of sandy brown hair from side to side. "He came from a very well-to-do family. Only I think they disinherited him, or something along those lines. After his release, he went back home and stole all the family paintings off the walls. Sold most of them for a small fortune, too. Anyhow, Dr. King arranged to have Max come live with him up there."

"You mean in Dr. King's home?"

"Yep."

"But Max doesn't live up there."

"He did for a while. Only when Sarah came—let's see—back in the early fifties, I believe—well, they just couldn't see eye to eye. That's when Max moved into Dr. King's ranch house. Kinda looked after the place. Sort of a caretaker there, like Carl Gustafson is here."

"A ranch with horses?" Richard asked.

"Some of the most beautiful horses you ever saw in your life. I used to take care of 'em. Feed 'em and groom 'em. Yeah, those were the good ol' days. Had some wild times there," he said behind a grin. "I was in charge of all the horses and—"

"All the King's men?"

"What?"

"Whatever made you leave the ranch, Marvin? How come you work up here now?"

"Well, the long and short of it was that Dr. King sold the place some years ago. You see, he had no one to share the things he once enjoyed. Besides, who ever heard of a ranch foreman by the name of Marvin?" he said with a chuckle.

"I don't know," Richard said, glaring down at the green tile floor. "What about a family, Marvin? Do you have a wife and kids?" he asked uneasily.

"Oh, that was a long time ago. I have a little girl somewhere. Only she's not so little anymore. About as old as you, I'll bet." Marvin stared out the window, toying anxiously with his ring of keys.

"Marvin?"

"Boy, you certainly are full of questions today," he said, turning away abruptly. "Come on, now. Let's go downstairs. I promised your mother I'd have you ready to go."

"Marvin, was I ever at Dr. King's ranch that you recall?"

Marvin averted Richard's eyes, staring over at the pictures on the bureau. Pictures of the young acrobat. The picture of the boy in the cowboy hat.

"Well, was I? Was little Dicky and Mother ever at that ranch fourteen years ago?" he insisted. "Tell me it wasn't just a nightmare, Marvin. Tell me I'm not completely out of my God-forsaken mind."

"I don't know," the attendant snapped. "How the hell am I supposed to remember fourteen years back? If you want to know the truth, I was pretty well liquored up half the time. Worked hard all day and boozed all night. Just remember that you're not the only one in the

146

world with problems. I got a daughter somewhere who doesn't even remember me at all."

Richard reared back and whinnied before trotting the few steps toward the bed.

"Whoa there, partner," the attendant reined. "Where do you think you're going?"

Richard curled up on the bed. "Back to finish a bad dream," he said while shivering, pulling the corner of a sheet over his head. "PRETENDING IT'S ALL A NIGHTMARE!" he screamed.

"Hey, come on now. Listen. I got no secrets from you. You keep too much in that head of yours. Let it go. That's the secret of getting out of here. If I kept everything locked up inside, why I'd be in the room next to you. Hey, look at me. Have I ever steered you wrong? You're beating a dead horse. Come on now. Your mother is waiting for you downstairs."

After a little coaxing, he and Richard rode the elevator down to the lobby. The doors opened, and Marvin led him into a waiting area. The smell of expensive perfume filled the air. Mother was seated at one of the tables near the door. Staged in high heels. Legs crossed in ladylike fashion. She wore a dark cotton skirt hiked high along a shapely thigh. A white laced-collared blouse with ruffled three-quarter sleeves completed the outfit. She sat there pensively, carefully checking her hair and makeup in a coral-colored shell before looking up with some surprise.

"Oh, there you are," she said, appearing a bit relieved, clicking her compact closed. "I was afraid you weren't coming down."

"Richard's all ready to go, ma'am," Marvin said, patting Richard squarely on the shoulder from behind. "Well, you have a nice time now, and say hello to Sarah for me."

Mother smiled, standing up slowly and pushing down the material of her skirt. "Thank you for bringing him down, Marvin."

"My pleasure," Marvin said politely, taking his leave.

Mother removed a comb from her handbag. "Now, dear. Kindly step over here and let me fix your hair," she instructed and fussed, running the comb through Richard's clay-red curls.

"I understand we're going to Dr. King's house for dinner again."

"Yes, that's right," she said so happily. "It's going to be a very special evening, and I think you'll be surprised."

"Oh, I'm certain of that, Mother."

"Now listen to me."

"I listen very carefully."

"I don't want you to ruin this evening for me. Do you understand? Dr. King has something very important to say tonight, and I want you on your best behavior."

"I really don't want to go to Dr. King's."

"My God, what is the matter with you? I should think that you would want to be out of that wretched little room up there and be eating dinner like a civilized human being. I should think that by now you would want to try and make things work," she entreated. "And please try to keep the hair out of your face." Mother reached back into her bag and removed a hairbrush, stepping forward and passing its bristles roughly through his curls and to the side.

Richard recoiled. "I'm not your little plaything, Mother dear. I'm not your little doll that you can just brush aside whenever you're through playing mother."

"Oh, you're so ungrateful, Richard. You forgot how I used to run down to that school to fight for you. How I fought to protect you. They told me you were difficult. Still, I ran for you until I was blue in the face."

"No! What you mean to say is that you went tramping around the town of Lake Hiawatha, all dolled up with little Dicky, hand in hand. Flirting with the liquor store owner, or the pharmacist who'd smile and joke and try to fill your pants behind the counter. Telling you that you were sweeter than $C_{12}H_{22}O_{11}$. Well, you certainly are sweeter than sugar because you've become $C_6H_4COSO_2NH$. You have become positively *saccharine*, Mother dear. You see, things are beginning to click. Tell me. Who ever heard of a ranch foreman by the name of Marvin? Have you? He was in charge of all the King's horses and all the King's men. Yes, there were lots of men," Richard declared, prancing around the area excitely, his fists extended from his crotch as if riding a stick-horse through the air.

Mother grimaced. "Sometimes I really thing you are a little cuckoo."

"Neighhh," Richard whinnied, moving through the space while whacking an arm insanely at his side.

"Stop it! Do you hear me?"

Richard finally settled down and calmly recited poetry:

> "The cuckoo is a pretty bird
> She singeth as she flies;
> She bringeth us good tidings,
> She telleth us no lies;
> She sucketh all sweet flowers,
> To keep her throttle clear,
> And every time she singeth
> Cuckoo-cuckoo-cuckoo!
> The summer draweth near."

"Look, dear. Let's not fight anymore," Mother pleaded, holding back her tears. "Please come to dinner with me. Dr. King is our host. Just listen to what he has to say. Okay? He's the only one we really have left, you know. Open up to him. He wants to be your friend. I try to be a good mother. Only I can't do it alone. I need your help, too. Darling, please just talk to him. That's all your mother asks."

"I talk to him all the time now, Mother. I tell him everything," he said and shivered.

"I know, sweetheart," she said so soothingly, touching one of his burning cheeks. "Come. Sarah and David are expecting us. Do this for me," she pressed, leading him toward the door.

Once outside, Mother opened her flowered umbrella and gently took his hand in hers. Hand in hand along the flowery path to Dr. King's house they strolled. A light rain fell softly upon the ground, and a brilliant rainbow bridged the horizon in the distance.

Sarah was busy in the kitchen preparing dinner when she looked out the window and saw Mother and Richard coming up the garden path. She waved excitedly, hurrying out back to greet them.

"Who's that handsome devil?" Sarah said grinning, laughing and wrapping her arms tightly around Richard as they approached. "I swear I's gonna steal that fellow fo' myself, Miss Vicki. Ah, hee, hee, hee. Com'on inside. Com'on, com'on," she said excitedly. "I got nice hors d'oeuvres waitin' for everyone. And a special cheese for Richard, too."

"As long as it's not Limburger," Richard said, wrinkling up his nose. "Stinks."

"Got Brie," she whispered and winked. "And I knows how ya love that cheese."

"How do you know that?"

"Oh, a little bird we know told me so."

Richard nodded knowingly. "Marvin said to say hello."

"God, when is this rain ever going to let up, Sarah?" Mother questioned, giving Sarah a hug and a kiss upon the cheek, the three of them stepping inside the house. "Wipe your feet, Richard," Mother bade behind a tight-lipped frown.

"Needs to rain to make things grow, Miss Vicki."

"I suppose," she said, following Sarah inside.

"Besides. These steady showers bring May flowers, 'long with somebody's birthday I know."

Mother smiled and caught the aroma off the kitchen. "Oh, does that ever smell delicious, Sarah. I'm absolutely famished."

"Dinner be ready in a jiffy," Sarah promised. "Now shoo. Both of you," she ordered, escorting her guests past the kitchen and down the hallway toward the living room. "Now you's two go inside and relax. Dr. King be down in jus' a minute."

"Are you sure I can't give you a hand with something, Sarah?"

"Everythin's set, Miss Vicki. Besides, I wants it to be a surprise."

Richard stood by the staircase. "Sarah."

"What is it, honey?"

"May I keep you company in the kitchen?"

Sarah narrowed her eyes, placing her hands firmly on her hips. "Now, if I's didn't know any better, I'd swear you got a crush on ol' Sarah," the old woman swore and laughed, going over to Richard and giving him another great big hug. "But first you gotta promise not to tell a soul what's cookin'," she stipulated, grinning from ear to ear. "Hear?"

"I promise."

"Can't win around here," Mother declared.

"Not with Sarah, you can't," Dr. King agreed, bounding down the stairs in dark slacks and a white dinner jacket, kissing Mother affectionately on the cheek. "Hello, Richard," he greeted, extending his hand warmly.

"Would you excuse me?" Richard said rather curtly, turning

away and following Sarah toward the kitchen.

Mother and Dr. King headed for the living room.

Sarah stooped before the oven door, basting the bird with a large spoon of drippings from the pan. "You know, Richard. Yo' mother and Dr. King makes a lovely couple. Don't ya think?"

Richard sat in the corner as quiet as a mouse, nibbling away at the cheese.

"What's the matter? Cat got yo' tongue?" she teased.

"I guess what's good for the goose is good for the gander," he answered, staring down blankly at the bird.

"Ah, hee, hee, hee. You's too much, Richard," Sarah sounded, straightening herself up and closing the oven door. "Now how'ds you know that was a goose 'stead of some other kind of bird? Marvin and his big mouth, I'll bet."

"Sarah, how come you never went back into missionary work? Why do you stay here with Dr. King?"

"What's ol' Sarah look like, a spring chicken?" she declared. "My teachin' and preachin' days is over. Besides, I found me a home here. I's all worn out from fightin' a losin' battle with them so-called messengers of God. Of course, you could say I got me a whole congregation down there to look after," she began to explain, gesturing toward the buildings in the distance. "Taught Althea all 'bout her ancestry. You know Althea Blythe, Richard?"

"Mrs. O'Brian told me a little bit about her."

"Only history she ever know'd 'bout her people was slavery in Colonial America, taught in white schools by white teachers like Mrs. O'Brian. But I's given that girl and others like her their heritage. Rich as any kingdom," she added proudly. "Now I's bes' be getting' this bird outta the oven 'fore my goose be cooked," she decided. "Why don't ya tell everyone that dinner's 'bout to be served in the dinin' room. You can take that bowl in with ya. Careful though 'cause the bottom's hot. I's be there in a jiff."

Richard took hold of the bowl near the rim, carrying the steaming dish of dark rice down the hallway and into the dining room, setting it down on the table upon a trivet. A moment later, Sarah carried in the golden-brown bird, its crisp breast draped with narrow strips of succulent-looking bacon. Dr. King carved the goose then poured some white wine while Sarah served the juicy slices upon a bed of stuffing made with mushrooms and long-grained wild rice, along with a cold and colorful aspic concoction on the side. When everyone was finally settled, Richard spoke without lifting his eyes from the plate.

"Sir, did you know that the female of the true Old World cuckoo sometimes visits the nests of other smaller birds whose eggs match her own in size and color, replacing an egg of the host with one of her own?"

"No, I didn't know that, Richard," Dr. King remarked, taking a sip of wine.

"Then an extraordinary instinct comes into play after the egg is hatched," Richard went on. "The young cuckoo, being somewhat larger than the others in the brood, works its back beneath its nestmates, ousting them one at a time along with any unhatched eggs, leaving them to perish on the ground below, claiming itself *victorious* and sole beneficiary of its foster parents' care. Of course, each species of cuckoo has its own particular mode of parasitism."

Mother glared. "We are eating goose, Richard. Not discussing the habits or instincts of cuckoos at this table."

"Oh, but indeed we are, Mother."

"Haven't I made myself clear?" she insisted.

"That's exactly my point, Mother dear."

"Hold on now," Dr. King said calmly. "I think Richard is trying to tell us something."

"Only that Mother has nasty nesting habits."

Mother cringed. "You may be excused, Richard."

"And you may not, Mother."

"You better listen to me and—"

"All right now," Dr. King interjected firmly. "I believe there are some things that have to be set straight from the start."

Sarah set the gravy boat down precariously in front of Mother, unsure of whether to leave the room or remain.

"Richard, I think I can understand how you feel." He paused a moment. "Your mother and I have something we'd like to announce."

"David, I don't think this is the time," she interrupted.

Dr. King raised a finger judiciously. "Your mother and I are planning to be married by the end of the summer, Richard. We'd like your blessing, and we'd like you to take the name of King."

"Oh, my Lord, Miss Vicki!" Sarah exclaimed excitedly.

Mother beamed ecstatically. "Well, Richard. Do you have something you wish to say in response?"

"'A little more than kin, and less than kind,'" Richard replied, reciting the very first words spoken by Hamlet in William Shakespeare's tragedy, *Hamlet, Prince of Denmark*. While staring down blandly at the cooked bird, Richard chorused from an anonymous source.

> "The cuckoo is a giddy bird,
> No other is as she,
> That flits across the meadow,
> That sings in every tree.
> A nest she never buildeth,
> A vagrant she doth roam;
> Her music is but tearful—
> Cuckoo-cuckoo-cuckoo!
> "I nowhere have a home."

"Richard, I'd like for you to listen very carefully to what I have to say," Dr. King continued. "Please hear me out. In less than a month, things are going to get very hectic here at the Foundation. I've got construction starting here in June, then the annual picnic celebration in July, and by the end of summer, your mother and I are going to be married."

"A picnic celebration," Richard echoed and mused.

"Yes. We have one every Fourth of July; patients and employees. For many, it simply marks another summer. For us, it could mean a new beginning. What I'm trying to say, Richard, is that I'd like very much to see us living and working together as a family before the end of summer rolls around. Your mother is going to be moving into the house shortly, and she'll have her own room downstairs until we're married. I need her help around here. Quite frankly, I could use your help, too."

"Use, you say. Yes. A very interesting word, Doctor. And how, exactly, would you *use* me here? By helping Mr. Gustafson in the garden, pulling weeds?"

"That's not what I had in mind. You see, I know the way you

work with figures."

"How do you know that?"

"Oh, from the things your mother has told me. And from some other sources, too."

"Such as?"

"Your records."

"Records?"

"Well, your school records, for one. And you do remember a Dr. Roche, the psychologist at the parental home in Bayonne?"

"So?"

"Well, I recall speaking with him at great length about you. It's no secret that you have an extraordinary ability in dealing with figures; quite an analytical mind."

"Probably genetic. You see, my real father was an accountant, and very good with figures. Wouldn't you agree, Mother?"

Dr. King ignored the comment. "It would be a shame to waste that ability, Richard. If you really wanted to accomplish something, there's no telling where your talent might lead. Business. Engineering. Science. You seem very interested in astronomy. Those concepts of an expanding universe you talked about last time have been explored by great minds. I could get you all the books you wanted. We could go to the planetariums together. Even meet some of the astronomers if you like. And there's plenty of work to be done here at the Foundation. The possibilities are endless. You have a fine mind, Richard."

"Yes, board certified by the American Psychiatric Association, I suppose."

"People get well, Richard. The key is will. Along with an understanding that those around you care. And believe me, we do care. We all care very much."

"May I speak frankly, sir?"

"By all means, Richard. Please do."

Richard looked Dr. King squarely in the eyes. "I see you as a manipulator."

"RICHARD!"

Dr. King raised his hand. "No, let him have his say."

"A user, to use your own word. Sarah got well, I see. Well enough to function as your chief cook and bottle washer. She makes your beds and washes and irons your underwear and sheets. Scrubs your sinks and bowls and tiles and tubs. Washes your floors and vacuums your carpets. Polishes your furniture and *objets d'art*. Takes care of your plants. Mr. Gustafson got well enough to cultivate your gardens and dump your garbage. And Mr. Wyszynski got well enough to frame your photographs and build you shelves and cabinets whenever his services were needed. That is, until he really went under. I understand that chauffeur of yours, Max, was a former patient, too. You have a hold on everyone here, Dr. King. You use them. You exploit them. And now you're going to use Mother. I guess we all use one another in different ways. But what galls me is this sham, this mockery, this pretense that you are helping people. This crazy world of make-believe in which you have become a maleficent Walt Disney, pulling all the strings. Look out there sometime. There's Mickey, and Goofy, and Donald Duck. And now you want Snow White. Queen for a day? I understand that your first wife died in childbirth along with the child. Was she a former patient, too, or was she just plain crazy over you?"

"THAT IS ENOUGH!" Dr. King shouted.

"Not nearly."

"Leave this table immediately, Richard."

"Last Supper, Judas?"

"I said leave," Dr. King insisted.

"May I be excused now, Mother?"

Tears fell down Mother's face as she ran from the room with Sarah trailing behind her on old bowed legs.

Richard stood up from the table. "Before I leave this fantasy world of yours, Doctor, I will make a mark upon your FOUNDATION," he declared, bringing his fist down firmly upon the table. "I shall leave you with a permanent and everlasting impression."

"I'll have someone take you back to your room," Dr. King stated angrily.

"Oh, and thank you for that touching speech on caring, Doctor."

Dr. King picked up the telephone behind him and spoke with someone briefly. Within minutes, two attendants came for Richard while Dr. King went off to comfort Mother, too. The two men whisked Richard away in a van.

"Wee! What a ride!"

Late that evening, when most everyone else was fast asleep,

Richard climbed quietly out of bed. Kneeling at the foot of the metal frame, as if in prayer, he lifted one end of the bed, carefully removing a wad of paper from a hollow tubular leg, catching the aluminum canister in his palm; like a miniature garbage can, he thought. He gently set the bed back down and crawled into the corner near the door. Slowly, he unscrewed the little cap, being careful not to spill the highly toxic compound. Moistening a finger, he transferred but several of the crystals to the tip of his tongue, tasting the deadly almond fixer and laughing silently up his sleeve, the grin of madness plastered across his handsome face.

Chapter 17

SURPRISES

Richard kept to his room for nearly a week, staring down at the sunny grounds by day, gazing up at the moon and stars at night. The world spun all around him in a brilliant bath of light. He had learned from Marvin Gitlin that Mother would be moving some of her things into Dr. King's house around the middle of the month. Richard figured that the special day would probably fall on Mother's birthday, so he thought he'd better make amends, and soon.

Through Dr. Bianco, Richard sent word out to Dr. King, apologizing for his actions at the house the week before, explaining that he wanted to try and make things work from that point forth. Just as Mother had wished. Of course, Dr. King was positively thrilled, although he played it rather cool. It wasn't until an hour before Mother was scheduled to arrive that Dr. King invited him for the day: Sunday was Mother's birthday and Mother's Day as well.

Early that afternoon, the black limousine came barreling through the gates and up the private road. Around the circular drive it shot, screeching to a sudden halt in front of a pair of fluted columns extending from the front porch.

"Here they are. Here come Miss Vicki now," Sarah said excitedly to Richard, hurrying outside while Dr. King went quickly up the stairs and out of sight.

Sarah moved along on old bowed legs, waving to Mother and shaking her fist at Max. "Good Lord," she declared, peering into the car at the piles of clothing lined along the seats. Gowns and dresses draped the side rear windows on either side. Hat boxes, boxes of shoes and handbags covered the floor in both front and back. "Why, you's got more clothes than the Queen, Miss Vicki."

"And much better taste, I might add," Mother teased, holding her head majestically as Max stepped forward and helped her from the car. Mother stepped out of the limo wearing white pedal pushers and halter top, peddling her ass for sure.

"My, my, my-my, my," Sarah rattled off emphatically. Then the two of them laughed to no end and embraced each other warmly. "I's jus' so excited," Sarah affirmed most sincerely, beaming brightly two rows of perfect white teeth.

"Oh, I am, too, Sarah."

"I'll take the bags in first, ma'am," Max said, opening up the trunk.

Mother smiled merrily. "That will be fine, Max. You're such a dear."

Sarah shifted her eyes with contempt toward the chauffeur. "Max is a crazy driver, Miss Vicki. A real cowboy. I wouldn't let him take me from here to the corner after how he drove the other— " she trailed off, about to give away part of the big surprise.

Max turned to Sarah, addressing her in a condescending tone. "Then the next time you ask me to do you a favor, old woman, do flatter yourself and take a cab."

"Oh, hush up, you ol' fool."

"No fool like an old fool," Max acknowledged, chuckling while carrying in the first of several sets of luggage.

"Sarah, where's David?" Mother asked.

Sarah laughed lightly. "Now I jus' knew you was gonna get 'round to askin' 'bout the man of the house. Fact is, the man of the house done become the boy of the hour. He been runnin' 'round here all mornin' makin' ol' Sarah crazy. Com'on, follow me, Miss Vicki," she insisted, leading the way inside.

Mother passed by the doorway when Richard suddenly appeared as if from out of nowhere, wearing a childish grin. "Happy birthday, Mummy!"

Startled, Mother took a step back. "Oh, for heaven's sake, Richard! You gave me quite a start. What on earth are you doing here?"

"It's my surprise to you. I told Dr. King that I'm going to try and make things work from now on. I really am."

"Oh, dear child; I'm so proud of you. Come here and give me a great big hug. Part of any journey is taking that very first step." The two embraced and gave each a hug and a kiss. "Now, where's David?" she asked, stepping back rather abruptly.

"You see soon enough, Miss Vicki," Sarah answered. "Now, up the stairs and follow me. Com'on. You too, Richard. Right this way. I feel like an usherette working a matinee," she said and grinned broadly, climbing past the series of plants suspended along the windows. Reaching the top of the stairs, the old woman paused just long enough to collect her breath. "Now straight on down the hall and to your right. Come'on," she coaxed excitedly. "Last door on the left."

Mother followed Sarah to the end of the hall. "In here?"

Sarah nodded excitedly.

Mother opened the door.

"Surprise!" Dr. King announced delightedly, seeing the shock upon her pretty face.

"Happy birthday, Miss Vicki!" Sarah added.

Dr. King was standing in the center of the newly carpeted room. "Say cheese," he teased, squeezing the rubber bulb of the hem-marker next to him. A cloud of white powder shot forth, settling lightly upon the new rose-colored carpeting.

Mother took in the freshly painted blush pink walls. Beneath a sunny window stood a large table, its surface neatly organized with pairs of shiny scissors and boxes of tiny pins; packages of needles and thread; a pressing board and a steam iron; marking chalk and measuring tape; and a large fabric sewing basket sitting beside a lavender clock radio. And in the far corner of the room stood a handsome wood-grain sewing cabinet, wrapped with a single giant red bow. In front of that exquisite piece of furniture sat a matching upholstered chair. Mother stood in awe.

"Well, don't you like your new sewing room?" Dr. King asked. "It would have been a little difficult to wrap, darling," he joked.

"Oh, David!" she exclaimed, completely overwhelmed. "I can't believe it," she cried, shedding genuine tears of joy, rushing into his arms. "It's absolutely beautiful! You knew it's what I've always wanted. What a wonderful surprise," she said, showering him with a million kisses. "Thank you, thank you, thank you, David. I just can't believe all this." Mother wept tears of joy, turning around and giving both Sarah and Richard another hug. "Thank you all for making me so very, very happy."

"And I have yo' room all ready for you downstairs, Miss Vicki," Sarah said, practically on the verge of tears herself.

"Of course, those are only temporary quarters," Dr. King warned good-humoredly. "I wouldn't want you getting too comfortable there."

"Oh, I wouldn't dream of it," Mother assured him with a giggle.

"Well, now that's jus' somethin' you's two gonna have to work out for yo'selves," Sarah said, turning to leave the room.

"Where are you going, Sarah?" Dr. King asked.

"Gonna help that ol' fool put Miss Vicki's clothes away. I stays 'round here any longer, you gonna see ol' Sarah blubberin' like a baby."

"Sarah."

"Yes, Miss Vicki?"

"Thank you again."

"Oh, shoo," Sarah said, flagging her hand with annoyance at not being able to hold back the flood of tears streaming down her coal-black face.

"Sarah, how are you going to behave at the wedding come the end of summer?" Dr. King teased.

"Like an ol' fool," she swore and sobbed, hiding her face in embarrassment. "Like a sentimental ol' fool."

Mother went over and put her arms around Sarah once again.

"Now, why you want to see an ol' girl like me cry fo' anyways?"

"Shh," Mother whispered, stepping back and gently brushing aside the old woman's tears. "Or else you're going to have me starting up again, too."

Sarah sniffled and nodded her head up and down. "I be fine in jus' a minute. Now I bes' be checkin' on that ol' fool downstairs."

"We'll be right down, Sarah. I just want to show Victoria her new sewing machine." Dr. King led Mother by the hand across the room like a happy child.

Richard stepped from the room.

"David, I can't believe all this. It's a dream come true."

"It's no dream. Come here, I'll show you."

"DAVID!" she exclaimed. "Stop—I'm—you know I'm ticklish." Mother sighed and squirmed. "You—ummm. David, the door is wide open. Ohhh." She put her arms around him tenderly. "Oh, I do love you, David."

"I love you, too, Victoria." He kissed her long and passionately there in the newly decorated room, holding her ever so close, sewing thing up rather nicely.

Richard watched them from the hallway, his mind a rousing, stirring, whirling pleasure dome of madness as the moment came and went most magically.

Breathless, the two stepped back from one another.

"You were going to show me the sewing machine," she reminded.

"No, you must have misunderstood. What I meant is that I wanted to sow some oats."

Mother giggled girlishly. "Oh, is that what you meant?"

"I think I'd better show you that machine."

"I think maybe you'd better," she agreed, leading him gently by the hand.

"Oh, by the way, before I forget. When Sarah shows you your room, I'd like you to make a big fuss over the curtains."

"The curtains?"

"It's supposed to be a surprise. It'll mean a great deal to her. All right?"

"Of course, David."

"Now, let's see here," he said, stepping over to the machine and removing the satin bow. "The salesman tried to show me how this works," he said, scratching his head and laughing, staring down at the cabinet quizzically. "Ah, yes. First we remove this piece like so," he began, lifting off the polished cover and setting it upon the chair. "Next, we lift this arm, like so. And presto! So, what do you think?"

"Oh, it's beautiful!" she exclaimed, examining the elaborate engraved machine and all its features.

"Then you simply set this dial for whatever stitch you wish. See?" The two of them leaned forward, toying with the dials and buttons like inquisitive children.

"Oh, David, it has everything."

"Do you really like it?"

"Like it? It's absolutely fabulous. And this room! You must have spent a fortune on all this."

"Are you truly happy?"

"Ecstatic, David. Truly."

"You're so beautiful, Victoria." He brushed aside her lovely auburn hair.

"David." She took his hand in hers. "I can't get over Richard's behavior today. I never saw him so relaxed. He's like a different boy."

"Now, didn't I tell you that everything is going to work out just fine? He's starting to come around, but as I told you before, it's going to take some time. That's why I need you here now instead of at the end of the summer."

"I'm just so surprised. I think this is a turning point, David. Yes. I can feel it. Everything is beginning to come together."

"Listen to me, Victoria. All Richard needs is some time to get adjusted to things. I want him to see that you have your own room downstairs. I want him to understand that we care about each other and that we care about him. That's what's important, Victoria. You remember Mr. Wyszynski? He was making progress by leaps and bounds. He was functioning, and he was productive. Then one day he realized that those he loved and counted on most didn't care anymore. Richard has got to know we care. He's here because we care. And if everything goes smoothly, say by July, right after we have the Foundation's annual picnic, well, maybe we can move him out of A Building and have him here with us. I have to be in Boston that weekend for a convention, but if he can behave himself, he's more than welcome to spend some time here with you and Sarah. Besides, it might be a good idea that I'm away. Sarah will be pretty busy with the picnic planning, so it'll give you and Richard a chance to be alone together. How does that sound?"

"Oh, David, I wish I had listened to you years ago," she said, holding him close. "I was very foolish and selfish, and I let you slip away from me."

"And now you're here forever."

"Yes, David. Forever and always." As they embraced, they could hear Sarah and Max arguing downstairs. "I think maybe we'd better go down and see what's going on," Mother suggested. "It sounds like those two are at each other's throats again."

"Those two wouldn't be happy unless they were fighting. Believe me, they thrive on it."

"Come. We'd better go referee."

"Well, let's do it from the sidelines. I make it a point never to get caught between those two if I can help it."

"Come on," she said, laughing and pulling him playfully by the hand.

Sarah and Max were standing in the living room hollering back and forth at one another as Dr. King and Mother came down the stairs.

"What is going on down here?" Dr. King insisted.

"A rodeo. That's what's goin' on down here," Sarah said angrily. "This ol' fool thinks he's at a rodeo."

"I'm afraid I don't' understand, Sarah."

"He's the one who don't understand," she screeched and scowled, narrowing her eyes at Max. "He carryin' Miss Vicki's evenin' gowns over his shoulder like he was carryin' 'round a pair of saddle bags. I tell him he gotta hold 'em straight, that he gonna get them all wrinkled. I tell him to take the rest of the suitcases out of the trunk, and that I take care of everythin' else. But no; he gots to do everythin' by hisself."

Max stared at the ceiling in frustration. "I told that old woman I would have the car unloaded before she ever quit her gabbing. She gabs more and says less than any woman I ever met in my entire life."

Dr. King shook his head from side to side. "What am I going to do with the two of you?" he chided with a patient smile. "Tell me."

"You can start by havin' that ol' fool recommitted," Sarah decided with a frown.

"If I had an old sock, old woman, I'd stick it in your mouth," Max declared.

Sarah placed her hands squarely on her hips. "And if I was you, ol' fool, I'd mind that smart mouth of yo's 'fore somebody put their foot in it," she challenged, tapping her foot firmly upon the thick carpeting.

"All right now, you two. Enough is enough. Sarah, why don't you show Victoria to her room while Max and I get the rest of the things from the car."

"But everything's been brought in, Dr. King. That's what I've been trying to tell the old battleax. Clothes are all hung up in the closet, and the suitcases are on the shelf along with all the boxes and bags. I told that old woman I'd be finished 'fore she could quit her jabbering."

"Well, I'm sure everything is just fine, and I want to thank you both," Mother said pleasantly, trying to assuage matters.

"So then there's really no problem. Now is there?" Dr. King put forth more as a statement of fact than a question of concern.

Max looked at Sarah amusingly. "Only problem is with that old woman. She just can't cotton to the fact that underneath all her

163

meanness lies a soft spot in her heart for old Max."

"Only soft spot 'round here is in yo' head, fool," Sarah retorted, shaking her fist in Max's face. "And the next time you grab ol' Sarah's behind, she gonna let you have it real good."

"Now, I just knew you were my kind of woman," Max said with a mild chuckle. "Sarah's finally going to work some of her old black magic on Max."

Dr. King and Mother tried to keep their grins and laughing eyes from growing any wider, lowering their faces to conceal any sign of mirth or merriment.

"Don't you pay no mind to that ol' fool," Sarah said disconcertedly, realizing they were having a laugh at her expense. "Max is a wild man. He drives like a cowboy and behaves like a fool." She stared at Max coldly. "You should be ashamed of yo'self. I's an ol' woman."

"And I'm just an old fool," Max maintained.

"Oh, by the way, Max," Dr. King interrupted, deciding it was time to put the matter to rest. "I'd appreciate it if you would take Mrs. Geist into town tomorrow so that she can do some shopping if she wishes. I'm sure she'd like to see some of the lovely boutiques."

"Yes, sir."

"Good. Now, why don't we show Victoria to her room, Sarah. She's been riding in a car for hours, and I'm sure she'd like to freshen up and relax a bit."

Sarah stood with her arms folded across her chest, staring deliberately up at Max. Max ran a finger along his bottom lip, staring down at his highly polished shoes.

"Sar-ah!"

Sarah looked up into Dr. King's smiling dark eyes. "Yes, sir," she replied obediently. "Please come with me, Miss Vicki. I jus' know ya gonna loves yo' room."

Mother smiled at David. "Charmer," she whispered, fluttering her eyelids with exaggeration.

Dr. King mouthed the word *curtains* as a reminder, pointing anxiously down the hallway toward the room.

Mother rolled her large brown eyes up inside her head so that only the whites were visible, hung her tongue out like a dead dog, then ran a threatening finger across her throat. "*Curtains*," she mimed, turning and following Sarah down the hall.

Dr. King slowly shook his head from side to side anew before addressing Max. "And you. What am I going to do with you, Maximilian? You're incorrigible."

Max shrugged his shoulders and grinned. "I like that feisty old woman," he made perfectly clear.

Dr. King laughed. "Well, I'm sure she likes you, too, Max. The only problem is that the two of you are going to have to find another way to show your mutual admiration."

Richard came up behind Dr. King and asked if it would be all right to have a look at Mother's room. Of course, he said it would, smiling and leading Richard down the hallway.

Mother and Sarah stood before the door to one of the rooms. "Close yo' eyes now, Miss Vicki. And no peekin'."

"I don't know how many surprises I can take in one day, Sarah." Mother smiled, closing her eyes tightly.

Sarah opened the door and guided her inside. "Well, here you is, Miss Vicki. You can open up yo eyes now."

Mother opened her eyes in another place and time. Another world, it seemed. A fantasy world. A world of make-believe. It was a room with all the room in the world, decorated with scores of dolls in dresses from foreign and familiar lands. Several dolls sat staged upon some shelving while the multitude stood on ceremony within large black lacquered showcases that lined a mirrored wall. Mother looked around the room in total disbelief before crossing over to a huge four-post canopy bed, sinking dreamlike beside two sun-drenched, cloud-like pillows.

"Oh, my God, Sarah! It's positively heaven. And just look at those curtains!" she exclaimed, getting up and going over to the sunny window, touching the delicate lace. "Why, they're positively exquisite. They make this whole room."

Sarah's smile filled the entire room. "I made them, Miss Vicki," she added excitedly.

Mother turned to Sarah with genuine surprise. "Made them! How on earth did you ever make them, Sarah?"

"Why, upstairs on yo' sewin' machine," she confessed. "Of course, Dr. King was furious when he hears what I's up to. He come flyin' up the stairs thinkin' ol' Sarah gonna sew her fingers together fo' sure."

"But where did you get this magnificent fabric?"

"Well, the day after yo' bed arrived, I asked Max to take me into town. Last time I ride with that cowboy, though. I be in the backseat bouncin' 'round like a buckin' bronco. Next time, ol' Sarah gonna take a cab 'cause that man is absolutely crazy behind a wheel, Miss Vicki. But you already know all that. Anyhow, they got this fantastic store in town."

"You're incredible, Sarah."

"You're not mad that I used yo' machine to make the curtains, now are ya, Miss Vicki? Because I really wanted it to be a surprise," she said, hanging her head in doubt.

"It's a splendid surprise," Mother insisted, wrapping her arms around the woman warmly, setting her mind at ease. "But I never knew you could sew. And so beautifully."

"Oh, the machine do all the sewin'," Sarah said most modestly. "She's a real humdinger."

"*You're* a real humdinger," Mother maintained quite seriously, hugging Sarah tightly. "I'm so happy we're friends."

"Me, too," Sarah agreed while wiping away her tears of happiness. "Me, too."

Richard and Dr. King smiled satisfactorily, standing there together at the threshold of Mother's magnificent room.

Chapter 18

SECRETS

Three weeks since Mother's birthday and Richard was still on his best behavior, a model patient who had practically total freedom of the grounds. He took in each and every moment with a very special sort of interest, waiting patiently for just the right moment.

Mother strolled along the splendid gardens in a flowing white summer dress and matching flats. She was certainly more beautiful than all the June flowers one could gather in that month alone. She watched Theresa Martinez playing with her doll near the gazebo as the young girl did most every day for hours on end. Theresa's outfits were always remarkably crisp and clean. On that particular afternoon, she wore a beige top, matching shorts, and sneakers that contrasted sharply with her dark hair, olive skin, and expressive brown eyes. Large and attractive doll-like eyes.

"May I sit down here?" Mother asked politely, walking over to the little girl that afternoon.

Theresa Martinez looked around for a bench, a rock, a seat of any sort; something that the girl supposedly thought Mother had meant to sit upon. "Where?" became the puzzlement.

"Right here," was Mother's answer, sinking slowly to the ground in a swan-like pose and graceful split, the hem of her dress held back and high with an outstretched arm before both limbs came together like a pair of wings to form a V, the backs of long slender fingers touching to form a second, head erect, eyes closed, bearing an inviting smile upon her lips.

"Good gosh." The girl cringed, folding her fingers in her mouth, gnawing away most nervously on their tips.

"Oh, my!" Mother exclaimed, opening her eyes wide, holding the pose for a moment longer before turning over on her stomach, reaching back and grabbing the tip of an open-toed shoe, touching it to the top of her head. "What do you suppose is the matter with your pretty little friend?" Mother asked, directing the question into the doll's face held level with her own. "Hum?"

Theresa Martinez clutched her doll protectively, drawing it

upward and forming a cradle in her arms. "You're going to get grass stains all over your pretty dress that won't wash out. I guess you're too big to be spanked. But my mommy would spank me if I came home with grass stains on my dress."

"Is that so?" Mother questioned.

Theresa nodded her head most assuredly.

"Well, if you were my little girl, I'd fall head over heels for you. Like this," Mother beamed, springing to her feet in a single motion before falling forward into a somersault, one after another, rolling across the grassy grounds and winding up in a perfect split, freezing and framing the action as if posing for a picture. "What would you say to that?"

Theresa Martinez giggled with delight, lowering her doll gingerly upon the grass in similar fashion.

"That's very good. I didn't know that Ruthie knew acrobatics."

Theresa quickly brought her doll back to the safety of her arms. "How did you know Ruthie's name?"

"Oh, Dr. King told me," Mother answered straightaway. "And I know that your name is Theresa. That's a lovely, lovely name. And you're such a pretty little girl, too," she cooed.

"What's your name?"

"Victoria."

"Mrs. Victoria?"

"No. Victoria is my first name. But you may call me Vicki, if I may call you by your first name, Theresa—since I'm sure we're going to be friends."

"Mommy said I must be very careful of people who want to be friends right away."

"And your mommy is a very wise woman," Mother said, rising to her feet most magically. "Still, I wouldn't spank you if you came home to me with grass stains on your dress. No, indeed. Instead, we'd go off together in the greenest of meadows and get as grassy as we could," Mother boldly remarked and laughed, wheeling across the grounds in a series of handsprings. "Why, I'd bend over backwards to make you as happy as I could," Mother swore, leaning backwards until her head rested upon the ground. Suddenly she shot up into a handstand, her cotton dress closing down all around her like a precious flower pulling in its petals for a spell. "Where did you go, Theresa?

Ruthie? Are you two hiding from me?" Mother teased.

Theresa laughed, lifting the inverted cotton canopy and peeking just beneath. "Here we are. See?" Theresa said, inverting her doll, pushing its dress down around its head; its long thin legs stuck straight up in the air like Mother's.

"Ah, yes. There you are, indeed."

"Would you let Ruthie come with us to the greenest of meadows and get all grassy, too?"

"Why certainly," Mother answered assuringly, although her head was certainly upside down, appearing like a frown. She lowered herself to a headstand, her shapely legs spread wide apart, and then again together, pedaling through the air, faster and faster, peddling her charm. "Do you and Ruthie like riding bicycles, Theresa?" came the muffled voice beneath the umbrella of material. Grass stained, pink panties clung sensually to Mother's loins; leg muscles pumped away a mile a minute.

"What did you say?"

"I said, do you and Ruthie like riding bicycles?"

"Yes, and you look like a funny kind of parachute."

"A parachute, you say?"

"Yes, and I have a brand new bike at home."

"Well, did you ever ride one upside down?"

"No," Theresa laughed hysterically, as though a million squirmy worm-like fingers were tickling her to death.

"It's easy. See? Would you and Ruthie like to come for a ride with me?"

Theresa Martinez suddenly stopped laughing, her expression turning rather cold.

"I can't hear you, Theresa. Does that mean you two don't want to go for a ride with me?"

"A bad man took me and Ruthie for a ride," Theresa said quietly. "And the bad man put his pee-pee thing up Ruthie's *dupa* in the car."

Mother came to her senses, settling back down to earth, straightening her dress and fixing her hair. "Oh, I'm so sorry, Theresa. I didn't mean to—"

"When I came home, Mommy saw bloodstains on Ruthie's panties and took us to see the doctor. The doctor said that Ruthie had been raped. He asked me and Ruthie a lot of questions before he called

169

the policeman. Ruthie told Mommy and the doctor that some of the things the man did felt nice, except when he pushed his pee-pee thing into Ruthie's *dupa*. Ruthie wiggled to get away, but he was very, very heavy on her back. 'Please. Please. Please,' Ruthie cried. 'Do the other thing, not that.' That's when Mommy slapped Ruthie again and again until the doctor made her stop. When we got home, and after the policeman and a policewoman were gone and everything, Mommy told Ruthie she was sorry, just like the man said in the car. The man told Ruthie he was sorry that he hurt her, and that he was very sick. Ruthie asked him if he had a stomachache. Then the man began to cry, just like Mommy did. It was very strange. I never saw a grown-up man cry before. And then my daddy cried that night when he got home from work. He didn't make the sounds like crying, but the tears were falling down his face—like yours are now," Theresa said, falling forward into Mother's lap and sobbing softly, too.

Mother sat there with Theresa for a long time, gently stroking her hair, caressing the top of her head, patting her shoulder gently as the girl continued crying.

"Shh," Mother whispered soothingly. "Shh. Let me tell you a little secret," Mother said after a while. "Of course, you have to promise not to tell a soul."

Theresa nodded her head, still buried in Mother's lap. "I promise."

"When I was a little girl, maybe a little bit older than you, my daddy came into my room one night. I shared a room with one of my younger sisters then. She was fast asleep. Daddy was standing there in the doorway with a towel wrapped around his waist, fresh out of the shower. Then he invited himself into the darkness and touched me in a very private place." Mother had a faraway look in her eyes. "He told me something I'll never, ever forget. He told me I was the prettiest of all his daughters. He told me that I was something special. Me! Special. Can you imagine that? Then he put my little hand around his hardness and placed a finger in my mouth. In and out of my mouth he ran it. I felt his hardness throb. We did many things there in the darkness. Secrets of the darkest kind. And this went on for quite some time, until one night my sister Helen awoke to a rather upsetting scene. But I convinced her it was nothing but a dream. A rather unpleasant dream. That morning, and from that day forward, nothing was ever said. And Daddy never came into my room again.

"At first, all kinds of things went through my head. I remember running to the church for some kind of an answer, but I didn't know how to put the question. I almost went to Mother for help, but then wondered what the problem really was. Suddenly, I realized, all by myself, that I was a woman! A woman trapped in a child's body. But a woman nonetheless. And that's what you are, my dear Theresa. A woman. A little lady. A pretty little lady with a lovely name. A child with all the charms and loveliness of a mature woman who draws men to her like a pretty flower attracts the honeybee. A curse you carry with you, and one with which a billion foolish women wish they could be blessed. For the grass always seems greener in some other meadow, sweet Theresa. Boys will be bothersome, and men will flock to you like senseless sheep. But you will learn to somersault away until that very special day. The day you truly fall in love. It took me all these years to realize that I have a very special man."

"Is he handsome?"

"Well, you tell me."

"How can I do that? First I'd have to see him."

"But you already have."

"I have? You mean I know him?"

"Indeed you do. His name is Dr. David King."

Theresa raised her head from Mother's lap. "Do you mean Ruthie's mind doctor?" the girl gasped.

"I do."

"Oh, he's a nice man. Mommy told me that Ruthie should tell him everything—except the part about the nice feelings. Only I've told you so much more."

"That's because they're secrets, and secrets are only shared between two very special friends."

"Are you going to ever tell Dr. King what I told you? I mean about the part of some of the things feeling nice. Mommy made Ruthie promise not to tell that part. Everything else but that."

"Cross my heart and hope to die if I should ever tell a soul."

"Do you really and truly and positively love him?" Theresa asked, rolling over on her back with her head back in Mother's lap, pairs of doll-like eyes fixed upon each other.

"I really and truly and positively do."

"What's love like?"

"Well, it's a feeling inside that makes a mockery of words; in other words," Mother said sadly, "you can't explain it so that it can be truly understood. It's something wonderful that you feel inside, and that feeling is written upon your face for all the world to see."

"Then how come you look so sad right now?"

There was a pause. "Hum?"

"I said, how come you look so sad right now?"

"Because my Dr. David King is dying."

"Dying?"

Unable to look at the little girl directly, Mother simply nodded her head, staring down at the doll instead.

"Why is he dying?"

"I'm afraid that's another secret. A nasty little secret both Sarah and David are trying to keep from me."

"I won't tell," the little girl assured her. "I promise."

"It's his heart."

"Is he old? Dr. King doesn't look that old."

"No, silly," Mother answered, forcing a little smile. "I told you how it took me many years before I finally realized that I had found that special someone. Dr. King fell in love with me when I was a patient here years ago. Just like you. Only I was quite a bit older than you, my dear. I think I broke his heart when I walked out of his life."

"But you're back now. Right? Doesn't he feel better now that you're back?"

"Broken hearts never really repair themselves, Theresa. They never quite heal the same."

"How do you know his heart hasn't healed?"

"Because Sarah keeps hiding his medicine from me. She's really quite clever about it, too. I think Dr. Bianco also knows. I can see it in his face. I never suspected a thing until I found a prescription bottle in the glove compartment of David's car. You see, I know the medicine because a very good friend of mine died from the same heart condition. I do believe that I broke his heart, too."

Theresa said nothing, holding her doll's hand, and then taking her newfound friend's.

"Want to hear another secret?" Mother asked.

"Sure."

"I always wanted a little girl just like you," Mother said, reaching for the doll's free hand to complete a circle—a closed circle. "I have a son. But I would have much preferred a little girl. Maybe you'll meet Richard one day."

Richard had seen and heard every word from within the flowery garden situated no more than twenty yards away. Slowly, he slithered through the fragrant bed upon his belly, like a serpent in the grass. He was barely breathing. Oh, he was destined to meet that little girl, all right.

Chapter 19

THE PICNIC

It was a pleasant morning, and the day would prove to be just perfect for what Richard had in mind. It was the day of the Foundation's twenty-fourth annual Fourth of July picnic celebration. Richard stared up at the red, white, and blue banner strung high above the entrance gate.

Carl Gustafson was busy setting out several large trash containers for the occasion when he looked up and saw pretty dark-haired Theresa Martinez coming out of C Building. The young girl strolled along the garden path, holding her doll guardedly by its little hand. Carl gave Theresa a friendly greeting as she passed, bidding her good morning.

Theresa practically froze in mid step, clutching her doll protectively as a mother would a frightened child. "Come along, Ruthie," she insisted. "You must listen to Mother and never talk to strangers. Never ever let them take you for a ride. If they offer you sweets, you run away and hide." She moved cautiously aside, cutting across the path.

"And here's a banana for your monkey," Carl hollered, pulling suggestively at his crotch. "YOU LITTLE TWIT!"

Paul Johnson, black as a bull and built like a linebacker, muscles bulging beneath his short sleeved khaki shirt, marched immediately over to the caretaker. "Good morning, Carl. What seems to be the trouble?" the attendant inquired.

"Trouble? What trouble? Where do you think we are, River City?"

"Yeah, sure is a great day for a picnic," Paul said with a smile. "It's supposed to be in the eighties this afternoon. You like volleyball? Maybe you could help me set up the net later on."

"Just what we need around here. A social director."

"Party pooper," Paul replied with a pout.

"How about pooping this?" Carl suggested, bending over and grabbing the seat of his dusty pants, flatulating loudly.

"Hey, do you know that Dr. King is driving up to Boston today?"

Paul asked, changing the subject and ignoring Carl's behavior, which would surely lead to a confrontation if pursued. "That's my old hometown," the attendant stated pleasantly. "Ever been in Boston, Carl? You'd like it. It's a beautiful city. Know what they've got there?"

"*Ja.* Boston blackie and baked beans," Carl remarked sarcastically. "Ever been to its municipal zoo? Gorillas there look just like you."

The attendant glared at Carl menacingly. "How would you like to spend the afternoon sitting in your room instead of enjoying the picnic? It could be arranged, you know."

"The only thing you could arrange, ding-a-ling," Carl retorted, stepping forward and ringing an imaginary bell near the man's ear, "is to have my bags brought down here at once! This isn't the only rest home in the area," he declared, storming off in a huff.

"Morning, Paul," Dr. Bianco called, walking over to the attendant. "Carl getting your goat?" the psychiatrist asked amusedly.

"Ah, you know Carl."

"Know him? If I knew him, maybe I'd be able to help him. Thank God he's Dr. Schwartz's headache," he offered candidly, turning toward movement near the end of a hedgerow. "Richard! Well, you're certainly looking fit this morning" he said cheerfully. "What can we do for you?"

"Good morning, sir," Richard said courteously, stepping around the bush. "Nurse Marlow said I should let you know that I'm on my way up to Dr. King's house to give Sarah a hand getting things ready for the picnic."

"All right. But I'd like to see you here this afternoon enjoying yourself, too. We're going to have one hell of a barbecue."

"And lots of games," the attendant added. "Do you like games, Richard?"

"Yes, sir!"

"And tonight, we're going to have a fireworks display. That's something you really wouldn't want to miss," the psychiatrist assured him.

"No, sir."

"Well, go ahead then. Say hello to your mother and Sarah for me. I'll see you at the picnic later on."

"Thank you, sir," Richard said politely, disappearing back

behind the thick covering.

Dr. Bianco shook his head uncomfortably. "I think Dr. King is going to have his hands full with that one."

"Seems like he's coming around, though. Sometimes all they need is time."

"I don't know, Paul. This whole business gives me an uneasy feeling."

Both men looked up to see a procession of trucks and other heavy equipment moving along the south wall toward the building site. Concrete mixers with their huge revolving drums rolled noisily into the area. One behind the other. Teams of men were everywhere, setting up chutes and directing the machinery over to an assemblage of boards that formed a giant wooden structure.

"Looks like they're finally getting ready to pour the foundation today, Doctor," the attendant commented. "I'm surprised they're working on the Fourth."

"Dr. King's been after them for weeks to get this project off the ground. They were supposed to have started in June, but it's just been one delay after another. He had hoped to have all the buildings completed and fully occupied by the end of fall. We'll be lucky if they finish by next summer."

"Seems like things are going to be pretty hectic around here today."

"Yes, we'll have to be sure to keep everyone away from that area. We don't need anyone wandering off and getting hurt. I think we should move some of those benches a little closer to the pond."

"Well, not too close," Paul said and laughed. "You remember last year? Mrs. Zammitti insisted there were ducks in there and went wading in after them."

"Silly goose."

Richard moved along the hedgerow. In the distance, he saw the Martinez girl strolling carefree along the gardens with doll in hand. Suddenly, a mangy mongrel lit across the grounds, startling the little girl. It ran past Richard, making a beeline toward A Building, its crazed eyes blazing with alertness, its cropped ears folded flat against its head.

By noontime it was hot. Extra tables and benches had been placed in shady spots across the grounds, and patients were filing out of the buildings one by one.

Young Tommy Molsen, a rather obese lad with a disproportioned head and body, stood on the tips of his toes atop a picnic table set beneath an apple tree. With hands clasped behind his back, neck outstretched, Tommy devoured the unripened fruit from a leafy branch as though he were engaged in some sort of inverted bobbing-for-apples contest. He ate voraciously, taking gigantic bites but being extremely careful not to pull the green fruit from its stem. In no time flat, scores of apple cores hung above his oversized head like tiny skulls. As he ate, he watched a group of children setting off fireworks in the park across the way.

Carl and Mrs. O'Brian were making a futile attempt at burying their differences by trying to communicate with one another for the first time in many years, arguing their points of view concerning art and life.

"But art lives on forever," Carl insisted.

Mrs. O'Brian shook her head defiantly while humming the theme song from *Cabaret* with a forefinger finger planted firmly in each ear.

At the base of a flagpole, an elderly tattooed man wearing slippers and a sleeveless shirt stood with his head craned back, saluting and singing *Stars and Stripes Forever.*

Althea was opening packages of hamburger and hot dog rolls when she looked up and saw Sarah coming down the path. The young woman waved excitedly. Sarah smiled and nodded anxiously, her slender arms wrapped around a huge bowl of salad.

Mrs. Ackerman paraded past the gardens in a flowery red dress, wearing her long and lovely hair down in public for the very first time. She trailed a large plastic garbage bag, policing the area around several of the tables. Althea eyed the bag suspiciously, watching the woman's every move.

"Ah, Mrs. Ackerman. It is a fine day. Vouldn't you agree?" Mr. Schimmel asked in earnest, smiling and inflating his chest, thumbs tucked snugly within the pockets of his paisley vest, fingers fanned across its breadth. Proudly lifting the silver timepiece by its chain, he opened its cover with a thumbnail, consulting the timeless face. "Ve have a mission," he mumbled more to himself, walking back and forth along the garden path.

Mrs. Zammitti stood near the north gate, preoccupied with the endless flow of traffic moving steadily back and forth along the busy boulevard. Her attention shifted to a resounding click of the traffic signal hung above the avenue. The light turned to amber, and the world just outside the iron gate wound down. Red. Everything stopped. Suddenly, a car shot from out of nowhere. There was the screeching of brakes followed by a crash. Mr. Wyszynski went wild and had to be brought inside A Building. Mrs. Zammitti looked around in confusion before going up to the gate for a closer look, witnessing two middle-aged men scrambling frantically around their damaged cars, screaming and cursing at one another outrageously. Songbirds hopped frantically from branch to branch high above her. The light turned green. Horns blared, motorists shouted, and the two men shoved each other fiercely. Mrs. Zammitti's attention was diverted by the flutter of small birds fleeing the treetops.

Mrs. O'Brian hurried over to the gate and raised her arms as though she were about to conduct a symphony orchestra, pinwheeling them excitedly as the two men flailed their fists, hitting each other furiously about the head and shoulders. The smaller man fell to the ground while the other stood over him, kicking the cowering form mercilessly. Mrs. O'Brian swung her arms and kicked her legs erratically. Tommy Molsen laughed hysterically, tears streaming down his flaccid cheeks as he thumped a heavy leg upon the table beneath an umbrella of tiny, tanning apple cores.

"All right now; let's all move back away from here and not concern ourselves with what's going on out there," Dr. Bianco instructed. "Come on, Tommy. Off that table before you break it . . . you fat fuck," he mumbled the latter beneath his breath. "Let's go. You're going to get sick eating all those goddamn apples . . . asshole," he added in *sotto voce*.

"Ah, Dr. Bianco. It is a fine day. Vouldn't you agree?" Mr. Schimmel remarked, anxiously winding his timepiece as he hurried over to greet the psychiatrist.

"Yes, I certainly would agree, Mr. Schimmel. So why don't we all go on back and enjoy the picnic. Sarah and Althea have lots of hot dogs and hamburgers ready."

"Burger! Burger!" the corpulent youth responded excitedly, climbing off the table and waddling across the grounds toward the barbecue area.

Sarah was busy cooking before a large stone barbecue while Althea helped Mrs. Alvarez with a green salad and beverage.

"Burger, burger," Tommy panted, tugging impatiently on Sarah's sleeve.

"Here you go, Tommy," Sarah said, putting a hamburger and bun into the boy's hand.

"Burger," the boy pleaded, holding out his other hand.

"Ah, hee, hee, hee. You certainly are a hungry devil." Sarah handed him another. "And when you's all through with that, you come on back for some of Sarah's potato salad and a nice cup of lemonade. Ya hear?"

Tommy smiled and nodded anxiously, taking gigantic bites from each fist before waddling off to find himself another shady spot.

"Who's next here?" Sarah called out, turning over several hamburgers with a long spatula, maneuvering away from the wavering white smoke.

"Sarah, may I please have two hot dogs?" Mrs. Alvarez asked politely. "One for me, and one for my good friend Mrs. Ackerman, over there," she said, gesturing toward the woman sitting at a nearby table with her bag of garbage.

"Two hot dogs comin' right up," Sarah said enthusiastically, reaching for a set of napkins and paper plates. "Gotta have some of Sarah's potato salad, too," she insisted.

Mrs. Alvarez downed her beverage then carried over the plates of food, sitting next to her friend. "Here you are, Lillian."

Mrs. Ackerman grabbed the hot dog, discarding the roll into the bag of garbage. Gripping the steaming frankfurter in one hand, she lifted her dress high and slid the wiener firmly between her legs.

Mrs. Alvarez giggled.

"That's not very nice what you're doing, Mrs. Ackerman," Dr. Bianco scolded, pulling her hand away and straightening the woman's dress. "If you can't behave yourself, you'll have to go back inside," he warned.

"Oh, leave her be, Doctor," Mrs. O'Brian insisted. "Can't you see that she's finally let her hair down? Or haven't you bothered to notice? Men! I'll just bet if that were your hot dog she was holding, you'd be singing a different tune."

Mrs. Alvarez and several other women seated at the table chorused in agreement.

"Mrs. O'Brian, would you please mind your own business and see if you can give Sarah and Althea a hand?" the psychiatrist suggested, losing patience rapidly.

"Why, I should say not! I am a guest here. Not a handmaiden."

"Mrs. O'Brian, please try and cooperate."

Mrs. O'Brian shook her head of silvery hair. Taking a deep breath and closing her eyes tightly, she plunged an index finger into each ear, humming quite loudly. "HUMMMMMMMMMMMMMMMM—MEN!"

"Dr. Bianco, I vould like a vord vith you," Mr. Schimmel insisted, practically standing on the psychiatrist's heels.

"What is it now, Mr. Schimmel?"

"I vould like a verd vith you concerning that Nazi you have verking in the garden."

Dr. Bianco noticed several of the staff converging in front of C Building. He saw Nurse Marlow waving to him urgently. "You'll have to excuse me a moment," he interrupted, hurrying off in her direction.

"Don't you be abrupt with me, Doctor," Mr. Schimmel said excitedly, wringing his hands together. "That's not the vay you're supposed to act," he hollered. "You help me. I help you. Von hand vashes the other and both hands vash the face. My own brother. You know vhat he tried to do to me. Said that I vas all vashed up. That I vas finished. *Kaput*. That's a brother? A partner? He thought he vould take everything away from me. Still, I advised him during the last years of his life vhile he made a shambles of the business—running around vith some *shiksa* from Hoboken, New Jersey. How does anyvon meet anyvon from Hoboken, New Jersey? Hey, vhere do you think you're going? Ve have a mission. People listen to me. Even the *goyim*. I vas an influential man out there. I vas president of the temple. I vill get all the patients together and vote you the hell out of here, Mr. Big Shot Doctor. Charlatan! QUVACK-QUVACK," he shouted, flapping his arms at his sides like a lame duck.

Mrs. Zammitti looked around in confusion then went running off in the direction of the pond with several nurses and attendants chasing after her. "QUACK. QUACK," she cried, leaping feet first off the grassy embankment and hitting the lily padded surface with a splash, surfacing immediately with both arms beating the water wildly as if desperately trying to demonstrate the very principles of lift and thrust.

"MAYDAY! MAYDAY!" the tattooed man shouted, kicking off his slippers and wrestling with his top.

"Come on now, Mrs. Zammitti," Paul Johnson coaxed, running into the water and helping the heavyset woman from the shallow pond. "You are not a duck, and there are no ducks in here. See? Nurse Connors here will show you some ducks in the magazine after we get you changed. All right?"

"Is she okay?" the old man asked excitedly, still struggling with his top.

"Keep your shirt on, gramps," Paul heeded with a good-natured smile while leading Mrs. Zammitti back to one of the benches.

"Paulie."

"Yes, Mrs. Zammitti."

"Why are there-a-no ducks in-a the pond?" the woman asked as the attendant helped her over to a bench.

"Oh, I imagine for the same reason that there are no door knobs above the first floor," he explained. "They just don't belong there."

"Oh."

"I'll take her back to her room in a minute, Paul," Nurse Connors said, sitting down beside the soaking-wet woman. "Well, Mrs. Zammitti. What have you got to say for yourself? Hum? Enjoy your swim, dear?" the no-nonsense, freckled young woman asked.

Mrs. Zammitti looked at Nurse Connors with annoyance. "I punch-a you face," she said, making a tight fist under the nurse's chin.

"Now, now, Mrs. Zammitti," Paul said firmly. "You promised Nurse Connors and me that you were going to be good."

"I did?"

"You certainly did," he insisted.

Mrs. Zammitti looked around dumbfounded. "I be good, Paulie," she promised, making the sign of the cross across her drenched blouse, divulging rather large and well-defined breasts. "Honest Injun. I no punch-a nursey's face," she scowled, casting a rather grotesque expression that quite belied any assurances whatsoever.

"That very good, Mrs. Zammitti," Paul said with satisfaction, taking leave as the nurse took charge, the attendant's soggy shoes suddenly making funny squeaking noises as he strode away.

Mrs. Zammitti stared down at the ground in horror. "OH MY GOD!"

"What's the matter now, Mrs. Zammitti? What are you doing?" Nurse Connors asked alarmingly, unable to stop the frightened woman from climbing up onto the narrow, wooden bench.

"Mice in-a the meadow," she shrieked, pointing toward the ground near Paul Johnson's feet.

"There are no mice in the meadow, Mrs. Zammitti. Now please get down from there."

"You no tell-a-the truth!" the woman categorically decided, trembling while smashing the flat part of a fist firmly against the palm of her hand. "You lying-a-rat-a fink. Get away from me before I smash-a-you furry face with-a-my bare hands," she threatened.

"But they're all gone now," Nurse Connors insisted, gesturing for Paul to pick up his stride. "Paulie's frightening them away. Listen."

Mrs. Zammitti listened intently to the squeaky sounds fading in the distance as the attendant continued heading toward the barbecue area.

"You see, they're all gone. Paulie's chasing them far, far away from here, and they'll never be back again," she swore. "Come on now. We'll go back upstairs and change, and then I'll show you some ducks in the magazine."

"Promise?"

"Honest Injun," Nurse Connors assured her with a winning smile.

"Cross your heart?"

"Cross my heart," she said, running a finger down and across her chest.

"And hope to die?"

"And hope to die."

Mrs. Zammitti climbed down from the bench with the nurse's assistance.

Richard arrived on the scene pushing a wheelbarrow containing a cooler filled with marinated chicken and ribs that Sarah had been busy preparing for days.

"Oh, here come Richard with the good stuff," Sarah announced, grinning from ear to ear. "He help ol' Sarah in the kitchen this mornin'. He's a fine young man, you know," she told Althea and Paul.

"Yes, siree. A fine young man."

"Sarah," Richard spoke, lifting the cooler out and onto a picnic table. "Dr. King would like to see us both before he leaves."

"You go ahead, Sarah," Paul insisted, removing his shoes, pulling off and wringing out his socks. "I'll take care of things here."

Mr. Schimmel stepped forward. "Ah, Richard, my boy," he greeted. "It is a fine day. Vouldn't you agree?"

Richard smiled amicably. "Oh, it's more than that, sir. It's a glorious day," he replied. "A new beginning, you might say."

Yes. Yes, it is indeed!" Mr. Schimmel agreed. "Tell me, is Dr. King at home?"

"Yes, he is."

"Good. I vould like to have a verd vith him."

"Excuse me, Mr. Schimmel," Paul interrupted. "Dr. King is very busy right now getting ready for a business trip. Couldn't it wait until after he gets back?"

"VAIT? VE CAN VAIT NO LONGER. VE HAVE A MISSION. VE MUST ACT AT VONCE!"

"I was only suggesting—"

"Are you avare, my good man, of Dr. King's open door policy? The rules clearly state that if a patient has a grievance, or simply vishes to chat, he need only—"

"All right, all right," the attendant surrendered, good-naturedly. "Sarah, Mr. Schimmel here is looking for an audience," he expressed with a wink and a smile. "Would you and Richard be so kind as to escort this fine gentleman up to the house?"

"Why certainly," Sarah agreed. "It would be our pleasure. Come along, Mr. Schimmel."

"Thank you, my good man," Mr. Schimmel declared haughtily, calling out and waving as if signaling for a taxi before climbing into the wheelbarrow to everyone's surprise. "I vill put a good verd in for your people, Mr. Johnson."

"That would be terrific," Paul replied, staring curiously toward the group of doctors, nurses, and other attendants assembling in front of C Building as Richard wheeled Mr. Schimmel away.

Mr. Schimmel craned his neck and addressed Richard. "Dr. King's residence, please," he instructed. "And step on it. Ve have a mission, my good man."

"Yes, sir."

Mr. Abraham Schimmel sat with Dr. King on the back patio. The little man finished a full glass of iced tea in several gulps, setting the glass down firmly upon the table before him. "I vill come right to the point, Doctor. I vant to know vhy it is that you have that Nazi verking for you in the garden," he asked excitedly, "vhen I'm sure ve could find for you a nice colored boy through the YMCA?"

Dr. King smiled and explained to Mr. Schimmel for the hundredth time that Carl was not a Nazi, reminding him of the fact that the man was Swedish, and an American war hero to boot. "Carl fought against the Germans in both World Wars, Abe. And almost lost his life."

But Mr. Schimmel dismissed the notion altogether. "Too many people forget the past so easily. No von must ever forget," he vowed. "For if ve forget the past, ve allow for the past to repeat itself. Ve must never ever forget the past."

Dr. King agreed that the past must never be forgotten. "But by the same token, Abe, you have got to realize that we are living in the present. The world goes on, my friend."

"No! The verld goes around, Doctor," Schimmel argued, orbiting a finger through the air. "Listen to me," Mr. Schimmel insisted. "I didn't vant to bring it up, but being ve are on the subject anyvays, I vill tll you vhat a real *meshumod* he really is. Yesterday, he comes into my library. So I say to him, 'Good morning, Mr. Gustafson. It is a fine day. Vouldn't you agree?' You know vhat he says to me? 'Jew really think so, Mr. Schimmel?' having me believe he substitutes his Y's for J's. You understand vhat I'm saying, Doctor? 'You are a Jew, Mr. Schimmel' is vhat he vas saying to my face. Believe me vhen I tell you a *meshumod*. You don't believe me? Vell, do not take my verd for it. Ask Wyszynski. Alvays with the ethnic jokes about Polacks and Jews. And you should see the vay that Nazi looks at the vomen."

"How is that?" Dr. King asked with mild amusement.

Mr. Schimmel dismissed the question with a wave of his hand. "Ah, don't ask."

Dr. King smiled, setting down his glass and glancing at his watch.

"And I vill tell you something else," Schimmel continued

excitedly. "The books he reads. Books. Such books you vouldn't believe. *Communist Manifesto, Das Kapital, Mein Kampf. MEIN KAMPF!* Vould you believe? Vell, it vasn't on the shelf, so he vants to know vhere the hell it is." Mr. Schimmel pulled his chair closer to Dr. King's, lowering his voice to a near whisper. "I don't mind telling you that I von't keep it on the shelf. I don't even vant it in the same room vith me, but I have no choice. So I keep it on the vagon buried beneath the returns. Then he vants to know who checked it out? Vhen it vould be back? Vould I reserve it for him? I tell him I am a very busy man. Do you know he vent through every vagon until he found it. Then he tells me I should have more than von copy around!"

"Abe, listen to me," Dr. King implored. "Carl reads everything he can get his hands on. He borrows what—three hundred books a year? Yes? You don't want people to forget the past. Isn't that what you said a moment ago? Those books are an important part of the past. They are there as documents for people to read and remember. Abe. Look at me," Dr. King tried to reason. "Carl attends to the grounds during the day, then goes to his room and reads. He wants to read. He wants to garden. How can he hurt anyone?"

"HOW? I'll tell you how," Schimmel stated gravely. "By sowing seeds of hatred. That's how. Hitler had a garden high in the Alps before he started planting Jews across Europe. I VAS THERE!" he shouted angrily, pulling up his sleeve and pointing to the faded, vein-colored numbers scored along his forearm. "I VAS THERE. SEE?"

Dr. King saw all right. He saw into the mind and memory of a man consumed by fear and hatred. He saw, by God, into the very soul of the living dead, haunted by the dread of anything so horrible ever happening again. Dr. King looked down at the bony arm then took the man's trembling hand in his steady grip, nodding understandingly.

Sarah stepped out onto the patio and refilled Mr. Schimmel's glass. "Here you go, Mr. Schimmel."

"Ah, thank you, Sarah," Schimmel said, gulping down the icy beverage. "You are a fine woman, and a credit your race."

"And you, sir, are a real gentleman. And *you*," she said, scolding Dr. King, "bes' be gettin' yo'self in high gear, 'less you wanna be late for that convention. Hear?"

"I hear something," Dr. King replied with a grin.

Sarah looked over at Richard who was busy reading at a table in the corner. "Com'on over here and say good-bye to Dr. King, young man."

Richard came over carrying the book.

"Vhat are you reading, my boy?" Mr. Schimmel questioned.

"*The Little Prince*, sir."

"Ah, Saint-Exupéry. A children's classic for children six to sixty," he declared, "and von of my favorites. You see, Doctor? A story vich concerns itself with duty, love, and humanism. Not ideas of destruction. Vill you answer for me a question, Richard? Who's your favorite author?"

"I have more than one, sir."

"So name me more than von."

"Steinbeck and Twain, sir."

"You see the difference, Doctor King? Books vith concerns for the downtrodden and the oppressed; not obsessions vith vorld domination or the destruction of Jews. Books vith vit and humor. Books that help us make some sense out of the growing madness in this vorld," he stated solemnly. "You ever read Sholom Aleichem, Richard?"

"No, sir."

"I asked Mrs. O'Brian the same question. You know vhat she says to me? 'Who wrote it?' You know vhat I said to her? 'Harold Robbins.'"

Dr. King laughed heartily. "Listen, Abe. We'll talk some more when I get back, all right?"

Mr. Schimmel stood up. "Before you go, Doctor, I vould like to give you von last vord of advice. You could put a *schvartze* in the garden for half the trouble of that Johnny Appleseed. Vhen you get back, you see Wyszynski. VE HAVE A MISSION. VE MUST PUT A *SCHVARTZE* IN THE GARDEN!"

Sarah was busy watering flowers along the patio when she looked up and heard what could only be Dr. King's limousine racing up the drive. "I guess Miss Vicki and that cowboy's finally back from town," she announced, stepping off the patio and walking around toward the front of the house.

"Tell Max I'll be there in a minute," Dr. King called after her. He turned to Richard. "Go ahead, son," he said, getting up and placing a hand upon the young man's shoulder. "Tell your mother I'll be right there. I just want to say good-bye to Mr. Schimmel. Then you and Sarah can escort him back to the barbecue."

Richard went around to the front of the house but suddenly stopped short when he saw Sarah standing at the edge of the driveway with her hands cupped over her mouth, watching as Max lifted a naked form off the front seat, its small breasts pointing toward the sky.

"What in tarnation!" Sarah exclaimed.

"It's a mannequin," Mother explained, seeing Sarah's surprise. "You should have seen the people on the boulevard gawking at us," she said through a girlish giggle. "Max insisted on sitting her up in the front seat with him. I swear I never laughed so hard in all my life. But I'm afraid we caused a little accident back there. Nothing serious, I'm sure. The car alongside of us ran a red light and hit another. Then two men got out and started fighting, so I guess they're all right. But don't tell David," she whispered. "He has enough on his mind right now. Anyway, Max and I stopped by the post office to pick up stamps for the wedding invitations, neither of us realizing that it was closed for the holiday. I tell you, Sarah, I'm just so excited that I can hardly keep my mind together. Oh, and we brought back more ice and soda for the picnic. That's when I saw the mannequin in the store across the street. This gorgeous man was closing up his shop for the holiday when I told him I just had to have it. And before he even had a chance to think," she paused and giggled, "Max was dancing with it in the street. I'm telling you, I almost died."

Max averted Sarah's eyes, leaning the mannequin against the limousine before going around and opening the trunk filled with packages and paraphernalia.

"See, like a big doll," Mother beamed, posing beside the life-size figure. "Isn't she marvelous?"

Sarah marveled at the naked form propped against the car. "Jus' as skinny as you, fo' sure. What's you gonna do with her, Miss Vicki?"

"Why, she's going to help the two of us fashion the most exquisite wedding gown you've ever seen, Sarah! Of course, we'll have to use a dressmaker's form, but I have this revelation. And wait till you see what else we bought. Come, I *must* show you this fabric," she prattled like a happy child.

Max removed one of the bolts of material from the trunk.

"You put Miss Vicki's material in the trunk along with ice and soda?" Sarah screeched in disbelief.

"Oh, Sarah. Max was very, very careful. So please don't fret. Now, Max, if you'll just hold this here—like so. Good. And follow me over to my new companion," she instructed happily, peeling off yards of exquisite embroidered cotton. "Let's see, now. If you would just step back some, Sarah. Just a bit." Sarah stepped back carefully. "Yes, right there. The whole idea is to see oneself the way others do," Mother explained, draping the white transparent fabric over the naked form. "Well, what do you think?"

"I think you'll make a lovely bride, Mother," Richard announced, stepping forward and giving her a peck upon the cheek.

"Oh, Richard darling. You just made your mother's day." She turned as Dr. King came out from the front of the house. "Ah, there you are, David." She walked over and gave her man a great big hug and kiss. "I'm so glad I got back before you had to leave. I'm really sorry that we ran a little late, but Max and I got so involved as you can see," she began explaining, laughing at the chauffeur posing in his summery suit and shiny shoes, standing there rigidly with his arm around the mannequin's waist.

"What's all this?' Dr. King remarked.

Sarah went over and directed Dr. King back inside the house, insisting that it was bad luck for the groom to see the bride in her gown, even if it was a dummy clad in partial fabric and the wedding was still many weeks away. She told Max to bring down Dr. King's bags and to pull the other car around while she and Mother brought the mannequin and material inside the house and out of sight.

At the last moment, Dr. King decided to take his set of golf clubs on the trip. So Sarah sent Max to the basement to bring the cart while she waited at the head of the stairs. Max went over to the washer-dryer and started wheeling Sarah's laundry cart past the foot of the stairs and over to the set of Bilco doors.

Sarah hollered down in sheer frustration. "Not my laundry cart, you simpleton! Dr. King's golf cart, behind the stairs," she called, heading down the steps on old bowed legs.

"Then say what you mean. What you mean is a caddie-wheel pushcart—you old war-horse."

"I mean cart, moron. A caddy is someone who goes around with the golfer."

"But you didn't say anything about golf, old woman. Besides, a cart is what a golfer rides around on."

Sarah went around to the back of the stairs. "This is what I'm talking about, ninnyhammer," she carried on, rolling out the caddie cart and bag of clubs. "See? What do you think this is? A giant arrow quiver on wheels? How many times have you packed his clubs?"

But Max insisted that Dr. King does not use a caddie-wheel pushcart when he golfs. "Dr. King rides around the greens in style with his caddy. He doesn't push a cart, you old shrew."

Sarah sighed in exasperation. "That's when he golfs at *his* country club here on Long Island, chum for brains. But he's traveling up to Boston to play a different course. He needs the cart to carry his clubs from the trunk of his car to the clubhouse. He's drivin' hisself; he won't have you around to lend a helpin' hand. Get it?"

"All you had to do was say *cart* for golf clubs, ya old crow."

Sarah told Max that she had a mind to use those clubs on him. If looks could kill, the chauffeur would have been driven to hell and back and holed away in some godforsaken corner . . . perhaps in Sarah's old steamer trunk, Richard entertained, stored beneath and well-forward of the set of basement stairs . . . a large oak and tin Victorian dome top antique trunk containing secrets of the darkest kind. Secrets concealed for years beneath its padlocked cover. A cover strewn with dust and intricately webbed with the fine spun threads of time. A treasure-trove of mystical oils and ointments and powders along with books of spells and chants that no lock and key could seal forever.

Max carried out then wheeled the bag of irons past the limousine and over to a shiny silver Rolls Royce. Collapsing the wheels of the cart, he carefully placed the set of clubs in the trunk beside the expensive leather luggage. Dr. King slid behind the wheel and gave Sarah and Max some last minute instructions. He kissed Mother good-bye, then took and shook Richard's hand. Everyone smiled and waved and wished him a safe and pleasant trip as the car went down the drive. Sarah went back inside the house. Max went back to the limousine.

"Well, now," Mother rejoiced, holding Richard at arm's length. "Tell me. What do you think of Mother's doll?"

"Well, to tell you the truth, Mother dear, I think you're a little too old to be playing with dolls. Yes?"

Mother lowered her arms, stepping back from her son. "I don't

189

know, Richard. I just don't know anymore," she replied ambiguously, heading inside.

"Come on, Richard. Give me a helping hand," Max said, handing him one of the cases of soda from the trunk of the limo, grabbing a heavy cooler filled with ice. "Need plenty of ice and soda for the picnic. Not like last year. Last year we ran out early. Dr. King told me to load up this time. Of course, Sarah hollers whenever anyone drinks too much soda. But I like something with a little fizz. Guess that's why I like ol' Sarah," he said through a laugh.

Richard set the case down and grabbed another.

"Say. I have an idea!" Max remarked. "Let's go down to the basement, very quietly, and borrow Sarah's laundry cart to carry all this stuff. The two of us can pull together as a team. Be a lot easier than pushing everything down to the picnic in Carl's wheelbarrow like I generally do. This way, we'll make one trip instead of two. Certainly be a lot faster than my driving all the way down and back around the area because we'd still have to carry everything over from the parking lot once we got there. Got to use the old noggin," the chauffeur said, tapping a finger upon a balding head.

A few minutes later, Max and Richard ascended the basement through a set of Bilco doors. Together, they filled the laundry cart with the cooler of ice and cases of soda, alternately pushing or pulling it down a narrow asphalt path toward the picnic area before returning to the house.

Sarah was busy in the kitchen cutting up slices of watermelon when the phone rang. Wiping her hands on her apron, she picked up the receiver and answered cheerfully. Sarah's face grew troubled as she listened to the voice on the other end. A moment later, she hung up and hurried down the hallway to Mother's room.

"That was Dr. Bianco on the phone, Miss Vicki," Sarah said, standing just outside the bedroom door. "Theresa Martinez is missin'. They can't seem to find her anywhere," she added, turning and hurrying back along the hall.

"Missing? You mean my precious little friend?" Mother said excitedly, rushing to Sarah's side.

"Yes. I tell 'im I hadn't seen her around here this mornin'. Of course I was busy in the kitchen preparin' fo' the picnic like I been doin' fo' days."

"What about the gazebo? She likes to play there with her doll."

"They already checked there. But I'm gonna have me a look see jus' the same."

Mother looked around uneasily. "Wait, I'll come with you," she insisted, appearing quite upset.

"Maybe you bes' stay here, jus' in case the phone ring, Miss Vicki. I told Dr. Bianco that Dr. King already left fo' Boston, but that you was back from town. He say he don't want no one else comin' up to the house while Dr. King's away. Now, I gonna be right back," she said, heading out the rear of the house.

"Maybe I can see her from an upstairs window," Mother called aloud. She was halfway up the stairs when she thought she heard a child's voice coming from the study. She paused. "Theresa. Theresa, is that you?" Mother listened for a moment then came back down the staircase toward the room. She could hear voices coming from behind the partially open door. "Theresa?" The room fell silent. Mother placed her hand on the knob when suddenly the door flew open. "RICHARD! Oh, you gave me quite a start. I thought you were with Max. You know you shouldn't be in here alone."

"But I'm not alone, Mother," he assured her. "Come see," he coaxed, leading her happily by the hand.

Mother saw her mannequin lying face-up on the floor in the center of the room. She saw Sarah's tea service set with cups and saucers and little cakes all around the naked form. "Richard, what in God's name is going on in here?" she demanded.

"Why, we're having a tea party, you and I. Kind of a picnic all our own. And we're working things out like I agreed. Would you like to see? See, we're finally talking, you and me." Richard sat down beside the naked form, fondling its breasts. "First, I ask you a question, like, 'Would you like a cup of tea, Mother?' And then you say, 'Why thank you, Dicky,'" he answered, imitating his mother's voice flawlessly.

"Oh, my God!"

"But you must first rise to the occasion, although I see you're not inclined," he flared, jumping up and pulling the mannequin roughly off the floor, propping it upside-down between the cushions of a chair, its legs up in the air. "There. Now from here on in, we must weigh things very carefully," he stated calmly, picking up a box of graduated weights, placing several different sizes on one side of the apothecary scale. "Next, we must see how sweet you really are," Richard assured her with a slick, sick grin as he knelt before the low oak table, measuring out heaps of sugar from a silver bowl. "See?"

Mother saw the seesaw motion, watching the scale balance perfectly. "Richard, I'm going to call Dr. Bianco," she insisted, crossing over to the phone.

Richard stood immediately, taking a firm hold of Mother's arm. "I'm sorry, Mother, but I'm afraid Dr. Bianco is very busy at the moment."

"Let go of my arm, Richard. You're hurting me. How dare you start up with me like this. That Nazi-father of yours abused me, but I'll be goddamned if I'm going to let you start abusing me, too. You just remember that I'm still your mother. Your father never wanted you. All he ever wanted was his junk room. All he did was use me. Even my own goddamn sisters used me. Dr. King is the only man in the world who ever made me feel like a woman."

"What did you feel like at the ranch when I was wee? You see, I'm beginning to put things together very carefully. I'm beginning to get the whole picture," he said, leading her roughly by the arm across the room. "Of course, we must stand back and examine things in their proper perspective. You see, that's been my problem all along. I've been right on top of things."

"Richard, take the mannequin off that chair this minute."

"Why? Don't you want to see yourself as others do? The way that I remember you? Like the time we went away together to Dr. King's ranch house across the bay. I was only four, but all the hands there said that I made a fine young cowpoke. So I poked around the stable and found you with some hired hand. Every other day there was another man." Richard threw the mannequin to the floor.

"It was on a moonlit evening, Mother, when someone rode up to the ranch house, then came in and pranced around your room, asking if you wanted to go for a hayride and horse around a bit. I could hear the two of you laughing quietly. 'Not in here,' you said. So he swept you up and led you down the bridle path, the two of you trotting off together beneath the moon.

"So Dicky quickly dressed and strapped on his six-shooters, following the trail down to the corral behind the barn and beyond the bunkhouse for the hired hands. The sky was filled with stars, the moon all round and white. It was very clear that night. Lowering you to the ground, the man removed your skirt and spread your thighs. And what to your surprise! All those hands came forward. All those pairs of glaring eyes. Of course you fought courageously, whinnying in the hay, as Max took off your blouse, another man fondling your breasts." Richard fondled the breasts of the mannequin. "Then still a third, without a word, pulled your panties off and mounted you from behind, sending the other two away so that he alone could ride you bareback upon the hay." Richard turned the mannequin face down upon the floor and mounted it. "And as you swooned, the others formed a fucking line, laughing and joking with each other impatiently, enjoying you one at a time. And after everyone thought they were finished, you summoned forth the lot. But someone spotted little Dicky in the shadows.

"'Whoa there, partner! Don't worry about your mommy, son. She's fine. Having a good time,'" Richard panted, practically out of breath. "'You'll understand better when you grow up. Probably even forget all about this in time. Pay it no mind. Just pretend it's all a bad dream.'"

"It's all in your imagination, Richard. You had a nightmare. You always dreamed up things that weren't so. Don't you realize the effect you had on me? I can feel the strain right here in my heart," Mother said shivering.

"A weak heart but a strong back, Mother, to be sure."

"Oh, you're so very cruel to your poor mother. How you love to torment. I don't know why in hell I ever had you, Richard. You were difficult from the moment you were born. I thought my insides were being ripped out when they pulled you from me. You should have seen me before I had you. I was *really* something then. Men promised me the world. Only that Nazi never cared. He used me like everyone used me. I taught you everything, Richard. You were so far ahead of everyone in school. Now, I can't even talk to you."

"What would you like to talk about, Mother? Would you like to talk about that so-called father figure? Yes?"

"Your father gave up on you a long time ago. You never gave him a moment's peace. Not even during early retirement."

"That's really not true, Mother. Little Dicky was responsible for giving him a nice long rest. It was little Dicky who retired him to an early grave by telling him how sweet you had become. And we both know he wasn't my real father. Now don't we? Only we don't talk about those things. Do we, Mother dear? None of us really talked very much at all. To tell you the truth, I don't ever remember having a dialogue with him. It was either him telling me about electromagnetic induction, or me telling him about your escapades. Never an exchange of ideas."

"You were no son, Richard. Once he tried to talk to you like a real father, but you wouldn't let him near you."

"Why, I should say not, Mother. Not with the Limburger on his breath. The day after he died, you ran to the bank with Mr. Gladstone and cleared out the accounts, while I ran to the refrigerator and cleaned out that damned Limburger cheese, replacing it with Brie."

"Don't you realize that I did everything for you, Richard? That Nazi never wanted you. All he ever wanted was a free servant to do his dirty work. I never had a wedding, a honeymoon, or a vacation in all those years of so-called marriage. I even had to scrape together change from the food bill in order to take you places. He never took us anywhere. He just used me the way my sisters used me. Even that goddamn Nazi-family of his used me. Oh, I'll never forget them until the day I die," she swore, the tears welling up in the corners of her eyes. "You don't know wh-what that Nazi did to me while I was still ca-carrying you. He hit me in the face and th-threw me down two flights of stairs. DO YOU UNDERSTAND WHAT I'M SAYING, RICHARD? He hit me in the face and threw me down the goddamn stairs," she repeated, biting her hand viciously and pulling savagely at her face until it bled. "Your father ne-never ever wanted you. He already had one son of a bitch by his first wife. Never told me he was ma-married. Never. But one day I found a letter in his pocket along with an alimony check while I was ironing his fucking pants. Oh, he was so secretive, Richard. He even had a private post office box. All he did was use me to do his goddamn cooking, cleaning and ironing then drill a hole in my ass."

"Good, now we're getting somewhere. So let's talk about my real father," Richard insisted. "I never really knew about my real father until it was too late."

"You don't know what you're talking about, Richard. You're all mixed up. You were always a difficult child. You were like that all through school. I didn't have an easy life. You forget the times I ran down to that school to fight for you. They said that you were difficult, only I didn't believe them."

"Well, you know how mothers are," he said and snickered.

"Oh, you were so far ahead of everyone. I worked so hard with you. By the time you were five, you knew how to read and write and spell. I gave you quite a start. You had a chance to make something of yourself; instead, you threw your whole education out the window."

"Traveling is an education, Mother dear. And would you like to know what truths I have come to discover in my travels?"

"That Nazi never wanted you," she repeated, not knowing what else to say.

"I'm not talking about a NAZI, Mother. I'm talking about a JEW who was very good to you. I'm talking about a man who was very good with figures." Richard sneered, slipping his hands around his mother's waist. "I'm talking about an accountant by the name of Horatio Gladstone. A father figure, you figured. I'm talking about my real father. You see? Everything adds up. Or must I spell it out for you. I-L-L-E-G-I-T-I-M-A-T-E. A misbegotten soul."

"STOP IT!"

"CUCKOLD CUCKOLD," Richard crowed, beating his arms insanely about the room. "Coc-a-doodle-doo. Or any cock'll do, Mother dear?"

"STOP IT! YOU'RE MAD!" she shouted uncontrollably.

"Oh, indeed I am, Mother. You made me terribly mad. Remember how you pulled me by the hand and dragged me down the street. You didn't want me to hear what Aunt Helen had to say."

"It's all in your mind, Richard. You would always pretend. You always invented stories that weren't true. You always told such stories. Always."

"'YOU'RE A WHORE,' Auntie shouted. Only I couldn't find it in the dictionary under H when we got home."

"Ple-please stop it. You were just a child. How could—could you understand?" She wept bitterly, sinking to her knees. "Your Aunt Helen didn't know what she was talking about. She was all mixed up. She was always jealous of your mother. I was the prettiest of all the sisters. Me! My very own father told me so. They were all envious of me. Your Aunt Helen couldn't have any children. Do you understand? That Nazi never wanted you. He never wanted a child. He ne-never— Oh, you were so ahead of everyone."

"There you go shifting gears again, Mummy. Yes! You drove so very fast that day. And I kept repeating Auntie's words over and over to myself, trying to forget that we were traveling at a terrifying speed. We were traveling faster than the birds, Mummy. 'CUCKOLD CUCKOLD,' they screamed down at me."

"Richard, please stop this!" Mother demanded.

Richard crossed the room to the bay window and observed a flock of sea gulls scrambling for mollusks along the distant shore. Suddenly, the birds took to the air, soaring high into the heavens, one with a single shell secured firmly in its beak; then, like a bombardier, it released the tiny dark projectile with deadly accuracy upon the targeted rock below, the fragile shell exploding as the other hovering forms swooped in frantically, fighting viciously for the clammy flesh. Richard watched in fascination. Those phantoms of the sea. Ghostly aery bodies. Euphoric. Narcotic. Floating. Gliding. Soaring. Sailing. Swooping down in profuse strains of premeditated art.

Richard could see Sarah searching for the little Martinez girl along the bed of bright flowers near the gazebo. Brilliant bulbs exploded everywhere. Yellow and white narcissuses trumpeted their silence, accompanying a gentle breeze that danced the fleshy leaves of red, white, and blue hyacinths. From across the shallow pool, tulips tolled their toneless knell. In the distance, he could see the heavy machinery turning and churning, chuting endless batches of concrete into giant, vertical formwork molds. Construction had surely begun.

Richard watched Althea rummaging through cans of garbage, approaching the single rusty barrel standing beneath a giant shade tree along a vine laden green-leafed wall. Suddenly, the young woman froze. What she saw made her knees buckle and the pit of her stomach ache. Althea slowly sank to the ground, her mouth wide open, her screams barely audible above the turning and churning of distant drums, certainly unheard at all from within the air-conditioned home. Althea screamed and screamed until she could scream no more.

From all directions, Richard watched as Sarah and others hurried towards Althea. Teams of construction workers looked up from their jobs, staring at one another apprehensively.

". . . Richard, look at me when I'm talking to you," Mother insisted.

Richard turned away from the window and went over to a small closet near the door, throwing it open wide and taking down a plastic poncho from a shelf. He unfolded and pulled the full-length garment down over his body, poking his curly red head through the top of the cloak, throwing back the hood. "BOO!" he shouted insanely, giggling and giving Mother quite a scare. Then he whirled around the room, slapping the plastic wrinkles free. "There!" Richard stood as still as a statue, garbed in angry gray. Sea-green eyes blazed with alertness.

"Richard, what on earth? It's eighty degrees out there," she said, wiping the blood from her face then staring oddly at the back of her tooth-marked hand, saying anything that popped into her pretty head, any words that would alleviate her fright.

"Yes, Mother, but it's a cool sixty-two in here. That's how Dr. King likes it. Real cool. But it's going to warm up in just about a minute. Just you wait and see. It's going to get as hot as hell in here," he promised, crossing over to the center of the room beside the parquet table, sweeping up the statue of Hermes from the highly polished surface, surfacing a childish grin.

"Richard, pl-please put down that piece immediately and listen to me," she insisted, trying to overcome her fear. "Do you hear what I'm saying? What do you think you're doing? That's a very expensive —oh my God," she uttered and shivered, staring at the hatred in his eyes. "Please don't. Ple-please don't hurt me, Richard," she pleaded, cowering into a corner of the room.

"Oh, Richard's not going to hurt you, Mother," he assured her. "Dicky's just going to knock you from here to kingdom come," he declared, raising the heavy statue high above his head.

"PLEASE. DON'T DO THIS TO ME, DICKY," she screamed as he smashed her violently to the floor, repeatedly hammering and caving in her skull, over and over again, till he was sure she lay as still and silent as stone.

Several minutes later, Richard sat beside her on the floor then dipped the index finger of his right hand into the pool of warm blood, sketching two stick figures of a mother and child holding hands. "Dicky met a nice girl today, Mummy," he said in a child's voice. "She was so sweet. That's how I knew that she was really you, you see. I

197

mean when you were wee. She had her little doll with her. I tried to tell her it was really me, but she insisted that it was little Ruthie." Richard took one of the honey cakes that Sarah was saving for dessert, placing it firmly in Mother's mouth. "Shh. Honey cake to keep you quiet," he stated, slamming her jaw shut tight.

Chapter 20

THE BODY

Uniformed police and plainclothes detectives were busy everywhere. Running pretty yellow ribbons all around the murder scene. Measuring and marking distances along the ground. Scribbling notes. Snapping pictures from every conceivable angle. Several detectives scoured the corner of the viny green-leafed stone wall, one of them carefully examining the large rusty trash barrel. Others in uniform stood behind them, glaring down at the body stuffed within.

One of the detectives nodded, and two uniformed officers stepped forward, carefully lifting Theresa Martinez's naked body from the heap. Up and out she came, the child's doll rising with her, its little hand held securely in the dead girl's grip. The officers gently laid the body upon a plastic sheet. Cold white eyes stared blankly back at the solemn faces peering down. The macabre expression revealed but a part of the grisly tale as the police photographer moved in for several close-ups of a silver object gnashed between the young girl's teeth.

"All yours, Lieutenant Lark," the man with the camera said.

Everyone stepped aside as the stocky moon-faced man moved in. As if in prayer, the detective knelt beside the body, examining the child's face, pressing the tips of his fingers firmly against her cheeks, feeling along the lower jaw, palpating the neck, passing his hands across her trim torso, down then up along those skinny little legs and arms before removing the battered doll clutched within the tiny fist.

Another detective reached deep within the barrel and carefully removed articles of clothing belonging to the pretty dark-haired girl, depositing them into plastic evidence bags. He also noted a small claw-like garden tool with a bloody wooden handle; this, however, was handled by another detective donning a plastic glove.

Lieutenant Lark looked up. "Come here, Sergeant."

Detective Sergeant Grear went over and stooped awkwardly beside the stocky form. "Yes, sir?"

"Feel. Rigor mortis appears to be confined to the facial musculature and outer extremities," he said, directing the sergeant's hand to the child's face, fingers, wrists, and ankles. "All the smaller muscles," he explained. "Now, over here. Note the difference?"

The young detective compared the area of stiffness to the supple flesh of the young girl's torso, thighs, and calves. He nodded uncomfortably, taking back his hand as if it had no business being there at all.

"It's only an approximation, Sergeant, but I'd say the child's been dead some four to six hours, considering the temperature as well as the shaded area along the wall."

Lieutenant Lark took into consideration other variables, too, guesstimating the time of death, for the time being, to have occurred around 9 o'clock that morning, explaining to his charge just how undependable this aspect of forensic pathology to be, especially without the compilation and assimilation of all the facts. But the few facts they did have seemed to be falling neatly into place, for Theresa Martinez had been seen by several nurses and attendants at around 7 a.m. in C Building, then about a half hour later, heading across the grounds with her doll toward Dr. King's estate as reported by Paul Johnson and Dr. Bianco.

Lieutenant Lark carefully turned the body over.

The sergeant turned his head away from what he knew he'd see: the child's bloody buttocks apparently violated by the handle of the garden tool; the narrow rake marks along the small of her back, apparently made by the metal implement. "Bastard," the detective said as though he were about to puke.

"What's the matter Sergeant Grear? You wanted homicide. Remember?"

"She's just a kid," was all that the young detective could say.

"Oh, I see. Next time out, I'll just tell the captain to have you cover senior citizens. All right? Or I can have him hand you a checklist to fill out beforehand: Violent deaths or deaths by natural causes. You can check off male or female along with age preferences, too. Even choose the neighborhood you want. How's that?"

"Come on, Lieutenant. I'm not quite that thick-skinned, yet."

Lieutenant Lark smiled. "Well, I'll let you in on a little secret, Sergeant. Neither am I," he stated matter-of-factly. "I just hide it better is all. You get used to a lot of things out here. But never this. Not with children," he affirmed, turning the child back over and, with his handkerchief, carefully removing the silver object from her mouth. Finally, almost religiously, he closed her doll-like eyes forever.

"Looks like a film container, Lieutenant," Sergeant Grear remarked, staring down at the crumpled mess.

The lieutenant looked up in mild amusement. "That's very good, Sergeant," he replied, assuming a condescending tone. "It's one of the reasons I take you with me on these outings."

Sergeant Grear said nothing.

Lieutenant Lark reached inside his jacket pocket and took out a small plastic evidence bag and a scrimshaw pocket tool. Unfolding an awl-like instrument from its handle, he meticulously probed the punctured surface of the tiny tin, holding the item just inside the pouch, scraping and collecting any particles that fell, carefully examining the crystalized compound set in coagulated blood and saliva. Next, he brought the object to his nose, sniffing the contents like a bloodhound taking up the scent. Lark dropped the canister into the plastic pouch, sealed its top securely then handed over the evidence to the sergeant. "Have the lab check this out right away," he ordered, then ordered the body bagged.

It seemed as though everyone at once was giving and taking orders in a kind of organized chaos when suddenly Richard appeared from behind a hedgerow, wheeling Sarah's laundry cart across the grounds.

"Hey, where the hell did he come from?" a detective hollered, hurrying over toward the young man. A couple of uniformed officers followed suit. "What are you doing here?" the detective stated gravely.

"It's all right," Marvin Gitlin waved, running over to the group.

"And who the hell are you?" the detective demanded, glaring ominously at the attendant.

"Marvin Gitlin," Marvin stated, pointing to a plastic badge pinned to the pocket of his shirt. "I work in A Building," he answered out of breath, gesturing toward the complex. "This is Richard Geist. He's visiting his mother and has the director's permission to be up here at the house."

The detective looked suspiciously at Richard, stepping over to the cart. "What's all this?" he asked impatiently, poking through the articles of clothing.

"Hand-me-downs," Richard answered up. "Mother and I were

cleaning out her closets. These are just some things she won't be needing anymore. She thought perhaps some of the patients could make use of them."

The detective held up a clean, crisp cottony section of cloth, all neatly trimmed around the edges with the help of Mother's shiny new pinking shears.

"Old pajamas," Richard explained. "I cut some of them into rags as you can see. You see, Mother went from rags to riches practically overnight," he said with a wide grin, looking over at several police officers who were busy combing the grounds for a clue.

The detective glanced from Richard to Marvin, then dropped the material back into the canvas bin. "Listen, we have to keep everyone clear of this area. You'll have to take him around the construction site and back to his room," he instructed. "His visit's over for now."

Marvin nodded obediently. "Come on, Richard."

Richard looked around in bewilderment. "Marvin, where is everyone? What are these men doing here? I thought we were having a picnic. What's going on here, Marvin?"

"There you go again, asking a million questions. Come on now. I'll tell you all about it on the way," he answered, helping Richard push the cart along the path.

"God, this seems awfully heavy. You sure you ain't got somebody in there?" he kidded as they detoured around the construction site.

"You said you were going to tell me what's going on," Richard pressed.

"I'll tell you. I'll tell you. Don't I always tell you everything?"

"I suppose," Richard said sullenly.

"Well, come on then."

Dr. Bianco came out the front of A Building to discover Mrs. Ackerman traipsing through the gardens, pulling out flowers by the fistful. "Get the hell out of there," he hollered. "What is the matter with you?"

Groups of patients were milling about the area, talking with one another calmly. Most of the doctors, nurses, and attendants were running around in a state of total shock. Dr. Bianco hurried over to Nurse Marlow who was busy trying to round up all the female patients.

"For Christ's sake, let's go. Let's get them back inside," Bianco urged. "This place is turning into a goddamn circus. Where's Carl?"

"The last time I saw him he was hoeing the garden by the shed," was the nurse's reply.

"Hoeing the garden by the shed!" Bianco echoed, shaking his head incredulously. "And why, in God's name, is he hoeing anything at all, pray tell? Don't you know that we've got an army of police officers and detectives scouring the grounds, looking for a maniac amongst a multitude of maniacs? And you tell me Carl is off hoeing a goddamn garden."

"I've only got two hands, Doctor," she said defensively. "We just finished securing C Building, for Christ's sake."

"Look," he said, "the police will be down here any minute. They want to talk to Carl."

"Carl?"

Dr. Bianco raked his fingers through his wavy hair. "Yes, Carl," he repeated irritably, gesturing toward the garden in front of A Building. "And wait until he sees what Mrs. Ackerman did to his flowers over there. You want to see murder?"

"They think Carl's involved?"

"Who the hell knows? All I know is that they searched his room, and now they want to speak with him. He had a few choice words for the Martinez girl this morning. I guess they've got to start somewhere. Only they're turning this place upside down. They've already stopped construction, and now they're questioning the crew. Dr. King's been pushing for weeks to get this project off the ground. He'll have a conniption when he finds out there's been another delay. Not to mention a murder. We've got to get ahold of him, and fast."

"'Not to mention a murder'? Do you hear yourself, Doctor? A little girl is dead, and all you're concerned about is Dr. King's project?"

"Listen. Don't put me on the defensive. I was only—"

"Only what? Go ahead. I'm listening."

"Only trying to emphasize the fact that if we don't have this project finished and fully occupied, say by next spring, we could both be looking for another job. This isn't one of those state-run operations you know. Savvy?"

"Oh, I savvy all right," Nurse Marlow assured him, walking

away in disgust. "I'll go look for Carl," she called back. "I leave the women to you."

Dr. Bianco turned around to see a green sedan coming up the narrow drive. Sergeant Grear suddenly reversed the car's direction and shot the official vehicle into a tight parking space. The sedan jerked forward, cutting its wheels steadily back and forth. The Plymouth's long antenna whipped steadily to and fro like a giant metronome.

Mrs. O'Brian looked up in fascination then began swinging her arms to-and-fro while marching mesmerically across the grounds toward B Building, keeping time with the series of rather hypnotic sweeps.

"All right now, ladies," Dr. Bianco ordered. "Let's all follow Mrs. O'Brian back inside the building. Come on Mrs. Alvarez, Miss Johnsen. We're all on parade."

"It was a lovely picnic," Mrs. Alvarez affirmed, falling in behind Mrs. O'Brian. "But kind of short. Are we going to see fireworks tonight? Last year we had fireworks."

"I do believe the fireworks have already started, Mrs. Alvarez. Let's go, Mrs. Ackerman. Fall in please. And pick up that bag of shit behind you."

Mrs. Ackerman marched right up to the doctor, handing him a large bouquet of flowers. The very flowers that she had pulled from Carl Gustafson's garden. "These are for the funeral," she stated solemnly.

Dr. Bianco stared down at the armful of black-eyed Susans, then back at Mrs. Ackerman. "That was very thoughtful," he said almost apologetically. "Why don't you take them inside and tell one of the nurses to put them in a vase."

Mrs. Ackerman nodded mournfully, cradling the big bouquet.

Sergeant Grear was talking on the car radio; Lieutenant Lark was busy flipping through some notes.

"All right," Bianco called out loud and clear. "Everyone inside. Let's go. No, not that way, Mr. Wyszynski," he said, redirecting the man toward A Building. "You're not one of the ladies. You, too, Mr. Schimmel. Follow your buddy. Let's go, Fowler."

Mr. Schimmel stood steadfast in defiance. "Some lunatic is loose and vhat is anyvon doing about it?' he demanded angrily. "That is vhat I vant to know. Somebody has got to be crazy to do such a thing like that. Such a vonderful little girl. It is horrible," he carried on. "I'm telling you it vas that Nazi. I varned you all. How else could a terrible thing like this ever happen here? How?" he insisted, staring vacantly at the sky . . . .

The little man traveled back in time to the evacuation . . . merely being told, 'points east.' He recalled the boxcars . . . the horrendous Auschwitz hell . . . his emaciated wife, slowly dying from exhaustion and starvation in another section of the camp. And he, alive with certain knowledge that there was nothing, nothing in the world that he could possibly do but die a living death. And then the word. The final word. The word that she was dead. DEAD. Leaving him all alone. Alone with all the memories. Memories of the pit. Oh, the pit he would never forget. Men. Women. Children. CHILDREN! Weeping. Everyone standing naked along the periphery of a pit at the break of dawn, before unmuzzled German shepherds and unleashed German soldiers. Muzzles held at the ready . . . aim . . . fire! The outrageous fusion of gunfire and flesh. Variegated blues and reds. Bodies torn asunder. Screaming. Falling. Crawling. Gurgling. Dying or already dead. Lying forever still. And he? Alive! A miracle. A living soul in the midst of all that madness. Buried alive in time. Alive, but barely breathing . . . staring vacantly through the mass of tangled limbs . . . a witness, witnessing the advent of the day . . . the day of liberation . . . the day time stopped for Abraham Schimmel.

"I vas not a coward," Mr. Schimmel cried, stepping back into the moment, observing several billowy clouds drifting eastward across an otherwise bright sky. "Ah, it is a fine day. Vouldn't you agree?" he suddenly declared, smiling ambivalently.

"Come along, Mr. Schimmel," Dr. Bianco coaxed, leading the trembling man by the arm when suddenly a tumultuous cry carried through the passageway between the buildings. The two detectives moved in quickly. Guns drawn. Dr. Bianco followed close behind.

A second later, a shabby looking German shepherd came shooting up the basement steps past the detectives and the doctor, stopping just short of Mr. Schimmel who stood shaking in his shoes.

Carl came to the foot of the stairs, kicking the air and stirring the animal into a further frenzy.

"KHHRRRR," the dog growled, spinning around toward Carl.

"KHHRRRR," Carl tormented, dropping to his knees.

205

The dog crouched low upon its filthy belly, crazed eyes firmly fixed on Carl. White teeth flashed, and spittle shot from its mouth as the shepherd snapped forward, barking away viciously at the top of the stairs.

Both guns disappeared beneath the detectives' jackets. Sergeant Grear spoke softly to the dog. "Easy boy. Good dog. Good fellow."

The animal swung back and challenged the detective boldly, its eyes acutely cautious, standing its ground between Carl and the others.

"Atta boy. Good fellow," Grear persisted, his voice calm and reassuring.

The mangy mongrel growled, brushed past Mr. Schimmel then scurried off across the grounds as one of the nurses brought the terrified soul inside.

Carl stood up, and the two detectives went quickly down the stairs with Dr. Bianco.

"Carl, these gentlemen would like to talk to you," the psychiatrist stated rather anxiously.

Carl eyed the two men suspiciously. "You from the A.S.P.C.A?"

"Homicide," the lieutenant snapped, flashing his credentials rather dramatically.

"Homicide!? I didn't kill the fucking dog. Just hit him upside the head with that broom handle over there," he confessed, walking over and picking up the can of toppled garbage.

"Let that go for now, Carl," Bianco said. "Lieutenant Lark and Sergeant Grear would like to talk to you."

Lark went right over to the caretaker, looking up into those sparkling blue eyes. "Do you work with chemicals in the garden, Carl?" the lieutenant queried, wiping the sweat from his brow with his handkerchief. "Any toxins, say? One of my men took the liberty of searching your room." The detective reached into his jacket pocket. "He found these," the lieutenant declared, withdrawing a clear plastic package, displaying a dozen or so 35mm film canisters. "We found one exactly like it crushed between the dead girl's teeth. The little girl you were hollering at this morning. Theresa Martinez."

"What the hell are you talking about?" Carl demanded, staring in disbelief at the two detectives.

"About murder, Carl. About the murder of that little girl," Lieutenant Lark stated flatly.

The caretaker stared at the plastic package. "Those are my seed containers! Dr. King gave them to me to keep my seeds in. They're all labeled: alyssum, begonias, black-eyed Susan, chrysanthemums, coleus, dahlias, geraniums, gloxinia, impatiens, marigold, primrose, and zinnia," Carl rattled off alphabetically. "I had them all in order. They were sleeping on my shelf. Dormant. You had no right."

"Lieutenant Lark and Sergeant Grear have to ask you these questions, Carl," Bianco assured him with a nod, adding something reassuring in Swedish, for he spoke the caretaker's tongue as well as several others.

"Questions? About murder? I'll tell you all about murder if you really want to know," Carl said angrily, pulling out a dog tag from inside his shirt. "I'll tell you about murder on a bloody beach. About how they mowed us like a lawn. I'll give you murder scenes galore. I WAS MURDERED IN YOUR WAR!" With a finger, Carl raised his upper lip, exhibiting an ugly scar cut high into the gum. "See? Marked for identification."

Lieutenant Lark and Sergeant Grear looked at one another then back again at Carl.

"I have one hundred seventy-seven stitches in all," he showed them, pulling up his shirt. "Yes?"

Dr. Bianco and the two detectives observed the twelve-inch scar across the caretaker's abdomen. They saw the riddled skin along his frame that gave his torso the appearance of a sieve. Suddenly, Carl dropped his pants in protest, revealing the prodigious scar across his groin. The scar which had rendered him impotent. The one that scarred his life forever as told by Mrs. O'Brian earlier in time. It was a scar received in neither of the wars but delivered in an ax fight within the private war of youth, back in some lumber camp before the wars of the world were ever fought; before he ever met and married Sonjia, seducing her with adoring words in several languages along with worthless promises, which charmed her but for a spell; before he lost her to the chairman of the Foreign Language Department; before he made her disappear forever for fear of losing her to any other man.

"I think maybe we better go inside," Dr. Bianco suggested, helping the caretaker get himself together. The psychiatrist spoke to Carl in Swedish so as to try and calm the angry soul. "Come along, gentlemen. We can go in through here," he directed, leading the three along the corridor and up a flight of stairs to the main level.

Near the reception area, a young dark haired woman stood screaming at Nurse Ryder who held her firmly by the arm. "JESUS. JOSEPH. HOLY MARY, MOTHER OF GOD. HELP ME! PLEASE HELP ME," the patient shouted. "They're peeking at me," she whispered in a macabre *sotto voce*, glaring at the vase of black-eyed Susans sitting on the desk. "They want to smell me. OH, GOD. HOW I MUST SMELL!"

"Come along now, Eileen. You know you belong in B Building, dear," Dr. King's receptionist-secretary insisted, leading the woman out the front door past a rather large man in a bathrobe who took tiny measured steps while staring wide-eyed and suspiciously around him.

"OH MY GOD! HE SMELLS ME," the woman cried.

"This way, Eileen. Come along now," Nurse Ryder coaxed, assisting the woman down the steps.

The two detectives followed Carl Gustafson and Dr. Bianco across the lobby and into a small room located at the end of a hallway. The space was confined and stuffy, furnished with a small table and two chairs. Dr. Bianco left the door open and directed Carl to one of the seats.

Carl moved cautiously to the other side of the table, refusing to sit. "Where is Dr. King?" he insisted.

"Dr. King left for Boston on business, Carl," Bianco explained.

"Business in Boston? Now? Oh, and I so revered that man. But I fear he has ridden off and abandoned me."

"Carl, no one is abandoning you. He's away on business."

"Business?" Carl cried. "YOUR BUSINESS IS HERE WITH ME, DR. DAVID KINGMAN," he screamed through cupped hands. "Oh, do not take it as a personal affront if your surname, sir, be Kingman. Simply have it abridged. Nose to the grindstone. That's the American way. YOU'RE STILL A YANKEE DOODLE DANDY, DAVID."

The psychiatrist ran fingers of frustration through his wavy hair. "Carl. Theresa Martinez was found murdered on Dr. King's estate. Paul said he saw you gardening this morning along the southern wall. You might have been one of the last people to see her alive."

"*Ja*. I figured you had the ace of spades up your sleeve," the angry Swede replied.

208

"Would you like to tell us what happened, Carl?" Lieutenant Lark suggested.

Carl sneered contemptuously at the detective. "What in the world would you like me to tell you about, Lieutenant? How about justice and fair play?"

Lieutenant Lark opened his jacket and loosened the knot at his throat, apparently quite uncomfortable from the heat and lack of ventilation in the room.

"Carl, these gentlemen are trying to do their job."

"Gentlemen? Dr. King I thought was a gentleman. And where is he now that I need him? WHERE ARE YOU NOW, DR. KING?"

"Carl—"

"Where is the justice in this mock tribunal I stand accused before?" Carl declared, hopping around in back of the table like a kangaroo. "Yes, I think we should talk about your so-called system of justice. Your judicial system, gentlemen, is one of bargaining and compromise, judged solely upon one's economic status," he ranted, gaveling his fist upon the table, warming up for his harangue. "'Order in the court,' Carl demanded. 'The Honorable Judge Divine presiding.'

"'Mr. P.J. Affluence, I hereby release you on your own recognizance to appear before me on April first, fool. What's that you say? Oh, you're going trout fishing upstate that week? Oh, my. Merciful me. Well, let's see now. We'll just have to move you up a bit. Put you down here on the calendar between the socialite who allegedly liquidated her assets along with that cantankerous old man of hers— and the caretaker who supposedly murdered some little twit at the King Foundation. Too bad we don't have the time to go on a fishing expedition into the patient's past. Which reminds me. I just love trout, and clout, and unforgotten favors,'" Carl's fictitious character carried on daftly.

"What the hell is he babbling about?" Lieutenant Lark asked angrily, appealing to the psychiatrist for help.

"Babel? Oh, for heaven's sake," Carl exclaimed, climbing up onto the table, towering over the others. "About one nation under God, for all Buddhists, Christians, Confucians, Hindus, Jews, Muslims, Shintos, Taoists, and Zoroastrians alike, is what I'm babbling about, Lieutenant."

Dr. Bianco shook his head regretfully. "I'm afraid you're not going to be able to get anywhere with him right now. Perhaps later on when he calms down a bit. He'll go on like this for quite some time," the psychiatrist assured them.

Lieutenant Lark stood gazing up at Carl in sheer frustration; Sergeant Grear stood by in apparent fascination.

"This way, gentlemen," Bianco said with a disarming sense of command, escorting the pair out into the hallway before securing the door behind them, leaving Carl to carry on alone. And carry on he did.

"WHAT ELSE WOULD YOU LIKE TO TALK ABOUT, GENTLEMEN?" Carl screamed, jumping off the table and peering out the little window in the door, pressing his nose against the pane of glass. "Prejudice perhaps? Like my answering a question with a question. Now, that's a mocking form of prejudice for you. You don't have to be Sherlock Holmes to spot an English Jew. Your young Watson, riding on your coattails, hasn't got a clue. You are an English Jew, are you not, Lieutenant?

"And you're a goddamn guinea traitor, Dr. Bianco," Carl went on. "Want to know the difference between a guinea and a Jew? Different church, same phew!" Carl affirmed solemnly, holding his nose with one hand, waving offensively with the other. "I hope to suffocate in this very room before I ever see the likes of you again."

It was late afternoon before Dr. Bianco and two other senior staff members finally finished discussing security measures with Lieutenant Lark and Sergeant Grear. They had reached a tentative agreement that seemed to have tested each man's mettle. Drs. Schwartz and Martin were the first to step from the office, appearing very much on edge. A moment later, Bianco and the two detectives came out. All five men were standing just outside the doorway when several nurses and attendants came trekking down the hall, assisting someone in obvious distress. As the group neared, one could plainly see a male figure doubled over, his chin lolling upon his chest, the front of his shirt covered with blood, his arm wrapped in a makeshift splint.

Nurse Marlow lifted Marvin Gitlin's badly battered face. "I found him unconscious near the construction site," she said excitedly. "I just finished setting his arm."

"Jesus Christ!" Bianco cried with alarm.

"Tell Dr. Bianco and the police what happened," Paul Johnson insisted. "Tell them who did this to you, Marvin,"

Marvin moved his lips, mumbling incoherently.

"Who did this, Marvin?" Dr. Bianco implored. "Did Carl Gustafson do this to you?"

Marvin moved his head from side to side, drawing a painful breath before he spoke. "Like a father to that boy. Told him everything. Hurt me."

"Who hurt you, Marvin?"

"Richard. Richard Geist," the attendant grimaced. "Murdered his mother. Put her—her body in Sarah's laundry cart," he winced. "Pushed her right past the police. Right under their goddamn noses."

Lark and Grear exchanged uneasy glances. Drs. Schwartz and Martin seemed to gloat.

Nurse Ryder shook her head. "He's delirious," she insisted. "Mrs. Geist called here only a few minutes ago. She's fine. And I reminded Sarah to make sure to keep all the doors and windows locked, and to call if she sees anyone who doesn't belong up there."

"Did you say Sarah?" one of the nurses asked incredulously. "You mean Dr. King's housekeeper?"

"That's right."

"But Sarah's been on the third floor of B Building for most of the afternoon looking after Althea. I just came from there."

"That's impossible! I'm telling you that I just spoke to her myself." Nurse Ryder looked around in bewilderment.

"What the hell is going on here?" Dr. Martin demanded.

"I think I'm beginning to get the picture," Bianco declared, examining Marvin's face and arm. "Johnson and Phelps. I want you to take this man to the infirmary," he instructed the attendants. "Nurse Marlow. I want you here with me. The rest of you, back to work. Let's go."

Drs. Schwartz and Martin shooed the others away.

Lark and Grear fixed their eyes on Dr. Bianco. "What are you thinking?" the lieutenant asked.

"I think Richard's in that house, Lieutenant. I also believe it was Richard who Nurse Ryder spoke with on the phone. Not his mother or Sarah."

"That's absurd!" Dr. Schwartz remarked, practically laughing in Bianco's face.

"Absolutely preposterous," Dr. Martin agreed.

"That's exactly why I'm sure of it. What's absurd," Bianco said, looking directly into Donna Marlow's eyes, "is how quickly some of us lose sight of the things that matter most in all this madness."

Donna smiled sadly yet understandingly.

"I saw Richard while you were busy questioning Carl," Dr. Martin remarked a bit testily.

"And why wasn't I notified immediately," Dr. Schwartz complained. "Carl Gustafson is clearly my responsibility."

"And why isn't Richard upstairs in his room while Dr. King's away, Dr. Bianco?" Dr. Martin pressed.

"Come on, Lieutenant," Bianco said, ignoring their questions, apparently taking charge.

"All right, let's all hold off a second. I'm afraid it's our picnic from here on in, Doctor," Lieutenant Lark quipped. "Now, here's *my* question. And I want all of you to answer very carefully. Does Dr. King keep any firearms in the house that you know about? Any handguns or rifles? Any weapons at all?"

Everyone emphatically agreed that Dr. King did not.

"Maybe we should ask the housekeeper to come with us," Sergeant Grear suggested. "I'm sure she knows that house inside and out. She could be of some assistance if we run into a problem. Of course, we'll keep her at a safe distance."

Dr. Bianco nodded in agreement. "I think that's an excellent idea, Sergeant." The lieutenant turned to the others. "It's one of the reasons I take him with me on these outings," he added, offering a moment of levity to the serious matter at hand. "Let's shake a leg, Sergeant."

"Dr. Bianco," Nurse Ryder called out from the front desk. "I have Dr. King on the line."

"Tell him I'll try and reach him later," he instructed, heading toward the side exit with Donna Marlow and the two detectives while the two psychiatrists went scrambling for the phone. "Then call B Building and have them send Sarah down to meet us."

"But Doctor, he wants to talk to you—you said the minute he calls—the mobile operator has him holding—what am I supposed—"

"Let me have that phone," Dr. Martin demanded, practically pulling the receiver out of the receptionist's hand.

"Let me have him after you," Dr. Schwartz insisted, removing his bifocals, wiping the thick pair of glasses anxiously on the corner of his coat.

Just around the corridor, Richard grinned gaily while toying with a plastic badge clipped to the breast pocket of a lab coat that he wore. He headed calmly out the back of A Building and across the grounds toward the king-sized house, keeping to the hedgerow, making the most of available cover.

Chapter 21

MUMMY

Richard had beaten the authorities back to the house by a comfortable margin, for they first had to collect Sarah and formulate a plan. He'd make it very easy for them; he wouldn't do anything at all except play a patient game. Everything was just about set. He knelt beside the figure on the floor in Dr. King's study, surrounded by empty boxes of gauze and circular tins of white adhesive tape with which he had practiced earlier, knowing exactly how many yards he'd need to properly prepare her body when the time was right.

Of course, a prop was needed here and there to set the scene. So he staged the sacred back and white ibis near the body's feet, its curved bill pointing to the blood-stained floor. At the head of Mother's figure, he placed the statue of Hermes, its caduceus missing from its hand.

"'That there's Hermes,'" Richard said in Sarah's voice. "'Messenger of the gods and conductor of souls to Hades,'" he recited eerily, sitting down beside the figure on the floor, flooding his mind with memories of long ago. "'That be the world of the dead, separated from the land of the livin' by the rivers Hateful, Forgetfulness, Woeful, Fiery an' the Wailin','" he intoned, methodically tracing all five digits with the index finger of his other hand. "'Ya see, the newly arrived dead was ferried 'cross the river Hateful, to be buried by a greedy ol' man who gots paid by a coin left in their mouths, 'long with honey cakes to keep them quiet. And anyone who tried to enter or leave Hades was challenged by the fearless dog, Cerberus: a three-headed hound that guarded its gates,'" he cited reassuringly. "'Then all the dead drank from the river of Forgetfulness, and the judges of Hades gave each soul its proper place. Now, the good and the heroic was rewarded in the Elysian Fields. Thems at the edge of the world. But the wicked gots sent to the lowest regions,'" he declared solemnly.

"'You see that there black and white bird nestled near your feet? That there's an ibis. Ain't no ordinary bird. No siree, bobtail. He be the embodiment of the Egyptian god, Thoth. A moon-god. He credited with the invention of writin', geometry, and astronomy. Darn tootin'. And when those archeologist fellows finds them Egyptian tombs where the mummies is kept, they finds them birds in there with 'em. Of course you know what a MUMMY is.

"'Well now, them mummies is all wrapped up like that 'cause one day their soul gonna come back to their body. Ya see, them Egyptian people, they believes in life after death. And Sarah gonna tell ya a little secret. Everybody wanna believes that. I mean deep down inside one's self. That be the hope of all mankind. Yes, siree. And I'll tell ya another thing. From what ol' Sarah can see, them Egyptian people spent so much time preparin' for death, why I don't see where they found the time for livin'. Ah, hee, hee, hee.'"

Richard stood up and crossed over to a chair, sitting back with his legs up in the air. He spoke of long ago. The voice was that of a child's. The voice of little Dicky.

"Say, do you recall the day the baseball came crashing through the parlor window in the Hiawatha house, knocking over your avocado pit? Of course you do, Mummy. Dicky certainly does, seeing as how the whole business became a metaphor for yet another kind of seed that never really took, for there was really very little hope for Dicky's proper growth. And I assure you that it had nothing to do with that Nazi knocking you down a double flight of stairs during pregnancy. Regardless, I remember you entering the parlor with your silly pit, as though you were carrying in some sort of precious pet. The tiny tail of a root had already broken through its protective shell. Actually, I thought the whole thing sort of resembled a miniature brain. Don't you think? You had stuck toothpicks around its convoluted mass, submerging half the pit in water just beneath the rim of the glass, placing it upon the window sill. I gazed in fascination. The water, of course, magnified its size. I pretended that it was Iceland, when suddenly the window was smashed to bits.

"Iceland looks very much like a brain, you know. Of course, you have to view it upside down or kind of twist your head around. Did you know that Icelanders read more books than any other peoples in the world, Mummy? So when you became volcanic and would start to erupt, I would travel thousands of miles away to Iceland. Once, you beat me for at least a quarter of an hour. And if I shivered, it was only from the cold. Do you remember all those times you planted me in the corner of the room and made me stand perfectly still? Like the line of avocado plants you started along the sill. I prayed they'd grow into a row of weeds. If you watched long enough, you could actually see their medulla oblongata descending the mouths of those glasses. Tiny skeletal arms extending from their spiny white crooked roots. Resembling the skeletons of fish. Brain food is what I'd fantasize about while standing in the corner of the parlor without any supper or sleep.

"Gradually the pit split. And from its top ascended a tiny stem. And it grew and grew, better than an inch a day. Then when it grew to seven, you'd cut it back a bit. Then the stem divided, and tiny branches shot out here and there and everywhere, unfurling tiny green leaves that grew and grew to great proportions till they surpassed the giant green-leafed pattern on the walls. You know that I'd gone mad, but still you nurtured *it*!

"And so, to grow too, Mummy, I built a private world all around me. And I'd pretend with my imaginary friend on whom I could depend. He'd do anything I wished him to. Though at times he got a little out of hand. You have to understand that Richard really tried to protect little Dicky from the madness all around. So frail and vulnerable was he. He tried so hard to make everyone see him as a fine young man. Quite a web was spun. But there was really only one. I realize that now because I'm finally cured, you see. The moment you died I was on my way to a speedy recovery. I know now that Dicky and Richard are really me. Invincible. You might even say, VICTORIOUS," he screamed, clicking his heels together and planting both feet firmly on the floor. "But I'll go on to do a little number and play it to the hilt. Actually, it's going to be a first rate performance. Just you wait and see.

"Do you know what your very last word was, Mummy? 'Dicky.' Yes, that's right. 'Oh, my God!' you said shaking. 'Please don't. PLEASE. DON'T DO THIS TO ME, DICKY.' Then you turned very white. Do you remember the very first word I ever uttered, Mummy? Of course you do. Why are you lying there so silently? I gave you a clue. In fact, I've given you the answer. That's right! MUMMY! Shh. Not a word now. Mum's the word."

Suddenly the phone rang, bolting Richard upright in his seat. He picked up the receiver, listening for the voice on the other end.

"Richard, is that you?"

"Dr. King? —No, it's me. —Dicky. —Oh, I'm so sorry that I missed your call earlier, but I just got back not five minutes ago. —No, Richard's not here. He's been a terribly busy boy. —Mummy? Oh, she's all wrapped up at the moment. Is that the reason you're calling? —Yes, she turned very white, you see. —I SAID, SHE TURNED VERY WHITE. She's all wound up. But everything is going to be all right now. —No, no. Everything is fine. She's lying here quietly beside me on the floor. —No, I don't think I could wake her if I had to. —No, sir. —But no need to worry anymore. —What's that? —No, Sarah isn't here. —The truth? You sound rather insane if you want to know the truth. Goodbye, Dr. King," he said, placing the receiver down abruptly before turning his attention back to his mother's body.

"Dicky did a terrible thing, you see," Richard said through a yawn then pouted childishly. "He didn't tell anyone he broke the serpent's wand when he knocked you to the floor. He told me not to tell. I think he wants to place the blame on me. Still, I feel obliged to protect that little rascal from himself. He's really quite mad, you know. Especially at Dr. King. Actually, he was going to make him into slaw, but I think I talked him out of it."

> Old King Cole
> Was a merry old soul
> And a merry old soul was
> Ah, hee, hee, hee.

"Hey! I have a great idea. Remember the anagrammatic games we used to play? Say! Let's play today. I go first, okay? Here we go. The word is LIVED. Are you ready? LIVED DEVIL EVIL VILE LIE VIE DIE. You took so long to die. Shh—listen. I think I hear someone coming."

The door to the study flew open as Lieutenant Lark and Sergeant Grear burst into the room. Revolvers drawn. Several police officers stood ready just outside the bay window off the patio, handguns outstretched at arm's length, leveled at Richard's back.

"FREEZE!" Lieutenant Lark commanded.

"BRRRR," Dicky said shivering, drawing two gun fingers from his hips. "BANG—BANG! YOU ARE DEAD. SIX·TY BUL·LETS

IN YOUR HEAD," he chanted madly.

Moments later, Dr. Bianco and Nurse Marlow stood comforting Sarah just outside the doorway. Sergeant Grear pulled Richard to his feet, securing the young man's arms behind his back, clicking on a pair of handcuffs. The old woman narrowed her eyes and covered her mouth in fright, staring down at the figure lying on the floor alongside the pool of blood. "Oh, my God! Miss Vicki."

"No. Shh. It's all right, Sarah. Mummy's going to be all right now," Dicky assured her with a grin.

Lieutenant Lark knelt beside the body, a look of bewilderment written across his face as he began unraveling the enigma. "What the hell is this?" he exclaimed, stripping yards of white adhesive from around the head. "It's a dummy!"

"It's a mannequin," Dicky declared. "Although it's Mummy's figure to a T. Wouldn't you agree, Sarah? The whole idea was for her to see herself the way others do. You see, we were playing a game while waiting for all of you. Anagrams. They're lots of fun. We were about to switch to homophones: words that sound alike but differ in meaning, regardless of whether they are spelled the same or not. Though in school they called them homonyms. Nevertheless, I'll go first, okay? MANNAKIN MANNIKIN MANIKIN MANNEQUIN. Oh, I see that you really don't want to play."

A uniformed officer entered the room and walked over to Lieutenant Lark; he reported quietly. "We found the laundry cart by the construction site, Lieutenant. There's no trace of her. But we found this buried at the base of a bush alongside the house. The ground is freshly turned." He handed over a piece of broken marble: a winged staff with two serpents entwined around one another.

Lieutenant Lark stooped down and matched the caduceus to the broken, bloody statue on the floor. "Where is she, Richard?" he asked, motioning his men to search the house.

"You see, Lieutenant, M-A-N-A-K-I-N-S are the beautifully colored, songless, passerine birds of the family Pipridae, which inhabit the warmer parts of the Americas, particularly the forests of Central and South America." His voice was no longer that of a child's. It was Richard's voice, sounding almost scholarly while standing there in Dr. King's laboratory coat. "M-A-N-N-I-K-I-N-S, on the other hand, pertain to the estrildine finches which inhabit parts of Asia, Australia, and the Pacific Islands. M-A-N-I-K-I-N-S, however, are the anatomical models used for demonstrating surgical operations. And, of course, M-A-N-N-E-Q-U-I-N-S are representations of human forms that you see standing in fashion windows, or like the one you see *lying* before you," Richard concluded with a smile.

"Where is your mother, Richard?" Dr. Bianco entreated.

"Why, she must have flown the coop, sir."

"Oh, please tells them, Richard. Please tells them where Miss Vicki be," Sarah cried.

The telephone rang, and Dr. Bianco picked up immediately.

Richard grinned, his face taking on a devilish glow. "You really did think it was Mummy; didn't you? I mean, just for the teeniest moment. Yes? You see, they all tried to take her away from me. Birds of a feather."

Dr. Bianco muffled the mouthpiece in his hand. "Dr. King is on his way home. He wants to speak with you, Lieutenant."

Lieutenant Lark took the phone.

"What think ye of me?" Richard chanted. "Whose son is he?" they'll say. 'The son of Hermes, pray?'" He stared out the bay window, snapping his head back and abnormally to the right. "Everything is beginning to come together. The darkness, the light; the black, the white. The day is gray, however. Leaden. Heavy. Everything is closing in. Even the birds are flying low today. Foul. Wouldn't you say?" Richard slowly backed away from the window to the center of the room.

Sergeant Grear took hold of Richard's arm to prevent him from taking another step.

Richard looked down at the arm then spoke in something of an unearthly whisper. "Get your filthy fucking hand off of me now, you two-bit slimy piece of shit," he intoned in a voice that left no quarter for discussion as the words fell freely from a mouth that made but not the slightest motion, past lips that moved but not a hair.

Grear lowered his hand cautiously, sensing imminent danger behind those desperate eyes.

Lark could sense it, too, hanging up the phone and sending out a signal to his partner to just relax.

"Thank you," Richard said politely, without the faintest trace of fury upon his face or tongue, without the slightest glimmer of rage within those sea-green eyes. He moved cautiously toward the far corner of the room, experiencing not the slightest bit of protest from a soul, for Lark had gestured to his sergeant to simply let Richard be. Into an open closet he stepped then suddenly sat, lithely slithering and slipping his buttocks, back legs, ankles and feet through the handcuffed loophole, sliding his arms forward in an empty embrace. With wrists still chained together, Richard reached for and spread one of Mother's more comfortable robes across his shoulders, holding it close to his neck like a cloak.

"Oh, where is she, Richard? Where's Miss Vicki?" Sarah pleaded.

"Where? Beneath the laurel and pachysandra. Asleep. No, 'neath the thorn and thistle where serpents creep. They beguiled her, and she did eat. Shh. Her voice crieth unto me. Listen:"

> "Secrets stored in a basement,
> Sarah.
> Magic within a trunk,
> Potions and lotions and notions,
> Sarah.
> Concealing the scent of the skunk."

It was Mother's voice, and Sarah swore it up and down. Hysterical she was, insisting the trunk was nobody's business but her own. Crazy she became and had to be assisted from the room by Nurse Marlow and another attendant.

Lieutenant Lark went over to the patient-prisoner standing in the closet. "I'll ask you one more time, son. Where is she?" the detective demanded.

Richard looked up blankly. "Am I my mother's keeper, Lieutenant?" he asked, dropping the garment along with the sergeant's shiny set of handcuffs to the floor. Standing before the lieutenant, Richard stuck out his tongue. Upon it lay the sergeant's key.

Grear pulled out his key ring and stared down in utter amazement.

Dr. Bianco summoned for further assistance, and two attendants stepped into the room, one of them carrying a straitjacket.

"I want this son of a bitch under heavy guard," Lark snapped.

"Day and night."

"Are we going away somewhere?" Richard asked, extending his arms cooperatively. "I'll bet it's awfully cold in there," he said shivering while slipping into the white jacket then wrapping his arms across his chest. "BRRRR."

Lieutenant Lark looked Richard in the eyes. "You have the right to remain silent. Any statement you make may be used against you. You have a right to the presence of an attorney, either retained or appointed. You may knowingly waive these rights." He turned to Dr. Bianco. "All right, now get him the hell out of here."

Chapter 22

THE SEARCH FOR TRUTH

Dusk had settled in quickly, and shadows loomed across the lighted court below. Richard stood by the window in his room, glaring down at the foreboding forms coming and going. In the distance, he observed a brilliant fireworks display. Showers of bursting, splintering, fragmenting light were flaring up again and again in a wild array of color and fascination that only he could comprehend. All the colors of the rainbow, the colors of the flag, the rich red blood of Mother's clothing, not to mention the daytime explosion of a hundred little dolls outfitted in brilliant dresses from foreign and familiar lands—now but a host of headless hussies scattered about her four post canopy bed. Richard watched the fireworks display with enormous pleasure, listening intently to the night.

Suddenly, he heard the harsh metallic click of a key inside the lock, followed by the grating sound of the heavy steel door swinging open along a cranky hinge. He turned around slowly, squinting in discomfort from the hallway's glaring bulb, his arms bound securely in the ghostly stark-white jacket. "BRRRR. It's as cold as ice up here," he said shivering. "Like Iceland."

A bold yet weary figure stood framed in the doorway, resolute and unshaken. "Where is she, Richard?" the voice commanded coldly.

"Why, Dr. King. I see that you're home early. How was your trip, sir? I know how you hate to fly."

Dr. King stepped inside the room. "Where is she?" he demanded, glancing at the wood-framed photographs sitting on the bureau. Photographs of Richard and Mother.

"She?"

"Victoria! Your mother!"

"Oh, yes. Mother."

"Where is she, Richard. I want the truth."

"Truth? Oh, good evening, Lieutenant. Sergeant," Richard said and nodded politely to the others waiting in the wings. "I'm sorry I didn't see you standing out there. One's eyes have to adjust to the light, you know. Please do come in. Only button up your coats as it's awfully cold up here. There are pictures of Mother on the bureau over there. I'm sure you could use them for your investigation. Of course, you'll have to view her upside down, or kind of twist your head around," he said with a frown, tilting his head to one side and then the other. "They're in frames as you can see. Oval. Ornate. Ordinary. But you may remove them if you like. Mr. Wyszynski gave those frames to me. Small frames, and frames of infinite dimension. Square frames, and large rectangular ones."

"I asked you a question," Dr. King snapped. "Where is she?"

"Why, I thought she was with you. She was always with you. Always. If not so much in body then at least in mind."

"I said I want the truth," the psychiatrist stated resolutely.

"Doctor! Whatever could the matter be? Truth, you say? These rooms are filled with those who wanted truth. But the truth deceived us all, you see. What of justice? Do you want justice, too? Mr. Schimmel wanted justice before he came here. And Mr. Gustafson once believed in the American way. Only none of us were supermen, although we all fought never-ending battles. For there is a universal sickness. A potpourri of prejudice upon which madness feeds. Feed a cold, starve a fever. Chili dogs and Coca Cola. Yankee pot roast and red cabbage. Coffee, tea, and egg creams. And everything is apple pie. My, my! The American way. Have you had your soup today? Hooray! You're still a Yankee Doodle Dandy, David. Hoorah! Oh, say can you see? Over here by the window. Bars and stars and stripes forever," he remarked above the cannonade. "And down here—everyone *so* busy. Searching everywhere."

"What did I ever do to you?"

"Do, Doctor? Little did you do. Dr. Doolittle, I presume? No, no. That can't be right. Wait a minute. Don't tell me. I have it on the tip of my tongue." Richard giggled gleefully. "Ah, yes. Dr. Livingstone. Dr. David Livingstone. Right? Dr. Livingstone, I presume? Me, Stanley. You, David. Oh, I can see that you really don't want to play. But that's okay. You see, I've learned to entertain myself in Mother's absence so as to while away the hours. Dr. David Livingstone: Scottish missionary and African explorer. Credited with the discovery of the Zambezi River in 1851; and in 1855, Victoria Falls. You can hear her roar and see the mist from twenty-five miles away. Sarah can tell you all about that. She's taught and traveled extensively through Africa. 'Been all 'round her, too. Darn tootin',"" Richard declared, capturing Sarah's likeness and her lilt, ambulating around the room on bowed legs. Around and around the room he circled.

"'From the Gulf of Guinea off the Ivory Coast, on up and through the Straits of Gibraltar to the Mediterranean; down the Suez to the Red Sea, 'long the Gulf of Aden to the Indian Ocean,'" he added assuredly. "'Then south through the Mozambique Channel. Finally, 'round the Cape. Yes, siree. The Cape of Good Hope. Ah, hee, hee, hee,'" Richard went on, imitating Sarah eerily.

"And our Doctor David, here, took her in and made her well, you see. Well, well! He's had a free servant to clean his crap for all these years."

"How could you, Richard?" Dr. King questioned and quaked, apparently shaken. "I've worked so hard with you. What did little Theresa ever do to you? You knew Althea would find her, didn't you? Why, Richard?"

"Why? Why, don't you see? Althea would be spending the rest of her life rummaging through cans of garbage. Can after can. The world is heaped with garbage. Mrs. Ackerman collects it. Mr. Gustafson dumps it. And Althea searches endlessly through it. For her, the search is over. She won't be searching anymore. I cured her. Me! But you can take the credit if you like."

"Why Theresa, Richard? What in God's name did that little girl ever do to you?"

"Theresa?"

"YES, THERESA! You were having tea together at the gazebo this morning. YES?"

"Tea together? Oh, no. She had tea. Tea for one. It was very pleasant just sitting there beside her on the couch. She was so sweet. That's how I knew it was really Mother. I mean when she was wee. You see, I had taken some of Sarah's honey cakes and went for a little walk up to the gazebo where Theresa likes to play. Then I invited her and Ruthie inside and put some water up for tea. Of course, she asked for sugar, so I handed her the tiny container that I had hidden in my sock. She poured in the whole amount. Only it wasn't really sugar. Nope." Richard shook his head from side to side. "KCN. Oh, that's potassium cyanide. Extremely poisonous. White. Granular. The faint odor of almonds. I handed her one of Sarah's honey cakes to mask the taste. I don't think she really noticed any difference. If she did, she didn't say anything. You see, they use it in developing. To make an image permanent. A fixing agent. You could say I fixed her."

"What in God's name did that little girl ever do to you?" Doctor King repeated, obviously quite distraught.

"What did she ever do? Oh, I'll tell you what she did if you really want to know. But I think you'd find it rather titillating if I told you what little Dicky did to her. I can give you all the sordid details if you like. First, she told me she was really a big girl now and didn't want any of old Sarah's lemonade; that she was a little lady and wanted a cup of tea; a little lady, and wanted to be treated accordingly. So I obliged her." Richard giggled. "I told her that she could meet and play with little Dicky if she promised not to tell. I spoke to her of long ago and how Dicky remembered Mummy standing naked on a chair before the closet in his room when she thought him fast asleep, and how it affected his little thing. God, it was hard to explain. So he had Theresa put her little hand upon it, asking where she got her pretty little doll. 'From Mommy,' she answered faintly, and told him how a bad man had put it in Ruthie's *dupa* in a car. She fondled little Dicky affectionately and promised not to tell a soul, practically falling off the couch without a sound.

"She seemed so sleepy lying there. She coughed a little. Dicky told her how pretty she looked. Sugar and spice and everything nice. Finally, she struggled for her breath and fell. So he carried both her and Ruthie outside and rolled them in a rusty barrel down the hill. All the way down to the viny green-leafed wall. Whee! What a ride. Then Dicky yanked them out and pulled them both behind a tree, tearing all the little lady's clothing off before he really went to town, putting it up her *dupa* without a sound, riding her to 'kingdom come, thy will be done, on earth as it is in heaven,'" he recited in a solemn tone before breaking into merry song. "Don't sit under the apple tree, with anybody else but me, anybody else but me, anybody else but me . . . Such a tight little tokus, too," he swore and giggled. "So we had to open it up a bit with the blunt end of Carl Gustafson's garden tool, but only after stroking her passionately with its claw. Foreplay, I guess you'd say. She didn't even cry out or anything. Just laid there like a rag doll next to her own little dolly playing dead."

Dr. King grabbed Richard firmly by his straitjacket. "YOUR

MOTHER, RICHARD. WHERE IS YOU MOTHER? I WANT THE TRUTH!"

"Truth with a capital T? And the truth shall set you free. Why, you're more a prisoner here than I. Truth without the T. Ruth! That's what Mother called her doll, you see. Of course, I tried to tell the little dear that it was really little Dicky. I mean, when he was wee. She wouldn't hear of it, though. That's when I became quite mad and stuffed the two of them upright in the trash."

"WHERE IS YOUR MOTHER, DAMN YOU?"

"Doctor! Dicky's analysis is quite complete. For he remembers everything at long last. Like that summer in a kingdom by the sea. Things seemed so foggy then. Except for one hot summer's night. The sky was filled with stars. The moon all round and white. Dicky thought he saw Mother sitting in a chair. Her legs up in the air. All twisted 'round someone, like those serpents 'round the staff. Only it wasn't Mother after all. No, sir. It was the painting Max had given Sarah that triggered the madness in Dicky's mind. Some dark and solitary secret locked away in time. So, the debauchery didn't happen at your gazebo high above the bay. Nay. It happened somewhat earlier in time. Down at your ranch house where you kept your horses and your hay. That's what threw me off at first, only Marvin Gitlin set me straight. Yes. It was on an earlier moonlit night. The time you had to go away. The night the groom came to Mother's room and carried her away.

"Marvin was your foreman then. Only it wasn't Marvin who stole her away, although he was certainly hot to trot and, like the others, enjoyed her acrobatic feats, riding her to kingdom come. Up and down and all around. Till Dicky finally drove them from his mind. But I made Max and Marvin tell me everything. Of course, I had to jar their memories quite a bit," he assured the good doctor with a knowing grin. "Maximilian was the groom who came for Mother and rode her away that night, beyond the bunkhouse built for your hired hands, Dr. King. You'll find him in the basement beneath the stairs in Sarah's steamer trunk. I tell you, though. He's not a very pretty sight," he warned, dropping his head to his chest as if it were fastened by a hinge. "Of course, the detectives will have to try and figure out how I managed it. I mean, what with all the dust and years of cobwebs still intact. That should keep them busy for a while. You should have given Max the ax many a year ago, Dr. King."

Dr. King shook his head insistently. "No. What you're saying isn't true. Oh, God!"

"Oh, yes. Every word. You see, Max's family made oodles of money in real estate, supplemented by breeding and racing thoroughbreds. Take a close look at the paintings in your dining room, Dr. King. You'll see that some of those faces bear a close resemblance to Max, before I finished with him, that is. A family of wealthy light-skinned blacks parading prize-winning creatures as fast as the wind itself. But you know all that. You also know that three of those paintings are worth a small fortune. But we'll just keep that under wraps. So. Who knew horses better than he? Hey? Max was the stallion, and Mother was the mare. He was the light-skinned black who rode her away that night on horseback. Past the barn and beyond the bunkhouse for hired hands. After a little horseplay, all those hands came forward, ordering Max to the back of the line. He was the last to ride her, but he rode her harder and faster and longer than anyone. And the others laughed and cheered him on before they finally pulled him off, realizing that he'd remain in the saddle forever if they'd let him. That's when Mother surprised them all. Shall I tell you how many cowboys she rounded up at once? SEVEN!

> "Coralled there all around her,
> With one buckaroo from behind,
> A bird in each hand
> And one in her bush,
> Plus Max in her mouth made five.
> Two other cowpokes holding their breath,
> Shooting her teats galore.
> Add everything up,
> And what've you got?
> Nothing less than a perfect score."

"YOU'RE A LIAR," Dr. King screamed. "Your mother's right. You always invented stories that weren't true. Always. You better tell me where she is, Richard. DO YOU HEAR ME? You'll tell me what I want to know. I have the key to unlock that twisted mind, you son of a bitch!"

"You know, Doctor. It's like the mind and the universe are one and the same. Darkness and light. Mysterious. Close your eyes for a moment. Go ahead. Close them tight." Richard closed his own eyes. "Now tell me what you see. You really can see, you know. A veil of madness across a galaxy. Zillions of tiny lights exploding so fast that you don't have time to focus. It's not 'nothing' you see, but eternity. The ultimate truth clearly revealed through the abstract. Aprons of darkness and light. The image firmly imprinted, if you'll only dare to look beyond that final curtain of madness. Molecular beams and dreams. Amoeba-like forms, falling and crawling through space. Of what matter the mind? An extension of the universe? A contraction of mindlessness?"

"TELL ME WHERE SHE IS."

"Close your eyes tight. What is the shape you see? Tell me of its geometry. Is it square? Is it rectangular? Does it have rounded edges? You're looking right at it, and yet you can't tell me. Can you? How far does its blackness tunnel? Does it have an edge? Some line of demarcation between here and a beyond? Is it finite and bounded? Is it limitless and therefore infinite? Or is it finite, yet unbounded? Can you conceive of that? Or would you say that one necessarily contradicts the other? It would appear that way on the surface of things. With that I'm sure you would agree. But things aren't always as they appear. Now are they, Lieutenant?" Richard questioned, winking at the cop.

"Yes, gentlemen. There is something within our world that is finite, yet has no boundary. Something very familiar to us, indeed. You give up? I gave you a clue. In fact, I've practically given you the answer. It's the face of the earth, gentlemen. The Earth's surface! It is a fixed and finite area, yet it has no boundary. However, we are so used to living in a rectangular world where surfaces are viewed as strictly two dimensional that we focus only on its lengths and widths. We don't ordinarily concern ourselves with its convexity because it lies in another dimension. Time is another dimension. Yes, I almost forgot about time. What time is it? It really doesn't matter. I have plenty of time. Say! Would someone like a cup of tea? It's getting awfully cold up here."

Dr. King turned away angrily. A badly shaken soul. He headed for the door, but Lieutenant Lark held him with a stare, the detective's moon-like features melding in a bath of light, moving his head ever so slightly from side to side, conveying a subtle message that Richard might, at the very least, offer a hint as to his mother's whereabouts. In sheer frustration, Dr. King moved away from the door, stepping back into the room.

"Now, let's see. Where was I?" Richard continued. "Oh, yes. Dimensions. Geodetic surveying takes into account the third dimension. The process is called triangulation, distinguished from plane surveying in that it enables us to measure the curvature of the earth's surface. We must conceive of all dimensions if we are ever to perceive our world concretely. If we are ever to comprehend the laws that govern us. If we are ever to fathom the order of the universe. Concrete impressions!

"Did you know that in 1962 our government put a geodetic satellite into space? Seven hundred miles above the earth. The same year Eichmann was hanged. Mr. Schimmel remembers that quite well because he said that it was the first time since the war ended that he had slept peacefully. Well, I want to tell you that I haven't slept peacefully since the day the surveyors arrived in early spring. I watched them scribbling notes and running tapes along the ground. So busy. Measuring up and down. Just like the police did earlier today. Of course, Dicky became so excited when the trucks rolled in this morning. 'VROOOOM—RRRRRR,'" he uttered with a throaty rasp, trilling his tongue and creating the sound of roaring machinery. "Dicky's favorites are the concrete mixers. He watched them with utter fascination pouring the foundation today. Concrete!" he added, remarkably capturing the sounds of churning drums and chuting cement.

"You understand, Doctor, that we are all governed by concrete impressions. Mrs. Ackerman has her garbage, and Mr. Wyszynski has his frames of reference. Yet, he's lost within the very framework. Oh, I don't mean to imply that he can't find his way along the halls and corridors because he's lost his mind. I'm only suggesting that it has been reduced to an immediate and concrete level. Concrete impressions. Yes. Mother was always quite impressionable, you know. Although I think she's finally settled now. And so today, Doctor, I leave you with a permanent and everlasting impression as promised: a monument by which to remember your beloved Victoria—my mummy dearest."

Dr. King's heart pounded fiercely in his chest as he lunged for

Richard. "YOU'LL NEVER GET OUT OF HERE!" he swore, struggling violently with the men who held him back. "NEVER EVER GET OUT OF HERE! DO YOU HEAR ME? NEVER! NEVER EVER!" he screamed insanely.

"Of course, another possible concept is that the universe is infinite, yet bounded. Oh, but that's difficult. Mother always said I was difficult. Infinite, yet bounded. Systems of stars receding at a velocity proportional to their distance from us. Dispersing into an ever expanding universe. Infinite, yet bounded. Like Mother's soul. Making its remarkable journey through time. Bounded within a perfect frame of mind," Richard stated solemnly, staring vacantly at the framed photographs on the bureau.

"NEVER. NEVER EVER GET OUT OF HERE! NEVER! NEVER EVER!"

Richard crossed the room back to the barred window. Brilliant lights exploded everywhere, and his eyes lit with an admixture of madness and cunning. Below, the grounds lay dark and empty.

"I'm all right," the psychiatrist told the two detectives, and the pair relaxed their hold. Dr. King called to one of the attendants standing just outside the door. "Secure him to the bed," he ordered, walking unsteadily from the room.

The attendant entered the room with additional restraints, stepping over to Richard, directing him to the metal rack and tattered mattress.

Soon everything grew black and silent.

Richard awoke early the next morning to the jarring sound of jackhammers pounding in the distance. He smiled satisfactorily, for he could hear the sound of heavy machinery rolling into the area, moving huge mounds of earth and stone along the southwest wall, breaking up messy, mortared blocks around the construction site. He knew they were out there searching for her. Looking everywhere. He also knew that others would be coming for him in a little while. Searching for the truth. Probing for answers. He'd tell them nothing. Oh, he could tell them stories all right. Only no one would believe him. Tales of how she'd go cavorting after other men. Or like the times she beat him till he shivered from the cold. Brrrr! He wasn't very old.

Richard lay strapped to the bed with his arms tightly bound

across his chest, shivering violently within the stark-white jacket. Shadows fell across his face as he whispered into his pillow. Clay-red curls contrasted sharply against a cotton pillowcase, along with stark-white sheets and walls. Sea-green eyes danced insanely in his skull as he glared ominously back at the black and white photographs that sat on the bureau in small frames. Five photographs of Mother, and one of her only son. "You'll never find her," he stated calmly. "Not with all the earthmoving equipment in the world."

At 6 a.m., several attendants came and transferred Richard to another floor, wheeling him down the hallway into a sterile little room.

"Whee!"

Nurse Marlow stood beside Dr. Bianco as he filled a syringe from a small inverted bottle in his hand. Richard glared up at the two of them while struggling against the restraints that bound him to an enamel table. He shut his eyes tightly as the psychiatrist inserted a needle into his arm.

"Trying to unlock my mind? So blind. Might is right!" he babbled. "Truth? You're looking for the truth in there? You dare! Prying—trying to unlock my mind . . . . " Richard resisted with all his might. A moment later he relaxed.

"Can you hear me, Richard?" Dr. Bianco questioned.

"Might is right!" the patient babbled over and over again.

"I'd like you to count—"

"One, two. Buckle my shoe."

"Can you hear me, Richard?"

"Three, four. Shut the door."

"Richard?"

"No, it's me—Dicky," a child's voice answered eerily.

"Where is your mother, Dicky?"

"Mummy?"

"Yes, Mummy. Where is she?"

"Far, far away."

"Far away where?"

"Beyond a care. Up there," Dicky answered, his eyes fixed firmly on the ceiling.

"Where up there?"

"'In an expanding universe,' I think he said."

"Who said?"

"Richard said."

"What else did he say, Dicky?"

"That he's going to save Mummy's soul."

"Is she dead, Dicky?" the psychiatrist asked gravely.

"Yes!"

"Did you kill her?"

Dicky rocked his head violently from side to side. "No."

"Then who, Dicky? Who killed Mummy?"

"Richard killed her," Dicky said devilishly.

Nurse Marlow backed away from the table.

"Where did Richard put her body, Dicky?" Dr. Bianco pressed.

Dicky's eyes searched the ceiling frantically. "Mummy's finally gone!"

"Gone where? Where did she go, Dicky? Where did Richard put her? Tell us where."

"Where? I'll tell you where," he fought in a final effort to free himself. "OUT OF MY MIND FOREVER," he screamed insanely.

It was the last thing that Dicky said before his expression went blank. Frozen. A kind of plastic immobility transformed the young man's body and limbs into that of a mannequin as they unstrapped and carried him silently from the room; his tongue tacit; his mind a vociferous maelstrom of meaningful verse.

> The cuckoo is a witty bird,
> Arriving with the spring,
> When summer suns are waning,
> She spreadeth wide her wing.
> She flies th' approaching winter
> She hates the rain and snow;
> Like her, I would be singing,
> Cuckoo-cuckoo-cuckoo!
> And off with her I'd go!

Chapter 23

ONE WEEK LATER

Richard beheld a bird's-eye view of the world below. From his new perch atop the maximum security ward in D Building, he observed the detectives' green sedan arriving at the south gate, stopping for a moment before continuing steadily up the narrow drive. Lark and Grear drove by a group of nurses heading down the walkway toward the parking lot. Starched white caps clocked 180 degrees as the Plymouth passed. Drs. Schwartz and Martin were walking just behind the nurses. They, too, turned and stared. Dr. Schwartz removed his bifocals, wiping the lenses upon the sleeve of his lab coat. Dr. Martin stood rather rigid in a stuffy three-piece tailored suit.

Attendants, casually clad in khaki trousers and matching short-sleeved shirts, suddenly looked up. Several wide-eyed patients stood and gaped, while others paid no mind at all. Many simply milled around the magnificent gardens, lost in its colorful splendor.

Near the end of the walkway, Mr. Schimmel stood shaking in his shoes, staring at the car in apprehension, his thumbs tucked deep within the pockets of his paisley vest. Tattersall knickers draped his bony knees, clashing with sandals and socks. One sock red. The other blue.

Alongside the curb, an elderly man blew into a silent whistle hung around his neck, excitedly waving the car ahead. Another poor soul stood dialing an imaginary phone.

Sergeant Grear approached the corner slowly, turning left and maneuvering the vehicle into a space in front of A Building. Lieutenant Lark looked up from his notes, staring back at the small groups of people gazing in his direction. Patients, staff, and personnel alike stood transfixed, absorbed in kind of trance that took them back to the Martinez girl's murder and Mother's disappearance the week before. The detectives' reappearance on the scene apparently served as a sharp reminder. And so, for the moment, there seemed to be no significant difference between keeper and kept.

The man appearing on the scene must have thought so, too; a rather distinguished looking individual in white loafers and smartly pressed tropical trousers, sporting a dark blue double-breasted blazer adorned with bright golden buttons that caught the late morning sun. He was barely recognizable. Not even Mrs. O'Brian noticed the nuance although she stared down oddly at the pair of matching wicker suitcases that Carl held in each dry-cracked calloused hand, the very same bags with which the caretaker had first arrived nearly a quarter of a century ago. She raised her eyes to the clean-shaven gentleman with short dark hair combed flat and parted in the middle.

"Good morning, Doctor," she beamed, wearing a winning smile, fluffing her silvery head of hair. "You're new here," she flirted.

"Ma'am," he nodded, watching Lieutenant Lark shift his stocky frame from seat to sidewalk as Sergeant Grear fell in behind. The two detectives headed toward A Building.

"I'll bet I know who you are," Mrs. O'Brian declared, giggling as everyone resumed their talking and rumors flared anew. "You're the new director they appointed while Dr. King is resting."

Carl Gustafson raised a finger to his lips.

"I just knew it!" the woman said excitedly, scrunching her shoulders to her neck. "Now, don't worry. I won't tell a soul. Believe me. I know how to keep a secret," she assured him. "We heard that it was going to be Dr. Bianco. But he's too young, and very, very fresh. I told everyone here that they were bringing someone in from the outside. They hardly ever promote from within, which causes such disharmony," she announced with a pout. "That's why I blew up the administrative offices in the school where I taught," she whispered, hurrying off to tell a group of women sitting on a nearby bench about the new arrival.

Carl cracked a crooked grin and walked away, heading toward a distant row of trees. Sandwiching both suitcases under an arm, he tried focusing the pair of horn-rimmed glasses back and forth along the bridge of his nose. The glasses belonged to Dr. Schwartz. The shoes and clothing were taken from a two-suiter belonging to Paul Johnson, who had planned on leaving for vacation directly from work that afternoon.

Carl followed the path around the gardens, stumbled once and almost fell. One of the suitcases flew from his hand. He recovered quickly then set the cock-eyed glasses straight, picking up the wicker bag before continuing along a shady lane behind another garden. His favorite. A prized rose garden. The garden set away from all the madness. Setting both suitcases down, he gently reached for the thorny, slender stalks that lined the walkway.

"Farewell, my little friends," the caretaker said and smiled sadly. "I am going to miss each and every one of you. But I must go away now. Far, far away. Even if I could take all of you with me, it would be too long a trip, and you would surely die. But here you will live out the season. And in here, forever," Carl swore, tapping his chest. "Here in my heart I will always hold a special place for you." He leaned closer, enjoying the fresh fragrance before relinquishing his precious friends. Or did they, in fact, release him from any further obligation, Richard wondered, observing the touching scene from the window high above. As if in answer, the entire bed of bright red roses bowed their slender bodies in a mild breeze before the caretaker. Carl returned the gesture most gracefully.

Moving into the shadows of the trees, Carl looked around to see if the staff parking area was clear. People were passing by on foot.

How strange he appeared, crouched behind a large tree. No longer sporting that bountiful head of snow-white hair. For Carl had given himself a rather decisive crop with a pair of garden clippers. He had also dyed his hair from a dark concoction that he'd been preparing for a week. A solution made by boiling the bark from an oak tree. It was a process that he had learned in his youth, an operation for blackening shiny new steel traps set out along the Finnish border during the years he trapped for both fun and profit. Mrs. O'Brian once said that he had spent a happy and healthy childhood hunting, fishing, and trapping furry creatures within the great forests which had been his home.

What must have been the most difficult part of Carl's disguise, that morning, was the sacrifice made with regard to that splendid pepper-and-salt handlebar mustache of his, rendering him as vulnerable as on the day of judgment when he stood half naked before his accusers; namely, Lark and Grear, who initially believed the caretaker was, indeed, the murderer of the little Martinez girl.

Suddenly, several cars appeared along the shadowy, tree-lined drive. Carl went flat upon his belly. Surely, he had to have felt like some sort of disabled cat. Trapped. Lying there without its trusty whiskers. Disoriented. Unbalanced, to be sure. Cars were pulling out of the staff parking lot. Across the way, another was just pulling in. Carl waited patiently.

Lieutenant Lark and Sergeant Grear waited in the reception area of A Building for their scheduled noon appointment. It was 12:15 p.m. Both men looked around the room impatiently. Lieutenant Lark sat, and Sergeant Grear stood.

Seated comfortably on a sofa directly across from the two detectives was a young couple casually fondling each other. Off to the left sat a father and son engaged in serious conversation. To their immediate right, talking away to no one in particular, stood an elderly man.

Sergeant Grear observed the five individuals as though he might possibly be called upon at some later date to give an accurate and detailed accounting. He often occupied himself in this manner, testing his ability to recall, even years later, significant information concerning individuals he'd set his mind to. But on that particular afternoon, the young detective found it rather difficult to bring to mind the concentration necessary in registering and storing such descriptive data. He found it difficult to concentrate because he realized that the couple on the couch was studying the two of them. Intently. The strangeness of it all was that they seemed uninterested in one another, as if their exploring hands and fingers were independent of any feelings connected with their play.

Lark and Grear waited impatiently.

Moments later, Nurse Ryder came by and escorted the two detectives down the hall past Dr. King's office, which Dr. Bianco was somewhat reluctantly in the process of taking over. Dr. Angelo T. Bianco had been appointed director and head of administration the week before. Appointed by Dr. King himself.

"Sorry for the delay and any inconvenience, gentlemen," Bianco's receptionist-secretary said most pleasantly. "Dr. Bianco is not quite settled in as yet. Both offices are a mess because we're still moving some things around," she explained, leading the way out the back of the building. "Dr. Bianco is waiting for you in D Building." Nurse Ryder directed the pair toward the maximum security building located across the narrow drive; the building to which Richard was confined. "Seventh floor. Ward B. First elevator on the right as you enter. An attendant will be there to take you up," she instructed, excusing herself and heading back inside A Building.

Just inside D Building (which could have stood for Dungeon from all appearances, Lark entertained), the two were met by a rather fit looking Korean who unlocked the elevator and took the detectives up to the seventh floor. From there, he led the pair down a long corridor, passing them through two steel doors, unlocking and relocking each with a separate key.

"Dr. Bianco waiting for you here," the man directed in broken English, pointing to the door.

There was a significant reason why Bianco had picked D Building to hold the meeting. It was virtually a fortress. And the new director wanted to reinforce that point, to let the detectives and anyone else know that Richard Geist wasn't going anywhere. Not yet, anyway. Besides, it wouldn't cost the state a cent to keep Richard where he was for the time being. Of course, Lark and the department knew that Richard was quite secure, or they would not have chanced the patient remaining there a second longer than necessary. It was only a matter of time before Richard would be transferred to North Shore State Hospital for the Criminally Insane over in Havenwood. As instructed by Dr. King, Dr. Bianco would fight to have his patient remain at the King Foundation for continued treatment. Ironically, Lark, too, would do whatever it took to postpone the inevitable, but for very different reasons to be sure. He wouldn't tell Bianco that he was in accord, for the lieutenant felt he had to keep the new director on his toes. Politics would certainly rear its ugly head. Therefore, cop and shrink would be engaged in a game of one-upmanship. Richard, however, would be playing a game of cat and mouse for keeps.

Carl teetered from behind a tree and out into the parking lot, ducking down between two late model automobiles. From inside one of the wicker bags, he removed a wire coat hanger, untwisting it and reshaping its handle to form a V. He slid the length of wire past the rubber seal atop the car window on the driver's side, maneuvering the V down toward the mushroom-like door lock post. After several attempts, Carl hooked and pulled the flanged stem upward, unlocking the door. Suddenly, he heard someone coming up behind him.

"Ah, Doctor. It is a fine day. Vouldn't you agree?" Mr. Schimmel asked exuberantly, his expression gradually changing the moment Carl turned around.

"It certainly is, my good man," Carl stated cheerfully, assuming an English accent and patting Mr. Schimmel good-naturedly on the shoulder, trying to focus beyond the librarian to see if anyone else had followed.

Schimmel stared up at Carl queerly, then down at the wire in the man's hand. "Vhat is that?"

"Oh, you see, I locked myself out of my car," Carl explained, adjusting the glasses, amused that Schimmel appeared as odd to him as he to Schimmel. "I'm afraid it is becoming an unfortunate habit. Now that I have gotten in, I realize I do not have my spare key that I usually keep in the glove compartment. Say! You don't suppose that you could do me a favor?"

"Favor?" Schimmel asked cautiously.

"Yes, a favor. Perhaps you could go over to A Building and ask Nurse Ryder to entrust you with the spare key that I instructed her to keep in the top drawer of her desk for just such an emergency," Carl invented on the spot.

The librarian reached inside the pocket of his vest and proudly produced a single brass key. "See," he beamed. "Dr. King has entrusted me vith this key for the past tventy years now. It is the key to the library, of vhich I am in charge. I open every morning and lock up every night."

"That certainly is a considerable trust," Carl agreed. "I knew I picked the right chap for the job. An honest soul. A modern day Diogenes," he assured him, staring apprehensively over the man's shoulder.

Schimmel nodded excitedly.

Carl looked Schimmel squarely in the eyes. "Listen to me, my good fellow. When I return, I am going to entrust you with more than just that key you carry. Or for that matter, the key to my car. Yes, sir! When I return, you and I will make some changes around here," he said, tossing the wire hanger and suitcases upon the backseat.

"Mrs. O'Brian told the vomen that you're the new director, Doctor," Schimmel stated with some degree of doubt.

Carl smiled mischievously, suppressing the sudden urge to twirl his forsaken handlebar mustache, deciding to play Mr. Schimmel along for all its worth. "I'm sure by now you've heard of Dr. King's—shall we say—recuperation?"

Mr. Schimmel nodded affirmatively.

Carl leaned forward, commanding the man's full attention. "Well, I'm afraid that's just a bloody rumor," he whispered confidentially. "I'm afraid it's a little more serious than that. Poor chap," he stated solemnly, circling an index finger around his ear. "I'm afraid he's a bit balmy in the crumpet as we say. Not quite right in the upper story. Mad as a weaver, to be blunt."

"*Vy iz mir!*"

"Yes. Very sad situation, indeed. Anyhow, I am the new head of this Foundation," Carl stated with authority. "I am in charge here."

"*VY IZ MIR!*" Schimmel announced in awe.

"But not a word about Dr. King's condition to anyone. I want to save him from further embarrassment when I bring him back to health."

"Not von vord," Schimmel swore, affirming their secret as though it were a sacred oath. "Ve have a mission," he stated anxiously. "Ve must put a *schvartze* in the garden."

Carl looked down in amazement at the little man. "A *schvartze* in the garden," he mused with delight. "Yes, a capital idea. Positively smashing!"

"Yes," Schimmel stated, ready to burst apart at the seams. "Yes, indeed!" Then the little man asked the inevitable question. "Vhat is your name, Doctor?"

"Dr. Bullshitski from Liverpool," Carl answered straightaway, taking and shaking the man's hand vigorously. "Well, you run along now, and I'll wait here for your return. Cheerio. Ta ta."

Schimmel nodded obediently, scurrying off in the direction of A Building.

Carl waited until Mr. Schimmel was out of sight before opening the door and sliding in behind the wheel. Removing those horrible glasses and opening up one of the wicker cases for the tools he needed, he quickly went to work beneath the dashboard, cutting and splicing wires with a pair of small pliers, rewiring this and that. A moment later, the car was purring like a happy kitten. He put everything away, setting the suitcases on the floor of the backseat.

Putting Dr. Schwartz's glasses back on then sending down the window for some air, Carl carefully shifted through the gears, for it had been many, many years since he had driven an automobile. Slowly, he approached the stone booth at the far end of the parking lot. He smiled pleasantly at the young man standing alertly at his post. Immediately, the guard shot up his hand. Carl stopped short.

The guard came over, noting the decal on the windshield, shaking his head from side to side. "Your parking ticket has expired, sir. May I have your name, and I'll see to it that you have a new one in a day or so."

"Doctor Gustafson," Carl answered up enthusiastically. "That's G-u-s-t-a-f-s-o-n. I'm leaving for vacation, so there's no need to rush."

"Have a nice vacation, Doctor," the guard said, jotting down the name and waving him ahead.

"Oh, by the way. Do you know Dr. Bianco?"

"No, sir. I only started here a week ago."

"Well, you'll meet him soon enough. And when you do, you can tell him I'm off to Sweden for a spell and that I'll send him a postcard. He speaks my language fluently. Actually, we're both multilingual. Would you say *farväl vän* to him for me? Would you do that for me, please?"

The guard picked up a pen and slip of paper.

"That's f-a-r-v-ä-l, space, v-ä-n," Carl spelled out. "Umlauts over the final ä of each word."

"F-a-r-v-ä-l v-ä-n," the man jotted down. "Umlauts over the final ä of each word," he repeated. Will do, Doctor."

"Much appreciated, my good man." *Farewell, friend,* the caretaker translated silently, driving out the gate with Dr. Bianco's caring and friendly countenance etched into the patient's mind forever.

Mr. Schimmel ran into A Building, completely out of breath, communicating the *new* director's instructions to Nurse Ryder to a T, requesting the spare key from the top desk drawer for Dr. Bullshitski's automobile. Needless to say, Nurse Ryder had no idea what Mr. Schimmel was talking about, for Dr. Bianco was still in a meeting in D Building with Lieutenant Lark and Sergeant Grear. At first, Nurse Ryder ignored the excitable soul. But when he persisted, she placated him by promising to handle the director's request personally, explaining that she simply could not hand over a key to just anyone without the express permission of Buildings and Grounds. Boss or no boss. End of conversation. But Mr. Schimmel shook his head stubbornly, practically standing over the woman while pleading to merciful God.

Finally, Nurse Ryder pushed her chair back from the desk, pulling open the top drawer and removing the single key. She stood abruptly. "All right, Mr. Schimmel. But first I want you to go to the library. Now! And put away any books that you see lying around on tables and chairs. Last I looked, the place was a mess. *I'll* take care of the key myself."

This seemed to satisfy Mr. Schimmel to a degree. Nevertheless, he went over Dr. Bullshitski's instructions once again. When the librarian finally left the building, Nurse Ryder smiled and shook her head, buzzing for one of the attendants who came immediately.

"I'll only be a minute," Nurse Ryder said, taking up her purse. She went around the corner and, with that very key, unlocked the door to the ladies room, if only to powder her nose.

Lieutenant Lark and Sergeant Grear sat across from Dr. Bianco, listening to the psychiatrist's clinical evaluation of Richard Geist's condition of catatonia. The doctor fully understood the skepticism written across the lieutenant's face as the new director explained the patient's disorder as one of the forms of schizophrenia.

"So, Richard is in what we call a catatonic stupor or stuporous state," Bianco elaborated, "holding rigid positions for extremely prolonged periods of time. How long he will remain uncommunicative, I really can't say."

"It's all a goddamn act," the lieutenant snapped in frustration. "He knows we want answers, and it's his way of avoiding our questions. He understands everything all right; he just doesn't *want* to cooperate."

"Ostensibly you're correct," the psychiatrist agreed. "Although Richard may appear to be unresponsive to all outside stimuli, he does, indeed, understand. He sees, records, and retains. Only, he *cannot* act."

"Cannot, or will not?" Lark pressed.

"Outright refusal to act," Bianco stated.

"Well, that's exactly what I'm saying!" the lieutenant insisted.

"I'm afraid it's not that simple," the psychiatrist said

understandingly. "You're right, but for the wrong reasons. Allow me to explain. All right?"

Lark shifted impatiently in the chair. "Go on."

"First, Lieutenant, you have to understand that a person in a catatonic state may rationalize his refusal to communicate openly by actually believing that if he were to behave otherwise, if he did not resist all efforts, something devastating, something absolutely catastrophic might happen to him or, say, a loved one. It's important to understand that the patient believes that fully. Unfortunately, in Richard's case, we do not know what the underlying factors are yet. But what we do know, gentlemen, is that it has something to do with his mother's soul. A soul that he is desperately trying to save."

"Her soul?" Lark questioned and laughed. "Her soul, or his own skin? C'mon, Doctor. Do you expect me to believe—"

"I really can't expect you to believe anything, Lieutenant. What we're dealing with here is a very complex case. It seems that Richard had to kill his mother along with any *form* of her that ever existed. Like the mannequin, or mummy, if you will, that you yourself unwrapped in Dr. King's study; her alter ego. Or Theresa Martinez, who he believes was his mother's younger self, just as Dicky is Richard's younger self. Or Theresa's doll, symbolizing Richard/Ruthie during infancy."

"Richard? Ruthie?"

"Yes. A hermaphroditic syndrome. All rather complicated, gentlemen."

Lieutenant Lark stared at Dr. Bianco rather incredulously before shifting in his seat toward Sergeant Grear. "Well, what do you make of all this lunacy, Sergeant?"

Sergeant Grear glanced at his superior before addressing the psychiatrist. "Isn't it possible, Doctor, that Richard cleverly established the fact that if he does not act out this resistance, as you put it, that he may be found capable of standing trial and quite possibly prosecuted for his mother's murder as well as the Martinez girl's? Not to mention Dr. King's chauffeur, Max."

"Who, Sergeant?"

Sergeant Grear did not understand. "What do you mean, 'Who?' We're talking about Richard."

"Richard? Dicky? Or perhaps some other personality that has not yet surfaced?" Dr. Bianco challenged. "Look, Sergeant. If Richard clearly understands that compliance might result in fitness to stand trial, which he probably does, and that he might be held accountable and culpable, well, that doesn't exactly render him sane either. Now does it? Especially in light of the fact that it was Dicky, his divided self, who, under a very powerful drug, told us of Richard's guilt. You have to understand that Dicky sees himself in the clear when he spoke of Richard's deed. It's not Dicky who is assuming the responsibility for the murders. But, from where you're sitting, if one burns, they both burn. However, that's not the way the individual personalities of the patient see it; for they are just that. Individuals. Both sick as shit, for sure, but truly separate beings in his own mind."

"But it was Richard who tried to frame Carl Gustafson for the Martinez girl's murder," Lark quickly pointed out. "All very calculated. Don't you think?'

"That was only to throw us off track in order to gain the necessary time he needed to dispose of his mother's body, not to try and assign any permanent blame to Carl, or anyone else for that matter. He knew it was only a matter of time before we'd discover him." Bianco paused for their response, but there wasn't any. They weren't buying it. "For Christ's sake, Lieutenant, he was waiting for us in the house. And did Richard not confess to the murder of the Martinez girl as well as Max? What Richard fails to see, as apparently you do, gentlemen, is that he really is very sick."

Lieutenant Lark smiled sarcastically. "What I'm afraid you fail to see is that you are being taken in by a very clever young man who has the perfect cover and unwritten sanction of this Foundation to commit murder, copping out with an insanity plea. And may I point out, Doctor, that the records from Dr. King's office say absolutely nothing about a split personality, as you are more than suggesting here. There's nothing in Richard's file that even remotely supports your evaluation."

"Might I remind you, Lieutenant, that Dr. King was blinded by the love of a woman who had at one time suffered a most severe case of depression? A case that Dr. King treated successfully. A case where others failed. A woman whose entire family had a history of mental illness. A woman whom Dr. King planned to marry at the end of the summer. A woman, whose son, if successfully treated, too, meant the establishment of a family Dr. King so desperately needed. You have to understand, Lieutenant, that Dr. King could not afford to fail. But fail he did. His plea of impropriety is not so much a question of unethical behavior as it is of having simply become emotionally involved. His resignation is a clear acknowledgment of that unfortunate error in judgment.

"And let me also assure you, Lieutenant," Bianco continued, "that Richard Geist is clearly a divided personality. So strong is Richard's will to safeguard his mother's whereabouts, that he can actually dissociate his adult self and assume the personality of 'little Dicky' while under a powerful truth inducing drug. That's not playacting as you're suggesting, gentlemen. And when things became too hot, when we asked Dicky where Richard put his mother's body, when the world started to close in on him, he simply escaped to the security of a catatonic state. He may, in time, abandon the uncommunicative stage, speaking in fragmented sentences or isolated words, perhaps giving us some clue. We'll just have to wait and see what happens. We'll just have to be patient."

"I'm afraid that's going to be difficult, Doctor. The district attorney is not going to sit still for this. I'm sure you're well aware of the fact that, officially, Richard Geist isn't even committed to this Foundation. Dr. King's records clearly list Richard Geist as an outpatient since the beginning of July."

Dr. Bianco raked his fingers through his wavy coal-black hair in pure frustration. "That's because Richard was to be brought up to the house to continue his treatment just as soon as Dr. King returned from Boston. Before he left, he asked me to expedite the paperwork. Dr. King thought it was important for the patient to be settled in before the marriage. And I assure you, Lieutenant, that Richard Geist has been confined to this Foundation since the day of his military discharge and wasn't going anywhere," the psychiatrist stated firmly.

"Confined to this Foundation," Lark echoed with a biting tone, shaking his head firmly from side to side, pushing himself out of the chair. "Do you call patients roaming around this—this private country club you operate between here and Dr. King's estate, confinement, Doctor?"

"Only those patients who are of no threat to themselves or others have access to the grounds between here and Dr. King's estate,

Lieutenant."

"Oh, you mean like Richard Geist," Lark mocked with a scornful sneer.

"Dr. King made a mistake, Lieutenant. But I am in charge now. I am running this show, and I assure you that Richard Geist will remain here under heavy security."

"A *mistake*, Doctor? You're going to sit there and tell me that Dr. King made a mistake? We all make mistakes, Dr. Bianco. We all let our guard down occasionally," he said in a rather solemn tone, glancing over at his partner as a sharp reminder of Richard somehow lifting the sergeant's key and opening the handcuffs. "Sometimes we get lucky and it costs us nothing. Other times we pay a price. But we are not talking here about some minor mistake, Doctor, as you make it seem. We are talking about gross incompetence."

The newly appointed administrator pushed his chair back deliberately, rising to the occasion and angrily addressing the remark. "Neither Dr. King nor anyone employed at this Foundation is in any way incompetent. And I resent your comment," Bianco stated firmly.

"And that, Doctor, I believe is your mistake. For openers, Richard Geist belongs in a maximum security facility such as North Shore State Hospital for the Criminally Insane over in Havenwood. And I'm going to see to it that he's headed there. We'll be in touch," Lark said flatly, heading toward the door. "We'll see ourselves out, thank you."

Sergeant Grear sat staring gravely at the two men shrouded in their professionalism.

"Well, are you coming, Sergeant? Or do you need a written invitation?" Lark barked with one foot at the threshold.

Grear got up.

"Good day, Lieutenant—Sergeant," Dr. Bianco said evenly, pressing a button on the intercom before speaking in a foreign tongue to an attendant. Sergeant Grear quietly pulled the door closed behind the lieutenant and himself.

In the hallway, Lieutenant Lark expelled a sudden gust of breath that clearly spelled frustration. Disgusted, he walked ahead. "You know as well as I do, Sergeant, that Geist will never be found fit to stand trial. Not in his condition," he added angrily.

"I know, Lieutenant."

The Korean who had escorted the two earlier was coming down the corridor to meet them, the sound of keys jingling officiously off a thigh. He unlocked and led the detectives back through the set of double doors and over to a waiting elevator. As the three stepped within, the attendant used another key to close the doors, and the car started its descent. Lieutenant Lark remarked at how unusually quiet it was for a nut house. The Korean no sooner smiled up at the pair then let out with a blood-curdling cry that filled the space and put both detectives immediately at the Asian's throat. Suddenly, murderous shrieks and waves of hysteria came funneling through the elevator shaft and all around them as the trio tunneled past floor after angry floor.

"Are you out of your fucking mind?" Lark sallied, holding the attendant firmly against the elevator doors.

"Yep, I'm long-time trustee. Started here eleven years ago," he explained with a disarming laugh. "Don't get sore, Joe. Doctor Bianco told me to give you ride you not soon forget. Doctor no like you," he assured the lieutenant, directing their attention to the insanity all around. "Sound like nut house, now. Yes?" he questioned rhetorically. "Here we are, Joe. You come back again real soon. Hear?"

Lark made some offhand comment about the Korean War and let it go at that. Sergeant Grear soured and told the man he had better hold on to his keys.

Once outside the building, Lieutenant Lark took out a small notepad and pen from his jacket pocket. Impatiently, he flipped through several pages, stopping abruptly to peruse a single word. "Tablecloth," he said disturbingly.

"What?"

"Tablecloth, Sergeant. Remember last week when we asked the housekeeper if she noticed anything missing other than some of the mother's clothing? She told us that a tablecloth had vanished from the linen closet. A large white linen tablecloth. No scissors or shears from the sewing room. No drugs from the medicine chests or cabinets. No tools such as spades or shovels from the garage or the caretaker's shed. Only a tablecloth. One large linen tablecloth."

"She said that the chauffeur had probably stolen it."

"A linen tablecloth, Sergeant? No other linens or silver missing. You just don't steal one linen tablecloth."

"Maybe Max was starting to collect an item here and there before he bought the farm."

"No, he was around here too long. Stole galleries of expensive paintings from his family in the past. He wasn't a petty thief."

"Well, she did say that he wasn't wrapped too tight. Not that she's got both oars in the water either," Grear kidded.

Lieutenant Lark stopped stone still in his tracks upon the path, looking up at the sergeant. "What did you say?"

"Lieutenant, I was only kidding."

"No, no. Repeat what you just said."

"I said that the housekeeper doesn't exactly have both oars in the water. I only meant—"

"No, before that."

"What?"

"You said something before that."

"That the housekeeper said that Max wasn't wrapped too tight?"

"Exactly. Not wrapped too tight," Lark repeated. "That's it!"

"I don't get it."

"Of course not. That's why you're the sergeant, and I draw the big money."

"Lieutenant!"

"Come on."

"Where are we going?"

"They've got a library here. Right? We'll talk on the way."

"Yes, but I thought we were going back to question Sarah further, to find out more about all that stuff in the trunk, aside from Max."

"'Potions, and lotions, and notions', Sergeant. You remember what Richard said there in the study, and how upset the old woman became. Those are the real clues, Sergeant. Clues he knows she won't reveal. We find only what Richard wants us to find. Yes. I think things are beginning to take shape."

"So clue me in, Lieutenant."

"Look. You heard Bianco. Richard is on some sort of a soul-saving mission. Right? Safeguarding a resting place for dear ol' mom. Maybe he saw her as a kept woman, selling her soul for power or position. Whatever. In Richard's mind, she's a glorified prostitute. Okay? He's got to save her soul before it's too late."

"I thought you didn't buy into Bianco's story."

"It's Richard's story I don't buy, Sergeant. Sure. He's in the house. He takes the gauze and tape from Dr. King's supply closet and wraps up that mannequin like a mummy. All very neat. Nothing's missing. It's all there for us to see. The materials are all accounted for. Scissors and pinking shears are on the floor. Empty gauze boxes. Tape dispensers. He does a whole routine with cups and saucers and honey cakes. He's got a couple of statues keeping vigil. That bird—the ibis—fits right in with the whole goddamn ritual to convince us that he's bats. We have a weapon, Sergeant. The broken statue that he left for us. We have a motive. Wanton behavior on behalf of his mother. But we have no body, Sergeant. We have no body because he doesn't want us to have a body. We see only what he wants us to see. He gave Dr. King clues. All the wrong clues. He told King, 'I will leave you with a permanent and everlasting impression. Concrete impressions. I will make a mark upon your Foundation.' And what are we all doing? Breaking up freshly poured foundations for the last week. Digging up freshly turned soil, 'beneath the laurel and pachysandra where serpents creep,'" Lark mimicked. "Every place where Richard is telling us to look. Oh, and up there," the lieutenant said, pointing toward the sky. "I'm surprised we're not shooting missiles on some sort of soul-searching mission. Richard would really love that one. I'm telling you, he's laughing up his sleeve at us right now."

"And you don't call that crazy?"

"Crafty like a fox, Sergeant. Like a fox."

"I still don't understand the business with the tablecloth."

"A tablecloth, Sergeant. A linen tablecloth. That's what's missing from the house. That's our first real clue. All of that other crap of his is just a smoke screen . . . which wouldn't be necessary if his secret were secure . . . if she were tucked away safely . . . permanently . . . if he were truly finished with the business he started out to do. Unless I miss my guess, Richard's created a diversion for us. We're going to find other things missing from that house. Things that are not so obvious. Things you wouldn't normally miss at all."

"So why are we going to the library, Lieutenant?"

"You like history, Sergeant?"

"I was a pretty good student in school."

"Not me. Actually, my worst subject. Couldn't remember a

single solitary date. But it's not so much the remembering that's important, Sergeant. You can always open up a book. What's important is knowing *where* to look. Always remember that."

Inside the library, Lieutenant Lark and Sergeant Grear sat with half a dozen books before them on Egyptian civilization. They worked together as a team for hours. One reading aloud. The other taking notes. The two of them taking turns. Neither of them knew exactly what it was they were looking for, but they kept right on looking just the same.

Sergeant Grear came to a section on burial rights and customs. The lieutenant listened carefully as Grear carefully defined certain Egyptian words. The ka: one part of the spirit conceived as a dematerialized double of the deceased, and how the mummy was a home for the ka. The sarcophagus: a coffin for the mummy. And in the Old Kingdom, the mastaba: a tomb with flattened roof and crumbled walls, a permanent home. The serdab: a second chamber where objects of an afterlife were stored. Lark scribbled notes and asked the sergeant to repeat certain sections, or anxiously pulled the books away for a closer examination of a sentence, phrase, or single word.

After a while, Sergeant Grear got up to go to the men's room as the lieutenant read for himself the various methods of embalming, fascinated by the most elaborate, in which the deceased's brain was literally drawn out through the nostrils by means of a metal tool and certain drugs. Then on to how the contents of the abdomen were removed via an incision, the interior washed with palm wine and aromatics before being filled with spice.

What Lark read next intrigued him. The body was then placed in natron—a hydrated sodium carbonate—for fifty-five days, after which it was washed and wrapped from head to foot with bandages of fine linen cloth smeared with gum resin. The process took another fifteen days to complete before the soul could reenter the body through a ritual called the 'Opening of the Mouth Ceremony,' whereby a slit was made through the bandages across the mummy's mouth. Lark read on.

"Seventy days,' the lieutenant added aloud. "Seventy days from the day Richard killed his mother, less seven is sixty-three days."

"What's 'sixty-three days,' Lieutenant?" Sergeant Grear asked upon returning to his seat.

Lieutenant Lark pushed the book across to Grear. "Right there," he pointed. "Read, Sergeant. Richard took that tablecloth for the linen bandages he'll need to wrap the body. His mother's body. He's mummifying her! Sixty-three days from today."

Grear read the passage, grasping the lieutenant's point in part. "Only it says here that the body was wrapped in bandages after fifty-five days, not seventy."

"Go on, Sergeant."

"Well, Richard killed his mother on the Fourth of July. A week ago today. Which means he would have forty-eight days left to wrap things up," Grear punned, staring across the table at the serious face staring back.

"Sixty-three days precisely, Sergeant. Nine weeks," Lark stated emphatically.

Grear read the passage again, trying to follow the lieutenant's logic. "But according to this, the process takes another fifteen days before the soul can reenter the body, Lieutenant."

"Nine weeks from today, Sergeant," Lieutenant Lark repeated, flipping to the pocket calendar in his wallet.

Sergeant Grear shook his head in confusion, calculating aloud, working the problem backwards before looking up from the text and into the earnest face of his superior.

"There's nothing faulty with your math, Sergeant. It's your reasoning that worries me."

Puzzled, Grear looked back down at the passage, searching for some clue.

"Sergeant," Lark said impatiently. "Richard can't just walk freely out of a locked ward after forty-eight days, wrap her body in bandages, then calmly stroll back to his room in D Building and wait another fifteen days before he performs the 'Opening of the Mouth Ceremony.' Richard knows he'll have but one chance, and one chance only. Sixty-three days from today. Nine weeks to go. He'll wrap her body and perform the ritual that very day. That's providing we don't find Victoria Geist's body before—September 12th," Lark said, consulting the calendar again. "So, what we have to do now is try to figure out for ourselves where he put her body."

Grear stared at Lieutenant Lark skeptically, holding several gnawing questions in abeyance before returning to the page. "Sodium carbonate," he read aloud. "Washing soda. He could have gotten that from the housekeeper's laundry room. You think the body is lying in some sort of sodium carbonate solution? Or maybe salt water, Lieutenant!" Sergeant Grear said excitedly.

"Salt preserves. But I don't think it's salt water we're looking for, Sergeant. However, I do think you're getting warmer," he said behind a smile. "Think about it. The likelihood of preserving a body in Egypt is easier to consider than in most other countries, simply because of its climate. Especially during summer when the intense heat scorches the land. But if a body were carefully prepared and buried in dry sand, Sergeant, even here at the Foundation, it would probably dehydrate faster than it would decay, more than likely preserving an individual for months. Perhaps even longer. Got the picture?"

Grear sat saturated in an ambivalent bath of admiration, assigning renewed respect toward this uncanny puzzle solver. He had worked with Lieutenant Lark on several cases, and not once did this middle-aged unraveler of riddles cease to amaze him. It all became so clear whenever his partner finished imparting pertinent information, initially cloaked in theory, working backwards from its premise, like a person adept in origami, exhibiting an intricate bird or flower design, only to reveal, upon unfolding, a single solitary sheet of paper. So simple once you understood the scheme of things. Still, there were several unanswered questions.

"So, Victoria Geist is possibly buried in one of a hundred sand dunes somewhere below the cliffs," the sergeant inferred.

"I can't say for sure," Lark admitted. "But it's all we have to go on for the moment. It fits. It explains why we haven't been able to come up with anything out there," he said, referring to men and machinery breaking up heavy concrete blocks, not to mention teams of men digging up the gardens around Dr. King's home, especially the gardens in front of the house where they had found the caduceus belonging to the broken statue of Hermes. "Hermaphroditic poppycock," Lark snapped. "I believe he bulldozed us into doing all the work for him," the detective punned. "Now he has a dozen ready-made tombs in which to place her body whenever he's ready."

"You want me to put a team of men and some equipment along the cliffs?"

"No, Sergeant. Not without something substantial to go on. We don't head in there like gangbusters and disturb the environment. If her body is down there, we'll find it. Besides, there are only two ways of bringing in equipment. One is by craning it down the cliffs; the other is by boating it across the bay. The taxpayers would just love us for that. Not to mention the environmental groups that would be on our backs. No. What we'll do is put a few good men down there to simply look around, but I don't want anything disturbed. No equipment. If they discover anything suspicious, anything at all, I want to be notified immediately. This is the best we've got so far, and I don't want to blow it. And I want this kept quiet. I don't want the district attorney's office wondering why I only have a few men working on an important lead. Assuming we don't come up with anything right away, we'll have to stall. If they want to know whether we have anything concrete, tell them we have plenty of that. Otherwise, the official word is, 'No important leads as yet.' Tell them we're moving cautiously on this one because we're trying to cooperate with the new head of the Foundation. If they accuse us of dragging our feet, put it on Bianco's head. But put it charmingly. 'Can't cure madness in a month of Mondays, Alfred.' And if that pompous ass leans on you, you tell him that I said there'll be a body. Only it won't be the one he's looking for. Got it?"

"Got it."

"Well, I can see that something is still bothering you. What is it, Sergeant?"

"Lieutenant. Suppose we don't come up with anything ourselves and have to wait Geist out. How in God's name is he ever going to get out of a maximum security ward in D building to begin with?"

"Only one way, Sergeant. Only one way."

"Escape?"

"He's already done that. Bianco told us that Richard has withdrawn to the security of a catatonic state. Only now, he's planning his return. To the scene of the crime as they say. To the place where he has temporarily hidden his mother's body."

"But how?" Grear persisted. "How will he move if he's confined?"

"Perhaps, by getting well," Lark said enigmatically. "Look. I don't have all the answers yet, but there are certain things that I can sense within the marrow of my bones. I don't know exactly how he plans to do it, but Richard Geist is somehow going to try and keep his date with destiny. If we can't find her before September 12th, well, we're just going to be around here to make sure he leads us to her in sixty-three days, Sergeant. Nine weeks from today."

"You keep saying nine weeks, Lieutenant. But what if he doesn't move in nine weeks? What if nine weeks becomes nineteen weeks? Or nine months for that matter. What if he doesn't move at all? What if he's still in that catatonic state? What if you're wrong about all this?" Grear stated flatly.

Lark shook his head from side to side insistently. "Seventy days from the day he killed his mother, Sergeant. One week down and nine to go. Sixty-three days from today. September 12th. He'll try to do it quickly, just before he performs the 'Opening of the Mouth Ceremony.' But we'll be ready for him."

"Yes, but how can you be so certain?"

"Because Richard has a plan. And everything so far has gone according to plan. More importantly, Richard is exacting. Numbers are very important to him."

"Yes, I know. I read his file, too. But what I'm asking is how you can be so cocksure that Richard has the same information that we just gleaned from a few pages here?"

"Gleaned?" Lieutenant Lark needled. "You're such a showoff with words, Sergeant. I mean you're sometimes downright embarrassing. If you must know, I get surer by the minute. I'm not only sure that Richard has this information, but that he *gleaned* it from the very page in front of you."

Grear stared blankly down at the page.

"What does glean mean, Sergeant? Explain it to me."

"Lieutenant."

"Give me a definition," Lark snapped impatiently. "Give me the meaning of glean."

"Well, in this case—"

"We're discussing this case, are we not, Sergeant?"

"It means to collect knowledge or information, especially bit by bit."

Lark stood up. "Ah, bit by bit. I see. Then would you mind gathering the hairs recessed between those pages, and I'll arrange for patient Geist to have a haircut so that we can have the lab match them right away."

Sergeant Grear picked up the book, carefully bending back its binding. Within the crease, several curly strands of hair loomed out at him like a specimen under a microscope, brought suddenly and sharply into focus; clay-red arcs seemed to magnify the increasing shade of embarrassment settling into the sergeant's cheeks, like a chameleon soaking in the color chemistry of the world around it.

"Well, are you just going to sit there, Sergeant? Or am I going to have to do all the work myself?" Lark asked impatiently, lighting up one of the cigars that he had helped himself to in Dr. King's study. "Damn good weed the old boy smokes. Can't get them in the States, you know."

Grear just sat there mesmerized, contemplating the curly hairs before removing a pair of tweezers and a small plastic evidence bag from his pocket, having to remind himself why it was that he so admired this man who constantly berated him. His mentor. The man who helped him make the grade of detective sergeant. The man who had been passed over twice for promotion to captain because he flatly refused to involve himself in Chicago's dirty politics before his transfer came. The man who was not so much respected as feared by certain factions within his own department. The man with an uncanny ability to solve even the most difficult cases. The man who was rarely challenged or reckoned with. The man who truly was his own man. Lieutenant Milton Bernard Lark. The man.

Mr. Schimmel came over to the two detectives as they were leaving the library. His library. His domain. Suddenly and quite vehemently, the little man set forth a series of venomous attacks directed at the two outsiders. "There are going to be some changes made around here," Schimmel stated with assurance. "Ve do not vant strangers coming and going. Ve have a mission. Ve must put a *schvartze* in the garden—and get the *goyim* out of Galilee," he added arrogantly, staring up at Sergeant Grear. "Hey! VHERE DO YOU THINK YOU'RE GOING? *SCHLEMIEL. SCHLIMAZEL.* I AM A VERY IMPORTANT MAN HERE. PEOPLE LISTEN TO ME. I HAVE THE *NEW* ADMINISTRATOR'S EAR," he warned, pulling savagely on his lobe and screwing up his face in a fit of rage.

It was not until sometime after the evening meal that Carl Gustafson was reported missing. Mrs. O'Brian and Mr. Schimmel were questioned at length, revealing the little they knew about the *new* administrator. Dr. Bianco helped to sort things out quickly, calmly explaining that Carl had put together a disguise while assuming the role of the *new* administrator. Mrs. O'Brian smiled sadly and said she hoped that the authorities would bring the caretaker back to her, explaining that she would miss him terribly if they didn't. But Mr. Schimmel was still nonplussed. It took some time before that tormented soul fully digested the impact of what had transpired in the parking lot earlier that day, shaking his head in total disbelief.

"Betrayal!" was the one word Schimmel kept repeating. "A VOLF IN SHEEP'S CLOTHING," were the others that resounded across the courtyard, throughout the entire night.

Devastated, Abe Schimmel abandoned all hope of ever obtaining a position of influence he so desperately desired. Sleep, not undisturbed, finally took hold of him as the sun shone in the east, where, beneath the cliffs, policemen were busy combing the dunes in search of Victoria Geist, while others covered neighboring towns and villages for a stolen 1969 Mercedes coup and Carl Gustafson.

Chapter 24

THE PLOT

The following day, Richard stood still and silent in his room. Running things carefully through his mind. Plotting. It was a very simple plot, he thought, giggling delightfully to himself. A ground plan that he had laid out oh so carefully from the start. Though he himself was grounded, in a manner of speaking, he knew it was only a matter of time before he would fly the coop. He had all of that figured out, too. Well in advance.

First, they would cart him off to the infirmary for the self-inflicted injuries he'd cause. Of course, he knew he'd somehow have to muster up the strength to carry out the penultimate scene, having casted a host of characters who, unbeknownst to them, would play their parts magnificently well. Bravo! Yet, not a one among them would receive the slightest bit of recognition for their role. No encores or applause. Neither flowers nor a fen. He alone would take the first and final curtain call, and the moment would be his and hers to share forever. Surely, no one would dare accuse him of a pusillanimous or second rate performance. Certainly not he. Such a star! Scintillating. Soon to enter the limelight. But first the infirmary. Yes. The oldest building of them all. Everything was there. Unctions and all. Mother, too. Bathing in her balm. An embalming ritual practiced thousands of years before.

Richard had painstakingly orchestrated, directed, and rehearsed the scene to perfection. Soon he would be ready. The stage would soon be set. All the players in their place. The only trouble had been in staging Mother. But that, too, he had resolved the week before. Richard closed his eyes and replayed the preliminary and dramatic moment in his mind. The scene was the basement of Dr. King's home. And what a scene it had been.

After Richard had elicited Max's rather painful confession, a confession made barely audible beneath the chauffeur's diminishing supply of breath, justice was meted out swiftly. Richard delivered the verdict. Guilty! For Max, indeed, was the one who rode Mother away that night. Max, of course, pleaded for mercy as there had been little time left for any sort of appeal. Without batting an eye, Richard carried out the sentence quickly, cracking the man's neck about as passionately as one might crack a whip to sound attention. Then it was off to the races, delivering ice and soda to the picnic in Sarah's laundry cart. Back to the house he flew.

Max had been stashed in Sarah's steamer trunk. Theresa and her doll were tucked away in the trash. And Mother lay cold-stone dead on the floor of Dr. King's study. It was time for another delivery. So Richard had quite literally wheeled her away, using the very same laundry cart. It had been the perfect time to move Mother to the infirmary, for practically everyone was so busy looking for the little Martinez girl. He had to work quickly, though. The only problem, up to that point, had been the blood. But he had taken extra precautions to double bag Mother's body in large, black, heavy-duty Lawn & Leaf bags, which he had filched weeks earlier from Carl Gustafson's garden shed. So there had been no visible bloody trail to follow between Dr. King's estate and the infirmary. Infirm she was, both in body as well as mind as it were. But Richard was there to fix all that.

Richard had even fooled the police and taken care of Marvin Gitlin in the bargain, wheeling Mother quickly up the ramp and into the rear of the infirmary, chauffeuring her into one of the cubicles near the end of the hall.

"Whee!"

Before Richard had returned from the infirmary to Dr. King's house—in mock surrender if you will—after having murdered Theresa Martinez, Max, Mother, and maiming Marvin, he had pulled the bloodstained poncho from a plastic bag at the bottom of the bin, donning the garment anew and throwing up its hood. It had served quite satisfactorily earlier, shielding him from the gaping head wounds he had inflicted in Dr. King's study on that memorable afternoon. Once again, it would suit him nicely at the infirmary. Richard rehashed and relished every detail:

Having lifted Mother's corpse from underneath all the clothing in the cart, he had carried her over to the infirmary's large, circular therapeutic tub, placing her carefully within. There, he tore the protective plastic Lawn & Leaf bags free along with the bloody clothes she wore. He studied Mother intently, recalling everything that he had read regarding the "Ritual of Embalming."

From the pocket of the poncho, he took out several more black plastic bags of different sizes, unfolding and draping each one neatly over the porcelain rim of the tub. He knelt beside her body. With Mother's head closest to the drain, he had no trouble whatsoever removing her brain from the shattered cranium, especially after having brained her at the house. And it was certainly a lot easier than having to pass that convoluted mess through her nostrils by means of tools and chemicals. Talk about disgusting!

Working methodically, Richard had spooned the rest of the bloody gray-white matter from her skull before carefully pouring in a highly caustic solution prepared from agents stored beneath a sink. He burned away her brain, poking and dissolving the slippery mass with one end of a glass rod. Finally, down the wide-mouthed drain of the porcelain tub it disappeared. "Gulp, gulp," Richard sounded noisily as if he himself were swallowing the globular remains before opening the faucet full blast and forcefully running hot water down the drain, washing away any trace of sin and stain.

Pulling on a pair of surgical gloves, Richard withdrew a shiny blade from a stainless steel drawer. Leaning over the tub, he drew the scalpel skillfully down along her side, from one end of her rib cage to the top of the pelvic bone, splaying her open wide, spilling and filling a medium-sized bag (set within another) with viscera and other vitals, save the heart and lungs. In went the large and small intestines, stomach, liver, kidneys, bladder, and spleen, along with internal genitalia. Ultimately, the monotonous peritoneum membrane.

With the cavity clear, he quickly went to work along the thoracic wall, first breaking through the fibrous tissue, cutting her windpipe and esophagus in order to pull away the lungs. Whoops! Her heart did fall. Although considered the seat of intelligence and to normally remain inside her body, Richard weighed things very carefully before plopping it into the bag with all the other trimmings, for he couldn't risk a stench. Besides, there was a special formula in the *Book of the Dead* discovered in Sarah's steamer trunk that would renew the heart symbolically. So, in the tub, he rub-a-dub-dubbed, cleansing the cavity with a special kind of care, careful to exsanguinate each and every drop of blood and gore. But time was ticking away, and he had yet so much to do before he could even begin to properly prepare.

Richard quickly rinsed and ripped free the pair of gory gloves, dropping them into the bag, too. Hurrying downstairs to the basement, he grabbed an empty trash barrel. Back upstairs he came, setting down the container. Lifting the bundled remains from the floor, he secured the bag's corners with a double knot, thoroughly rinsing and wiping the package dry before depositing it as trash.

Next, he cleaned out the laundry cart, gathering up all the garments that had concealed Mother's body in the canvas bin, stuffing the contents into another bag, tying it off and pushing it down inside the barrel. Then back to the tub he turned.

Holding Mother up with one arm, he slipped two heavy-duty Lawn & Leaf bags over her head, pulling the 3-mil plastic down to her tippy toes, double bagging the body once again. Knotting the ends of the bags securely, he lifted the eviscerated form up and out of the tub. She was practically weightless. Such an oddity, he considered, carrying her over to the container . . . her parts so seemingly heavy; her body . . . ethereal. Yes. Ethereal. That was surely the word in a wisp.

Draping Mother across the mouth of the barrel like a Raggedy Ann, he wrapped his arms around the bulky container, lifted the weighty contents then descended the basement stairs. So as not to let her body out of his sight for even a second, he bore the cumbersome load along a corridor and up an exit ramp, making his way toward a large Dumpster just outside the building. The container became increasingly heavier by the second, or so it seemed. Finally, he set it down and cradled her aery body in a pair of leaden arms when suddenly she rose before his very eyes as though it were of her own volition. Of course, it was nothing more than an involuntary motor response from handling the far heavier weight, yet it unnerved him just the same. He laid her down then quickly dumped the bag of body parts and clothing deep within the Dumpster, placing the trash container inside the receptacle, too. Richard had things timed perfectly, for the infirmary's trash was scheduled for late afternoon pickup, holiday or not.

Taking Mother back into his arms, he again carried her inside the infirmary, heading toward the far end of a dimly lit corridor and around a corner that tunneled down a cool black passageway. He stumbled once but refused to curse the darkness, smiling brightly while inching his way carefully along the wall. He continued until there was no place else to go. Slowly, he sank to his knees before a stone frame set within a slate and concrete floor. A frame constructed of the same materials and ingeniously designed to fool the keenest eye of any devil in the dark; a door in the floor leading to a shallow subcellar used for storage many a year ago. Perhaps a root cellar. A place forsaken or simply forgotten. A perfect place in time.

Setting his precious package down, he worked the tips of his fingers beneath the heavy beveled corner of stone, prying up the cover, pushing it aside before disappearing in a hellishly shallow void. Instantly, he reappeared, reaching for and carefully pulling down the coal-black bag containing Mother's shell of a body.

Moments later, he crawled out and carefully slid the concrete slab in place. Back along the passageway and around the corridor to the ramp he sped. Up the stairs he flew to scrub, and rub, and mop the scene, turning the room back to its original, checking scrupulously for any sign of hair, or blood, or anything at all that might possibly give him away.

Soon, everything was spotless. Richard stood there garbed in angry gray. Somewhat satisfied. He was sweating profusely. It was as though it had been pouring pailfuls of perspiration from within the plastic poncho. Throwing back the hood of the garment, he returned to Mother's temporary grave.

Along the inside wall were all the things he needed to prepare Mother for her journey into time: sticks of wax with tiny wicks and matches with which to shed a lovely light. A bag of rags and riches. All the ointments and oils. Lotions and potions. Powders and salves. Notions like needles. Yes. Needles and thread. Bags of lime and nitrate that he had smuggled in from Carl Gustafson's shed over a period of time. And finally, the strips of fine white linen tablecloth he'd need for bandages to wrap her body from head to toe. It was clearly obvious that Richard had been there prior to the Fourth. Preparing.

Squatting there in the refreshing darkness like a giant toad, enjoying the cool dryness of the concrete floor, he opened the coal-black plastic bag and slid Mother out and onto a large section of burlap so that the body would easily breathe. Then he struck a match and lit a single candle.

Working there in the tiny light, he had everything at hand to turn the fleshy cavity dry, dusting it with special powders before filling it with handfuls of lime and nitrates scooped from several bags. Taking up a shiny threaded needle, he closed Mother up rather neatly. Yes. "A stitch in time saves nine," he said with a giggle, wrapping the corpse within the burlap shroud before extinguishing the flame. There in the darkness, he inhaled the exhilarating column of warm and waxy air.

Of course, there were a lot more things that Richard could have done if only he had had more time. For instance, he could have labored hours scraping and swabbing the deeper recesses of the ghastly cavity in order to minimize contamination. He could have paid particular heed to the stringent rules regarding the "Ritual of Embalming," concerning the preservation of her vitals into makeshift canopic jars. He could have secured her fingernails and toenails with a stitch or two so that they would not fall free. There were many more details he could have attended to, but time had been his enemy. Time was running out. And although these things were done to ensure the survival of her soul, Richard had his own idea. It was unique! Unprecedented. She'd soon be all his very own. Certainly not for shares. Her journey would be a very short one, he reassured himself. He would, when ready, summon forth her soul to him forever. He knew she'd accept *his* body over the decrepit remains lying beside him on the floor. Lying there in the ancient subcellar within those hellish, hallowed walls.

Naturally, he had been apprehensive about receiving a second sex to share his eternal soul. But *that* was what was so spectacular. So singular. So unique! He shivered there excitedly in the darkness, dismissing any doubt. She was, after all, his own Mummy—was she not? What troubled him, though, was the possibility that Mother just might try and take him over. Now, there was serious room for concern. Yet, Richard was sure that he and Dicky could put her in her place if she became too domineering. She would just have to learn to behave herself. Yes. He was positively thrilled by the idea. And then they'd have their fun with Dr. King.

Confined to a tiny cell-like room under lock and key and heavy security in D Building, Richard reopened his eyes to the glory of the scene, rehashing its brilliance till he thought the very sun would burst.

The next week or so had passed rather slowly, like an interminable intermission. He remained silent yet stirred about rather restlessly, not having slept for days. When sleep did come, Richard's ka would leave his body, traveling alone through aery space, setting forth to the infirmary to investigate his handiwork. For according to Egyptian myth and legend, everything that ever existed had its double. And although those nightly visits were nothing but a dream, Richard certainly knew, Mother's eviscerated body, lying in the subcellar beneath the infirmary, was very real indeed!

Chapter 25

THE CAST

July had finally drawn to a close, and the police were still no closer to uncovering Mother's whereabouts. Lark and Grear were either up at Dr. King's home asking the grieving psychiatrist and Sarah scores of questions, or down at the library poring over pages and pages of material for a further clue. Lark's men had found nothing after having searched the buildings and grounds numerous times, including acres of land beneath the cliffs. Nor had the police reported any lead on Carl Gustafson or the stolen car, both of which had vanished into thin air.

Lieutenant Lark had other problems, too. Pressure was being applied by the district attorney's office to have Richard Geist transferred to the state facility over in Havenwood, despite the fact that the patient had failed his 7-30 examination, a psychiatric evaluation given to determine a defendant's competency to stand trial. Needless to say, the situation was frustrating to the state. The district attorney's office had motive, method and means in order to establish a solid case against Richard Geist in connection with the murders of Maximillian Shane and Theresa Martinez. Furthermore, they had his confession. They had everything needed in order to prosecute on two counts alone. Concerning Victoria Geist, they had everything but the victim herself, incidental to the fact that they had plenty of physical evidence, which would essentially constitute the body. Word had filtered down from an assistant district attorney that if Richard Geist was going to cop an insanity plea, he was going to do his time in a state hospital, not within the walls of a private Disney World-like Foundation with ostensibly privileges galore.

Lieutenant Lark couldn't agree more, but he would not reveal his reasons for wanting Richard to remain at the King Foundation for the time being. Lark wanted Richard *in flagrante delicto*; to be caught red-handed with his mother's nearby body. Of this the detective was sure that her body had to be close by. Just had to be. Lark was certain, too, that if the patient was sent to the North Shore facility before

September 12th, there would be very little hope, if any, in ever finding Victoria Geist. That, he would not chance. He had to find her. It wasn't a question of pride or showmanship or track record or any of that nonsense. It was simply a matter of closure for Doctor King, the detective told himself. He had seen too many people like patient Richard Geist walk after several years of confinement, supposedly cured. And the law would set people like Geist free. Free to commit the same heinous acts over and over again. Admittedly, part of Lark's persistence and downright tenacity was simply the challenge, he knew. Yet the matter somehow went deeper than that. Suddenly, Lark realized that was all bullshit. Recovering the body wouldn't really change a thing. It *was* the goddamn challenge! And, perhaps, the chance to kill Richard Geist on the spot.

Somehow, he had to stall the powers that be. He didn't like to admit it, but his instincts told him that if there was any chance of ever finding Victoria Geist at all, they would just have to wait Richard out. Play the patient's game. Lark couldn't go to the top and tell them Richard had this date with destiny. He couldn't tell his superiors to be patient until September 12th. Things didn't work like that. Once things got put into the machinery, once the cogwheels were set in motion, the action-cart would bump along its bureaucratic way. But Lark knew how to slow down the gears of that machinery, to impede its progress. He knew how to expand upon the range of red tape that a judicial cart could carry, to tie things up in a trafficked nightmare. He had put his best men on the job. Men who owed him favors. Men who knew men who could manipulate the very weather if necessary.

One beautifully bright warm morning in early August, Dr. Bianco came by Richard's room in D Building to see his patient. A billion birds were singing, and a zillion flowers stood listening like an attentive audience.

"How about a nice walk this morning, Richard?" the psychiatrist suggested. "It's really terrific out there." He waited for a reply. Receiving none, he plopped himself down upon the cot. "The birds are singing," he said, trying to coax a response before going on about the weather and sports.

Richard stood in complete silence, his arms secured across his chest within a straitjacket, ignoring the chatterbox jabbering away. At

Lark's insistence, a plainclothes officer stood posted just outside the door.

Dr. Bianco got up and took Richard gently by the arm, turning him toward the door. "Really, Richard, it's grand out there. Give yourself a breath of fresh air. You'll feel better. Come along, you'll see," he promised, leading Richard just outside the room, locking the door behind them. The off-duty officer followed several yards behind.

Summer was in full bloom, and the birds were hopping excitedly from branch to branch, fleeing as the three men followed along a treelined path. It was the path that Richard had taken around the construction site to the infirmary on the afternoon of the Fourth. A paved path that made it impossible to trace the course of Sarah's laundry cart. A path that merged with others in all directions. Richard noted that construction was completely at a standstill. The site was literally an unsightly ruin. *Now, that was power!* he thought, smiling satisfactorily to himself.

Dr. Bianco noted that Richard was responding positively to the scene but in silence. So, he, too, walked quietly beside his tight-lipped killer who could, in an instant, extinguish his life or ravage limb. Although Richard was confined to a straitjacket, Bianco took comfort in Lieutenant Lark's assurance that his best man was on the job. Whereas the month before Bianco had resented their intrusion, he now felt reassured with this professional at his back.

A gentle breeze danced the flowers playfully along the lawn. "Nice," Richard whispered softly, throwing caution to the wind.

Dr. Bianco looked up with some surprise. But when he questioned Richard and received no answer, he didn't press, but simply made a mental note of it for his report, a confidential report that Dr. King had asked that the psychiatrist send him, keeping him apprised of any new developments regarding Richard Geist. Although Dr. King thought it best to relieve himself of the responsibility of running the Foundation, in light of the situation, he insisted on being consulted in matters concerning his former patients, as well as some of the important areas of management. With those two stipulations agreed upon, Dr. King had placed the care of his Foundation into the capable hands of Dr. Bianco.

Shortly after Dr. Bianco had accepted his new position, Dr. King received two strong letters of resignation from respected doctors of long standing: Doctors Schwartz and Martin. Dr. King simply refused to accept their resignations, signing and sending the letters back marked, *Denied*. Dr. Martin remained on staff; however, Dr. Schwartz packed and left in a fury. Actually, he left in a rented Plymouth Fury III, for it was Dr. Schwartz's 1969 Mercedes coupe with which Carl Gustafson had absconded.

Doctors Schwartz and Martin were not the only two to voice dissatisfaction. Nurse Harrigan hammered home her point, too, informing the other nurses that if Dr. Bianco ever used his position of authority to abuse her, as he had in the past, that she, Nurse Kathleen A. Harrigan, would, without reservation (swearing an oath referencing her mother's grave), drive a stake through his heathen heart.

And when word got back to the new director of her violent vow, Bianco informed the others, with utmost seriousness, that he, Dr. Angelo T. Bianco, would, without hesitation (swearing on his godfather's grave), take definite advantage of her position by driving his Sicilian salami between the chubby cheeks of her derriere.

He reflected on his own foolishness while continuing along the garden path with Richard, wondering why in hell Dr. King ever put him, the kid of kidders, in charge of things. Did Dr. King think he'd change? The underlying answer was clear. Bianco was changing. His new behavior simply lacked the playful form it had before. A few weeks ago he would have simply carried out his threat, accosting Nurse Harrigan in the halls as he had a hundred times before, before being given the responsible position of heading up the Foundation, before his significant increase in salary. It was a subtle trick he played upon himself. He couldn't change overnight, so he changed in small degrees. He didn't fool anyone, so he had to fool himself. He certainly sensed and understood his colleagues' resentment. Oh, he had more than sensed it. It was more than abundantly clear. His kidding around was not so funny anymore because—well—because now he simply cared. Not about the others but about himself. It wasn't their bitterness that bothered him. At least that was open and honest. It was a handful of sycophants with their phony smiles or pretentious laughter who suddenly wanted to be his friend. And then there were the others. Those who didn't say a word one way or the other and just went about their business. They were the ones who simply did not understand him, he told himself. Yet, somewhere deep within his being, he knew that they were the ones who only knew him too well. No! It was their jealousy, he suddenly insisted, sparring with the voice of conscience. In truth, he himself had been profoundly shocked when handed the awesome responsibility of administration:

"You will take over in my capacity as head of this Foundation, indefinitely," its founder had told him in very definite terms. "Salary commensurate with responsibility."

Bianco had wondered if there was some weakness of character that Dr. King would later play upon. The stipulations the man had set forth were not unreasonable. Schwartz and Martin would certainly have adhered. They knew the politics as well as he. There was absolutely nothing underhanded going on. *But why me?* he had asked himself initially. At first, Bianco thought that he might be made into something of a figurehead, at the very worst, a scapegoat. But neither was the case. Angelo Thomas Bianco was clearly in charge. Not autonomous. But certainly his own man.

Dr. King had been entirely candid and fully cooperative with the police, assigning blame to no one but himself while stepping down; not out of any self-effacing scheme, but with the sincere conviction that what he had done was wrong. The whole business weighed heavily on Dr. King's heart; he was too tired and torn to go on administrating effectively. Although he suffered gravely, he was not about to make those around him suffer, too. For those reasons, Dr. King had Dr. Bianco's complete admiration and loyalty. How could Bianco help but change from clown to administrative chief? Perhaps that was it. Perhaps Dr. King was giving him the chance to grow—to grow up, Bianco suddenly realized. But then, he was back to his initial question:

"Why me?"

Richard looked at Bianco oddly.

"I was just thinking aloud," Bianco said, turning around to find the police officer close behind, noting again that Richard was responding, wondering how to word the progress in his report without offering Dr. King any kind of false hope.

Dr. Bianco had been doing a lot of soul-searching of late, asking himself many sorts of serious questions. Questions concerning Nurse Donna Marlow for one. And serious questions often carried with them a host of others. Such as, why did she remain married to a man she didn't love? Or even more serious, why hadn't he ever considered the question before? Why all of a sudden was he thinking about these things? Why all of a sudden were there so many whys? he wondered.

Oddly enough, Bianco had sensed that Donna Marlow was becoming the target of a kind of abuse, an abuse directed at her by the other nurses. Probably instigated by Nurse Harrigan herself. It was hard to put a finger on it. There wasn't any sort of verbal assailing involved. Nor was it simply a form of mistreatment. It was, ironically, no treatment at all. A kind of distant disrespect. Intangible. There had been no overt cold shoulder shown but rather a subtle indifference emanating from the group as a whole. A kind of calculated coolness that was difficult to define. A paradoxical abuse.

After an hour of strolling quietly around the gardens and grounds with Richard, Dr. Bianco and the officer brought the patient back to his room. The psychiatrist made his rounds but couldn't take his mind off matters concerning Donna Marlow. He tried to understand what was going on.

Nurse Marlow understood it fully. She also understood that if the other nurses had ever treated Dr. Bianco the way they had been treating her, they'd be inviting big trouble. They wouldn't dare behave that way with him. What hurt her deeply was in knowing exactly why they thought that they could get away with it with her. The reason being was that she and Dr. Bianco simply did not share a *serious* relationship. Everyone at the Foundation certainly knew they played around. A purely sensual pact. And it was exactly that arrangement that made it safe for the others to aim their elusive sights at her. For she held no outright claim. For him, it had only been a game. He did not treat her as *his* woman, so he would not act in her defense. The fact that she was married had little bearing on the matter, for a good many of the married men and women at the Foundation fooled around. The problem was that Bianco portrayed the clown.

Even Nurse Ryder put up an invisible wall. Serving now as Dr. Bianco's personal receptionist-secretary, she had been instructed by Dr. King to fully assist the new administrator while he learned his way around, which she did competently. But whenever Donna Marlow came on the scene, Nurse Ryder, usually wide-eyed and winsome, extended anything but a warm reception. Instead, there was a professional coolness that prevailed.

Over the next few weeks, several remarkable things had happened. Dr. Bianco had asked Nurse Marlow out on a *serious* date. An evening in the Hamptons. Dinner and dancing beneath the stars. And Donna Marlow danced around the lobby of B Building in acute anticipation. Then there were the surprise theater tickets that Dr. Bianco had Nurse Ryder reserve for the hottest play in town. Not to mention the weekend bungalow on Block Island he had discretely arranged, carrying Donna across the threshold as though they were on their honeymoon. She was in such sweet ecstasy when she spied and smelled the fragrant bouquet of roses on the bureau near their bed, collapsing in splendid delirium into outstretched arms.

Only then, and almost magically, did that inexplicable cloud of coolness suddenly disappear. And Nurse Donna Marlow and the other nurses were united once again. Even Nurse Harrigan seemed to brighten up a bit. It was as though a spell that had been cast over Donna had suddenly been broken. As though it had never existed at all. And in her ecstatic state of mind, she questioned if in fact it ever had. Donna Marlow finally felt safe and secure, for Angelo T. Bianco had, indeed, become her man.

Another remarkable thing happened. Richard was really starting to come around. It seemed remarkable to everyone except Lieutenant Lark and Sergeant Grear. By now, the two detectives had put many of the pieces together. Although Carl Gustafson wasn't around to answer any questions, they were certain that small bags of lime and nitrates had been removed from the caretaker's shed by Richard in order to dry the body. And even though Sarah wouldn't say one way or the other exactly what was missing from the trunk, Lark and Grear knew that the housekeeper had at one time practiced a host of mythical and supernatural rituals, inclusive of witchcraft and voodoo. For they had found scores of ancient and modern books translated from several languages into English, along with notes in Sarah's own handwriting, recorded in earlier years. Books and notes buried beneath Max's broken black and blue body found in Sarah's trunk. Books and notes that spoke of secret formulas, potions, lotions, notions, and such. Books and notes that Richard had committed to memory. The only thing Sarah would admit to was the possibility that some of Mother's toiletries and jewelry had vanished from the house. And Dr. King positively confirmed that at least one bottle of his finest wine had disappeared.

Dr. King pretty much kept himself secluded in one of the upstairs rooms. Sarah had been especially attentive, even to the point of seeming obsequious if viewed by outsiders who did not understand the special relationship they shared. Of course, there was a very sound reason for Sarah's devotion to Dr. King, for he had literally rescued her from the mean streets of a concrete jungle in West Harlem's Hamilton Heights section almost twenty years earlier.

During the early fifties, it had become the practice of state institutions, starting with New York, to empty its warehouses (in lieu of its coffers) of the mentally ill onto its city streets, discharging hundreds of helpless souls who had neither families nor friends nor the means to support themselves. It was Dr. King who championed a cause, bringing to the public's attention another kind of sickness. Not the kind of illness you'd find confined behind institutional walls, but a proliferating disease manifesting within society itself. The madness grew out of a hierarchy whose irresponsible mistakes would eventually lead to the rewarehousing of patients into single-room shanties and shelters of Dickensian despicability. Ambitious, avaricious politicians and lawyers were the collective powers behind the insanity—groups of self-serving bureaucrats whose only consideration was to ravage purported financially impaired state treasuries.

"But not this way," Dr. King had vowed. And so, he took the first step. Down a set of filthy subway stairs he went, grabbing the first dysfunctional soul he found. Back to his home he brought Sarah Barnes. A raving, delirious, ravenous Sarah Barnes. He took her in and nurtured her back to health. Healing first her body. Then her mind. No pills or medication of any kind.

Dr. King made headlines as well as many enemies over the years that followed as the result of his crusade, namely, important members of the state's psychiatric institutions whose practice it was to medicate and release potentially dangerous patients back into the community rather than offer asylum. "Madness at its best," Dr. King would quip. "Our psychiatric institutions must not be allowed to drug and release and view their ephemeral success as some sort of permanent solution," he was often quoted by the press.

The police, of course, invariably played their repetitious revolving door role of recidivism, arresting the mentally ill, over and over again, frustrated by callous judges who'd release them time after time from hospitals and jails. And there was always—always the lack of communication between the psychiatric institutions and the police whenever Dr. King investigated on his own. He often tried to bridge the gap between the two worlds, but inevitably made even more enemies for himself. The criminal courts were a travesty, and liberal judges became the bane of his existence. The district attorney's office? A sheer disgrace! He fought them all. Finally, the public said, "Enough's enough!" And through private funding, Dr. King proudly expanded the King Foundation. But over the years, the armies had been amassing, and Armageddon was close at hand.

And so, Dr. King wasn't at all surprised that early August afternoon when handed a summons, commanding him to appear before the district court in mid-September to answer charges of criminal negligence. A political vendetta was mounting rapidly around him, yet he really didn't seem to care.

Instead of seeking legal advice in preparing for his case, or just getting the proper rest that Sarah would insist upon, Dr. King spent many sleepless hours going through the personal effects of his beloved Victoria. There were hundreds of pictures in albums and boxes to sort through, and he couldn't help but view the pictures of little Dicky, too. Pictures of the boy growing up. Pictures of Richard. But there was something that struck him quite odd. There was no smooth transition from adolescent to adult. In fact, the metamorphosis was quite abrupt as he himself had witnessed more than once in private sessions with the lad. But somehow the photographs told so much more. Like discovering a new dimension in a fine painting by standing at an appreciative distance or viewing it in an altogether different light. It was as though there was a split. A schism. A very distinct dichotomy. It wasn't as though he had failed in properly diagnosing the boy's disorder. He had, admittedly, failed in dealing with Richard's case objectively. He had, admittedly, failed in updating certain reports in order to hide certain truths from himself. Dr. King had somehow convinced himself that because he was at a later date personally involved, he could, in fact, deal with the situation satisfactorily. After all, did he not believe that he had successfully treated the likes of Mother, years before? Why not similar success with Richard as well? A curious thought in retrospect, and a most serious error in judgment, to be sure. For there could be no clearer reminder than in the photographs before him. Even his private sessions with Richard lacked the impact of those candid shots.

Lieutenant Lark had been indefatigable. Probing. Querying. Supposing this and that. Dr. King had become indifferent. Nothing really mattered anymore. His Victoria was dead. And that was that. The police reports certainly confirmed as much: the blood samples taken from the study; the statue of Hermes that Richard used to bash her brains in, covered with bits of hair and blood and bone; the fact that she was missing for practically two months; and the most unsettling fact of all, Richard's psychiatric profile, of which the psychiatrist was, finally, well aware.

Dr. King had insisted on all the details. He knew all he needed to know. All hope had been abandoned. The police simply would or wouldn't find her body. It wouldn't change a thing. It wouldn't bring her back. All that he had left were the photographs, the memories, and the overwhelming guilt he bore. He wept silently as he turned the albums' pages or sorted through a box. He wished to remain all alone in his room upstairs, having to be reminded by Sarah from time to time to take his medicine.

Chapter 26

THE INFIRMARY

The month of August had been especially hot, and Richard knew that the body was getting ripe. He was a bit apprehensive, but obviously the police hadn't found Mother, otherwise the authorities would have certainly shipped him off to North Shore State Hospital in Havenwood in a heartbeat. That he knew for sure, for he was only being held at the King Foundation because everyone concerned was hoping against hope that he'd reveal, inadvertently or otherwise, a clue as to the body's whereabouts. It was one of the reasons Lieutenant Lark had encouraged Dr. Bianco to walk the Foundation's grounds with Richard on practically a daily basis, and almost always in a different area, hoping that something as subtle as a sudden shifting of the patient's eyes might divulge Mother's location. Meanwhile, Lieutenant Lark would bide his time until the September 12th as he doubtlessly believed that Richard would somehow keep his date with destiny and actually lead them to her resting place in the penultimate hour. *But how?* was the perplexing question Lark perpetually entertained. Escape was the only possible answer, he realized. Could Richard possibly escape from his cell in D Building? Highly unlikely if not downright impossible. Could he somehow manage to flee by freeing himself of the overlong-sleeved garment that bound his upper body like a bundle as he walked about the grounds under custodial supervision as well as having an armed police officer at his back? Inconceivable. Then again, Richard had managed to nimbly slip his handcuffed wrists down along hips and buttocks to his feet, sliding each foot up and over the cuffs, bringing the pair to the front of his body before unlocking the set with Sergeant Grear's key, summarily displayed upon the patient/prisoner's tongue. An incredible performance and one that told the lieutenant that Richard Geist was potentially a formidable adversary and to be watched most carefully, which was precisely what Richard wanted from the police as well as the Foundation's administration. *Watch me guardedly*, was the signal Richard was sending to everyone concerned. Richard was no Harry

Houdini, but he was indeed a master of manipulation and deception.

From the clay-red curly hairs discovered within the creases of several books on Egyptology found in the Foundation's library, Lieutenant Lark and Sergeant Grear knew with certainty that Richard Geist had read many pages and passages, chapter and verse concerning ancient burial rites and rituals. For the hairs had unquestionably matched those of Richard's after the patient was given a haircut. Of course, this information as well as Lark's theory referencing the patient's plausible date with destiny was kept from the Foundation's administration.

In addition to his own men, Lark made certain that only personnel with spotless records and time-in-grade employed at the King Foundation be allowed to handle keys while escorting Richard Geist anywhere within D Building or any other facility for that matter —certainly not the Korean trustee who had accompanied the two detectives to and from one of Bianco's temporary offices initially.

Well, well, thought Richard as an attendant escorted him from the grounds and back to his room. A plainclothes officer was busy reading a newspaper outside the prisoner's door. Inside, the attendant removed Richard's straitjacket. When the man was gone, the patient/prisoner produced the attendant's comb, checking on the policeman through the barred window in the door. Richard sat quietly upon the cot and combed his locks, running things over most carefully in his mind. The afternoon was drawing to a close, so he decided he'd best get started, for sufficient time would be needed to effect his self-inflicted wounds as well as to heal to a degree before wrapping things up once and for all.

All his prearranging, and still he knew that it must be Mother's choice alone. Her ka could, of course, choose the horrid remains shriveling away in the infirmary's shallow subcellar, lying there cloaked in its burlap shroud in the nearby building. But he knew her better than that, as there were no priestly guarantees in this world or the next for one so vain. So she would be obliged to do his bidding, coming forth to share his very soul. And in return, he would do everything within his power to play the perfect host. For he had the magic to make her queen, as Dicky would be boy-king. How could she refuse? He was sacrificing everything. Surely, she would not be blinded. Surely, she would acquiesce. But it had to be her choice, and hers alone. That was of paramount importance and why everything had to be just so. He wanted Mother absolutely assured that the mummy he would finally prepare would be a valid home for her ka. That is, if she dare! Richard firmly believed that she would reject it in a second and, without question, come to him in a whisper when he performed the final rite of the 'Opening of the Mouth Ceremony.' He believed it with all his heart.

Richard sat calmly, pulling the tapered comb through his curly clay-red locks, deciding that it was finally time to pay a painful visit to the doctors. He was in good health and knew he would recover quickly. He contemplated the hard rubber comb, knowing it would be the perfect implement with which to put him in the catbird seat. It was a laborious task, but he managed to bend back and bite off two-thirds of its tough but pliant rubbery teeth. One by one. He started at the narrower end, leaving about a third of the thicker section. When he finally finished, it very much resembled a rattail comb. It was a satisfactory conversion and would suit his needs just fine. He got up and again checked on the policeman who was still preoccupied with the news. Richard huffed and puffed and counted aloud as though he were engaged in exercise, raising his voice to cover up any sound. The policeman went right on reading without a stir.

Richard ran the toothless strip back and forth against the rough-hewed wall. Picking up a pace. Frantically raking its hard black backbone in a feverish race against time. Back and forth. Faster and faster. Honing the hot little strip to pointed perfection, till he thought its very tip would flame.

Pulling down his pants and underwear, he plopped to the cot and began to masturbate, picturing Mother along the pictureless wall, projecting her acrobatic feats . . . flashing to the action of seven hired hands all corralled around her in the hay . . . riding her to kingdom come . . . up and down . . . faster and faster . . . pumping away rhythmically to the peak.

It was as Richard's own mouth opened wide that Dicky drove the sharp point downward, stabbing the supple flesh repeatedly, puncturing the curly red-haired region around his groin, filling Richard full of tiny holes as blood and semen shot forth simultaneously. Like little geysers gushing. Hot! Oh, Richard was percolating now! Red, white, and remaining true blue to Mother to the very end. Power in action. No longer dormant like sleeping bulbs beneath a wintry bed. No longer bottled up like energy entombed within those sealed glass tubes stored in dusty red, white, and blue RCA boxes. No! For some strange reason he felt more colorful than all the boxes, ribbons, and bows that filled Mother's parlor long ago. More vibrant than the flags and pennants waving freely through the air after the Yankees had won the pennant when little Dicky was five.

Richard stood up, feeling deliriously alive as his blood was spilling freely upon the waxed green wavy tile. His agonizing shrills filled the halls and corridors, bellowing to the rooftop, funneling through the floors. It commanded the full attention of the policeman posted just outside the door, summoning forth a parade of doctors, nurses, and attendants.

Unlocking and throwing open the door to Richard's room, they rushed immediately to his aid, managing to stop the bleeding before carrying him away. The moan of the closing elevator doors was the last thing he remembered before he slipped into a state of unconsciousness.

When Richard came to, he was exactly where he had planned to be. The infirmary! An old single-story structure dating back to the Civil War. He had a private room with a different kind of window in the door. Finely defined diamond-shaped wires ran diagonally across the frosted pane of glass. A small rectangular window with vertical bars was oddly set just beneath the ceiling, revealing nothing but the sky. He was in agony. Positively excruciating pain. And he let them know it, screaming mercilessly until they shot him full of painkillers. But his groin was still afire, so he sank his teeth determinedly into his lower lip, summoning forth Dicky to share the common pain. The two of them would get through this thing together, Dicky had insisted . . . easier than the one . . . easier than the . . . one . . . easier than . . . . That little trick alone cost him a dozen stitches in the lip and at least a quarter pint of blood.

Lieutenant Lark and Sergeant Grear were immediately notified, appearing on the scene and stationing several of their men in key locations just outside the infirmary for an around-the-clock vigil. The lieutenant knew that Mother's body had to be close at hand. And although his men had checked and rechecked all the buildings and the grounds, he had them check the area once again, especially the section around Carl Gustafson's shed which was but fifty yards away.

Lark posted a policeman just outside the door to Richard's temporary quarters, located at the far end of the building. The doctors assured the two detectives that Richard wasn't going anywhere for a while. Not in his condition. Not with those self-inflicted wounds. Not enough to require surgery, but enough to warrant a long recuperation period. He wouldn't walk on his own for weeks they swore. Lieutenant Lark smiled and doubled the guard outside Richard's door. He wasn't taking any chances.

Two days later, and feeling rather foolish, Lieutenant Lark took one of his men off the door, especially after seeing for himself that Richard could just about make it to the bathroom across the hall. And only with assistance. Besides which, Lark was still convinced that Richard wouldn't be going anywhere until September 12th. Well over a week to go. It was exactly that kind of reasoning that Richard counted on. Lark's reasoning like a cop. Richard truly was in terrible agony, but he had learned a long time ago how to deal with pain. He wouldn't be as good as new, but he'd have Dicky by his side to assist.

Richard slept for long periods over the next few days and nights, building up his strength. When he awoke on the evening of September 6th, he noted with a satisfactory grin that the temperature had taken a sudden drop, for fall was just around the corner. Ready to assist, an attendant helped him out of bed. And move he did. Very slowly at first. Step by step. Across the hall to the showers he went, doubled over in sharp pain that was clearly written across his face.

"No more sponge baths," the man insisted. "Up and at 'em. You've got to move those muscles. Doctors' orders."

The following evening proved to be rather provocative as paling gray clouds invoked their magic across the Sound. Moments later he could hear the wind howling just outside, imagining the kind of havoc it played across the land, blowing and pinning long grasses to the ground, stirring up the sands below the cliffs. Whining. Whispering. Winding its way further inland before turning positively wild. What he saw through the oddly placed window above him was a series of cumulus cloud formations passing rapidly by. "Moving pictures," he uttered and giggled aloud. From out of nowhere, a cloud with an anvil top swept in from the west. Richard knew that Lark's men were out there waiting. Suddenly, a violent September storm lashed out mercilessly, pounding the windowpane while seeming to wash away the very bars themselves. He had the men pictured in his mind as they turned their backs and raised their collars in angry protest. Richard grinned satisfactorily, awaiting his evening meal.

After dinner in bed, an attendant came by to take Richard across the hall, but the patient complained of severe pain, pleading with the man to forgo the shower. They were the most words he had said in over two months.

"Maybe later on," Richard pleaded, bending forward and coughing up a convincing storm, noting the hour on the attendant's watch. "Please. I really don't feel very well right now."

The police officer spoke to the attendant. "I can take him in later if he wants," to which the attendant agreed, handing the cop the key, for Richard apparently posed no threat. In fact, the policeman more than welcomed the diversion from his dull routine of having to sit or stand just outside the patient's room for hours at a clip. He would gladly supervise the prisoner's shower if Richard changed his mind. Of course, Richard had his mind set from the start.

Most of the hospital personnel were gone until morning. There was but a skeleton crew on hand, and it was unlikely that anyone would use the facilities across the hall as there were bathrooms off the reception area along the other wing. No one would be coming down to the end of the hall until the police officer's relief checked in. That would not be until midnight. Richard knew the whole routine. If anyone did come down to discover the policeman off his post, it would most likely be one of the night nurses who would assume that the officer was supervising Richard's hygiene across the hall. Everything would appear quite normal. Still, he realized that his success hinged, to a large extent, on luck. But Richard was born on February the 7th; how lucky could one be?

It was approximately 11:15 p.m. when he finally spoke up. "Sir. Sir, I'd really like to take my shower now," he said and smiled in the face of frosted glass.

There was a moment of silence before he heard the click of the key in the metal lock. The officer opened it wide then stepped aside while Richard took tiny measured steps across the hallway.

Just inside the doorway and to the left was the bathroom. The showers were to the right. Soap, shampoo, towel, toothbrush and toothpaste were kept out in the open on a shelf above a sink. They were the only articles Richard was permitted. He took what he needed and headed slowly toward the shower area.

After what seemed an eternity, Richard finally made it, thankful that everyone's guard was down. Not only had the lieutenant taken one of his men off the door, but even the doctors saw no need for a straitjacket, permitting him a hospital gown. So lucky, he beamed.

Richard hung the towel on a ceramic hook and stepped inside the shower stall, placing both soap and shampoo in one of the recessed spaces along the wall. He appeared to be having trouble with his gown. With his back to the officer, he asked for the man's assistance. But the officer remained standing where he was, somewhat leery of this request, although he certainly didn't consider the patient any threat whatsoever. Not in Richard's condition. Not on your life!

Richard finally maneuvered out of the gown, draping it in front of his privates. Acting very, very shy. He moved past the officer and hung the gown on a separate hook alongside the towel, stepping back inside, still with his back to the cop. He turned on the water full blast so as to muffle any sound. Then turned around. "LOOK!" Richard hollered, pointing to his groin. "NO BANDAGES," he bellowed in Lieutenant Lark's voice. A voice that seemed to echo from below.

Richard's groin was completely shaven, appearing like a sieve. The officer couldn't help but stare. It was as the cop stood gaping at the gruesome sight that Richard caught him off guard. The policeman looked up but never knew what hit him. A sudden shot to the center of the man's Adam's apple took his breath away. Another sharp blow with the heel of Richard's hand practically drove the man's nose into his brain. But it was far from over, and Richard desperately needed Dicky's help more than he ever needed it before. The officer was down but scrambling to his feet. So little Dicky knocked those legs out from under him, delighted that the man was still fighting to catch his breath. Leaping to where the officer was vulnerable, Dicky choked the man with all his might while Richard bashed and smashed the angry brown head hard against the shower floor. Until the man lay still. Richard could take the pain no longer, wanting to scream bloody murder. But Dicky told him, "No!" that there was unfinished business beneath the basement floor below.

Pulling himself together and rising to the occasion, Richard soaked and soaped his excruciatingly painful body so as to cool and calm his nerves, being very careful not to let the powerful stream of water hit his groin. He was practically out of breath, but thankful that the blood eddying down the drain was not his own, that his wounds had not somehow opened up—when suddenly a slippery hand grasped 'round his ankle fast. Richard almost jumped out of his skin, slipped and fell. But Dicky dashed over to the cop and ripped the man's revolver free, quickly handing it to Richard who hammered the officer's head repeatedly: "UN-TIL THE EYES EX-TIN-GUISHED LIFE!" Richard uttered in measured breaths beside the running water, banging away insanely as though he were pounding three-penny nails.

Physically drained, Richard fought the piercing pain as he dragged the officer to the opposite corner and out of sight, urinating upon the battered body while thanking Dicky profusely for all his help. Extending an arm so as to keep the revolver relatively dry, Richard stood beneath the shower, rinsing his soapy body before shutting the water. He somehow endured the terrible, terrible fire in his groin, making Dicky promise to take over for him if the pain became unbearable. Dicky promised, but reminded him that they would somehow get through this thing together. Richard moved excitedly to and fro, waving the officer's gun aimlessly through the steamy air, his brain filled with the sound of pounding blood.

Peering from around the corner and down the hall, Richard slowly dressed then paused for a moment, mustering his strength to reach the staircase. That would be the most difficult part of all. He was amazed that he wasn't bleeding. He was amazed that numbness was somehow setting in. The doctors were absolutely right in saying that you had to move those muscles, he giggled deliciously to himself.

Down the basement stairs and along the pitch-black corridor he disappeared, making his way along the wall, rounding the corner with his hand. Finally, he reached the very end of the hallway. Kneeling down, he found the frame in the floor, but somehow it felt all wrong. A seemingly tighter fit he swore as he tenaciously tried to pry up the cover with his fingers until they bled. Finally it gave, and he quickly slid inside, setting the heavy slab back in place above him. He felt a sharp pain tearing through the numbness as he crawled along the eerie blackness of that chilly charnel-like space. But the pain was somehow bearable.

What he reached for but could not find, practically took away his nerve. Frightfully, he fanned his palm along the corridor floor, searching frantically for the materials along the wall. It was only then that Richard realized he was on the wrong side of the wall was all, for he had become disoriented in his frenzy. So, calmly, deliberately, he crawled along on hands and knees to the opposite side of the shallow space. He was very angry with himself.

There he found the things he needed to perform the ritual. A place for everything, and everything in its place, he grinned satisfactorily, taking his mind away from the grueling pain. It was almost time!

Kneeling there in the darkness, he lit one of the little candles and very carefully unwrapped Mother from her burlap shroud, marveling at the sight and acting very, very proud—gazing down at the contrasting coal-white form resting peacefully in the glow, its skeletal arms folded across a shriveled sunken chest. Uncorking a bottle of fine wine, he washed his hands and began a quiet chant, eager to go to work.

Lieutenant Lark had decided to go to bed early that evening, but he had tossed and turned for more than an hour before finally falling into a trying, restless sleep. The storm disturbed him, but what disturbed him even more was the fact that he could not, no matter how hard he tried, sink into that slick, sick skull of Richard Geist. It had been eating away at him like a cancer. He just couldn't figure him. For whenever he tried to figure him, he failed. No! Not to try and figure him, but to become him. Yes! That was the key he told himself, over and over again, driving the thought back and forth across his mind, momentarily dismissing the notion as some sort of crazy head game. "Crazy," he said aloud and shivered, knowing immediately that he was on the right track. For Lark had taken the first step of the journey into Richard's demented mind. Lark dared to toy with madness of a kind, lying there upon his clammy sheets in sweat, immersed in the madness of his past.

Lieutenant Lark had been a streetwise, savvy cop for over thirty years, having solved some of Chicago's most baffling cases before his transfer came. From small-time hoodlums to Mafia chieftains. Revolutionaries. Hired assassins. Even cold-blooded killers of the opposite sex. But what in God's name did he have here? Labels. That's what he had. A schizophrenic; a catatonic (part and parcel). A multiple personality. A psycho. A nut! That's what he had in plain and simple language. But they had all been nuts, his childhood friend included whom Lark had no choice than to kill in the line of duty one tragic night, many a year ago.

Tossing there in bed, he brought to mind many an intricate case. But nothing like the one that had left a permanent scar. A case he rarely brought to mind. A case involving the shameless corruption within his own department back home. That was shortly before his transfer came. A transfer to another precinct within the Windy City. But Lieutenant Lark had decided to leave Chicago altogether, relocating to New York.

A fortnight after his first assignment on Long Island, Lark solved the case that had for months been baffling an army of detectives investigating scores of mutilated male bodies found along North Shore beaches. From Cutchogue on east to Orient Point. The serial killer turned out to be a middle-aged balding barber from Mattituck who probably cut one too many a head. What Lark saw, that apparently everyone else had missed, was the killer's trademark: a hardly discernible yet irregular clip made somewhere between a sideburn and a point behind his customer's ear. 'Earmarked for Death' was one headline the detective drew. Stories appeared in back copies, which Schimmel kept and Richard had read with special interest. Lieutenant Lark had become something of a local living legend overnight, going on to solve one case after another as he had back home. So many cases, he thought. But nothing quite like Richard Geist. Yes. They had certainly all been nuts in that they had all been determined souls. His childhood friend included. And Lark was going nuts right now, vacillating between troubled sleep and semiconsciousness when the thought suddenly flashed across his mind like the bolt of lightning resounding just outside the window.

"THE INFIRMARY!" Lark thundered, bolting upright in his bed. Yes! To keep his date with destiny. It was all perfectly clear. Lark had figured early on that the body had to be close at hand. But the body was probably right under their noses all along. Certainly he knew that Richard had caused his self-inflicted wounds in order to wind up in the infirmary. Not from which Richard would bolt to do his deed, but from within. And that was what had thrown him off the scent. Of course he had instructed his men to use their keen senses as he himself had smelled death many a time before. That sickening sweet fume of decaying flesh wafting through building doors and walls and windows. The putrefying bodies of the deceased who had been left alone to rot for days or weeks on end in their run-down tenement flats before finally being discovered by a friend, a pet, or next of kin. The smell was always unmistakable. The police had even brought in a dog used in cadaver work.

Still, Lark's men had reported nothing. He knew that Richard was very clever and would try to mask the deed. It *had* to be the infirmary. He could feel it in his bones. For all of the medical staff from that small hospital had been on the grounds that afternoon. The afternoon they found the murdered Martinez girl. Yes! The building had been virtually empty for a time. The time that Richard needed.

Swinging his feet off the bed, Lark sat peering at the clock radio. **11:59 p.m. Sept. 7** read the digital display in bright, bold red numerals before it flashed to **12:00 a.m. Sept. 8**.

"Twelve o'clock at night and raining cats and dogs," he said aloud with annoyance, wishing right then and there that he had become a dentist instead of a cop. He knew exactly what he would be doing during the first year of retirement, if he ever lived that long. Yes. Sport fishing in the Florida Keys during the day, and sleeping without interruption throughout a lovelorn night, he swore, switching on a table lamp before dismissing those pleasant notions. He fumbled for the small notepad and pen from inside the breast pocket of his coat that draped the mahogany valet beside the bed. The lieutenant flipped through several pages then dialed the Foundation's number, checking, too, through his list of men.

The phone rang once. "King Foundation, Nurse . . ."

Lark didn't catch the name, nor did he care. "Lieutenant Lark, here. Please connect me with the infirmary."

"One moment." There was a brief pause.

"Nurse Bayer. May I help you?"

"This is Lieutenant Lark. I want to speak with the doctor in charge."

Another pause. "Hello, may I help you?" a female voice replied.

"Yes, I asked to speak with the doctor in charge," he repeated impatiently. "This is Lieutenant Lark of Suffolk County Homicide."

"I am the doctor in charge, Lieutenant," the voice answered unevenly. "This is Dr. Harris. What can I do for you?"

Lark paused uncomfortably. "Would you please get me one of my men to the phone, Dr. Harris? Not the guard posted outside Richard Geist's room," he added quickly. "Do you understand, Doctor? I don't want my man off that door for a second. Get me Sergeant Luisi . . . outside . . . ." But there was static on the line.

"Come again, Lieutenant? Where outside am I supposed to find the man you're looking for? It's midnight and pouring out there."

Lark was losing patience by the minute. "Dr. Harris, I don't care if there's a fucking tornado coming through. Just get Sergeant Luisi . . . phone. Now, Doctor."

"I asked, where outside would you like me to look that I might call the sergeant to the phone? Or do I stick my head out the front door and yell, 'We know you're out there, copper; now get your ass in outta the pourin' rain 'cause we've got your lieutenant on the line'?"

Lark swore to himself that he'd remember Dr. Harris, jotting down her name with unnecessary pressure on the pen. "I said you'll find him by the shed where they store the garden equipment. It's to your right as—"

"I *know* where it is, Lieutenant. Hold on please."

Lark waited impatiently for Sergeant Luisi to come to the phone —and waited—and waited—and finally—

"Bizel here, Lieutenant."

"Where's Luisi?" Lark barked.

"I relieved him over an hour ago, sir. He's probably home in bed. Grear put us on three-hour shifts this evening because of the storm. Kilbride's inside on a regular four. I have Rebecchi relieving him now."

Lark glanced at the clock. It was 12:04 a.m. "Sergeant, I want you to make another check of the infirmary. There's something we overlooked."

"You want me to check the infirmary now, Lieutenant?" Bizel asked, standing there dripping wet in parka and boots.

"That's right, Sergeant. Now. There's got to be a space behind some wall. Some void between the ceiling and the floor. That building is over a hundred years old. The only building there without a set of plans. That's what Richard counted on."

"Hold on a second, Lieutenant."

Lieutenant Lark could hear confusion mounting in the background. A moment later Bizel came back on the line. "Kilbride's off the door, Lieutenant."

"What the hell do you mean, 'Kilbride's off the door'?"

"He's not around. Rebecchi went to look for him. He's not in the john. But the door to the patient's room is locked, Lieutenant. So don't worry."

"Get someone to open that door immediately. I'll stay on the line." Lark struggled out of his pajamas and into his pants and shirt, passing the receiver from one hand to the other, its cord rising and falling as though he were a marionette being manipulated by a single string.

There was quite a commotion as doctors and nurses bustled back and forth, fumbling in drawers behind the reception area for a duplicate key to Richard's solitary room. A room seldom used. Lieutenant Lark waited anxiously for what he feared he already knew. The commotion was growing louder. He heard Bizel's voice drawing near.

"Lieutenant?"

Lark knew. "Yes?"

"Kilbride's dead, Lieutenant. Murdered!" he added in a tone of disbelief. "We found him on the floor in the shower. Bludgeoned. Probably with his own weapon. It's missing. Kid's not in the room."

"Damn!" was all Lark could say, although a fury raged up inside him like a blazing furnace.

"How the hell did he get—get the gun away from Kilbride, Lieutenant? His gun! You don't go—you don't get near Kilbride," the officer said, apparently choked up.

"Now you listen to me," Lark commanded. "And you listen good. You and your men secure that building. No one in. No one out. And I mean no one. Any warm bodies other than our boys, you corral them in the lobby. I want that building sealed and searched from top to bottom. Starting with the basement, Sergeant. You got that? Starting with the basement. That's where I think he is right now. You check the basement and any substructure. Get extra flashlights. I'm telling you he's down there. No one, Bizel, moves in alone. I want my men in pairs. If Geist so much as blinks, you kill him where he stands! You make sure you pass that down. Got all that?" He didn't wait for a reply, setting the receiver down roughly on its cradle, grabbing for his sock and shoes.

Richard lifted the lower portion of Mother's shriveled body off the cool stone floor, raising the wizened, leather-like figure carefully for fear that she might suddenly crack before him in the light. Supporting her gently, starting at her thighs and trunk, he methodically wound wide, pre-cut strips of sticky white bandages. Around and around the middle of her body. Selecting narrower strips of bandages, he finally wrapped her entire remains from head to foot.

Somewhere above, orders were being carried out. Quickly. Professionally. Men were moving in. There was little time left. Richard quickly reached for a jar of ointment. He could hear their muffled footsteps dancing and prancing around in haste. But he was well hidden in the corner. They wouldn't find him until they finally uncovered the frame within the slate and concrete floor. "Perfect," he said quietly and smiled, snuffing out the little light. Richard beheld the darkness.

The police were on the far side of the wall from Richard when suddenly, eerie—no—unearthly lines of light shot through the shallow space, light beams bouncing off the floor. The stage was finally lit.

"SHOWTIME!" Richard shouted, bathing in the glow, crouching low and slitting open the bandages across Mother's mouth with a tiny, shiny blade, awaiting the ordeal of ceremony, wherewith her ka, her immortal soul, would have the benefit of choice. He held his own mouth open wide with bated breath.

"There he is!" someone shouted. "On the other side." And along the other wall they raced around in pairs while one angry devil steadily held the light. Richard could hear other footsteps directly overhead. Toward the end of the hallway, someone had opened a back door to the building.

Then a curious thing happened. A cool current of air swept across and down into shallow space, tarrying along the line of light while carrying with it a soft, caressing susurration; a murmur or whisper one might say.

"Shh," Richard ordered.

"FREEZE!"

Steel blue barrels glistened inches from his face as Richard swallowed hard the sacred, consecrated name: "Victoria," he whispered ever so faintly, taking in her faint but acrid scent.

"Hands on top of your head—otherwise you're dead," a grave voice swore.

Richard leered and laced his sticky fingers comfortably upon his curly head as rough hands grabbed beneath his shoulders, jerking him out of his hellish hole as though he were being delivered from one world to the next.

"Where's the gun?" another devil demanded.

"I see it over there, Sarge." A pause and then, "Oh, my God!" the man's eyes riveted to the scene, shining his light in the corner and staring unbelievably at the ghostly queen. Snow White. Lying there as pure as sin herself. A dark withered rose lay diagonally across her breast.

"Don't touch a goddamn thing," Bizel ordered, peering into the shallow abode. "Get him the hell out of here. Fast! Rebecchi, you stay here and wait for the lieutenant. I'll call the lab." Hesitating, he turned and called back to the group ushering the prisoner away. "Hold it!" He walked along the passageway and right on up to Richard. "I should have killed you myself," the cop stated with hatred blazing in his eyes. "But there are just too many witnesses; too many conscionable souls," he added, glaring at his men.

Richard just didn't giggle; he really, really roared. "I see your lieutenant was waiting till the Twelfth of Never, Sarge," he stated after he finally calmed down, grinning from ear to ear with perverted glee.

It took four of Bizel's men to pull him off the sticky youth, or surely he would have killed Richard precisely where he stood.

Chapter 27

OTHER VOICES

Under the watchful eyes of heavy security, Richard was cleaned up and brought back to his ward in D Building. But the administration put him into something resembling more of a box than a room. A box without a window. *A box without a bow*, he giggled. This time the authorities weren't taking any chances, for they ordered their patient confined in a straitjacket, then strapped him down to a hospital bed. "But what if there's a fire?" Richard roared. Aside from the pain in his groin and a few minor cuts and bruises here and there, he seemed otherwise all right, lying upon his back and staring oddly at the ceiling.

"Ka—Ba—Ma-Pa-Ra," Richard ranted, sounding out a cadence all his own. Two police officers stood posted just outside his door like sentinels.

It was the second time that night that Lieutenant Lark came by the Foundation, having just returned from Kilbride's family: a twenty-one-year-old bride of eleven months; a child of sixteen days. He was going to pay her the painful visit later that morning, but she had phoned at 2 a.m., insisting in knowing what had happened, why her husband had not returned home after his scheduled eight to twelve. Lark truly wished that Bizel had killed Richard. He wished it with all his heart. For his heart weighed heavy with hatred and grief. And horror, too. Such horror. Horror he had never seen before. Not so much the horror found in the shallow subbasement. He had expected that. Nor was it the horror in Kilbride's eyes. He had seen that too, many a time before. But nothing like the horror in Kilbride's wife's eyes. He felt as though he had aged a hundred years that night. He cursed himself for having pulled the second man off the door. Kilbride's wife had cursed him, too.

Lieutenant Lark came around the nurse's station to check on the two officers posted just outside Richard's cell. What he saw unnerved him. Both men stood still as statues, their heads pressed against the steel door. Listening. They did not move so much as a muscle as he approached.

"What the hell is going on?" Lark snapped. But both men shushed him. Actually shushed him! One with a gesture of an arm, the other with a finger to his lips. Lark was completely taken aback, listening, too. He listened intently to the conversation coming from just behind the door, for there were not only other voices, but the voices were seemingly arguing with one another simultaneously. There was a woman's voice. Lark stood baffled.

"Who the hell is in there?" the lieutenant demanded of his men. But neither of them answered. "Sergeants, I just asked the two of you a goddamn question."

"Just the kid."

"What?"

But they nodded their heads in unison, affirming that it was so.

"This *is* a crazy house," Lark insisted and went running for the key. A moment later, Bianco and Lark came quickly down the hall together.

"Five of us put him in there, Lieutenant," Dr. Bianco explained, "and the five of us came out. Your men were right there. He can impersonate others. You know that. You yourself heard him talking in different personalities."

"I'm telling you what I heard," Lark elaborated. "What we all heard. There was a woman's voice and at least two other voices were arguing back and forth. At the same time, Doctor! Distinct voices. All arguing at the same time."

Weapons were made ready and leveled at the door. Lieutenant Lark took the key from Bianco and turned it in the slot, throwing the steel door open wide.

Richard lay quiet, strapped to the bed, staring at the ceiling in a faint light emitted from the hallway. There was no one else in the room. There was not a single place to hide. Fighting off the feeling of foolishness and, yes, even fright, Lark ran the barrel of his weapon beneath the elevated bed as a magician would wave his wand around inside an empty box so as to cast off any doubt to a disbeliever in an audience. *See? No trickery here. Magic, pure and simple*, the illusionist would have his audience believe. The only thing Lark knew about magic was that it was all deception. Chicanery, pure and simple.

It was as Lark moved the muzzle of his revolver toward the patient's mouth that Richard shot his ready phlegm. Lark stood paralyzed, with strings of mucus hanging from a shocked but determined face. The detective shifted his forefinger from the trigger guard to the tongue of the weapon itself, triggering an awful urge to blow this wide-eyed devil to bits right then and there.

"Lieutenant!" Bianco exclaimed.

Once again, Lieutenant Lark brought the muzzle to Richard's mouth, pushing the barrel against the patient's sutured lip until it bled, prying open the tenaciously drawn framework. Looking for— something. All he got for his trouble, this time, was a string of giggles. Shouldering his piece, Lark took out a handkerchief and wiped his face and jacket clean. He looked up into the dumbfounded faces of Dr. Bianco and the two officers. All three fixed their eyes on the lieutenant in disbelief as though he were stark-raving mad.

There, in the dim light, Richard rolled his head around to face the four. "Dr. Bianco, is that you?" It was unmistakably Mother's voice. Clear. Distinct. Expressive. "You'll have to excuse me, but I've been through quite an ordeal as you can see. Would you gentlemen please tell Dr. King that I'm resting now? Pretty please? I'm sure he must be worried sick." It was preternatural; positively weird. Even Richard's features seemed to take on Mother's demeanor, mirroring a frightfully faithful image. "Oh, I must look a frightful sight. Can anyone lend me a comb and mirror? No? Oh, do promise me you won't let Dr. King see me like this until I've at least had the chance to powder my nose. I must have been in a terrible automobile accident. Is that why the police are here? Is Max all right?" It was a rather convincing performance. "Is this a body cast I'm wearing? Everything's snow-white," the figure fretted, drawing a bloody lip over perfect teeth, running the tip of the tongue along a row of prickly sutures, staring up at all of them in horror. "Oh, my God! Am I disfigured? Please tell me. Am I still pretty?"

It was really quite a scene. But was it a performance and/or the fact that Richard was positively mad? Did some supernatural, some spiritual entity actually invade his very soul? The four men standing there certainly seemed to be considering those possibilities. Even Richard wasn't sure, especially when Mother started doing exactly what he had initially feared; that is, taking over.

Dr. Bianco checked the restraints on both the patient's jacket and the bed then escorted everyone outside.

Mother and Richard had such a violent argument after the men were gone, for she suddenly changed her mind and insisted on seeing her Dr. King, no longer fearing what she looked like. She cried out several times during the night, pleading desperately for someone's help. Richard, however, insisted that she wasn't at all presentable, that she looked a terrible fright.

"But he loves me," Mother moaned.

By morning, news had traveled throughout the Foundation concerning Richard's bizarre behavior. It was bad enough that many of the patients were convinced that Mother had taken over Richard's body and soul, but one or two respected members of the staff who knew her, casted their votes as well, especially after witnessing the unmistakable demeanor the patient bore as police and doctors paraded the frightened figure down the hall. And Sarah, who came by D Building to say a prayer for Richard, swore that it was unquestionably Miss Vicki, reincarnated, the two of them weeping uncontrollably on seeing one another briefly in the hallway as the group led the hysterical creature off to Dr. Bianco's office for a memorable session.

"Tell Dr. King I love him, Sarah. And send him this for me," the prisoner pleaded, blowing a kiss her way. "I don't know why they're doing this to me. Am I still pretty, Sarah? No one will answer me. Are they all deaf?"

"Oh, Miss Vicki. You jus' as pretty as a picture. You's jus' as lovely as you can be," Sarah cried out, trying desperately to follow after on old bowed legs.

"I'm sorry, Miss," one of the officers insisted.

Nurse Marlow came over and took Sarah gently in her arms as the old woman wept bitterly.

That afternoon, while serving tea and trying to get Dr. King to eat something, Sarah related the scene to the disenchanted soul when suddenly he looked up from the table in disbelief.

"He said what?!" he asked alarmingly.

"She," Sarah insisted, rambling on. "She blew you a kiss like this." Sarah stood beside him and pursed her lips just so. "Her arms folded 'cross her chest like this, asking if she still be pretty." Sarah held the pose.

"Goddamnit, Sarah," Dr. King blurted out angrily. Sarah was taken aback. "Of course Richard had to have his arms folded like that.

291

He was wearing a straitjacket, for Christ's sake," he railed, not realizing at the moment that neither his housekeeper, nor anyone else for that matter, could have possibly understood its implication. For it was impossible that Richard, inadvertently or otherwise, had ever witnessed their lovemaking. Not Sarah. Or anyone! No one but he ever shared their secret, playful game, when Mother would come to him in the evening, her arms folded across her bare breasts, her lips pursed just so, blowing him a gentle kiss while leaning forward in the darkness and whispering ever so softly in his ear: *Am I still pretty, David? Am I your one and only queen?* ""Am I still pretty? Am I your one and only queen?' Are you sure that's what he said?"

Sarah nodded most affirmatively, deeply hurt by Dr. King's angry outburst. Never in all their years together did he ever yell at her like that. Annoyance, yes. But never this.

"Did he say anything else?" he pressed.

"Jus' that she loves you, which everybody knows. Oh, and, 'I don't know why they's doin' this to me,'" Sarah added.

"Anything else, Sarah? Did he say anything else at all?"

"Nope. That's all that be said, 'cept fo' a lot of cryin' and carryin' on between the two of us. If I was you, I'd go down and see fo' myself, 'cause I tell you sure as shootin' that she be Miss Vicki, reincarnated."

"Sarah! Richard's a very sick young man. Surely you know that now."

Sarah shook her head. "I knows what I know, and I tell you, I knows that he be Miss Vicki. And I knows somethin' else, too."

"What's that?" he asked, sensing a foreboding and distance in her tone.

"I knows we can't be friends no more," she said sobbing heavily.

Dr. King went over and took the old woman in his arms, holding her close, gently rocking her like a child. "Not even if I promise to go down there and see—her?"

Sarah was trembling in his embrace, tears streaming down her coal-black face. "Promise?"

"Promise." He stood there comforting her for a while. Not saying another word. Not really sure about anything. Not after that conversation. Not after what he would read in Bianco's report the following evening.

And read he did. First, the preliminary notes. A cursory sort of glance. Dr. King sank into a comfortable winged chair in a room just off the kitchen. Carefully, painstakingly, he digested every single word. That was bad enough. Of course, he had been briefed earlier with regard to Richard's escape and capture, having been spared the gruesome details pertaining to the police officer's murder as well as Mother's corpse. But what distressed him greatly was Bianco's psychiatric report covering the session with Richard the day before. In it, Dr. Bianco had recorded and transcribed the following.

KING FOUNDATION
1 North Seawall Avenue
Bayview, N.Y. 11935
(516) 261-7305

FOR: Dr. David King   DATE: Monday, 9/8/69

FROM: Dr. Angelo T. Bianco   PATIENT: Richard Geist
                                     BIRTHDATE: 2/7/51

DYSFUNCTION: Personality manifestation: Victoria Geist
          (patient's mother—deceased 7/4/69)

DIAGNOSIS: Multiple personality:
          1. Dicky Geist: adolescent
          2. Richard Geist: adult-self
          3. Victoria Geist: patient's mother

PROGNOSIS: Inconclusive (patient transfer)
TREATMENT: Patient to be transferred to North Shore State Hospital,
          Havenwood. Wednesday, 9/10/69.

The following is a transcript from a recorded session between the patient and myself.

BEGAN SESSION: 9 a.m.

"Would you please state your name for the record?"

"Victoria Geist."

"Is there a way you'd like to begin this conversation?

"Yes, I'd like to begin by giving Dr. King a special message for me. I'd like for you to tell him that I love him, and blow him a kiss like this."

"And why would you like me to tell Dr. King you love him, and blow him a kiss like that?"

"Because I do love him. And because he'll understand."

"Understand what exactly?"

"I can't tell you."

"Why?"

"Because it's a secret."

"What kind of secret is it?"

"Oh, I can see that you really are very good, Doctor Bianco. It's a secret of an intimate sort. And that is all I care to say on that."

"But Dr. King will understand, you said."

"Certainly."

"Then I'm sure he knows you love him. Yet, you made quite a point of telling me to tell him that."

"I want you to tell him that because he may not really believe it's me."

"Why do you feel he might not believe it's really not you?"

"Just look at me. I've been through a terrible ordeal. Look at this body cast. No one will tell me how serious my condition is. Or how long I will be here. Or anything that's going on. They won't even let me have a comb or a mirror because they said that I might hurt myself. Did you ever hear of anything so ridiculous? I know why they won't let me have a mirror. Because I'm probably disfigured. I can feel the stitches on my bottom lip. I can just imagine what the rest of me looks like. Tell me, Dr. Bianco. Am I still pretty? I really have to know."

"If I answer that question, and promise to deliver your message to Dr. King, would you try and answer one very special question for me?"

"Not if it's personal. Not if it's an intimate secret, I won't. And how do I know that I can trust you?"

"Well, what if I can give you guarantees that you will find, I'm sure, not only satisfactory, but quite pleasing? Would you then agree?"

"—Agreed."

"Nurse Ryder, would you please come in here for a moment? And bring your pocketbook with you."

*****

"Nurse Ryder, I'd like you to transcribe the tape of this conversation after we've finish here."

"Certainly, Doctor."

"Good. And would you also send a copy up to Dr. King as soon as it's completed?"

"I'd be happy to."

"Excellent. Excellent. Just one more thing. Would you happen to have a mirror in your bag?

"I have a compact with me—here you go."

"May I hold on to it for a moment?"

"Be my guest."

"Thank you, Nurse Ryder. That will be all."

*****

"All right? Now, let's see what we have here. There we go. See? You're still very attractive. Yes? — What's the matter? You seem upset."

"Richard."

"What about Richard?"

"He lied to me."

"What did he lie to you about?"

"He told me I was a frightful sight. He told me

295

that I looked like a shriveled up old prune—that I gave off a putrid stench."

"I'd like to ask you that special question now."

"Yes, Doctor?"

"Where are Dicky and Richard right now?"

"Now?"

"Yes, now."

"Well, I don't know about right now. I mean, I try to be a good mother and all, but you can't watch them twenty-four hours a day. When I left this morning, Richard was resting quietly in his room. And Dicky was in the garden making a thorny crown."

"I see. Is there anything else you would like to say to Dr. King?"

"Oh, yes. Yes, indeed, Dr. Bianco. Now more than ever. Thank God there are only a few superficial cuts and bruises."

"Anything else?"

"Why, yes. I'd like to ask him, 'Am I still pretty, David? Am I your one and only queen?' And now I'd like to be escorted back to my room to await his response while I get my beauty rest. I had quite a night last night and am truly feeling tired."

****

CONCLUDED SESSION: 9:07 a.m.

There was more to the report: notes and comments. But Dr. King could take no more. A subpoena, newspaper headlines, and threatening letters from angry civic associations would soon be headed his way. Last night alone had taken its toll. But it was nothing compared to this report. This was horrific. Unexplainable! How in hell could Richard have known? Dr. King's nerves snapped as Sarah dropped a steel pot onto the fieldstone floor in the kitchen, sending a shiver up his spine and causing the hackle at the back of his neck to rise.

There were certain factors involved that would compel Dr. King to see Richard before the authorities transferred him to the state mental psychiatric hospital in Havenwood the following day. One of those circumstances went far beyond his promise to Sarah. One of those influences involved unadulterated fascination. Pure and simple. There was also the element involving fear. Paralyzing, yet attractive. *Attractive*, he thought. It was curious that Bianco had used that word in his report: "'See? You're still very attractive,'" King read aloud. He was beginning to believe that what obligated him to consider seeing Richard at all was not really a combination of factors, but rather a single solitary force. He wrestled uncomfortably with such notions, weighing the powers of evil in his mind. *Nonsense. Folly, pure and simple*, he told himself. "Attractive," he said aloud, lowering the set of papers to his lap, bowing his head. He no sooner dozed off, being very short on sleep, when suddenly the phone jolted him upright in his seat. "—Yes?"

"Dr. King's residence," Sarah answered from the kitchen.

"It's all right, Sarah," Dr. King said. "I have it. Hello." Sarah hung up the receiver.

"Oh, David. Is it really you?"

Dr. King felt his flesh go cold as ice. "Who is this?" he demanded, definitely dreading the reply.

"Oh, David. I *am* still pretty!"

"Who allowed you to call here?"

"David. Why are they doing this to me?"

"DON'T YOU CALL HERE EVER!" he shouted, slamming down the phone, but immediately it started ringing . . . and kept right on ringing . . . and ringing . . . and . . . .

And Sarah was shaking him gently in his chair. "I's awful sorry to wake you Dr. King, but it's Dr. Bianco on the line."

Dr. King waved a hand in mild protest, bringing his fingers to his eyes.

"He says he mus' talk to you. He says it's urgent."

Dr. King leaned forward in a pool of sweat, putting the report aside. "What time is it, Sarah?"

"Goin' on eleven-thirty. You's been sleepin' for a spell."

Dr. King picked up the receiver. "Yes?"

"I'm sorry to disturb you," Dr. Bianco apologized.

"What is so urgent?" he asked annoyingly, unnerved by the disturbing daydream.

"It's about Richard Geist."

"What about Richard?"

"I think you had better come down here and see for yourself."

"And what am I going to see exactly?"

"Did you read the report?"

"I read most of it. What is this all about, Angelo?"

"It's something you must witness with your own eyes. Something you have to hear with your own ears. I can't explain it on the phone. I'm not even sure I can explain it at all. It's like a bad dream. Please, Doctor."

"I'll meet you in D Building in twenty minutes."

It was Bianco's plea rather than any mystifying message that made Dr. King agree. Or was it that solitary force coming back to haunt him? he wondered, throwing on a light jacket, annoyed with himself for even thinking such nonsense. He told Sarah where he was going and left immediately.

As Dr. King headed toward D Building, he felt his apprehension mounting along with the pounding of his heart. For a moment he wondered why Bianco hadn't handled this himself, why he had to involve him now. He had picked Bianco to take control because he felt that the young psychiatrist was the ablest of the lot, holding impressive degrees from universities around the country, speaking no less than half a dozen languages, fluently. More importantly, he chose Bianco because the man was effective, a damn good doctor, innovative in his thinking if not downright unorthodox. That's why he secretly admired him. Completely his own man. And certainly nobody's damn fool. Certainly not Richard's. Doctor King knew that Bianco would not have bothered him unless it was extremely important. Beside, hadn't he insisted that Bianco contact him with anything important concerning Richard? Anything at all? He realized that and felt bad for having been so quick with him on the phone. Additionally, Bianco was not one for riddles or exaggeration. He could be a jokester, but when it came to his patients, Bianco was all business. Given time and proper grooming, he would make a fine administrator, too.

Bianco was waiting for him just outside the building. Everything told of gravity. It was sculpted in his face. What had gotten to Bianco?

"You won't believe this," Bianco stated, trying to exercise control.

"You told me that already," Dr. King responded flatly, following the young psychiatrist inside. They rode the elevator to the top floor. Again, Dr. King grew irritated with himself for his unnecessary tone.

Dr. Bianco led the way down the hall and around the corner. You could hear a commotion coming from one of the rooms near the nurse's station. Two uniformed officers stood on either side of the door, obviously shaken.

The commotion was growing louder. The voices were distinct. Arguing and screaming at one another at the same time. Dr. King looked at Bianco in confusion.

"They've been at it for quite some time," Bianco explained.

"Who is, *they*?"

"They, is Richard."

"But—that's impossible!" King said in disbelief.

"That's why I called you down here. You don't explain this sort of thing."

There was a sudden crash against the inside door, then another off the wall. Richard was screaming at a woman while she pleaded with him to stop. The voice was unmistakably Mother's. Her crying and carrying on went uninterrupted as a child's voice gave her a piece of his mind, while in the background, Richard ordered both of them to grow up. But the arguing continued. As one listened carefully, one became fascinated with the unbelievable quality of sounds, the paradoxical harmony of it all.

"Open up this door, Doctor," King ordered, standing between the two policemen.

Bianco withdrew a key and gestured to the officers who stood unsure. He inserted the key into the lock, and all became still save the eerie whisper of weapons leaving the mouths of leather holsters on either side of him.

Click. The door swung open wide.

Richard stood all alone in the very center of the cell. A broken bed was propped against the wall. Canvas restraints dangled from its frame. The patient's stark-white jacket was loose but still secure across his chest. The patient's fierce expression began to disappear. Hardened features melted away almost magically. Eyes hypnotic. Dilated. Large and doll-like. The countenance all aglow. Lips inviting. Warm. Innocuous.

"David! Oh, darling, you came to me. See? I *am* still pretty,"

Mother's voice assured. Blood was trickling down one cheek. "Am I still your one and only queen?"

"He's letting them take you away to a state hospital tomorrow," Richard's voice broke in.

"You won't let them do that to me, David. Will you? You know that I belong here with you."

"A, you're adorable. B, you're so beautiful. C, you're a cutie full of charms," a child's voice chimed in sing-song fashion quite merrily.

"She was an **AWFULLY BITCHY CUNT**, you see," Richard's voice rose angrily.

"Don't listen to him, David. He tells such tales. You know the problems I've had with him. You know what I've been through," she cried aloud as Dicky drowned her out with outrageous bursts of childish laughter.

"Leave her be," Richard insisted nastily.

"Oh, David. Make them stop. Please make them stop," Mother begged, locking desperate arms across a fiercely beating breast. The men gazed in fascination as the figure suddenly bore more than a likeness to Victoria Geist—a figure sinking to its knees while looking up at Dr. King intently, sending a tender kiss his way. "Tell me I'm still pretty, David. Tell me I'm still your one and only queen," she whispered sensually. Wiggling her bottom. Opening her mouth suggestively and lowering her head. Moving it up and down. Slowly at first. Picking up a rhythm. Bobbing and teasing with a serpent-like tongue. Up and down and all around. Faster and faster. Sucking sounds echoed off the floor but were barely audible beneath bellicose shrieks of protest from Dr. King.

"NO! HOW COULD YOU KNOW?" Dr. King screamed, affirming by way of rage their most intimate, nocturnal scene.

"Physician, heal thyself!" Richard sneered.

It took all three men to restrain the psychiatrist. To pull the madding doctor from the cell. Dr. King's head and heart were pounding furiously till he thought he'd have a stroke.

"Please don't leave me, David," Mother pleaded, frothing at the mouth. "I never told them anything," she insisted, licking her drooling lips lasciviously, wiping away the drivel from her chin across the bib-like, confining folds of cloth. "Please come back. Oh, God! Please come back to me."

Chapter 28

THE DEPARTURE

Early the following morning, Dr. Bianco and Nurse Ryder were busy in the new office, completing some last minute paperwork for Richard's transfer when the psychiatrist noticed a Manila envelope beneath a pile of letters. It was the block of foreign stamps plastered in its upper right-hand corner that caught the doctor's eye. He pulled the packet out from underneath the other mail and saw that it had been sent from a city just outside of Stockholm, bearing the return address of some clinic. The envelope was postmarked a week earlier and directed to the attention of Administrator.

Upon opening the item, the psychiatrist found a letter along with several Swedish newspaper clippings, one of which carried a full-length photograph of a menacing-looking yet familiar figure wearing a wide-brimmed hat and chaps. Dr. Bianco smiled broadly as he recognized the unmistakable features of Dr. Schwartz's former patient, Carl Gustafson. The caretaker's towering stature and piercing eyes set behind Dr. Schwartz's frames were the giveaway. He noted, too, the somewhat younger appearance at the cost of Carl's magnificent handlebar mustache, sporting instead, a devilish if not distinguished-looking goatee. Bianco laughed heartily as he read about the man who called himself Willy Brennan, garbed in a dazzling sequined shirt and an elaborate buckskin coat. Twin holsters displayed a pair of ominous-looking guns slung low across the desperado's narrow hips, pistol grips turned outward and set in mother-of-pearl as captioned in the article. Boots with spurs added the finishing touch. A rather flamboyant outlaw to be sure. BANDIT TERRORIZES NATIONAL PARK, the headline read. Carl Gustafson had made it all the way to Sweden, by God!

The articles were brief accounts given by scores of vacationing couples all eager to tell of their ordeal involving a "gun-wielding madman" who forced his victims into shameful submission by demanding that the party stand naked before him before relieving them of fixed amount of cash and jewelry determined solely by how well each was physically endowed.

According to one report, a young couple had been picnicking at a roadside stop when out of the bushes the bandit appeared. At gunpoint, he ordered the man to "drop his draws," instructing him to make obscene gestures at passing motorists and other picnickers, ridiculing and humiliating the poor soul mercilessly for his shortcomings before finally demanding a forfeiture of all jewelry as well as the substantial sum of 2,000 kronor. His wife, on the other hand, had been politely asked to surrender but an öre: the equivalent of a fraction of a penny. "A looker with abundant charms," the bandit was quoted as saying. Bianco shook his head as he skimmed the other articles.

A week's worth of news coverage, involving similar escapades, appeared in four separate clippings. Its reporters (probably after considering that no one was seriously hurt) treated the matter rather humorously, turning the stories into something of a farce as couples of all ages, apparently fearing humiliation above the loss of life or limb, furiously disputed one another over the sum of money and valuables said to have been seized, each grossly deflating or flatly denying the actual value or amount, or so said the sensationalistic press. DESPERADO DEMANDS BOOTY, another headline read.

Even one of their more respected newspapers seemed to be treating the incidents lightly; that is, until the First National Bank of Stockholm was held up in broad daylight, and in much the same fashion as before, whereby the bandit, calling himself Willy Brennan, and brandishing pistols, ". . . seriously jeopardized the safety and well-being of men, women and children yesterday afternoon, forcing everyone inside the bank to undress," Bianco translated for Nurse Ryder, " while passing out copies of an Irish ballad and insisting that both tellers and officers of the bank perform a sing-along, finally demanding that every customer carry off as much 'gold and silver' as they could possibly 'cart off to them thar hills,'" Bianco continued reading. Nurse Ryder simply shook her head.

Apparently, the lunatic had chased the entire crowd of naked Scandinavian men, women and children into the street, stampeding the lot headlong through the city at breakneck speed, their angry fists greedily clutching cash and coin and clothing. A spokesman for the bank refused to comment on its loss.

The article concluded by telling how Carl had somehow

managed to barricade himself behind a large appliance in an outlet store for the better part of an hour before finally agreeing to surrender to police. But only under three conditions: (1) that the 'reward money' be divided equally among common folk; (2) that his 'wanted posters,' 8 x 10 glossies, remain on display indefinitely in the main post office; (3) that authorities install in the corner of his would-be cell, stocked with Swedish beer and ice cream, the same fourteen cubic foot, self-defrosting refrigerator behind which Carl had sought refuge, asking, too, for complete protection by insisting on at least a full ten-year unlimited service contract covering all parts and labor.

The Swedish police, having had time to cool off, good-humoredly gave in to all demands. Carl surrendered and confessed that he was not the Irish folk hero, Willy Brennan, giving his full name as Jesse Woodson James.

An enclosed letter, typed in English by one of the clinic's resident psychiatrists, explained how Carl Gustafson had finally been traced to the King Foundation. The doctor had also attached a psychiatric profile that told of several delusions of which Dr. Bianco was well-aware. Carl had informed the Swedish doctors that he had been improperly imprisoned in America for impersonating a Whig president, but that he was actually Sweden's sovereign king, 'King Carl Gustaf, returned. Duty above all!' When asked to comment on the fact that Carl Gustaf wasn't born until 1946, a person somewhat younger in years than the man they had before them, Carl simply dismissed the notion as a Fascist plot, insisting that he was heir apparent at the time his grandfather ascended the throne, and that any other pretender was simply that: an imposter. After being pressed for further information, Carl decided to remain neutral on the subject, insisting, now, that he was Tiny Tim, and inquiring whether or not any of the Swedish doctors had ever seen him married on American television's *The Tonight Show*, starring Johnny Carson.

Finally convinced that Carl had gained the clinic's respect and trust, he told his doctors that he had changed his name from Gustaf to Gustafson, and had been hiding out in America at the King Foundation, Long Island, New York, as a caretaker and part-time librarian, giving the names of Doctors Schimmel and Wyszynski as references.

The letter went on to explain that the psychiatrist had twice called the King Foundation, but that each time he tried to get through to Dr. Schimmel or Dr. Wyszynski, having to explain several times that he was calling from Sweden, and that they were holding Carl Gustafson, the secretary had slammed the receiver in his ear. The Swedish doctor closed by stating that Carl was in good physical health and that if either Doctors Stanislaw Wysznski or Abraham Schimmel cared to consult with him that he would be more than happy to hear from either of them before committing the patient to their institution in Stockholm—following a period of sixty days—for further evaluation and treatment.

Dr. Bianco grinned from ear to ear, knowing that Carl Gustafson would finally be at home in Stockholm. "Yes," he said aloud. "Certainly the last of a breed and truly one of the King Foundation's most magnificent madmen."

"Excuse me, Doctor," Nurse Ryder interrupted, avoiding Bianco's eyes altogether. "You have some papers to sign, and I'll need your report before Richard Geist leaves here this morning."

Bianco deliberately placed the letter and newspaper clippings under Nurse Ryder's nose. "Linda, is it you who was derelict in the performance of your duties by failing to put through two important phone calls from Sweden, regarding the admittance of Carl Gustafson to a clinic affiliated with a state mental hospital in Stockholm?" he asked in an even tone.

Nurse Ryder looked down nervously at the news articles and letter then nodded in the affirmative, staring at the picture of the figure she barely recognized at first. She apologized profusely for her misjudgment, explaining anxiously that she had thought it a practical joke played by someone here at the Foundation. "Please forgive me," she swallowed as though she were about to choke. "When the person asked for Dr. Wyszynski or Dr. Schimmel, then said that he was calling from Sweden, I—"

"Forgiven," Bianco said succinctly, smiling and assuring the woman that the matter was as good as forgotten. He gathered up the paperwork concerning Richard Geist's transfer from the King Foundation to North Shore State Hospital. "Well, I think we're about done here, Nurse Ryder."

"Yes, sir. And thank you," she said, taking her leave.

Doctor Bianco smiled warmly at a group photograph of Nurse

Marlow kneeling in the foreground, framed on the corner of his desk, admiring the way in which the soft light highlighted her lovely features, thinking that one day she would be old and gray and even wrinkled. So he beheld her beauty, committing an indelible impression with which to carry around in his mind and heart forever, vowing that they would one day grow old and gray and wrinkled together.

Dr. Bianco turned his thoughts back to the psychiatrist's letter, half serious in having *Doctors* Schimmel and Wyszynski respond to the Swedish psychiatrist themselves, explaining in their own inimical way why each believed they should keep Carl Gustafson exactly where he was, rather than have two friendly governments at odds over any sort of extradition proceedings. It would be a marvelous treaty. Perhaps a classic of its kind. He was certain that Carl would overwhelmingly agree, picturing the Swede smiling that mischievous smile of his from across the ocean.

Putting such silly notions aside, he considered the completed report before him. Police and the Foundation's personnel would be coming for Richard in a little while, and then things would hopefully be back to normal, he told himself. Outside a corner window, he saw Mr. Schimmel heading up a set of steps to open the door to the library. The man walked briskly, appearing a bit upset.

As the Foundation's library had grown over the years, Mr. Schimmel had long since converted from Dewey decimal to the Library of Congress classification system found in most centers throughout the country, having proudly organized everything himself, setting up his card catalogs by subject on one side, author and title on the other. This had facilitated matters nicely, for the library had added many more books to its growing collection. In his twenty years as librarian, it was doubtful that he had received more than a dozen complaints from anyone other than Carl Gustafson. But no sooner than that Nazi was out of his hair, did patients start complaining about the fact that they could no longer locate books on Egypt, Egyptology, embalming, or mummies.

Mr. Schimmel prayed for the hour they'd take Richard Geist away so that the others might forget about such books. He was becoming more and more agitated by the minute, knowing ghastly well what they were really after. At first, he put the blame on

Lieutenant Lark and Sergeant Grear who had borrowed many more books than they returned. But for the past two days it had been the staff who grabbed up anything pertaining to the subject. Anything they could get their greedy little hands on. Especially after the stories spread like wildfire concerning Victoria Geist.

Mr. Schimmel was busy putting away returns while trying to explain the situation to Mrs. O'Brian.

"But this is supposed to be the patients' library," Mrs. O'Brian complained bitterly, following the little man around the room.

"Oh, I know vhat you vant! Vhat you vant is blood and gore," Abe Schimmel challenged.

Mrs. O'Brian shook her head defiantly. "No. No. No!" she persisted, passing a noisy passage of air through distended nostrils. "I want to read about the preservation of a people."

"You vant to read about the preservation of a people? No! You vant to read of blood and gore. If you really vish to read about the preservation of a people, read the history of the Jews," he insisted. "Read about Auschwitz. Or Dachau. Or Buchenwald. Or even some of the lesser known camps. You vant to read horror? There you will find it all. *Ve* are the living dead!"

But Mrs. O'Brian cut him short, insisting that she wanted DT 62 M7 P25. *Wrapped for Eternity*, by Mildred Mastin Pace.

Disgusted, Schimmel swore that he'd *wrap* her. Searching one of the wagons, he found a different book. "Ange-Pierre Leca's, *The Egyptian Way of Death*. Pace is for children," Schimmel explained. "Leca is in depth. Actually, you should research the Chinese on the subject; they vere vay ahead of everyvon. Only the Egyptians advertised more," he assured her.

What Schimmel had said was indeed true. But Mrs. O'Brian was only interested in knowing how the Egyptians managed to pull the brain through the nose, at the same time complaining of her sinuses.

"Then you ought to try it," Schimmel agreed wholeheartedly, laughing up a storm. "I mean, vhat the hell do you have to lose? Can't hurt."

Mrs. O'Brian was on a short fuse that morning and started humming very loudly, drowning out the librarian's laughter by planting a finger firmly in each ear, finally threatening to blow Mr. Schimmel's precious library sky high with a case of dynamite she claimed she had cached away years ago and had been saving for a special occasion.

Inside D Building, Richard was being escorted around a corridor and off the ward to a waiting elevator, flanked by half a dozen police officers as well as several members of the staff. Once outside, the group headed across the narrow drive toward A Building. Dr. Bianco and Nurse Marlow were waiting inside by the reception desk.

"Ma—Pa—Pa-by-yo-Ma. Ka-Ba-Ra," Richard resounded, entering the building while calling cadence with perfect pitch, advancing across the lobby in a highly military manner, executing a series of flashy steps. "Ma—Pa—Pa-by-yo-Ma. Ka-Ba-Ra," he repeated.

Nurse Marlow wanted to know what the gibberish was all about, so Dr. Bianco explained to her the significance of Richard's cryptic chant. He explained how Ma and Pa were symbolic of the parents Richard felt he never had; figuratively lying next to one another in death was just a guess. "The ancient Egyptians believed the ka to the spiritual part of man, which gave the material part, the body, its personality, presumed to be born out of chaos," the psychiatrist tried to couch in simple terms.

"Ka?" she questioned in confusion.

"The Egyptians believed that the ka was actually man's double. In this way, Richard is able to justify his other self; that is, Dicky."

"And how does he justify his mother's personality?"

"Well, first you have to understand why he chose to adopt it in the first place. And that's the easy part."

"Sure. Because he wanted his mother's attention."

"TTEN-HUT!" Richard shouted eerily from the far corner of the lobby, certainly too great a distance for him to have heard the two conversing quietly by the reception desk.

Nurse Marlow looked over uneasily at Richard.

"Yes, attention rarely paid," Bianco agreed, looking over uncomfortably at Richard, too. "Compounded by an unrelenting jealousy of anyone who paid her any mind. He couldn't have her, so he became her. The rationalization is in wanting to save her soul. A positive act to justify the negative one of having murdered her."

"And what's this business with ba?"

"It gets more complicated," Bianco promised. "The ba, not the ka," he went on to explain, "was believed to be man's immortal soul, merging with the ka and the body in order to determine man's behavior. All very essential to one's survival in the other world."

"But why would Richard go through all the trouble of preparing a mummy if he knew he was going to assume his mother's personality in the first place?"

"Because Richard had to assure himself the act would be completely voluntary on her part. In Richard's mind, she had to be given the freedom to choose between the mummy he prepared for her or his own body."

"You're kidding?"

"Would I kid a kid?" he kidded. "What Richard is struggling with now is inner conflict because his mother has surfaced as the dominant personality."

"And Ra?" she asked, obviously impressed. "And those voices? How can he possibly speak as three?"

"Ra was king or supreme ruler of the ancient Egyptians. A symbol, if you will, for our Doctor David King. But those voices are quite another thing. Believe it or not, Mrs. O'Brian put me onto something. Harmonics. It's all physics; and very complicated. The science of musical sounds. Richard has somehow learned to control tone. It's positively weird."

"Weird isn't the word," she said, shaking off a sudden chill. "Tell me, how did he ever know about that horrible place in the infirmary?"

"Mrs. O'Brian knew about the substructure as having been a root cellar some hundred years or so ago. Probably mentioned it to Richard casually, although she says she really doesn't remember for sure."

Nurse Marlow shivered. "I'll be glad when he's long gone from here. He gives me the creeps."

"I guess we'll all rest easy once he's the hell away from here."

"Well, I don't know about that," she said. "I don't think that Doctor King will ever rest easy."

"AT EASE!" Richard ordered from across the room as an attendant checked and double checked the restraints on the patient's straitjacket.

One of the phones rang. Nurse Marlow jumped. Her nerves were apparently shot. Dr. Bianco gently drew her to him. Comforting her. Something he had never done in front of others.

Nurse Ryder answered the phone, gasped, then suddenly dropped the receiver as though it had turned dangerously hot.

"What is it?" Bianco demanded, bounding around to the other side of the counter. "What happened?" But the woman just stood there trembling. He picked up the receiver, sensing a different kind of trembling on the other end of the line. "Who is this?"

It was Sarah—barely breathing. "Dr. King is dead," she whispered. "Dr. King is dead!"

"RA!" Richard shouted, knowing exactly what was wrong although he stood some sixty feet away.

"No," another voice whined. "Oh, my God. No!" It was Mother's voice, clear as a bell but tolling rather pitifully.

"THE KING IS DEAD. LONG LIVE THE QUEEN!" Richard proclaimed. Then Dicky asked if he could be the little prince. And all three voices melded. All three spoke at once. One above the other. Two above the whine.

Bianco came back around the counter wondering how on earth Richard could know. The psychiatrist moved closer toward the scene. And closer. Listening. Searching for some flaw. Some trick. But there was none. The voices grew louder and more maddening, and in that second it seemed as though Bianco might lose his mind. His heart beat faster, just as surely as Dr. King's had stopped. It was as Bianco fixed his eyes upon the tortured soul that Richard spun violently around. Like a whirlwind. A maelstrom of madness. Stirring up a storm.

"Brrrr," he emoted and shivered as the police officers swept him off his feet, his voice suddenly shifting to a woman's sob.

Bianco raised his hand in protest to still them all. Everything grew quiet.

"Please don't abandon me, David. Please, not now. I need you more than ever. I need your help. Please help me," Mother pleaded.

"YOU ARE A QUEEN! YOUR KING HAS ABDICATED," Richard shouted.

"Oh, no," Dicky assured everyone. "You usurped his power. You pulled him off his throne. Just like you said you would. Just like you said you would," the child's voice taunted cruelly.

"You killed him, Richard," Mother's voice intoned in solemn oath. "You tore him up inside just as surely as if you had plunged a knife into his weakened heart. Why?" she pleaded. "Tell me why."

"Because he used you."

"No, he loved me. Oh, in God's name, how could you, Richard?"

"You are a queen. Now behave like one!"

"No, I am sick, Richard. Can't you see that? I feel so dead and empty inside," she cried out bitterly. "Please just let me die. Just let me go and lie with him forever."

"NO! You are a queen, and we are the heirs apparent."

"That's right," Dicky chided childishly. "We're ascending heirs."

"Yes, and we shall claim all our earthly rights," Richard vowed.

"YOU LOST YOUR RIGHTS. HE WAS YOUR FATHER, RICHARD!" Mother shouted hysterically. "I would have told you that in time," she said sobbing bitterly.

"WHAT?" Richard roared. "Dr. King? My father? You would have told me that in time? WHO IN GOD'S NAME COULD EVER KNOW MY FATHER? FOR THEY ALL HAD YOU IN THE HAY. MAYBE MARVIN IS MY FATHER. YES? Oh, you are such a violated queen."

"He was truly your father, Richard. This I swear. I never told David. I was going to tell him before the end of summer, but I never got the chance to tell him or anyone. Thank God I never told him."

"But what about Horatio Gladstone, Mother? You led me to believe that he was my father. I heard conversations."

"You heard only what you wanted to hear. A woman *knows* who the father is, Richard."

"Knows? How could you possibly know?"

"There was only one, Richard."

"Only one? THEN I SUPPOSE THE OTHERS PUT IT UP YOUR ASS!"

There was a violent struggle, and it took seven men to hold the tragic figure down.

Dr. Bianco gestured, and one of the attendants placed a hypodermic needle and a little bottle in his hand.

"DIRTY—FILTHY—DISGUSTING—VICIOUS—DEVIL," Mother's voice cried out as she writhed frantically and tried to bite the hands of those who held her fast, fighting them the way Dicky would like to have seen her fight fourteen years ago when seven men corralled her in the hay. "YES. YOU KILLED YOUR OWN FATHER,

RICHARD. YOU! DO YOU HEAR ME?" Then all three voices melded and tunneled through the room as though they had been shot out of a single large-mouthed canon: "DEVIL. EVIL. VILE. LIE. VIE. DIE," the voices boomed in unison. Mother fought courageously as Dr. Bianco pushed up a pant leg and plunged a needle smack into a calf. "Stop it!" she shrieked. "What do you think you're doing? Where are you taking us? We have a funeral to attend. I have to be here to bury my king. You had better let Richard remain here with me to see his real father for the very last time, or there will be hell to pay. Take your hands off of me, I say. Oh, if there is a God in heaven, please help us now."

The authorities led the demon away, having to half carry the limp body along the sidewalk and over to a car with a built-in cage. Opening the rear door of the sedan, they placed the groggy creature onto the backseat. Moments later, the car sped off, its siren screaming out the main gate.

Just outside the building, Nurse Marlow turned to Dr. Bianco. "Is Dr. King really dead?"

"Yes. I'm afraid he is, Donna. Sarah would know."

"Oh, my God!" she cried.

Once inside, one could hear the intermittent beep signaling trouble on the line—the line—the line. As soon as Bianco hung up the phone, it rang again. "Yes? —Yes, of course, Sarah. We're coming right away."

Chapter 29

POCONO REFLECTIONS

The past week had been especially tiring for Dr. Angelo Bianco. He had made all of the funeral arrangements for Dr. King. Relatives, staff, colleagues, friends, and even a few patients came to pay their last respects. Scattered among the faces were several of Dr. King's rivals through the years, men and women from both the state and private sectors who had questioned yet marveled at the man's success. But at a man's funeral, rivals, too, were simply tenants who held temporary leases in the game of life. Those among them who understood that came to pay their last respects; those who didn't, simply came to gloat. It really didn't make a damn bit of difference, Angelo thought. The only face he didn't want to see in the crowd was Richard Geist's, or any likeness of it that could take on Mother's mien.

But it wasn't Richard's face so much as it was those tongues that had troubled the new director throughout the week, tongues that had visited the physically exhausted and emotionally drained psychiatrist in his sleep, turning him over feverishly in his bed, speaking to him in a horrible language, a language he never even knew existed, let alone could comprehend; a language fired up with a series of whines and whispers; a language comprised of cries and chortles that sent his body shivering beneath a blanket and sheet. Yet, he somehow managed to withdraw from those maddening voices, maneuvering himself away from the fleshy flames that summoned him below, escaping those haunting, horrible instruments of hell. Finally, a sound sleep did come to him sometime in the wee hours. But what he couldn't escape was the horrendous heat.

Click sounded the radio alarm clock: ". . . with soaring temperatures through the weekend. News and complete forecast in a moment. But first an important message for those who suffer from acid indigestion . . ." Angelo Bianco hit the snooze button.

He had spent the last two days in bed with the flu, praying for the strength he needed for the very special moment close at hand. All week long the weather had been quite erratic; stormy but bright, unreasonably warm, cool and cloudy, sunny and mild, humid and hot.

It was no wonder he had gotten sick, he told himself, reaching for the thermometer on the table by the bed, shaking the instrument before popping it into his mouth.

Of course, his air conditioner had to be on the fritz during some of the hottest days in weeks, he complained, throwing back the sticky sheet as he got up slowly, crossing over to and turning on the unit with little hope that a cool current of air might somehow find its way through the circular vent. He reached over and pulled back the window shade a fraction, reading the outside thermometer. He stood peering down at the quiet, empty world below. For a moment, he believed in miracles. The unit was humming away smoothly before suddenly turning mean, making rather unhealthy sounds and blowing an unbearable stream of hot air into the room.

He shut the unit off in frustration and stood before the massive antique etched glass mirrored dresser that his parents had given him and his ex-wife as a wedding present four years earlier. It was the one piece of furniture she positively hated, claiming that it didn't fit in with the modern sets she had placed on order. Ordered without discussion. It was the only piece of furniture that he had taken with him when he finally decided to wrap things up permanently, moving out of their sprawling, heavily mortgaged home he could just about manage, terminating the intolerable relationship with his wife that he thought he could handle, putting an end to the interminable interference from his in-laws, which he knew he never would continue to allow.

Angelo reflected on the past while standing in full profile before the mirror, observing himself unflatteringly in the pair of stretched-out briefs that hung from his buttocks like a cheap washed-out café curtain. He removed the thermometer from his mouth and read it in the early light, delighted that his fever had finally run its course, glad that his nightmare was over, remembering it only in part. The recovered soul was thrilled that he felt well enough to make the trip he and Donna had planned well over a week ago.

He made the bed then took down an old piece of leather luggage from a shelf in the closet, recalling that it was the only other item he had taken with him (save some clothes and toiletries) on the day he stormed out of a rather shaky marriage. The bag she hated, too. A seasoned L.L. Bean bag handed down to him by his father. And when his wife had found him packing in a huff, she went over to the dresser drawer and helped him by removing fistfuls of his worn-out underwear, stuffing them into the bag with no regrets. The pairs of dingy white underwear she hated most of all, always insisting that he buy the expensive and fashionable colored sets he never wore.

Suddenly, it all made perfect sense to him while standing there fever free before the ancient dresser. Standing there in well-worn briefs and holding his father's faded bag. What his ex-wife had simply hated was anything outdated, weathered, or worn. Everything had to be modern, colorful and expensive. He thought it strange that it took him years to realize. Three years after the divorce.

He headed for the bathroom, hoping the flush and rush of cold water would somehow wash away the heat. He had called the superintendent at the beginning of the week to repair the air-conditioning unit, but the cranky individual informed him, in all frankness, that it was unlikely the maintenance crew would be able to attend to the problem for at least a week or two. Angelo made a mental note of attending to the superintendent's Christmas gratuity perhaps the following year. A refreshing thought in itself, he mused, urinating forcibly into the clean white porcelain pool. Flushing the toilet, he moved over to the sink, deciding to alter his morning ritual. Shaving before taking a shower.

"Damn," he muttered, staring fixedly into that reflective calendar of time. That damned daily reminder. That recording clock of ages. He examined, with sheer disgust, the dark bags beneath his eyes from lack of proper sleep. Opening his mouth wide, he looked down the back of his fiery red throat, cursing the hellish hole before gargling with warm salt water.

Lathering up, he listened to capsulated accounts of international and local news: Vietnam. Subway violence. Insanity from some terrace of a twenty-story building from which an infant was hurled. A teenage suicide pact. An outrageous local story of a dog stuck up a tree after chasing a cat—then on to reports of snarling traffic.

After a refreshing cool shower, Angelo stepped from the stall and wrapped a towel around his waist, drip-drying and splashing on cologne, double-daring the relative humidity hanging heavy in the corners of the room to touch his tingling, vibrant skin. He felt wonderfully alive, slapping his bare, wet feet playfully on squares of linoleum that he pretended were castle-like cool tiles. However, that invigorating moment melted away most magically, exacerbated by the promise of record-breaking temperatures well up in the eighties for the tri-state area; high humidity notwithstanding. With no relief in sight, the weatherman reported his infernal forecast with the same conviction an evangelist would deliver a scorching sermon on sin and the state of man.

Actually, it seemed a sure-fire bet rather than any sort of prediction on the part of the preacher of meteorology, for it was already eighty degrees outside, and the mercury had been climbing steadily since 6 a.m. So Angelo promised himself that he and Donna would stay as close as they could to inviting theme park water rides, frozen daiquiris, air-conditioned restaurants, and a mini-suite with a sunken tub during their next few days together at the Pocono resort area they'd be heading toward that morning. He'd be meeting her in a little while and realized that he had better move his butt. So move his butt he did. Across the hall and back to the bedroom he withdrew, behaving a bit insane, tearing away the towel from around his waist, drawing a waist-high section of red drapery deliberately at his side.

"*Olé!*" he shouted, pivoting decisively to the right as the thunderous and massive weight of the imaginary beast passed within inches of his frame. Multitudes of screaming spectators all rose to the occasion before him in the eighteenth century mirrored glass. Women swooned, and men expelled their breath in mixed relief. Then man and animal turned to confront one another in that spectacular moment of truth. The final curtain. The moment of madness. The bull: firmly planted on all fours. Head and horns held obliquely toward the cape. The matador: moving in for the kill. Angelo removed an illusory blade from behind the red fabric, dancing the curtain of death in an envisioned yet dramatic dream-like scene. The movement caught the bull's eye, summoning the bulk forth in a blind rage as Angelo *Romero Bianco* rose to his tippy toes, aiming along the length of flashing steel before suddenly thrusting the sword deep between the blades of bone and sinewy flesh. "Bull's-eye!" he cried, playing it to the hilt, withdrawing the blade to the sounds of outrageous cheering and applause as the prodigious black bull buckled to its knees in a cloud of dust rising off the arena floor.

Casting imagination aside for the moment, Angelo ripped open a new package of Jockey shorts, stepping into the soft white cottony cloth and snapping the waistband smartly against his gut. How snug it felt against his skin; quite unlike the stretched-out pairs he enjoyed wearing around the apartment, offering about as much support as a jock strap on a two-year-old, he entertained, picturing the infant on the news in a baggy cloth diaper falling twenty stories to its death.

Standing in profile before the mirror, he sucked in his gut beneath its banded, well-tanned cage, flexing his biceps like an assured athletic youth. Setting a confident chin upon a shoulder, the powerful body builder turned to face his fans. Filling his lungs and expanding his massive black-haired chest before thousands, the celebrity waved and most conceitedly accepted the Mr. Universe title.

"Not too shabby," he said aloud, exhaling and promising to exercise more often. Funny how a new pair of underwear could make you feel, he considered a bit boyishly, knowing it wasn't the briefs at all that gave him a sense of well-being that morning. Nor was it solely the security accompanying his most recent appointment as director of the King Foundation, spelled out clearly in an emergency meeting with Dr. King's lawyers earlier that week. Neither was it simply the power and prestige the position brought. It was, he realized, for the very first time in three long years, the sudden and surprising knowledge that he was finally free, free from the chains of a woman who had cast and held some sort of inexplicable spell over him. And as he moved away from the mirror, he saw himself set truly free. Free to pursue. To pursue the Poconos. Free to choose. Free as a bird that suddenly found itself at the door of an open cage.

Carefree, he flew over to the dresser and opened a small ice-blue velvet box, removing and examining the beautifully faceted stone that he alone had carefully selected and would present to Donna during a romantic dinner that evening in the Poconos. It would be a crazy kind of presentation. A proposal with flair. For he was in a crazy, carefree kind of mood. It would be a wonderful surprise. A declaration of his love for her. Together, they would map out their own plans and shape their own future. And no one, but no one, would ever meddle in their lives, he swore. He had no doubts about his Donna. No issues like the ones he had before. It all seemed so perfect. Like the diamond in his palm.

Donna phoned Angelo's apartment the moment she had the

chance, happy to hear that he was feeling better, surprised that he was packed and ready to go. Yet, she suggested they postpone their plans until he was feeling stronger, and that she'd come over and nurse him back to health with soup, and juice, and lots of TLC. But he insisted that he felt strong enough to move mountains and was raring to go. She laughed and said he sounded like his old self again and agreed to meet as planned, glad that she had taken her shower early and set her hair.

After they hung up, she really became excited. She needed a quiet weekend away from all the madness of the Foundation and the house. Just the two of them. She had no idea of what Angelo actually had in mind. No idea at all.

Sitting at the edge of her bed, she carefully slipped into a pair of nylons, pulling each along a long and shapely well-tanned leg. Standing up, she fastened the tops of her hose to a sexy mint-green garter belt which crowned a matching pair of panties. Stepping into a pair of taupe heels and cotton skirt, she stood before the vanity, studying herself, pressing a palm firmly against her stomach, tucking her tummy, turning her head smartly to one side and setting an assured chin squarely atop a slender shoulder. She stood there for a moment, admiring her trim figure and full breasts before flagging a hand that meant she could still stand to lose a few pounds. Moving closer to the mirror, she considered her features carefully. Classic, pretty, or plain were the images that flashed across her brain as she gave the mirror sultry sidelong glances. As if in a trance, she gazed into the looking glass, recalling certain cruel remarks made by her late mother, many a year ago:

". . . And when you were born, Di, darling, your daddy just stood there outside the nursery, repeating over and over again, 'Are you pretty? Are you plain? Or are you just plain ugly?' Oh, God, were you an ugly duckling, dear. What the Jewish people call a *mieskeit*." She could hear her mother laughing deliriously as though she were standing right beside her now.

"Well, baby, look at you now," Donna reflected, satisfied with the certain knowledge that she could still turn a few heads if she had a mind to. She thought about the crude and embarrassing remark her husband had made on the eve of their first wedding anniversary, babbling on about her erecting the dead whenever she strutted her stuff. 'Class ass,' he told everyone, staggering around their living room stinking drunk, belching in her face before passing out cold in front of a room full of guests. God, how she had grown to hate him. Oh, how she would strut her stuff before Angelo during their holiday weekend in the Poconos, she told herself. How she would strut her stuff before him and him alone. Forever and always, she swore. How this would be their special time together.

Turning away from the mirror, she suddenly started to cry, and she hated herself for doing so. She cried because the magic had gone out of her marriage soon after it had begun. She cried because her husband had told her that he didn't care whether she spent the next few days with her sister in Peekskill (as she told him she would), or on her back in some sleazy motel room, 'gyrating for sailors or gyrenes,' was how he put it. She cried because he simply shrugged his shoulders when she had asked him for a divorce earlier in the week. She cried because her parents had thought her an ugly duckling some thirty years earlier, hating her mother for having had the audacity to think the incident of anecdotal interest, having told that stupid story in detail to others outside the family as well. She cried because she was so sick and tired of being so goddamned sensitive all the time.

When she finally stopped crying, she dried her eyes and forced a smile, glad that she had not yet applied her makeup. Pleased that she was still vain enough to feel pretty and could wish to be beautiful. And when she finally finished working her magic in the mirror, highlighting her blue eyes and high cheekbones, when she finally finished dressing, tucking in a frilly blouse, she was just that. Beautiful! Pulling a comb quickly through her silky blonde hair, she left the house beaming and outshining the early morning sun as she strolled coolly down the steps and along the walkway toward her car.

Donna and Angelo met at a designated spot, parking their cars on a deserted street near a high school then arguing about whose car they'd take. Angelo reminded her that his was air conditioned. Donna said the air conditioning would make him sick. She also explained that she needed the mileage just in case her husband had checked her odometer before he left the house for a camping trip early that morning with friends. Angelo finally agreed to take her car but insisted on driving even though she told him that he still looked like hell and wouldn't mind driving at all. He told her that she'd have her chance to drive in a little while. It was to be the first surprise. Angelo brought the car up to eighty, for he loved driving fast. He wanted to beat the heat, to feel cool air racing along his arm. Eighty-five. He wanted to take the car up a mile per hour for every degree of temperature out there. Off to a Pocono park they flew.

It was a rather hot but exciting time for the two of them. Donna and Angelo played hard and fast among the crowds of happy people in the amusement park, excitedly racing miniature cars around an oval track, speeding along with scores of grownups whose children and grandchildren watched in awe and envy as uproarious adults behaved worse than any child imaginable, or so thought the Indianapolis 500 champion, taking to the inside track with tires screeching in the dirt, pistons pounding to the finish as the powerful machine and its driver defied death on a daily basis, when suddenly our hero swerved off the track, racing in his mind toward the body of an infant falling freely through the air, catching it at the last possible moment in outstretched arms before the multitudes, losing the race by meters but winning the hearts of millions during that glorious Walter Mittyish moment.

Stepping from the car and removing his helmet, Angelo *Andretti* Bianco bowed immodestly before the crowd of envious youngsters rushing past him and into the arms of laughing adults.

"Gotta get me one of these," Angelo said and smiled, grabbing up the tyke who had stumbled in front of him and almost fell on his face. He lifted the boy high into the air before setting him safely upon the ground in front of an apprehensive parent.

In the afternoon, Angelo and Donna changed into bathing suits and found themselves chuting down a towering water-slide behind a line of screaming happy children as parents and grandparents stood crowded together behind cameras of every kind, snapping stills or shooting miles of footage in the heat.

Deciding that it was time to trade one watery world for another, Donna and Angelo dressed and headed for their Pocono retreat. High up a winding lakeside mountain road they drove, distancing themselves from the action world below. After checking into the beautiful resort, delighted with their accommodations, the two of them quickly changed back into bathing suits, not wanting to lose a minute of the late afternoon sun. Angelo brought along two plastic glasses and a pitcher filled with frozen daiquiri.

He led her up a steep embankment and across a catwalk to a rocky pool beneath a magnificent waterfall. They could see its boiling madness crashing upon the rocks below. Level with the pool was an overlook that commanded an awesome if not dizzying view of a range of distant mountains to the west. As they approached the falls, they could barely hear themselves.

"You see that big globe-like bubble down there?" he roared, pointing to where the water cascaded off a ledge.

"What?" She could barely hear at all.

"The bubble. See?" pointing to where the water formed a large fishbowl ten yards out along a rocky wall. It was her next surprise.

She looked at him queerly.

"We're going behind and into it. I'll show you how."

"Oh, no!" she screamed, shaking her head violently back and forth.

"Follow me."

"You're crazy."

"I know," he agreed and led her by the hand as they inched their way along the narrow ledge with water blasting all around them.

It was his smile that gave her strength, but his eyes suddenly shown great concern, which scared her half to death. "What's wrong?"

"Daiquiris."

"What?"

"The daiquiris are getting diluted. Hold these." He handed her the pitcher and two stacked glasses.

"DON'T LET GO OF ME!"

"Just for a second. Here."

As she grabbed the items, he reached around and removed her bikini top then took the pitcher and glasses from her hands.

"What on God's good earth do you think you're doing?" she hollered, moving closer to the security of the wet stone wall.

"This way I know you'll follow me inside," he shouted, shielding the mouth of the pitcher beneath his chin before darting through the thinnest veil of water showering down closest to the wall.

"NOOOOO!" was all Angelo heard as he disappeared within the watery world. And no sooner than he put the pitcher and glasses down to fetch her, did his bare-breasted maiden appear.

"Ah, there you are," he said within the hushed, womb-like tomb.

He spoke in heavy sounding words that could be measured by the pound. A sort of weighty, hollow tone they tolled.

"Ahhhhhhhhhhhhhhh!" she screamed, and then calmly said, "Pour." She laughed lightly at her muffled tone.

"What was that for?"

"Pour, and give me back my top," she demanded, separating then holding out both glasses.

"I'll give you a drink, but I don't think I want to give you back your top just yet."

"Why not?"

"Because you look so sexy standing there. And because I love you," he whispered.

"I love you, too," she mouthed in silence.

Angelo read the words upon her lips just as clearly as though they had been echoed around the world, realizing in that moment how Richard Geist had picked up pieces of their conversation from across the lobby on the morning the police and personnel took him away. Richard could read lips. It didn't explain everything, but it explained enough. *So what were thoughts of Richard doing in their bubble two hundred miles away from home?* he scolded himself before sending such notions away.

"How did you ever find this place?" Donna asked.

"My parents used to vacation here when I was a little boy."

She wanted to tell him that he was still a little boy who never did grow up and probably never would. But she didn't. "Did they know you did this stupid thing?"

"I was never in here."

"You're kidding!"

"Nope. One afternoon I went exploring and saw something moving inside the bubble. It was all a blur. So I waited. After a while, two people came out, and I saw they were my parents."

"Your parents were in here?"

"Yep."

"You have crazy parents?"

"Yep."

Sitting together on the large flat rock in the very center of their private world that late afternoon, Angelo watched as Donna drank and ran her hand back and forth and lovingly along the ancient, well-worn wall and seated surface. He couldn't help but smile. The day was dissolving quickly. The child inside him tried to poke then punch a hole through the side of the thicker section of powerful waterfall, marveling at how nature's mighty force drove his hand downward and away. They sat protected. And a silent voice within him said that nothing would ever hurt them if they believed in the magic of the moment, for it was a magic place in time for the two of them. After a spell, Donna poured the last of the daiquiri and touched his glass with hers to toast their health and happiness, thanking him for giving her the most unusual sunset she had ever seen. They held each other closely and watched the fading, orange ball shimmering in the distance.

"I think we better get back before we lose the light altogether." Donna suggested. "Now, give me back my top."

"In a moment," he teased, standing and sticking the yellow item inside his trunks, placing one glass within the other and both within the plastic pitcher. "Remember, stay close to the wall on your way out."

"And where do you think you're going?"

Facing the center of the cascade, Angelo took a deep breath and one step forward before leaping through the seam of rushing water— falling ten feet to the pool below. A moment later, she saw him surface as the current caught and swiftly carried him down to the edge of an embankment before the flow relaxed and left him on his own.

Donna saw all this through eyes of disbelief, watching Angelo floating on his back while pouring mountain water from the pitcher upon his face. She saw him stand waist high and put the pitcher down upon a grassy spot, frantically searching his bathing suit for her bikini top, pretending it was lost forever before waving it like a flag, draping it over his head, finally stretching it across his chest and posing like a fool.

"Jesus Christ," she said, jumping to what she thought might surely be her death, exchanging both the safety and the silence of her crystal world for the maddening music of the falls while falling toward the bubbling cauldron of foam. Donna hit the soupy surface with her heels before disappearing into the absolute deafness of the icy pool, popping to the top like a cork, the current rushing her toward him as he handed her a line.

"Give me that, you," she said, grabbing her bikini top and taking it down to the underwater dressing room for a spell, circling beneath him while he wondered where she went.

Angelo waded out a bit when suddenly he felt his trunks race past his knees and around an ankle as he tried to hook and hold them with a foot. But she managed to knock him over and grab them firmly in her hand.

"Promise you'll never do anything like that to me again, or I swear you'll find these in the goddamn trees," she swore.

Emerging new as a newborn from the womb, Angelo headed up the path to the resort with Donna carrying plasticware and chasing after him, pleading with him to put his trunks back on. As he approached a group of trees, Angelo T. (for Tarzan) Bianco, Lord of the Jungle, leapt high into the air and grabbed onto a lower limb. He hung there, swinging gently, listening to her plea. Finally, he agreed to her request, but only if she promised to answer to the name of Jane. Hearing people coming along the walkway high above them, she agreed to anything, pushing up his trunks as the animal inside him let out a familiar savage cry that surely carried across the entire mountain range.

Attending a dinner dance that evening in the resort's swanky ballroom, Angelo pulled Donna up from the table and escorted her to the dance floor for one more merengue before their final course. When they returned, a fancy cart had been rolled up to their table, and dessert was being prepared in ostentatious display. Donna watched their captain put together a special coffee creation, creating theatrics that dazzled and delighted her.

Holding a large orange and small paring knife over a heated pan, their captain skillfully removed most of the peel with one continual slice. The colorful coil hung directly above the skillet. Donna watched in fascination as the man gently squeezed the fruit, blending its juice with brandy and a special liqueur being poured from a flask by an assistant. The concoction ran along the rind, reminding her of the water-slide she and Angelo had ridden earlier that afternoon, the two of them spiraling down its slippery surface like two happy children, splashing into the refreshing pool below. Suddenly, the pan burst forth in flame, startling her as a stream of fire rifled up its helical path.

Donna and Angelo applauded the performance, and her special coffee was served with a mountain of whipped cream along with warm and friendly smiles.

After a brief discussion concerning liqueurs, brandies, and fine wines from around the world, their captain politely excused himself. Angelo nonchalantly reached across the table and helped himself to a single cube of sugar, plopping it into his cappuccino. Then he slid Donna's special coffee creation in front of him, exchanging it for his cappuccino. She looked up but said nothing, thinking he simply wanted a sip.

"I put in a cube of sugar, but you'll have to stir it," he instructed. "Otherwise it'll be bitter."

"But I don't want your cappuccino," she protested mildly.

Angelo ignored her, taking up a heaping spoonful of whipped cream before sipping her special treat. "Ummm. Delicious," he teased. "But I think you'll find the cappuccino more to your taste," he insisted, handing her a tiny silver spoon. "Stir."

Donna stirred uncomfortably in her seat. "I'll be more than happy to share my coffee with you," she said in a whisper, "but I don't like cappuccino."

"This one you'll like," he assured her. "Stir."

Confused by his behavior, and not wanting to create a scene, she took the spoon and put it through the foamy head.

"Gently," he insisted. "You don't want to dissolve the cream. You want to sip the coffee through it."

As she stirred the coffee, she heard a clinking sound and felt a solid object against the spoon. Staring down queerly at the cup, she probed and fished out a brilliant oval stone. "Oh, my God," she cried. "OH, MY GOD!"

Patrons stopped their conversations in mid-sentence. Utensils and glasses were suddenly set aside. An alarmed waiter hurried over to their table, staring down in amazement at the engagement ring resting on the silver spoon in the shallow brown bath of cream and coffee . . . like a precious pearl just discovered in an oyster.

"Well, last year a customer retrieved her dentures from the *soup du jour*," the waiter said with a chuckle, relieved that the happening was a pleasant one. "She wanted to sue us, insisting that our broth made her teeth dance out of her mouth. No, that's a true story; I couldn't make this up," he elaborated, noting their skepticism. "And I thought we made unique presentations. *Mazel tov,*" he whispered, leaning closer to the table. "Don't tell anyone I said that, or they'll ship me back to the Catskills," he added wryly, leaving the two of them alone in celebration.

Angelo smiled as he took the ring from her, dipping it in his water glass, drying it with his napkin. Taking her hand in his, he slipped the sparkling stone gently on her finger. "Perfect fit. Yes?"

Patrons resumed their dining and conversation. And when Donna finally settled from the shock and leaned across the table to kiss him gently upon the lips, a young couple seated at a nearby table started tapping a set of water glasses with their utensils. A second later, other patrons got into the act.

Angelo laughed happily. "And I thought this would be a quiet evening,"

"And I'm still married," Donna whispered, giggling into her napkin. "I can't say yes, just now," she said, half serious.

"But I'm crazy about you," he insisted.

"Well, why didn't you say so?"

"Is that a 'Yes'?"

"Oh, yes," she cried so happily.

Glasses chimed anew while in the corner of the room an elderly couple sat quietly by, probing and poking their own cups of coffee, searching for some surprise . . . not exactly sure about anything anymore.

After dinner, Angelo and Donna went for walk along the private lake. They strolled beneath a trillion stars, deciding their lives, planning their future together.

That night, their lovemaking was special. Tender. Their moment was filled with hope and peace he prayed would never vanish with the years. He felt on top of the world, as though he could see forever and understand all things. It was like having the benefit of a thousand years of wisdom—wise before one's time without being subjected to life's pitfalls and pain. He felt good with her and the world at large, hoping that he might, forever, remain this noble child.

And between the sheets, she drew him close, asking nothing more than to be his, promising herself never having to ask him to promise anything save he be free to choose. Then, secretly, almost childlike, she wished that he could be her very first love, and surely his last romance, when all thoughts simply vanished, and a fountain of fluids profoundly flowed freely from them, sealing an inseparable pact, a bond between them. Forever and always.

Book III

Spirit

Chapter 30

VENTING HOSITLITIES

Fall was well into its first month, and North Shore State Hospital was busy turning back its clocks. Some of the patients seemed amused; others complained bitterly, wanting to turn back the hands of time still further, obliterating the entire decade. Most everyone agreed how violent the sixties had been, and how it would go down in history as the 'Angry Years.' Assassinations and Vietnam stood firmly fixed in everyone's mind as the decade was drawing to a close. A decade of decadence. Hellish. Even summer's headlines had been hot. July was Chappaquiddick: a travesty of justice involving Senator Ted Kennedy. August brought the Manson murders. It's not surprising that in our landing on the moon we shot for the Sea of Tranquility was the sentiment of several patients.

On the north wing of the maximum security ward, Richard Geist sat shivering in seclusion, his arms bound securely across his chest, listening intently to the noisy backward clicking of the clocks. Three o'clock in the morning suddenly became 2 a.m.

"Brrrr. It's awfully dark and cold up here," Richard chattered. No other person was in the padded cell, yet it was apparent that he was talking to someone in particular. "We were brought here to this hospital in a terrible, terrible rage. But Dicky told them that stone walls do not a prison make, nor iron bars a cage. Oh, it can all seem so very real if you let it; but illusion is the key, you see. Illusion will set us free. Of course, the doctors are going to confuse it with delusion and term it a mental disorder. Right? So we had just better keep this to ourselves. Understood? You look bewildered. Well, that's perfectly understandable. I'll try and make things as clear as I can as we move along.

"You see, we have some seven, maybe eight years before we'll even be considered for release. That's the hard reality of it! And if we don't find some way to obscure that time, if we don't entertain or at least amuse ourselves, we might go mad." Richard giggled delightfully. "Illusion. It's the key to our sanity. Look, I know you're a bit confused, but it wasn't my idea to spirit you away. It was all part of a compromise. Mother can explain the whole business to you later if you'd like. But first you're going to have to learn to communicate all over again. Starting with simple sounds. Now, I don't expect you to understand everything at once, but I do implore that you at least listen. I mean it wasn't exactly easy for me back there at your Foundation to accept the fact that you are my real father. Not any more surprising, I'm sure, than it is for you to acknowledge the fact that I am your son. And don't think that I haven't considered the possibility that this whole business is a trick. A trick on the part of Mother to bring you back. To resurrect you. If you want to know why I agreed, it's because I'm going to get answers, David. I know all about tricks. I have quite a few up my sleeve as you've probably gathered by now. So we're not going to waste any more time.

"The first thing we have to do is learn to vent our hostilities. Oh, I don't mean in the conventional sense exactly. It's more of a drill. And we must practice, for the dead don't speak, David. Or do they?" Richard smiled complacently. "But the dead certainly listen though, longing to communicate. I know the magic, David. It's the magic that Lieutenant Lark and you doctors missed completely. The conjuring up of a spell that you couldn't quite grasp. The necromancy of an androgynous strain. The sorcery of soul. It's most interesting that you doctors didn't hit upon it because it does have to do with psychology. It's a very simple trick. So, immediately you're thinking, 'If it's a trick, then it really isn't magic.' Well, the truth is that it started off as a trick. An illusion. But then that's the queer thing, David. You don't mind if I call you David, do you? Even Dicky had a little trouble thinking of you as Daddy. I mean this whole business has us going positively nuts. Anyhow, the magic just sort of took over by itself. It's not exactly the same kind of psychology magicians employ though. No! Pretending is one thing, but believing is quite another. And that's where the magic lies. In the believing.

"Take the magician, David. First, you have to understand that the audience will only see what the illusionist wants them to see. But that's only half the battle. The magician doesn't actually believe that he's performing magic, now does he? He's directing your eye here, while busy doing something over there. That's not magic. That's illusion. And that's great for the believing audience. But what about the performer? That shallow, empty shell of a soul leaves the stage a fraud.

"Now, take the ventriloquist." Richard grinned. "Venter of voices—in the sense of one who vents. It may be difficult, at first, to convince you that a good ventriloquist performs magic. Pure and simple. And that a great ventriloquist is positively the master of his soul. It takes years of practice and patience though. Of course, there are tricks, too. But I'll let you in on a little secret. After a while, the magic takes over on its own. For there are forces at work here. Sinister to be sure. Don't doubt it for a moment, David. The real magic lies in the believing. You see, unlike the magician, the ventriloquist must share equally in the believing with his audience. That's the most important distinction.

"Take your own profession for example, Doctor. You know that you can't be a good psychiatrist unless you believe in yourself and what you're doing. Your patients have to believe in you before they'll believe in themselves. And if you believe in yourself, if *you* really believe in you and what you're doing, well, then the magic is somehow summoned forth.

"It's really no different with the ventriloquist. In order for the ventriloquist to be believable to his audience, he must also believe in the illusion he is creating. A ventriloquist simply cannot pronounce, say a P, or an M, or a B, without first learning substitute sounds. For without substitutes, he would certainly give himself away.

"Watch my lips, David." Richard smiled brightly. "Ready? Pa. Ma. Pa by your Ma. You see, it necessitates bringing your lips together. Right? I think what we'll do is start you off with a plosive pa sound, until you get the hang of it. All right. Watch again—and listen: Pa," Richard promulgated, pairing his lips and pushing forth a current of air that would certainly have extinguished a candle flame no less than a foot away.

"Now, if we want to reproduce that sound without moving our lips, we must substitute Pa with Ta. Understand? Ta equals Pa. To do that, you touch the tip of your tongue to the soft palate near the back of your top teeth," Richard chattered in a highly alliterative tone, enunciating every single syllable distinctly without the slightest movement of his lips. "Then you POP the T, if you'll pardon the pun," he continued in like fashion. "Teter, Teter, tunkin eater, will transform itself. Listen: Peter, Peter pumpkin eater. See how easy? And if you

believe in the magic, if you really believe that you're saying Peter—
Peter Piper picked a peck of pickled peppers," Richard's voice
proclaimed through motionless lips, echoing from different corners of
the cell, "then, a peck of pickled peppers Peter Piper positively
picked," a child's muffled voice mimicked, seemingly from beneath
the matting of Richard's rubber room.

"So you can see that there will be a lot of necessary drilling,
David. I think it apropos that you practice with Pa. Don't you? You'll
have to work on those plosives as I've illustrated. Next, we'll move on
to the labial M. Ma. Then on to the labial plosive B. Ba. When you
become proficient, we'll work on some alternate ways of producing
substitute sounds. The Ka variant for the F sound is very important,
too. Anyways, it will all fall into place with a little bit of drill. You see,
I've worked out a very clever exercise." Richard smiled modestly.
"Actually, it's really rather ingenious if you want to know the truth."
Richard stood up and started marching around the cell.

"Ma—Pa—Pa-by-yo-Ma. Ba-ka-Ra. See how simple? They'll
just think you're counting a crazy kind of cadence, then try and
explain it away with a lot of psychiatric gobbledygook. One—three—
Three-by-yo-left. Left-right-left. Double-to-the-rear — — march.
Duggle equals double. Get it? Duggle-u is your W, David. I'll run
through the alphabet. When patients and doctors are running about,
you can count cadence normally, getting them used to your
shenanigans. Then when you're certain there is no one else around,
why, you're free to practice your drill without moving your lips, and
no one will be the wiser. You see? Of course, it would be better if you
could see. I mean if you could practice in front of a mirror. Mother
tried to borrow one the other day, but the doctors wouldn't hear of it.

"Do you remember my telling you about Mother's mirrored
tables in the parlor? I'm really not quite sure whether I mentioned it or
not. I seem to recall telling someone. Anyhow, one afternoon, Dicky
took Mother's lipstick and wrote all over the reflective surfaces. Of
course, she beat him and made him wipe them clean. Then a curious
thing happened, David. As Dicky knelt before one of the tables, wiping
the waxy red substance away, a strange image appeared before his
eyes. Oh, I don't mean unrecognizably strange. Nothing queer like
that. There was absolutely no question that it was me. But at first it
scared the living daylights out of little Dicky. For when he rubbed one

away, in a clockwise fashion, the image appeared years older. Then when he rubbed in the other direction, the image became younger again. If he wiped frantically, I'd disappear altogether. It was a positively fascinating phenomenon. And when Dicky finally spoke to me, I answered back in a voice that ranged from baby talk to quite a level of sophistication. I'm sure it was me all along doing all that talking. But it surprised the hell out of little Dicky that he could even do this thing. And this went on for quite some time. Whenever Dicky needed Richard's companionship or help, he'd go quietly over to one of the mirrored tables with Mother's dusting rag and slowly wipe away. Sure enough I'd reappear, and we'd talk things out together. I don't remember everything, though, because whenever he'd wipe in those wide circular motions, it was like going into a trance you see. Like being hypnotized. Yes, I'm almost positive about that.

"After a while, it got to the point that Dicky didn't need a mirror anymore. He could simply have me appear or wipe me from his mind at will. As Dicky grew older, he felt he didn't need me around anymore. He tried to make it a one-man show. Tried to brush me aside. He had forgotten all the times I was there when he needed me. How whenever things went sour, he'd try to place the blame on me. Not the true-blue comrade in arms you might imagine. But he's been getting better lately. We've been working together as a team.

"Oh, David, I know these are the very things you wanted me to try and talk to you about. But it's just so much easier telling you now that you are dead. I mean, you're not going to get up and tell me that we're out of time, or that you have other patients to see—now are you?

"Well, back to business. I'll be your mirror, David. And like a mirror, I'll give you dimension and depth. Only I can't make you whole again, simply because the prognosis isn't sound. It's not like I have your body to work with, you know. I probably couldn't even do it if I wanted to; that is, fuse you into a solitary sense of self. But we'll make the best of things. So, come on now. Put on a happy face. Smile. You're going to have to practice that a lot, too. It's all part of the drill.

"First, I want you to separate your lips about a quarter of an inch. Very important, David. Beginners usually start with simple vowel sounds; however, my method will make you a pro in no time. Now, let's try the word, *Poconos*, without moving our lips. Dr. Bianco and Nurse Marlow went to the Poconos last month." Richard smiled handsomely without the slightest movement of the lips.

"Anyway, after you master what we call 'near voices,' I'll tutor you in distant and muffled tones. It can really come in quite handy at times. Like that evening back at your infirmary when the police officer escorted me into the shower room. I was experiencing a little trouble and a lot of pain, trying to remove my robe, so I asked the officer for his assistance. But he just stood there, very cautious and alert. I knew I'd have to be quite clever to catch him off guard. So I wriggled out of my gown, hung it on a hook, then turned on the water full blast in order to muffle any sound; actually, to distort the sound I was about to produce, just to be on the safe side. Did you know, David, that sound is the least reliable of our senses? Anyhow, I turned around stark naked and made eye contact with him. Eye contact is absolutely essential to the training. 'LOOK!' I hollered, pointing to my punctured groin. He dropped his eyes in fascination. But to ensure his attention, to hold him there for a split second longer, I added, 'NO BANDAGES.' Only I vented in Lieutenant Lark's deep-sounding barrel-like tone. Baritone. 'NO BANDAGES.' He stood positively paralyzed, staring down at my pecker as though it were a puppet or a prop from which his boss's voice bellowed from below. That's how I caught him off guard before rendering him senseless, slamming the edge of my hand hard against those wing-shaped plates of cartilage projecting from his throat, sending him flying back against the tile. Tough old bird, though. Second shot broke his beak.

"Tricks, David. Illusion! But to take three souls, think of it, three souls that are verily embodied here within, and to infuse them with life, with voices that can chime, and rhyme, and ring with the richness of a thrush nightingale on a moonlit night—well, that's positively magic, David. Did you ever hear such poetry? I can have it sing with such abandon, or simply cancel its celebrated song, chortling croaks instead of chords. In or out of concert with the world at whim. That's not serendipity, David. Listen!" A single sound of beauty filled Richard's cage. "There it goes. A nocturnal songbird. Soaring behind the moon. Gliding across a darkling plain. Its music melding harmoniously with the night. How do you account for that, David?" Suddenly, Richard's cell was filled with the fluttering sound of countless songbirds. Distant but defined.

"Oh, sure. I can trill my t's, dancing my tongue along the

alveolar ridge. I can duplicate the melodious flight song of the skylark long after it has ascended into the heavens, hidden from the naked eye. I can imitate flawlessly the lark or the nightingale. But to have a chorus of my faithful feathered friends all trilling together in choral composition—well, I ask you. Is that trickery? Illusion? Or forces of the darkest kind? Stretch your imagination, David. I've taken mine across an abyss so wide that spanning its yawning gulf required the reserve and cloven hooves of the Devil Himself.

"Don't be disappointed in me, David. I tried God, only He tried my patience. I mean, I was positively beaten. Hell, I was shivering to beat the band. And I prayed, too. God knows how I prayed. And do you know what I got for my trouble?" There was a pause. "That's right. Silence. Like the sound of one hand clapping. Know what that's like? It's maddening.

"I don't think you really knew what kind of secrets Sarah had tucked away in that trunk of hers, David. I'm talking about books from Africa and Haiti. I'm talking about books with spells, incarnations, and formulas. I'm talking about potions, lotions, and notions. I'm talking power, David. Power that can alter the world as we know it. Books on black magic. Magic of the darkest kind. A purely perverted pact I made. And if I'm crawling along the bottom of some pit, if I've really reached the very floor of hell, slithering lower than a silken serpent within its sallow skin, then I'll at least have the satisfaction of knowing that I'll never be cold again." Richard giggled devilishly, huddled there in the corner of his cell.

"Now, I can't give you earthly flesh and fire, David. But I can give you spirit. However, I need some sign—some signal that you at least acknowledge the things that I've so painstakingly set forth. Some sign or signal, David," Richard repeated.

Richard sat in silence. Patiently. He strained his eyes along the windowless wall while sinking to the padded floor. Waiting. He waited for what seemed an eternity before he saw a reddish-green glow grow out of the blackness like a single eye—then fade—then brighten again —when a familiar odor wafted through the inky night. It was the unmistakable smell of Dr. King's cigar! The very same odor that had settled permanently into the doctor's clothes and cars; his couches and his chairs; the curtains and carpets in both his office and home. Oh, there was no mistaking that cigar all right.

Suddenly, Richard saw an eerie cloud-like genie rise. He watched in fascination as the gray fume unfurled, bowing and weaving through degrees of darkness palling at the door. Curling and climbing. Curving and carving through aery space. Drifting. Evanescent. Richard had only to ask for some sign, some signal. Doctor David King, deceased, was communicating with him from the grave. Doctor David King, his father, was sending him smoke signals! It was truly more than he had bargained for. And it frightened him. For he shivered violently before the glow finally faded.

What the patient seriously considered in that quiet, solitary cell for some time afterward, was a certain knowledge that he, Richard Geist, was unquestionably in league with dark forces, forces that could ultimately destroy him if he were not careful. He sat for a spell with his back flat against the cushioned wall before he finally relaxed and closed his eyes.

Richard wasn't sure how long he had slept, but when he awoke, he knew with certainty that the night had been very real, indeed. He knew it by the behavior of the black attendant who entered the cell bright and early, sniffing around like some sort of bloodhound, poking his nose where it didn't belong, frisking and staring up at the patient suspiciously, turning him around roughly and checking his restraints until the man finally seemed satisfied that everything was secure and that Richard had no contraband. And when Richard was certain that the attendant was finished with him, Dicky's voice resounded from the far corner of the cell.

"Over here, cocksucker!"

The attendant turned around in bewilderment.

"Dicky's the one with the cigar," Richard vented. "I told him it would stunt his growth. Watch it—he went behind your back," he warned and gestured with his eyes, stepping backward from the man.

"Hey, that's not fair," Dicky mumbled in a tone that rose up from behind the attendant.

The man swung around violently, then back again as Richard leaped high into the air, screaming, "LOOK, MA. NO HANDS," delivering a deadly kick to the center of the man's throat before he could ever utter a sound, excepting his collapse.

"Dead shot, partner," Dicky declared. "I'd applaud that in a minute if only I could. You know I would."

"Yes, if you only could," Richard said evenly.

"Oh, why, Richard? Why do you do these things? Why?" Mother's voice whined mercifully, moaning from a corner of the cell.

"Because I'm still venting my hostilities, Mother."

"You said you'd try, Richard. You said that you'd be good. You promised me that you'd bring David back. Is this what I can expect? Empty promises? More killing?"

"David was here this morning, Mother. At least I think he was. I mean the cigar odor isn't in my mind. You can smell it, can't you?"

"Why, yes! Yes, I can, Richard," she said excitedly. "But why didn't you let me know? Why did you let me sleep? Oh, Richard, how could you?"

"I had to be sure."

"YOU HAD TO BE SURE?"

"It was only his spirit for Christ's sake."

"Only his spirit. I . . . I worshipped him," she stammered and sobbed bitterly. "I worshipped and loved—you promised me, Richard. You swore to me that—"

"—that I'd bring him back to you. In time, damn you. In time. I can't produce flesh and blood. I don't have his corpse to work with, you know. I'm not a goddamn miracle worker. I wasn't even sure if it was him or some deadly apparition that might endanger our very souls."

"Apparition? For God's sake—what are you talking about?"

"I don't think there was anything God-like about it, Mother. I think it was all rather hellish if you want to know the truth. Then it all went up in smoke, Mother. Cigar smoke."

"Richard."

"Yes, Mother?"

"I'm afraid they are going to hurt you for what you just did," she said, sinking slowly to the floor in a graceful split beside the body, holding her head erect. Eyes closed.

"Why is that, Mother?"

"Because you just *killed* a man, Richard. Do you really think that they are going to allow you to keep right on killing people? Do you?" she insisted, rising most magically to her feet.

"But I'm crazy, Mother. You said so yourself. You made me terribly, terribly mad."

"You are always trying to put the blame everyplace but where it actually belongs."

"And where does it belong, Mother?"

"THERE! ON YOUR SHOULDERS," Mother's voice cracked violently, sending Richard reeling across the cell.

"Listen to me, damn you," Richard insisted.

"Listen to you?"

"Yes, to me! For once in your goddamned life, listen to me." There was a moment of silence. "That's better. Now. We haven't got much time. People will be coming in a little while. And you may be right. They may want to hurt me. So you must listen very carefully to what I have to say. I have an extraordinary plan to help you find peace with yourself. But first you're going to have to wake up from that fantasy world of yours, Mother. You can't keep going on the way you have."

"Richard, what in the world are you talking about? I have absolutely no idea what you're trying to say."

"Let's not go through this pretense again. Please. I'm talking about the men in your life. I can see everything clearly now. If you tell me that Dr. David King is my real father, then I believe you. But I just want you to think about that father figure you paraded around the house for years. Not to mention Horatio Gladstone or the scores of other men. I want you to think about your wanton display of acrobatics in the hay when all those hands came forward. Do you have any idea of the effect that had on me? Not knowing. Not understanding. At the tender age of four. I tried to save you—toy guns blasting away insanely because I thought they were hurting you. Then back at the guesthouse you tried to make me believe that it was all a bad dream, consoling me. 'A nightmare,' you insisted. They were your playthings, Mother. But you know damn well that you had to have the creature comforts and luxuries that those younger men could not provide. You couldn't find someone with youth, looks, money, and power all rolled into one. So you rolled around with everyone. Well, I found someone for you, Mother. He's had a bad marriage, too. He thinks he's in love with one of the nurses at the Foundation. Nurse Marlow. But you know yourself that he's interested in you. He finds you rather attractive. He even told you so in his office. Remember?"

"Richard!" she exclaimed incredulously. "Are you referring to

Dr. Bianco?"

"Yes, Mother. Dr. Angelo T. Bianco."

There was a long pause. "Do you really think he finds me attractive, Richard? Or am I simply a curiosity?" the voice queried demurely.

"I believe he finds you quite attractive. And I don't think I need remind you where that man is headed. We'll just have to turn his head a little," Richard made clear. "Catch as catch can, I believe is the cliché. I'm the curiosity, Mother. He couldn't possibly resist the challenge. I'll make sure of that. And he's smart, Mother."

"Oh, I don't know, Richard. I *so* miss David."

"Your David is dead, Mother. Let's let him rest in peace. But you're alive in me. Together we can build a kingdom greater than any one man could ever offer. You will take control and seize the power in the name of love, Mother. Dicky and I will be there to support you all the way."

"I'm the heir apparent," a child's voice chimed in.

"I'm so confused, Richard. I know they'll be coming soon, and I'm so afraid for you. Is it too late to tell you that I'm sorry and that I love you? I've been a terribly selfish woman. A very foolish woman, too. But I do love you, Richard. I've always loved you."

"Is that true, Mother?"

"You are my son, Richard. And you're my darling Dicky, too," she cooed, leaning forward and sending down a kiss.

"Then it's not too late, Mother. We shall be victorious. You will find love again as you have never known. This I swear. And we will have our mother back. It is only fitting for you to hold on to the memory of David, as I, too, will mourn the death of Father. But we must build a new kingdom upon the foundation of our future, not upon the weakness of the past."

Mother remained silent, and Richard could hear steel doors opening and closing along the corridor.

"They're coming to get you," Dicky taunted as noises were drawing near.

The sound of carts rolling down the hallway at that ungodly hour signaled breakfast on the run. Little angry wheels wobbling violently to and fro stopped abruptly outside his cell. Stacks of Styrofoam trays along with cups and tiny piles of pills to start one's day came into view as an attendant pondered the opened door.

"What the hell is this?" the attendant gaped, throwing the steel door open wide, staring down at the body lying on the floor. He hollered for the others.

"You think that maybe we're beyond socialization?" Richard questioned, sitting calmly in the corner, his arms wrapped securely across his chest. "Perhaps you had better throw away the key."

The attendant got out of the doorway as three other men stormed in. A moment later one of them pronounced his fellow worker dead.

Richard looked up gleefully into four coal-black faces. He wasn't even the least bit scared. After the initial fear of seeing them, the rest was easy. "Oh, and if you need to know why his fly is open— well, Mother wanted to satisfy her curiosity concerning shades of black."

Richard was swiftly swept off the matted surface by the largest of the four. The powerful man slammed his shoulder against the patient's body with the momentum of a wrecking ball, sending his adversary clear across the cell. Richard crashed into the cushioned wall but bounced back easily, giggling before delivering a knee and two swift kicks in quick succession to the middle of the attendant's groin, dropping the big man instantly. As a second man moved in, Richard whirled away from the wall and brought the heel of his right foot squarely across the man's face with a powerful roundhouse kick that practically took the attendant's head off his shoulders, or so it seemed. But a third brute caught Richard with a foot sweep, knocking him to the ground, smashing the patient's body with terrific blows. The attendant near the door still stood in shock, shaking his head in disbelief as the biggest of the four was busy climbing to his feet, demanding that the other stop.

"Motherfucker's mine," he insisted. "Stand him up," he ordered, stepping forward in terrible, terrible pain, locking an inverted fist firmly against his side. Richard shot his foot up and out, but the man easily warded off the blow, parrying another before planting a series of short, spiraling punches into Richard's gut. Richard folded in two. "I said stand him up," the black giant commanded. Pairs of hands grabbed the back of Richard's jacket and hair, holding him erect. The next shot was a devastating roundhouse kick that caught Richard upside his head. So severe was the force that it ripped the patient's body from their grip. Richard flew across the cell. The man went after him like a fiend. As Richard tried to twist away, he heard an awful cracking sound as a column of pain shot severely through his spine. Another terrible blow caught him in the side before he fell. Richard lay helpless on the floor. But the huge black man kept right on kicking, and punching, and pounding away brutally. Two others joined in. Richard's punishment went on for more than a minute. Suddenly, voices were heard down the other end of the hall. The men immediately stopped. One of them dragged the battered body into a corner. Richard lay there like a shattered doll.

"Get that jacket off him, fast!" the punisher demanded. And pairs of hands quickly went to work on those restraints. "We say he had the jacket off when we came in here. Otherwise, they'll hang us high. Understood?" he insisted, breaking Richard's arm in an instant for added measure.

Three black faces nodded in agreement, and the four rehearsed their story before attending to the body lying in the other corner. The body of their brother. *A soul brother*, Richard giggled inwardly before passing out.

Chapter 31

RETRIBUTION

Richard regained consciousness in a private recovery room late that night. A room with a view, but not exactly at the top. Inverted bottles carried sweetener to his veins. He squinted out the window through swollen eyes; eyes that could barely open. Yet it didn't seem as dark as it could have been; not with the panorama of artificial lights strung all along the horizon. Another light came from a night lamp mounted in the corner near the floor. Richard glared at the bars. The bars along the window. The bars along the bed. Surely he was dead. But he listened to his heart beating. His own beating had been severe. Actually, it was so much more than a beating, for they had meant to kill him. He knew that. What had prevented it? He believed he knew the answer to that, too. Intervention. Yes, devilish intervention. *Where are all the stars?* Richard wondered. They were always just beyond the bars at the King Foundation. Millions of tiny lights suspended in the ceiling of the world.

Almost magically, a moon-beamed face fell out of the shadows just above his own. "Hello, Richard." Lieutenant Lark said and smirked. "Got your own private quarters I see. I've been waiting for you to come around. Although I wondered if you really would. It certainly would have been less complicated if you had simply died," he affirmed. Lark continued smirking, shaking his head sadly from side to side.

"What in hell are you doing here?" Richard asked with hatred in his heart. His whole body hurt when he spoke.

"You know, they call this a recovery room, Richard. You're supposed to rest in here until you recover. Until you're well. Well enough, that is, to be transferred back to your ward. But you and I both know we can't let that happen. Now can we?"

Richard stared hideously at the detective. "Get out."

"You caused too many people too much pain, Richard. Yourself included. Just look at you. Your arm and ribs are broken. Your face is a fucking mess. And this morning they had to remove your spleen. There were some other serious complications, too. Only, I'm unhappy to report that you somehow beat the odds." Lark lit up the last of Dr. King's cigars. "I've been watching you, Richard. And you want to know something? You really are insane. I didn't think so at first, but you convinced me otherwise," he stated with conviction, puffing on the cigar and blowing a cloud of smoke down in Richard's face.

"You know. It's a crazy world, Richard. You carry with you such death and murderous destruction. You've created a dark world in which there is no future left for you. Yet, the state is compelled to keep you safe, to feed you, to give you medical attention, to provide you with a roof over your head and clothing on your back. You take life, and the state hands you back your own. Why is that? Of course, we both know the answer, Richard. It's because God-fearing men and women are afraid to pull the plug. But they don't see what I see. Oh, they may read or hear about garbage like you secondhand. And they hope and pray that nothing will ever happen to them or their families. I, Richard, am not a God-fearing man. I, Richard, am here to stop you. Now! Before it's too late."

"Oh, God," Richard cried weakly. "All my daddies are dead! Where are all the stars, Lieutenant?"

"Where they always are. Out there. Only this is not the country club you're accustomed to. This is a state facility. It's all lit up. See? There are no stars left for you to wish upon. You relinquished all hope back there at the King Foundation."

Richard grimaced and spoke through broken lips and teeth. "How do you figure to get away with it? The doctors will know. They must know that the attendants worked me over." The patient shook his head slowly back and forth. "You can't risk it, Lieutenant," he said, sounding rather sure.

"You were beaten by the attendant you killed, Richard."

"No! He was already dead, Lieutenant. Three of them beat me until I couldn't breathe. Especially one big black bastard. I'm sure you know that."

"It doesn't matter what I know," Lieutenant Lark declared, clamping the cigar between his teeth, pulling a smooth-skinned work glove onto his right hand.

"What are you doing?" Richard questioned nervously, realizing that the door to the room was closed. Perhaps even locked.

"Putting an end to pure evil, Richard."

343

"Then you're no better than I am," Richard posited with a grin. "You'll burn in hell, Lieutenant. You'll be a murderer just like me." Richard took a painful breath. "I know you don't believe in God, Lieutenant. But—"

"I didn't say I didn't believe in God," Lark interrupted. "What I said was that I didn't fear Him. Let's get down to cases, Richard. I'm sure you've thought a great deal about what happens to a soul once you die. Yes? Well, I don't believe in the soul in any sort of traditional sense. I don't believe it really leaves your body when you die. I think of the soul as more of an influence man has on those he leaves behind, an effect one has on others over the course of time. Marks and memories are all. What marks or memories are you to leave behind, Richard? You leave behind a trail of death and horror."

"Aren't you going to ask me about the web, Lieutenant? Aren't you even the least bit curious about how I managed to open Sarah's trunk without seeming to have disturbed a single thread? The lock was nothing. But what about the web, let alone all that dust? Wouldn't you like to know the magic? Wouldn't you like to hear the story about how my friends the spiders—"

"No, Richard. Your story days are over. But I've a yarn to spin for you. It's a story about stories. I understand you like stories."

Richard said nothing.

"My father, may he rest in peace, was a very young boy the day his father died, so I really never got to meet my grandfather. Not face to face anyway. But I did get to know him over the years, though." Lieutenant Lark puffed on the cigar. "I got to know him through my father's stories. They were wonderful stories. Some of them were quite fascinating, too. Especially for a boy as young as my father was when they were told to him.

"But there was one story that actually frightened my father as a young boy growing up in Brooklyn. It was the story of how my grandfather killed a man whom he knew would never be brought to justice. An untouchable who scoffed at courts of law because he had the protection of powerful people, bought and paid for with a family fortune amassed through a network of illegal operations.

"One day this gangster, who fashioned himself an industrialist, made the mistake of putting out a contract on a young lawyer who was making life a bit rough for him. A lawyer who couldn't be bought off and who simply wouldn't go away. The lawyer, my grandfather's niece, was found garroted outside her apartment door in the hallway. Next to her was the body of her nine-year-old daughter, her throat cut open from one end to the other. Bags of groceries were strewn across the hallway. Supposedly, no one saw or heard a thing.

"Of course my grandfather knew immediately who was responsible. Everyone did. But my grandfather set out to prove it beyond a shadow of a doubt before he would ever take the law into his own hands. He gathered evidence that took over a year to obtain. It also took his entire savings along with large amounts of borrowed cash. Finally, the trail ended at the doorstep of our industrialist who had put out the contract. My grandmother begged my grandfather to take the matter to the police, but he knew what would happen in a court of law. There was corruption leading all the way to the top. Instead, my grandfather typed the man a note. It read, 'Dear Mr. Manno. You cannot threaten or frighten off a dying man. I am coming after you from the shadows of a grave. Most sincerely, Bernard Lark.' I have his middle name, Richard," Lark added proudly. "I also have his cancer. I've been told it skipped a generation and landed in my lap. Actually, I believe my grandfather would still have killed him even if he hadn't had terminal cancer. I just don't think he would have signed the note is all," Lieutenant Lark added with a chuckle.

"Anyhow, my grandfather picked off our industrialist at one hundred and fifty yards from a rooftop in the Bay Ridge section of Brooklyn as the man stepped from his chauffeured limousine with packages of fruits and vegetables. Blew his head open like a melon the moment he returned from market. How's that for poetic justice? He also found and killed the hired assassin that very afternoon. My grandfather died a month later, long before that messy business would have gone to trial. And my father went on to become a rabbi.

"There are many more stories about my grandfather, Richard. But I never told that particular story to anyone. You see, you're privileged. Private room and private story. I hope you enjoyed it because it's the last story you'll ever hear. Oh, but there is a point to my telling you the tale. My father was eighty years old when he died. And do you know what his one concern was? 'Milton,' he said to me, 'there is such evil in this world, and our laws render us powerless to fight it effectively. So many criminals use our laws against us, then turn around and spit in our faces. I have asked myself why is this, Milton. I have asked myself why things have not changed in all the years. Have I wasted a lifetime serving as a rabbi, Milton? Or should I have been more like your grandfather?' It was a test question, Richard. I know it hurt my father greatly in that I could not, or rather would not, answer him straightaway.

"Eighty years old, and he still remembered each and every story. And do you know what story I'll remember until the day I die, Richard? Do you know what deep dark secret I will be left to live with and cannot share among a living soul, so help me God? No! No heaven or hell, Richard. Just the dark," Lieutenant Lark said gravely, glaring ominously down at the helpless soul.

"They'll know. The doctors will know," Richard tried to reason.

"Know what, Richard? They won't know I've laid a glove on you. You should see yourself. Your face is almost unrecognizable. They won't be able to tell where one blow landed and the other left off," he reassured him, leaning over and pressing a wide patch of adhesive across the gaping mouth. Hatred filled Richard's eyes, and he struggled painfully against the restraints that held him fast. Lieutenant Lark leaned closer and pinched the patient's nostrils, watching as Richard's eyes turned from hatred to sheer terror before the cop spoke up again. "Now, you just simmer down. Hear? I'm going to send you to your Maker in just a moment," Lark said and smiled deliberately, chomping on the cigar. "But first, just nod your head if you want God to know that you're sorry for your sins."

Richard nodded his head frantically. "Mmmmmph!"

"That's good," the lieutenant declared and winked, puffing away calmly before releasing his clamp-like fingers from the patient's nose, blowing another cloud of smoke Richard's way.

Richard gasped and raised his head high off the pillow, practically sucking in the ceiling while filling his lungs with sweet, sweet smoky air as Lieutenant Lark smashed a powerful gloved fist of retribution against the eighteen-year-old's temple, reeling Richard's skull abnormally to the right.

"That one's for Kilbride," Lieutenant Lark asserted, drawing back his fist and almost knocking over the stand that held the IV bottles above the bed. "And this one's for his bride," he repeated, landing another terrific blow. "Let's hear those voices now, you murdering son of a bitch. Where are those voices now?" Suddenly there was a voice. It was a voice that rose up out of the darkness. *Don't you dare lay another hand on him, Lieutenant*, it commanded righteously.

Lark froze. The voice did not come from behind him, or from one of the darkened corners of the room. The voice sounded familiar. Authoritative. Like Lark's father's voice. Only it wasn't. It called for the detective to stop. It was the voice within him. Shaming and warning him. It was the voice of conscience. Lark's conscience. But he would not heed, delivering another devastating blow. Then a thousand voices ushered in from floor to ceiling, sounding from heaven and hell —that Lark refused to intellectualize as they begged for him to show mercy—that Lark refused to listen to as he delivered blow after powerful blow that exploded against Richard's face and rendered him unconscious, blood pouring from the patient's nostrils, oozing from the corners of the tape. And as the beating continued, the voices grew louder and louder until Lieutenant Lark thought he'd surely gone mad. Suddenly, something inside him snapped as he felt a presence touch— his soul? Lark stood still. Listening. The voices were suddenly gone. He placed his head upon Richard's chest. The boy was barely breathing.

Lieutenant Lark removed his glove then ripped the tape from Richard's mouth. Blood spilled freely onto the patient's garment and sheets. Lark withdrew a compact scrimshaw folding knife from his jacket pocket. It had been a special gift handed down to the oldest male child in Lark's family for generations, beginning with his great-grandfather who had been a tool and die maker and machined the marvelous piece. Lark recalled his father reluctantly handing him the heirloom on the day the boy became a man, on the day Milton B. Lark was bar mitzvahed, for Milton's father detested knives and guns and anything that could be classified a weapon—tool or no tool. The boy treasured the gift. Milton was the last of the line, but he knew to whom he would pass the gift. Someone he thought very much of as a son. He held the ivory handle in his palm, carved and engraved by his great-grandfather, too. A handle that housed a small but razor-sharp blade. Lark brought to mind July Fourth, and how he had used the back of the blade to probe the canister taken from Theresa Martinez's mouth.

Prying Richard's mouth open wide, Lark fought to grab hold of the slippery, bloody tongue as it slid between his gloved fingers each time he pulled. Using his handkerchief, too, he took a firm hold, pulling the tongue forward, intent on slicing across that instrument of evil—when a sword of wisdom suddenly cleared and calmed his mind. Folding and putting the knife away, Lark again pulled the patient's tongue outward to its limit, clearing his fingers by a hair before slamming Richard's lower jaw shut tight with the heel of a meaty hand, gnashing the fleshy flap flat before ripping the reedy red vessels free.

"Tell you tale now, storyteller," Lieutenant Lark dared, stuffing the severed section of the organ, handkerchief and bloody patch of tape into the mouth of the glove, shoving the incriminating evidence into a small duffle bag that he carried over to the sink. Lark extinguished the cigar as he thought hard about extinguishing the little life left in Richard's body. *Last chance saloon*, he considered quietly. Lark cranked out lengths of paper towel from a wall dispenser, wetting and squeezing the white squares firmly in his fist. He wiped the blood from the leather handles of the bag, crumpling the cigar inside the paper wad, depositing everything within.

Lark quickly washed and wrung his hands with hot soapy water, watching the bloody swirl eddying around the pitted porcelain sink. Down, down, down it whooshed then gurgled in devilish decline before finally disappearing—deep—and away forever. He splashed cold water on his face while taking full account of himself there in the metal mirror fastened above the sink, cranking out another length of paper towel to dry his face and hands. Dispensing and dampening still another handful, the cop went around the room, methodically, cleaning and tidying up here and there. Finally, he checked Richard's intravenous. Satisfied, he stuffed the mound of bloody paper in the bag and zipped it shut.

Digging into his pants pocket, Lark removed a single key and unlocked the door. Opening it slowly, he peered out. The corridor was clear. He stepped from the room then closed and locked the door behind him, turning and heading toward the bank of elevators. He had the key to that, too. Lark waited for what seemed an eternity. Finally, it arrived. He stepped inside. Alone. Lark rode the car down to the first floor and got off, walking briskly toward a stairwell that led him to an exit door off the lobby. When he reached the walkway, he placed an anonymous call to the lobby.

Down the block from the institution, Lieutenant Lark found Sergeant Grear exactly where he had left him, seated comfortably behind the wheel of the green sedan, studying for a test. Lark tossed the bag onto the floor of the backseat.

"Patient resting comfortably," was all the lieutenant said as Sergeant Grear closed his book and started up the engine, heading the vehicle out of the lot and along a deserted street. It was all either of them said on that cool October evening.

Chapter 32

THE VISIT

November 1st, 1976
3 a.m.

An exhausted Donna Bianco awoke from a restless sleep shortly after collapsing from the couple's seventh wedding anniversary celebration. Angelo lay sound asleep beside her. The room seemed unusually cool. A sense of concern shone upon her pretty face as she focused dreamy eyes upon an open window. She reached for the lamp, switching the three-way bulb to low. Suddenly, she sat up straight, staring across the room, screaming and climbing insanely about the sheets and blankets, clawing and drawing them to her naked breasts.

Angelo shot up like a jack-in-the-box, confused and disoriented. Instinctively, he grabbed for her, focusing on the large rectangular eighteenth century etched glass mirror affixed to the massive dresser set against the wall. Crudely scrawled across their reflection, in red lipstick, was the name, Victoria Geist. Below the name were two stick figures of a man and woman.

"Oh, my God, they released him," Donna spoke in a horrified whisper that seemed to shock him even more. "Why didn't they tell us?" she implored, grabbing his robe off the floor and running down the dark hallway. "Why?"

"I don't know," he snapped excitedly, following close behind. "Maybe he somehow escaped," he considered, flicking on a wall switch.

Donna entered the room off to the right when suddenly stark-white bones loomed out at her. She clasped her mouth in terror. Hanging on a door of an open closet was their son's skeleton suit worn yesterday afternoon. Blanched bones seemed to dance upon the pitch-black background as beams of light from a passing car traversed the curtains and the wall. On a little chair sat the child's plastic jack-o'-lantern, heaped with treats that the six-year-old had collected door-to-door. Snuggled in his bed, safe and sound, was their precious sleepyhead.

"Oh, thank God," she cried, covering her son who lay nestled snugly against the headboard. She crossed over to the window, pulling down the shade to meet the sill.

Beside the boy's bed stood a brand new baseball bat. A Louisville Slugger inscribed with Ted Williams' signature.

"Where did he get this?" Angelo asked, picking up the bat from the shadowy corner when suddenly the headboard moved before them like an eerie tombstone.

Donna grabbed her son. Angelo raised the bat, ready to kill. And their sleepy dog moaned and stretched and crawled out from underneath the bed.

"I asked you to fix that damn headboard a hundred times," she snapped and sobbed, lying the boy back down and returning to her husband's arms. "He was coming up for a hearing," she recalled. "Damn them. Damn them all. Oh, how I wish Lieutenant Lark were still alive." And then it hit her like a cold towel in the face. Richard Geist had not simply left a message telling them he was out. He had actually been there in the night. In their home. In their very room. Maybe even watching the two of them make love that evening. Watching their son as he slept. "He wants you!" she said shivering, goose bumps traveling rapidly across her flesh. "I can feel it."

Angelo Bianco held her close, but there was little comfort in her husband's arms on that cool November morning.

Later that morning:
Suffolk County Police Department
Yaphank, New York

"Lieutenant."

"Yes, Sergeant?"

"There's a Dr. Bianco on the phone asking for Sergeant Grear," the detective said with a smile. "I told him we occasionally promote around here."

"Bianco?"

"From the King Foundation."

"Yes, of course."

"On 03, Lieutenant."

Lieutenant Grear pushed the button and picked up the receiver. "Dr. Bianco; how the hell are you?"

"Seven years older, Lieutenant, and not a hell of a lot wiser, I'm afraid. I hear congratulations are in order. When did you make lieutenant?"

"Three years ago. Shortly after I saw you at the funeral," Grear related, instinctively reaching in his pocket for his predecessor's scrimshaw pocket knife. "How's Donna and the little fellow? Everything all right?" he asked, leaning back in his chair complacently, toying with the heirloom Lark had presented to him as a gift on the detective's deathbed.

"It's the reason I'm calling. We need your help. It's about Richard Geist."

"What about him?" Grear asked flatly.

"He's out."

The lieutenant snapped forward in his seat. "What do you mean, he's out?"

"Out. Like in, in-and-out."

"They released him?"

"Not exactly. He was on some kind of a conditional pass to visit Dr. King's grave, but under heavy security. Yeah, right."

"What the hell is that all about?"

"It appears there's now conclusive evidence to support Richard Geist's earlier allegation that Dr. David King was the boy's father. Victoria Geist left Long Island, and more specifically Dr. King's estate in late 1950 to secretly have the child. DNA testing confirms that Dr. King was, indeed, the boy's father."

"What does that have to do with anything? And who and how and why were samples taken to begin with?"

"I don't know. All I know is that Geist somehow escaped from them yesterday afternoon at the cemetery. They're not saying much. I have a contact over at North Shore State who's worked with Richard over the years. She says ever since the publication of his book, he's become something of a celebrity."

"Yes, I read one of the reviews. He's got all of us in there as I hear it." *Which may explain a lot of things*, Grear quietly considered.

"Lieutenant, he was actually in our home while we slept. Donna and I awoke to his artwork on the mirror, signed Victoria Geist. He's added an epilogue to his goddamn published book, which he left by the phone in the living room just before I called the hospital. It's like he's paving the way for a sequel or something. Like he's actually turning his fiction into fact because it's practically what happened word for word—except our dog wasn't under my son's bed. It was tied up in the basement because he's not potty trained yet. But how the hell does he even know that I have a dog or a six-year-old son? And he left David a baseball bat, for Christ's sake."

"Okay. Whoa. Hold on now."

"I'm sorry, Lieutenant. I know I'm not making any sense. But he's even got this conversation scribed in sum and substance penned in longhand on a yellow legal size pad left by my fucking phone, like I said. Of course, he knew I'd call you."

"Where are you now?"

"I'm at home."

"Let me have your address. My partner and I are on our way," Grear assured the man, signaling to his sergeant from across the room.

"Thank you, Lieutenant," Dr. Bianco said sincerely. "Thank you," he repeated.

Grear took down the address and hung up.

"What's up, Lieutenant?" the sergeant asked.

"Ever hear of Richard Geist?"

"Geist? Sure. He's that whacko over at North Shore State Hospital who wrote that bestseller. My wife says it's a blockbuster."

"Grab your coat, Sergeant."

"Where are we going?"

"To pay a visit to his former psychiatrist."

"No kidding? That Dr. Bianco fellow?"

"That's very good, Sergeant," Grear teased.

"You know, I know a little something about multiple personality, Lieutenant."

"Is that so?"

"Sure. My wife reads, and I listen."

Lieutenant Grear smiled warmly. "Well, it's one of the reasons I take you with me on these outings. Come on, Sergeant. Let's shake a leg."

Epilogue

What started out as penning a feature-length story on mental illness for the *New York Newsday Sunday Magazine* section, Robert Redler, an obscure freelance writer with residences in Bayside, Queens and Riverhead, Long Island, interviewed Richard Geist a good number of times by phone while the teenager had been confined to the King Foundation.

Richard Geist's back-up plan, should his manuscript be lost, stolen, or merely long forgotten, was Redler's solemn promise to scribe a series of articles covering the events of what Richard referred to as his "madness in the making." It was not long after Richard's escape from North Shore State Hospital for the Criminally Insane in Havenwood that Robert Redler was offered a book contract with a small publishing house for Richard Geist's *unauthorized* biography.

Robert Redler somehow knew that he would one day meet Richard Geist up close and personal. Robert did not know when or how or even why. He simply knew that he had this date with destiny.

That Richard Geist knew this, too, was indeed an understatement.

Robert Redler was not a superstitious man, nor was he religious or prone to violence. Yet his belief that he and Richard Geist would someday cross paths—and possibly swords—fell well within the parameters of what some might consider preternatural.